MW00908833

ATOMIC AGE
CTHULHU

Also from Chaosium:

ATOMIC AGE

CTHULHU

EDITED BY BRIAN M. SAMMONS
AND GLYNN OWEN BARRASS

ATOMIC AGE CTHULHU:
Tales of Mythos Horror in the 1950s
is published by Chaosium Inc. This book is copyright ©2015
as a whole by Chaosium Inc.;
all rights reserved.
Stories are copyright ©2015 by the authors.

All other stories are original to this collection.

Edited by Brian M. Sammons & Glynn Owen Barrass
Cover Illustration ©2014 Victor Leza

Similarities between characters in this book and persons living
or dead are strictly coincidental.

www.chaosium.com.

FIRST EDITION
10 9 8 7 6 5 4 3 2 1

Chaosium Publication 6053
Published in April 2015

ISBN-10: 1568823983
ISBN-13: 9781568823980

Printed in the USA

CONTENTS

INTRODUCTION

So why *Atomic Age Cthulhu*, why bring Lovecraftian horror to the 1950s? Because few other points in history seem so tailor made for the paranoia and fear that is so important to the Cthulhu Mythos. While many places in the world were still recovering and rebuilding from the Second World War, this was a good time for America in many ways. The economy and industry were roaring, the middle class exploded and it seemed like everyone could own their own home, car, or perhaps even one of those new amazing televisions, and the nation was filled with pride over a hard won victory. Very few, if any other decade is remembered more fondly and viewed through thicker rose-colored glasses than the 1950s is for Americans. It was a time of innocence where the music, movies, cars, and everything was just so much better than anything before or since. It was a time of progress and strong moral values and optimism. The future never seemed brighter. And yet, all that was largely a façade. Just below the shiny surface of "everything is great" there was a festering fear that wrapped its clammy tentacles around everyone regardless of race, sex, or age.

Never before in history did the world face a global threat as it did in the shadow of the A-bombs, and later the even more devastating H-bombs. Mankind had always waged war, but now humanity had the power to eradicate all life on the planet with the press of a button. Educational films were made to show how to survive a nuclear blast, and at the movie theaters the classic monsters of the 30s and 40s were replaced by the horrors spawned from that atom. Children were instructed to crawl under their desks at school if "The Bomb" was dropped, as if a few inches of wood would make any difference. Many regular families either had new bomb shelters dug into their back yards, or converted existing basements and storm cellars into something with a more grim purpose.

Then there were the unseen dangers, the enemies that were everywhere, even in our midst. There were the usual cultural threats, exemplified in this decade by devilish rock n' roll, morally corrupt books like *Lolita* and *Catcher in the Rye*, disgusting nudie magazines like *Playboy*, and then there were the sinister comic books that were corrupting the minds of the youngest readers. A real world monster from Wisconsin named Ed Gein shocked the country with his vile crimes to such an extent that he would spawn fictional nightmares for decades to come such as *Psycho*, *The Texas Chainsaw Massacre*, and *Silence of the Lambs*.

But books, movies, and even the rare psychotic predator were one thing, the threat of a very real but unknown army of people, striving to overthrow the entire government and strip away all personal freedom, was quite another. This cabal of evildoers were everywhere, could be anyone including you neighbors, friends, politicians, the actors you idolized in cinema, the entertainers that sang to your children, or maybe even your family members. Of course we're talking about the dreaded Red Menace, the godless communists. Those dastardly Reds were spreading all over the globe in the 1950s; they were even reaching into cold depths of space by the end of the decade. These commies had to be stopped by any means necessary, lest the good people of America lose everything and if that meant undertaking an old fashion witch-hunt of American citizens, then that was a small price to pay for safety.

So in the 1950s you have people thinking that everything is A-OK, but in reality you've got a global threat that could change the world as we know it, one that can't be fought against and if ever unleashed, barely survived. There's an insidious corruption growing, spreading, influencing the young and easily led. Not to mention a virtual cult of secretive people working in the shadows to further their own nefarious ends. Sure sounds like a place and time perfect for the Cthulhu Mythos to us.

So here you have *Atomic Age Cthulhu*, bringing Lovecraftian horror to the postwar golden age. Within the pages of this book you will find stories about creeping, crawling menaces far more foul than any communist. Movies, music, television, and comic books have the potential to corrupt the minds, dreams, and sanity of people in ways never even thought possible in *Seduction of the Innocent*. The devastating nuclear weapons are a very real threat, but here you will learn that they pale in comparison to the horrors of the Cthulhu Mythos when unleashed.

This is *Atomic Age Cthulhu*, remember to duck and cover.

Glynn Owen Barrass and Brian Sammons

BAD RECEPTION
BY JEFFREY THOMAS

The 1954 RCA Craig with its seventeen inch screen had cost Stan a whopping $190. Sometimes he regretted not going for the Barton with a twenty-one inch screen, but that would have been fifty bucks more. He made a fair wage at the vast Plymouth factory on Detroit's Lynch Road, but that didn't mean he could afford to squander it.

He was grateful he had passed the automobile plant's required medical exam. As a Marine, seeking shelter in a trench from North Korean mortar fire, he had sustained a head injury that had required the insertion of a large metal plate in the front of his skull. His head there was markedly depressed. Despite his admission that he suffered chronic headaches, he had passed muster. Furthermore, his supervisor at the auto plant was a World War Two vet, who had taken an immediate liking to him. Maybe it was pity, Stan thought. In any case, he had been working at Plymouth for three months now, his first job since his release from the VA hospital.

Generally Stan was a frugal man, living alone in a small second-floor apartment, eating Swanson TV dinners in front of his new TV, but a television was more than an indulgence these days; it was a necessity. Especially for a man living alone, with no wife and children.

Stan's wife was Lucy Ricardo. His sons were David and Ricky Nelson. His best friend was Joe Friday. His dog was Lassie.

Like any good husband, father, friend, and master, Stan often had to undertake extra efforts to ensure the company of his loved ones… to coax and cajole these cathode ray phantoms into their visitations. In that way, his TV was a modern day ouija board. Though the Craig featured 'ROTOMATIC TUNING' to 'pin-point your station for you *automatically*,' and 'MAGIC MONITOR' circuits to 'screen out interference'. Stan relied on a set of rabbit ears resting atop the box-like TV case, without which he'd be a medium without a planchette. This device consisted of a small black sphere from which sprouted two tele-

8

scopic "ears," acting as conductors, and between them something like a twisted wire helix. Making adjustments was such a standard routine that Stan barely noticed himself having to set down his TV dinner or bottle of beer to rise from his lumpy armchair and tweak one or both of the antennae just so. One didn't question the limitations of technology when that technology was all one knew.

Stan thought the dipole antenna's black orb with its twin insect feelers resembled the helmet of some outer space monster, poking its head up from behind the TV to gaze back at him as he sat in his otherwise darkened living room with the television's gray illumination fluttering over him. On weekends, and sometimes even during the week, he would fall asleep there in his armchair with a bottle of Schlitz still in hand. He lied to himself that the beer dulled the pain of his headaches, when in fact it only intensified his suffering by leaving him with crippling hangovers. At least it helped wash down the aspirin.

Tonight, while slumped back in his chair, he dreamed he was at the plant—but whereas in his daily work he was on the team that installed the steering column, steering gear mechanism, steering wheel gearshift, and even the rear bumper of fish-faced American cars—in his dream he was instead helping to assemble hulking Sherman tanks of the type that had been used in Korea. In fact, the Plymouth plant had supported war-time efforts in the past by manufacturing trucks for the military, though Stan had never been part of such an operation. He had also learned that in a special clean room at the Plymouth facility, a team of Chrysler engineers had developed a cost-saving process for the military, electroplating steel drums with nickel in order to help refine uranium for the creation of atomic bombs, including the very first atom bomb. But Stan had of course never witnessed this project, either.

Working on the tank assembly, just as in Plymouth's real-life operations, was a mix of men and women, white and black. One of these workers was Alice, a young black woman with warm eyes and a bright easy smile. He had dreamed of Alice before. Standing on the far side of the tank they currently labored over, she looked up and gave him one of those big white smiles. Encouraged by this, Stan overcame his shyness to ask her, "Say, Alice, what are we making all these tanks for, anyway? I thought the war was over."

"There's another one coming, honey," she told him. She called everyone honey, but it made Stan's heart give a little kick every time, even in dreams, as if she only ever said it to him.

"Always is," said Frank, another worker close by. "Another war, that is," he clarified.

"This one's gonna be different," Alice told them both. "Don't know why we're even gonna bother, though. No way we can win this one."

"The USA not winning a war?" Frank said. "You're out of your mind."

"We'll all be out of our minds," Alice said, no longer smiling. "When we see them."

"Who is 'them,' Alice?" Stan asked her.

She turned her now solemn gaze to Stan, and she was so pretty he almost didn't notice the fear in her eyes. "Can't tell you that, honey."

"What's it, a secret?" Frank taunted. "You damn Negros gonna rise up against us, is that it?"

"Can't tell you who they are," Alice repeated, unblinking, not taking her eyes off Stan's. "Couldn't if I tried."

Stan woke from this dream to the Indian Head Test Pattern on his seventeen-inch screen, blurred as if it weren't tuned in properly, when in fact the blurring was from the pain that fizzed like static in his skull.

***

Stan slouched in front of his TV with his third beer in hand. He couldn't be bothered to shove a TV dinner in the oven tonight.

Framed in the Craig's glass screen, a window onto an easy make-believe, the world was all black and white.

Tonight Lucy and Ethel had somehow wound up atop the Empire State Building dressed as Martian invaders, in bizarre costumes with insect-like feelers and wearing prosthetic noses, jabbering in some weird outer space language. The tight costume emphasized Lucy's bust, and Stan found himself becoming aroused, just as he had in that episode when burglars tied Lucy up with rope and put a gag in her mouth. The beer in him made the scene all the more surreal. He was torn between changing the channel to spare his brain—already filled to burst with agony both literal and figurative—or unzipping his fly to alleviate his frustrations.

He had lost his job today.

He blamed Frank, of course, but he also blamed the pain in his skull. A storm had begun rolling in late in the afternoon, the summer sky weighted with iron gray clouds, and he could swear that changes in barometric pressure, and maybe changes in the air from dry to damp, had an effect on the steel plate in his skull. His headache today had sent spots of burning color swarming across his vision, like weird organisms viewed through a microscope.

He should blame Schlitz, too, because he'd had to endure a hangover at work this morning, but mostly it was Frank.

At work they called Stan the Gorilla. He had overheard it behind his back, but sometimes the other workers like Frank had even teased him to his face. It was not only because Stan was tall and heavy-set, but because the way his metal-patched cranium dipped radically, it gave his head a concave slope like that of a gorilla. He'd tried to ignore these jokes, had even laughed along self-consciously that time he had caught another worker holding a piece of steel up in front of his own forehead and staggering around with a slack expression, like a zombie, while the other men snickered. But today they had gone too far.

Stan had cornered Alice at a time when there was apparently no one else around, just as the workers were returning from lunch break, at her station where she helped assemble instrument panels. He had been summoning the courage to ask her out for weeks, and today he had finally stammered, "Hey, Alice, I was wondering if, uh, you'd like to catch a movie with me sometime. They say *On the Waterfront* is really good. You know…Marlon Brando? Or, um, *The Atomic Kid* with Mickey Rooney sounds fun."

Alice had looked at him with a mix of surprise and sympathy. Or was it shock and pity? And not without a dash of horror. Stan figured the shock was partly from being asked out by a white man, and mostly from being asked out by a disfigured white man. After a stunned second or two she said, "Aw, honey, I'm sorry but I already have a fella. Thanks for offering, anyway…that's awful sweet of you."

"Yeah, sure," he said, immediately looking away, no longer able to meet her eyes. He shrugged. "I just thought. Anyway…sorry. See ya around." And he had quickly turned to shamble off toward his own work area.

But someone, probably one of the white women Alice worked with, had obviously overheard him…and told others what she'd heard. Because in no time, some of the men in Stan's own area were laughing loudly and gesturing toward him. When Stan looked up from his work, there was Frank in front of him, saying to another worker named Jack, "You see how it is, Jack? If you can't get yourself a nice regular white woman, you go for the next best thing, figuring she ain't gonna be as picky."

"Hey," Mike said, chuckling, "it ain't no surprise the Gorilla would want to go with a monkey."

Stan didn't consider his reaction, and didn't hesitate in acting. He straightened up, took two strides toward the men, clapped each on the side of the head with one of his big hands, and forced their skulls together with a loud thunk. Mike dropped like the proverbial sack of potatoes. Frank managed to shuffle back a few steps, staring at Stan in dazed disbelief, before he went down.

Stan's boss took him aside later and was very stern, though he could have been worse about it, because he told Stan he was sorry when he fired him. Stan didn't see Alice as he was walked out, but he supposed the story would get back to her. He wondered how she'd feel about it. He only hoped she wouldn't be harassed by her coworkers henceforth.

On his way out Frank, now awake and holding a cold wet towel to the side of his head, had shouted after him, "You're crazy, you know that? Battle fatigue, huh, Stanley? Is that it?"

***

Fred burst into Ricky's living room, wearing a WWI style helmet and carrying a pump-action shotgun, breathlessly warning Ricky that he had heard about an invasion from outer space.

Outside the twin windows of Stan's living room, in the night, thunder growled as the storm that had been building for the past few hours broke at last. Two things happened at that instant: Stan's TV picture filled with snow, turning Ricky and Fred into grainy shadows—drowning out their voices with static—and unseen knives stabbed Stan in both temples. He actually dropped his mostly empty beer bottle to the floor and hunched forward with his palms pressed to the sides of his head. For an irrational moment he wondered if a bolt of lightning had shot through the nearest window and struck him, attracted to the metal plate under his skin.

Peripherally he saw another flash of lightning outside his windows. The thunder followed only a second later, indicating the storm was already directly overhead; a massive boom that made the walls vibrate. Stan felt as though he were again ducking down in a steaming trench gouged into that hellish Korean battlefield. He pulled his head into his neck, waiting for the shrapnel to hit him, though the plate in his skull was like shrapnel already, bigger than the chunk that had struck him on the battleground.

He lurched up from his chair somehow, staggered to one open window and then the other, shutting them just as a torrential rain was unleashed upon the city. Crashing down like a Biblical flood in the making. It slammed his windowpanes as if it were an angry, sentient force demanding admission. Stan pulled the shades down, to further shut out that malignant force, before he turned and fell back into the armchair with a groan.

When Stan managed to lift his head, which seemed to have tripled in weight as if its entire mass were now made of metal, and focused his watery burning eyes, he saw that horizontal bands were now rolling up his TV screen from bottom to top and the snow had intensified, so that Ricky and Fred were even harder to distinguish. Or was that Lucy and Ethel? The two distorted figures were weirdly elongated, gesturing in dripping blurs, black holes that were probably their mouths stretching wide. Snatches of metallic voices could now be heard through the hissing static, but they were incomprehensible... unless that was Lucy and Ethel imitating Martian talk again.

Another detonation of thunder. The glass in the windows rattled. The plate in his forehead felt like it was rattling in its frame, as well. Stan moaned again.

The tinny, garbled voices were like ice picks in his ears, fingernails on the chalk of his spinal column. He braced his hands on the grips of his armchair and once more shoved himself to his feet. As he stumbled to his TV, the static jumped louder in a crackling burst and the horizontal bands quickened to a flutter. He took hold of the left antenna of the rabbit ears, changing its position slightly. The rasp of static diminished to a milder hiss of white noise, the unsettling voices gone. He nudged the right ear next, and the horizontal bands slowed. As he stepped back to look down at the screen, the horizontal bands stopped altogether and the veil of electromagnetic interference lessened dramatically. Stan realized then that his proximity to the TV made the reception worse, somehow, so he backed away further and reseated himself to gauge the results. Sure enough, the snow cleared to the extent that he could view the television's images pretty clearly, and though there was still no proper sound, the fizzing static was just a whisper, almost lost under the pummeling of the rain outside.

I Love Lucy must have ended, however, and another program begun. Whatever this show was, it was not centered on some cheap interior set, some painted outdoors backdrop. The backdrop appeared to be an actual city, but a city half reduced to its constituent parts, its components, its bricks and blocks. Rubble and rebar, wafting smoke, and Stan was reminded of the destruction in Seoul or Pyongyang or Wonsan. Was it a documentary, then? An exposé on war? But which? Only technology differentiated wars. His war? Earlier, maybe...WWII? A lot looked flattened there in the background. Nagasaki, then? Hiroshima? Stan didn't know that this year—the same year the war in Korea had ended—the US had proposed a plan called Operation Vulture, in support of the French in Indochina, that if it hadn't been rejected would have allowed for the use of three atom bombs dropped on Viet Minh positions. Otherwise, he might well have believed this to be the aftermath.

In the middle distance, a dirty white sheet fluttered by on the wind, dragging its tattered ends across the floor of pulverized debris. Or maybe it was a torn-away canvas awning, or a futile white flag of surrender.

Yet another rumble of thunder, like a freight train barreling through the apartment overhead. The plate in his head hummed as though an electric current were being passed straight into it. And—as if the lightning storm, the electrical field of his own body, and the television were all connected—the TV screen went all snowy once more, but this time in a negative image of static: a field of seething black sparkling with glitter, like time-lapse photography of galaxies of stars being born and expiring in the briefest flicker of existence.

When the avalanche roar of thunder had passed, and the vibrating hum in his head had receded, the screen cleared to show a different angle of perhaps the same destroyed city. A church steeple stood in puny defiance, but the rest of it was a carbonized shell. There was still a faint degree of snow to the reception—yet then Stan realized it was not interference, but actual snow drifting down on the blasted city. No...no...not quite. It was a lazy fall of ash, sprinkling across the city from the churning black ceiling of cloud that capped the sky like an encroachment of deep space itself. Inky space pressing down on the atmosphere of the Earth, crushing the air, the friction of these opposing forces burning the oxygen itself into ash.

Several more ragged-ended sheets came fluttering along on the wind, one further in the distance than the other. The funny thing was, the plumes of smoke rising into the air everywhere from the piles of shattered rubble were being carried in the opposite direction.

The scene was depressing Stan on top of his pain, overcoming his curiosity about the nature of the program. He had learned all he wanted to learn about war—any war—firsthand. Before some orphaned tot with her face smeared in soot could stagger dazedly into the frame, Stan took advantage of the abatement of his suffering to get up from the chair yet again and reach out to turn the TV's dial to a different channel.

The next channel revealed a new image, but this image was a third angle of the same demolished city. He clicked to another channel. Another view of the same subject matter. Click…click…click. Only the perspective changed; the annihilation remained the same. In fact, Stan was finding that channels not normally active were receiving the transmission. He made several full circuits of the dial, as if futilely trying to crack a safe, and found that every channel featured the broadcast…only the point of view altering, as if he were receiving live feeds from a dozen or more TV cameras dispersed around the city.

Something of great import had happened, then…but where, exactly? And what, exactly?

When he'd drawn close to the TV to change the channel, his nearness had again caused the reception to grow grainy and noisy with static, but the various city scenes were only obscured, not fully erased. He gave both rabbit ears a few hard, impatient shifts that lessened the video and audio interference, but it wasn't until he retreated to the armchair that the picture was clarified and the sound went mostly quiet. He had settled on one channel arbitrarily: the one that showed the blackened church steeple. He had been tempted to turn the set off altogether, but he had to know what was going on. Whatever it was, it was obviously of profound significance. Would some announcer finally come on to explain what the hell he was witnessing? Along came yet another bed sheet (had an exploded laundry dispersed its contents across the city?), blowing into the scene, but it stopped in the middle of the street…and hovered there. And hovered there. Hovered there, with its torn ends stirring as if it swam in place. Its surface rippled or pulsed or undulated, and the sheet was not so much dirty white as cloudy gray, with the faintest metallic sheen. As he stared fixedly at it, the floating shroud raised itself up a little, its membrane appearing to stiffen with alertness, and Stan realized then it was not a bed sheet or any other inanimate object, but some kind of living thing, however primitive its protoplasmic amoeba's body; a sentience manifested as a raw scrap of primal tissue. And it had stiffened in alertness because, just as Stan had understood on some deep intuitive level what he was seeing, the thing had seemed to understand him as well. It was seeing him. Or sensing him, in whatever manner the thing perceived the material world. And even as Stan recognized that it was aware of him, the tattered membrane started moving directly at the camera. Directly toward his screen. Toward him.

Stan launched himself forward, thrusting his arm out. The membrane was sailing at him quickly as well, as if trying to intercept him before he could touch the dial. As he came at the screen the reception worsened, but unfortunately it wasn't enough to blot out what he was seeing.

Stan realized he had given out a wild cry, a blurt of panic, but before the thing could reach the thin windowpane of his screen—the flimsy bubble film that separated the two of them—his fingers found the dial and snapped it.

Another channel. On this street, none of those hovering, parachute-like bodies. Blending together, ash and popping electrical bugs filled the smoky air. The static roared like a raging fire.

Stan fell to his knees, his fingers still gripping the dial in case another of the apparitions came out from a shadowed alley of the ruins. He heaved with gasps, shaking badly, feeling as if he had just emerged alive from a firefight…but most of all he felt pierced by the eyeless, faceless creature that had spotted him, as if its awesome sentience had burned a hole straight through him. A lingering aftertaste of that inhuman, alien sentience seemed imprinted on the metal plate in his skull as if it were photographic film. Had the plate attracted that mental force, or had it in fact *shielded* him from it? If not for that little chunk of armor, might the creature have burrowed into his mind to consume it, or replace it with its own?

Through his shell-shocked terror and confusion, Stan belatedly registered a few details about this particular scene that had escaped him on his previous circuits of the dial. Framed within the TV screen was a downed camouflaged helicopter, crumpled by the side of the street. Despite the damage it had sustained, it was clearly unlike any such machine Stan had ever seen; certainly nothing like the choppers he'd known in Korea, such as the Sikorsky H-19. And now he more consciously took in the charred and gutted bodies of cars he'd only noticed peripherally before. Scattered everywhere, often half buried, many crushed, some upside-down—as if they had been borne high aloft on fiery winds before plummeting back to Earth. Despite their deformities, they too were of styles unfamiliar to him. Smaller than any of the big, solid American cars he had helped construct at Plymouth. More compact, more toy-like, more...*futuristic.*

He had another of his strange intuitions. This prescient instinct told him that he wasn't witnessing a catastrophic event occurring now at some distant location of the Earth. He was witnessing a catastrophic event occurring at some as-yet distant location in time.

But all these considerations had distracted him. He'd let down his guard. Suddenly, there it was: another of the jellyfish-things, appearing like an extrusion of ectoplasm from behind the crashed helicopter itself. It might even be the same entity that had tried to reach him before.

"I'm going crazy," Stan muttered to himself, quaking all over and close to tears. "It's battle fatigue, that's all. And I drink too much. And that shrapnel scrambled my brains. I'm still watching *I Love Lucy* and I just don't know it."

But he had made a mistake in speaking to himself aloud. The creature had heard him; he could tell by the way it lifted a little and its membrane stretched more taut. It stopped drifting, spun to face him facelessly, and as before began whisking toward him.

Click! The next channel. Stan was whimpering. In this shot, a scorched tank rested in the center of the road. Again, it was some impressive make that had yet to be invented. Not impressive enough, though, to have defended the city from the threat that had come. But where were the bodies of the soldiers, the citizens? *What had they done with the bodies?*

There, at the end of the street: three of the jellyfish glided into view, pale against the black smoke, almost glowing. Now four of the creatures...five. They hadn't noticed him yet.

Stan had seen enough. Enough. He reached his hand to another knob, and turned the RCA Craig's power off.

But the image didn't vanish. The static kept rasping. The only thing he accomplished was to make those five phantoms at the end of the street whirl around in the air to direct their attention his way.

Stan jumped to his feet and darted to the wall near his two windows, where the set's power cord was plugged into an outlet. He jerked it out of the wall socket, then turned and looked back at the screen.

Because he had moved away from the set, the reception had improved. That was the only change. The black and white vision of destruction remained, with the five entities approaching him steadily.

He thought of fetching a hammer and smashing that seventeen-inch screen. But what if that only opened the window? Let them into his reality, here in the past?

A flash of light outside his windows, like a bomb igniting. There were several beats of delay before the accompanying peal of thunder. The storm was moving along, then. Good...*good!* It was the storm that had opened the way, wasn't it? Some triangular relationship between the electrical storm, the TV, and the conductive metal hatch bolted so close to his brain. If that triangle could be broken again, *that's* what would really cut the power to his set.

But he was afraid the storm wouldn't pass in time. The five entities would have reached him by then. He had to take more decisive action. He was a *soldier*, damn it. The war was not yet over; hell, it was a long way from beginning. Maybe he could change the outcome—keep the invaders from entering his world right here and now.

So Stan rushed to meet the enemy. Charged his TV as if to hurl himself onto a sprung hand grenade to save his comrades. What he had learned was that he could disrupt the signal; it was probably the steel plate that was doing it. So he snatched up his TV antenna and bent his head forward and pressed his indented cranium against the twisted metal helix that jutted from the black orb between the two rabbit ears.

That did it, all right. The surge in static was almost deafening. The TV screen turned entirely to snow, as if a sandstorm were raging inside that little box. He could not see the creatures, and they could not see him. Right? The snow formed an obstruction, a wall…and blocked this way, the invaders could come no closer.

Right?

He closed his eyes, squeezed them tight, and held his position until the lightning storm could truly pass, to cinch the deal. Held his ground like a good soldier.

***

Stan opened his eyes at last, and what enfolded before him as his lids lifted was like watching an idle TV power up for the day's first viewing.

Static still sizzled in his ears, but maybe that was flames crackling, because fires still burned here and there all around him, sending smoke twisting into the air. He looked above him, making an inarticulate sound deep in his throat, and saw the black clouds that formed a near-solid cataract across the sky, as if to encase and trap this insignificant little world, an insect preserved in amber. Falling ash alighted on the skin of his upturned face and came to rest delicately on his eyelashes. Was it his imagination that the ashes smelled of death, as if they were the thinnest parings of human flesh?

Looking down again, he whipped around to glance this way, then that. He was standing out in the open in the middle of the street. Then he raised his hands in front of his face and examined them. His skin was utterly colorless. The world here was black and white.

A tiny disturbance in the air like an unheard whisper or rustle reached him, and he whirled again to look down an intersecting street. Hovering toward him was something like a burial shroud, a winding sheet instead of a bed sheet, carried on the wind. But there was no wind.

He spun to look down an alley on his other side, from which two more of the airborne membranes were emerging. The enemy forces were advancing on him from every direction. And that was when Stan had one more of those intuitions that the creatures themselves, perhaps, were putting into his head, with its special receiver. This intuition told him these were not so many individual beings, but individual *cells*—numbering in the millions, the *billions*—that in their totality constituted one great, single entity. God was too small, too humble a word for it.

"I'm going crazy," Stan sobbed loudly, as if protesting to the nearing cells themselves. "It's battle fatigue. And I drink too much. And that shrapnel messed up my brain. I'm still watching *I Love Lucy* but I just...don't...know it!"

He dropped to his knees there in the middle of the street as the circle around him tightened, as if he were the center of some TV test pattern...the hub of a complex geometry...an integral figure to complete an unfathomable equation...a vacuum tube to be inserted into a faulty television set. They had lured him. They needed him. And he would, thankfully, never know why. It was beyond human comprehension.

Stan threw back his head, palms pressed hard to his temples, and wailed to the crushing sky. The encircling entities converged on him... making it time to cut away for a commercial break.

UNAMERICAN
BY CODY GOODFELLOW

The tenant in #9 at the Tahitian Arms had a Doberman named Adolf. It barked and howled all night long, its owner said, ever since it stopped doing live sex shows for Howard Hughes at the Beverly Hills Hotel. The tenant in #7 was an old Borscht Belt ventriloquist recovering from a stroke. His dummy shrieked all night long at the dog, taunting it in Yiddish until it attacked the bedroom wall of #8, where Hugh Talbot lay on his narrow twin bed while other people slept.

When Talbot came in at ten, the sheets were still twisted in a sweaty noose from when he got up. But now a man in a raincoat and a green Stetson fedora sat on the bed, smoking Talbot's last Lucky Strike.

"How's the stag film business treating you, Tarkovsky?" His smile was like a leather bag overflowing with loaded dice. Picture Jack Oakie on a Benzedrine drip and nine years without slumber.

"Can't complain," Talbot said. "Beats the hell out of jail." His starch only held out for a few seconds before he rolled his eyes at the ruddy, acne-scarred face of the panty-sniffing peeper who wrecked his life.

"You're not as big a surprise as you make out," Talbot said.

"What gave me away?"

"The studio head tried to write me a kiss-off check with a broken arm tonight, so I figured I must be due."

Cooley smiled sadly and tapped ash on Talbot's pillow.

Talbot patted himself down and threw up his hands in surrender. "You must be tired, you didn't even trash the place this time," he said.

"We don't have to go through that, pal." Cooley got up and moved like smoke between him and the door. "We're old friends now, right? Friends don't keep secrets."

Sweat popped on his brow. His feet kicked chips off the cracked linoleum. "You fingered me and blacklisted me and all you could prove was that I fought for my country, I voted for Eisenhower, and the most radical group I belonged to was the Writer's Guild. Why do you still do it?"

"You should've represented yourself, 'stead of wasting all that dough on that sheenie lawyer." Pulling a nightstand drawer, the man took out a dull brown box, flipped it open with his thumb. The Bronze Star looked like a cheap Xmas ornament in his big, callused hand. "She let you keep all this? Man, she must've been sweet on you, even after all the dirt you did her. Maybe you should go back and try to patch it up. I could swear an affidavit you ain't getting any on the side, now."

The dummy in #7 was singing that Marlene Dietrich song from *The Blue Angel* in an awful, mocking falsetto. The dog in 9 barked and bit the wall. The dummy screamed, "*Cock zich oys, nudzi!*"

Cooley picked up the nearest heavy thing—a Writers' Guild Award for *Best Written Film Concerning Problems with the American Scene* in 1949—and threw it at the wall. It went right through the flimsy sheetrock and shattered something expensively loud in 9. The Doberman whined.

Dropping the spent cigarette on the floor, Cooley blew smoke in Talbot's ear with his next, whispered words. "How'd you like to work in real pictures again? Maybe even direct…"

Talbot's gaze roved all over Cooley without finding his eyes. "I don't know any more than the last time you kicked my door down, Cooley. And I'm still no belly-crawler."

"You won't have to go in front of a committee. You won't have to go on *Last Man Out* or write a mea culpa for *Red Channels*. You just have to do what you do. Make pictures. Come in with me now, or when we subpoena you tomorrow morning. You don't want to see the matinee show."

A fountain made of four big concrete clamshells drooled indigo-tinted water in the center of the Tahitian Arms' tiki-infested courtyard. Fritz lurched out at them in his bathrobe, holding an ice pack to his head. "Who the hell you think you are?"

Cooley waved a badge at him like a fastball. "Special Investigator from the House Committee for Un-American Activities. Uncle Sam sent me to kick your rotten kraut dog to death."

Fritz popped a vein in his temple. "That dog is a champion pure-bred, he pour the pork to Lana Turner, you should some respect to show…"

Cooley kicked Fritz in the crotch, grabbed his breadstick neck and threw him headfirst at the fountain. Fritz broke the bottom shell with his face and flopped under the syrupy trickle of too-blue water.

Adolf came barreling out the window screen of 9 and padded right past Fritz to leap through the saggy screen door of 7. High-pitched, asthmatic screams and weeping followed Adolf as the Doberman came back out and sped away from the Tahitian Arms with the mutilated ventriloquist's dummy dangling from its jaws.

***

Talbot refused a shot of bourbon at the Timbuktu Room on Normandie. "Just as well," Cooley allowed. "They piss in the white man's drinks. But if you'd rather be seen at the Brown Derby or the Beachcomber on my arm, we can do that thing, instead." To the bartender, "Just the bottle, Buckwheat."

"You forgot I don't drink," Talbot shouted over the noise. The club was a bottomless cavern, blue with smoke more grass than tobacco. On the tiny thrust stage, Pharaoh Jones and the Nile Crocodiles turned 'Caravan' into a ferocious jungle fertility rite. Half the brass section dropped their horns and picked up machetes and hatchets, which they banged on tin pails. Pharaoh Jones kicked over his vibraphone and produced a scythe, spinning and whipping it over the conked heads of the jumping, crazed crowd.

Cooley poured a shot of bourbon and knocked it back. "What if you could do it over?" His yellow teeth clenched as his gag reflex kicked in. It was a near thing, but he kept it down. "If you could go back, would you just name some names and get it over with?"

"I'd tell you the same thing I told you in '47. Go shit in your hat."

"You know all those excellent comrades you had in that artists' colony back in England, after the war? We found them all, the ones who came back. Your excellent friends rolled over on you. You know what they told us?"

"I was only there for a month! I was tired, I needed to get away and some friends led me out there. When I was there it was…well, it wasn't innocent, but it was none of your—"

"Your cute little English 'artist colony' was a nest of Communists, anarchists and sexual deviants. After '47, they ceased to exist, and since the Limeys have this brilliant thing called the Secrets Act, they don't even have to tell us what happened to them."

Talbot just shook his head, watching the flash of blades striking sparks onstage. Pharaoh Jones held up a white chicken.

"You never knew anything worth knowing, Talbot. We always knew that." Cooley offered Talbot a shot. "The one who fingered you first was a pro... She didn't know you or your Limey friends. Probably just threw you in to pad her list."

Cooley sighed at the untouched shot glass and went to claim it. Talbot threw an uppercut which Cooley caught, twisted and used to lift Talbot off his barstool.

"You knew I was clean, so why did you ruin my fucking life?"

Not even mildly upset, Cooley twisted Talbot's wrist until he somehow had Talbot whimpering at his feet. "Clean?" He picked up the bottle as he dragged Talbot to the back door.

In the alley, Cooley let him fall and gratefully hug filthy concrete. "Because you were a pinko fellow traveler of dubious character and foreign ideas. Because you threw the First Amendment at a special Congressional investigation, and so violated the *Smith* Act. Because you held your ideals above your own skin, even over your own country."

Inside, Pharaoh Jones did something that made the crowd scream like the club was burning down.

"America is the only bright candle in the endless night, and a storm is coming. You need to see how dark it really is out there, before we can let you go back to work."

Cooley pulled him to his feet and offered him the bottle.

"You go to hell. I served my country..." Talbot grimaced as he took the bottle and swigged from it. His deep-set eyes were ringed with shadow but glowed in the red neon light. "I've never even met anyone who wanted to overthrow the government. You tarred me as a subversive. Why would you do anything for me?"

"All writers are subversive, see? What do you do, but make up lies for a living? Better a hundred of you 'innocent' moral termites go down, than one real Soviet operative goes free to do real harm to this great democracy." A deep sigh and a hurricane of wet coughing. He snapped his fingers and peeled the cellophane off a fresh pack of cigarettes. "They're eating us alive from the inside out, and weak sisters like you are letting it happen."

Talbot hugged his arms, trying not to shake. The muscles of his jaw bulged like he was cracking walnuts.

Cooley stared at him with a tired smile. "Do you love your country?"

"Even now…yes, I do."

"Good for you. Then you might just be able to help save it."

Cooley looked away as someone came out of the club. A short young Negro in a green sharkskin suit saw Cooley and spun to go back inside, but Cooley caught him and pinned him to the wall.

Rifling his pockets, he rubbed a shiny green bundle in the kid's face. "What'd I tell you about selling this shit?"

"Man, they all grasshoppers down here. I just sell what they want…"

"You sell what you're told to sell." Stuffing his pockets with bags of white powder, he shoved the kid towards the door.

"Man, nobody want that shit…it's…it's evil…"

"You push it hard enough, they'll want it more than air." He herded the kid back into the club, turned and caught Talbot by the shoulder. Driving him down the alley, Cooley pressed the bundle of sandwich-paper envelopes of grass into his hand. "Smoke up, Hubert. I didn't forget. We've got a long drive and lots to talk about."

***

Prowling westward on Sunset, they hit clubs, restaurants and bars. Cooley braced busboys, pinched pushers, shook scandal rag sheet-sniffers. Passing white powder, demanding answers. Where is SHE? Talbot hid under his hat in the car.

Waiting down the block from the Formosa Room, Talbot fidgeted with the door latch and looked up the street. Some kind of red carpet gala was gearing up. Arc lights swept the sky from two theaters around the corner. The lights and the noise were constantly on the edge of some almost ecstatic climax. Every night like we just won a war.

And why not? With every release, we nuke the impossible. Fix history. Fuck the future. Teach our enemies to adore us, and our allies to fear us. Steal their dreams and force-feed them our own. Who cares if we got handed our asses in Korea? John Wayne will keep winning World War 2 forever. The Russians got the Bomb? They'll never get Marilyn Monroe. Hollywood even slew the HUAC dragon, if only in its dreams. Gary Cooper left it to die with lead in its guts in *High Noon.*

Clearing his throat, he said, "Thank goodness for movie stars."

Cooley spat. "America finally has some royal feet to kiss."

"Bullshit," Talbot said. "With movie stars, we got walking talking gods."

Cooley chuckled. "Must've been a hell of a kick, playing puppeteer and making all those fancy little tin gods dance and say your stupid words, eh, Tarkovsky?"

"You know how it feels." His eyes were red, his face stupidly beatific, but his hands still shook when he wasn't trying to strangle them.

"You can go back to work wherever you want. After..."

"After making agitprop for the American way of life. The American worker is the grease that lubes the gears of this great nation."

"That's the ticket. We don't need to push the propaganda; we just need to make something everybody will watch, that'll open the right doors in their heads so the real program gets through."

"The real program?"

"It's subliminal, Mr. Talbot." The woman's voice, husky and languid, came from close behind him. "The Chinese call it *xi nao*, or 'brainwashing.'"

Cooley jumped out of the car. "Ah, here's our missing comrade. Now it's a Party." Whistling the *Internationale*, he came around and opened the door for the woman who stood on the curb.

Her platinum hair was a shock of spun sugar curls wrapped in a red scarf. Her figure was a secret closely held by a fur-trimmed burgundy frock coat. She smoked a black cigarette in a long red holder. She had a wide, lush mouth and migraine-colored eyes. She glanced at Talbot with a calculated flash of frigid heat, but she demurred at introducing herself. She slid into the front passenger seat and Cooley slammed the door.

"Hugh Talbot," he brayed as he started the engine, "may I introduce Her Majesty the Red Queen of Hollywood, Miss Lila Corliss. I do believe you are acquainted with each other by reputation..." He winked at Talbot and made a lewd hand gesture.

Talbot turned away and began to roll a reefer. The grass kept spilling out onto the floor tiled in stained issues of *Variety*, *Hush*, *Aware*, *Red Channels* and *Police Gazette*. The carpet underneath was red-black and sticky and stank like a butchers' shop.

Swinging out onto the road ahead of an Italian sport coupe and a howling pack of taxis, the royal blue '53 DeSoto Fire Dome Deluxe sedan left smoking black rubber on the red carpet in front of the Formosa Room. Talbot left a racing stripe of vomit on Doris Day and Howard Keel.

***

Driving up winding Coldwater Canyon, they ditched the city. Burnt orange Chinese lanterns adorned green-black eucalyptus groves filled with parked cars with curtains. Halloween shadows gilded a long line of looming, impressively ugly palaces like an audition for *House of Usher*. Talbot wanted to pull over to be sick again. Cooley told him to hang out the window.

"You know what America's real weakness is? Well, any modern superpower, I mean." Cooley killed the dregs of the bourbon and lit a cigarette. "It's not a nation of people bound by blood, see, by a common culture. It's just a bunch of strangers tied together by an *idea*."

An oncoming convertible filled with drunken beach bunnies swerved to pass the DeSoto. Cooley tossed the bottle to smash their windshield.

"You look at the War. Germany kept fighting 'til we came knocking on Schickelgruber's bunker, and the Japs had to be atom-bombed twice before they folded."

Talbot rolled up the window and laid down on a back seat the size of a prison bunkbed. "But their fascism couldn't hold a candle to ours."

"Do go on," said Miss Corliss.

"People's loyalty to an idea is paper-thin when push comes to shove, see? There are foreign powers—shit, you don't even want to know—that would seek to infiltrate our civilian population and adulterate it. Our borders are like a fucking sieve, and more of them creep in every day to suck us dry. They've even tried to strike at us through our drinking water."

Talbot sat up and wiped his mouth on his sleeve and rubbed his eyes. "Boy, when you go crazy, you don't stop halfway for a manicure."

Cooley turned and raised a fist just high enough to make Talbot flinch. "It's true. The Russkies do it to their own satellite countries to stunt their mental development, see? But they use a crude fluoride-based system. We've had to take steps to protect our water supply, and fortify the civilian populace who consumes it."

Lighting a cigarette and running his fingers through his dirt-encrusted hair, Talbot said, "*We* put fluoride in our water. Is that a Communist plot, too?"

"It only looks like fluoride. These mineral molecular chains, they're pretty rare in nature. They tweak the blood chemistry just so much… it's untraceable, but it'll change you just enough so we can know really who's one of us, and who's a foreign agent."

Miss Corliss fitted a new cigarette into her holder. Her expression of polite interest had not changed since Cooley began his drunken civics lecture. "That's a fascinating idea, Mr. Cooley. Why, one could immunize the working class against disease, and…"

"Sure, one *could*, if this was Red China." Cooley guffawed like a mule. "But this is a question of national security. If you grow up with our tap water, it makes you unable to knock up, or get pregnant with, a foreigner. Pretty soon, Americans will be more like each other than like anyone from outside. We'll be a true American race…hell, someday, our own species."

"Sure," Talbot groaned, "that'll fix everything."

Corliss smiled a big million-dollar grin. "Is it just you who believes this, or are all of you experimenting with that new Swiss hallucinogen…"

Cooley blinked at her, genuinely alarmed. He stared at his hand on the wheel as if counting and recounting his fingers. "Not much farther now," he mumbled.

They emerged from the canyon and turned west on the twisted spine of Mulholland Drive. The heavens below them were crazed with stars. Talbot scrubbed his eyes, but it was still upside down. The stars lay in the basin of a vast valley, while the defeated sky above was an empty vault of dishwater-colored dust.

They cruised along the ridge until they couldn't see another light. They sailed through a gate with a couple armed MP's standing at attention with German shepherds on leashes. Cooley threw them a Nazi salute, whistling the "Duck and Cover" jingle through his crooked teeth.

Low, beige Quonset huts and shadowy mounds of machinery passed by. "Nike missile base," Cooley said, "on the surface." The DeSoto stopped beside a row of cinderblock bunkers with their own electrified fence. Talbot looked over the seat and immediately started shaking his head, moaning, "No, no, no."

"Oh, so you figured it out, already?"

"Oh no, you want somebody else."

"No, we need *you*."

"But I can't—"

"You said you wanted to go back to work. Here's your chance."

"I won't. I can't...not like that..."

"What's the matter with it?"

Talbot pointed at the red and white transmitter tower looming overhead. "There is no goddamned way I'm working in television."

***

Inside the main building, their driver's licenses were taken, fingerprints checked, and a lock of hair and a vial of blood taken from each of them, including Cooley. Then they got in an elevator and went down three floors.

Beyond the armed guards and the bank vault doors, it looked like the front office and bullpen of a TV station. A morgue filled with reels of film and a transmitter room filled with looming towers of blinking lights and whirring fans fed off the bullpen, but there were no studios, no sets or other signs of life.

"What station is this?" Talbot asked.

"Channel Zero," Cooley said. "Whole operation is underground, buried in lead. Officially, they only go on the air when the bombers knock out everything else. Stay put. I'm gonna go see a man about a horse." He slipped out of the room.

Corliss went over to the water cooler and filled a cup. Sipping it with her lips puckered, she started to turn away when Talbot came over.

"So, you're part of this cabal of zealots? I would've thought..."

She smiled frostily. "Thought I was just another lapsed Communist turned professional informer..."

Talbot shrugged over to the water cooler.

"But now you're thinking I'm a lady G-Man, or even a double or triple agent... Well, go on, what *are* you thinking?"

He filled the cup, drained it and refilled it. "I'm struggling to give you the benefit of the doubt, because we've never met and you're

29

rather swell in the flesh for a stool-pigeon, but I can't figure why such a nice girl would name someone she never met—"

"Oh, so you know."

"As luck would have it, yes."

"Please don't take it hard. It wasn't my idea; I didn't even know your name until they fed it to me in executive session. They said you were involved with some English radical group after the war. I had to give them what they wanted. It wasn't just a question of working or not…"

"I've never seen you in anything, have I…?"

She gave him a tired, flattered smile, but looked away and covered her eyes. "I'm not an actress. I'm a scenarist, just like you. Or I was… Now, I seem to've become more of a gossip columnist."

"A parrot as well as a stool pigeon. You're quite a catch."

"I didn't have any choice. And the pay is nothing to save the family farm, but I had to sell scripts through a male front long before there was a blacklist. Any girl who won't submit to the casting couch is a radical, in this town."

"Alright, it's tough all over. But why are you here, now? What did they tell you?"

She bit her lip as she loaded a cigarette. Red-black lipstick smeared on her teeth. "That something was going to happen. I write a column, I have a program on KABC, and I… I wield a certain degree of influence in the ex-Communist community. Cooley said I would have a role to play, so I came. I do what they tell me, and you should, too."

As she touched his hand, she dropped a tightly folded note into it. He went to the bathroom and sat on the toilet before he read it.

Please don't be angry with me. There's no time.
I know that one of us is going to be recruited to work for them, and the other is going to die. Not even they know, yet, which will be picked. Nobody knows the rules to this game… but if we work together, maybe we won't have to play.

He shredded the note and put it in his mouth, chewed it and spat it into the toilet.

***

They adjourned to a dimly lit screening room. Cooley sat in a chair in the back and mixed highballs at the wet bar while a stooge in a lab coat ushered Talbot and Corliss to the front row of seats.

An older man in a doctor's smock came out the door beside the screen and bowed deeply. "Doctor Fleming, ah…Tiverton," he said with a lipless peck at Lila's extended hand.

Picture a short, bald, asthmatic geezer with thick glasses and a wispy mustache like catfish whiskers. He looked like Peter Lorre, if Lorre were nearsighted and addicted to skin cancer. The other man, who only introduced himself as the station engineer, wore grubby coveralls and didn't look like anyone at all.

"Mr. Talbot, Miss Corliss," Tiverton lisped, "we have offered you the opportunity to assist us in an urgent mission for the cause of national security. Your discretion would, naturally, be compulsory. Now, ah… We have devised a very effective method of conditioning the viewing audience to insure order in the event of an emergency…"

"Brainwashing them, you mean," Talbot cut in.

"No, ha ha, quite the opposite. We were initially charged with finding a foolproof method of inculcating American values into the broadcast signal itself. Television is the greatest vehicle for such work. The viewer's attention passively rests on a single point instead of roaming and sorting out distractions. With our carrier signal added to all channels, the forebrain all but goes to sleep, allowing the program to saturate the deeper, more primitive regions of the brain.

"Not to make them slaves, but to set them free, or as free as anyone would really want to be. They are subliminally conditioned by rhythmic distortions in the cathode radiation to internalize the program's overt messages about the American way of life: hard work, respect for private property, rewards for initiative and individual achievement…"

"And a healthy dose of blind patriotic fervor, no doubt," added Miss Corliss.

Tiverton nodded like he was shaking off a bee. "Indeed! The old CONELRAD—the Control of Electromagnetic Radiation network— allows us to relay the alert signal to the nation's TV and radio frequencies. The new Emergency Broadcast Signal system will allow us to directly seize control of the entire broadcasting spectrum.

"The new EBS tone acts as a post-hypnotic trigger to induce an orderly civil response to an atomic exchange. But many of our test subjects have a poor reaction to the activating tone. They disregard their programming and seem to, ah…regress…"

Way off across the room, Cooley whistled the Star-Spangled Banner. He loped over, pushing a projector on a cart. "Don't tell them. Show them."

The lights went down and the projector lit up the screen. Tiverton stood in the glow as the numbers counted down to zero. "Now, these test subjects were, ah, paid volunteers…but they could not, of course, have been told of the true nature of the, ah, test…"

A TOP SECRET graphic flashed over the civil defense logo, then a proper title: CONELRAD EMERGENCY BROADCAST SYSTEM STRESS TEST No.107-LA-11f

"They were participants in a civil defense test in which we simulated a real atomic attack upon Los Angeles. This subject family unit took shelter immediately after hearing the fortified CONELRAD signal."

"They thought it was real?" Talbot asked. "How could you—"

"Shut up," said everyone.

A starkly lit concrete bunker viewed from high up on a wall, through the grate of a ventilation shaft. Below, the floor hidden under opened, half-empty cans and smashed bottles. A middle-aged woman with a bloodied face presses into a corner between a wall and a bunk bed, holding a young boy to her bosom and screaming as she points a revolver at the man of the house, who crouches holding his bloody shoulder and bobbing, looking for an opening. A hammer in his hand trembles and then flies at the mother. As it hits the wall beside her face, she fires and hits him in the throat. He falls, and the mother looks to her son, half-eaten but still, somehow, alive. Singing something—reading lips, it comes clear (O'er the la-and of the free) just before she resumes eating (and the home of the brave) his face.

Cooley applauded. Talbot buried his head in his hands and dug red furrows in his forehead with his fingernails.

Tiverton stepped in front of the screen as it cut to the film's tail leader. "This family self-destructed on day eleven of the simulation. They were the last group to implode."

Talbot asked, "Out of how many?"

"That's classified," Tiverton said.

Talbot looked around, from the engineer to the doctor to Lila Corliss to Cooley, lurking at the back of the room, nodding like he'd seen this film a hundred times. "You made them think… Jesus… Okay… I just don't see how, even if this thing does what you say it does…how is this going to help fight Communism?"

The engineer spat tobacco juice into a wastebasket. "Who gives a shit about Communism?"

"Show him the control group," Cooley said.

"I don't see how that would, ah…help."

Cooley made the geek in the lab coat change the reels on the projector.

Over the countdown, Tiverton's thick glasses reflected flaming pinwheels. "This is not a representative sampling, but a most interesting anecdote. All of our control groups outlasted the fortified groups, but, ah…after three months, they all either committed suicide, starved to death or tried to leave the shelter. This one group in our last round of subjects…"

There was no title.

Another bunker, much tidier than the last. A woman lies on the floor inside a triangle within a circle drawn in charcoal. Her arms and feet are outstretched, and a man hunches over her hand. A young girl holds her other hand. An old woman, somebody's mother, kneels at her feet and holds one up to her lips, and a little boy, barely old enough to talk, holds the other, seeming at first to be reverently, if not lustily, kissing it.

The woman's blouse is open and her chest and belly covered in geometric designs and symbols like in Medieval alchemy manuscripts. Her breathing is slow and measured, her lips moving in a mute incantation.

The father looks up and wipes his mouth. Blood pours out of a hole in the palm of her hand, blood and something solid and not at all recognizable as part of a human body pools in stigmata in her hands and feet. By turns, each member of the family pauses to give thanks for their feast.

"Jesus," Talbot said, and went to be sick in the wastebasket.

"The control groups were chosen from the migrant Mexican population, because they've never been exposed to our television or radio. This one started out like all the others, but a few days after the food ran out, they prayed until they seemed to go into a trance, and then they started doing this. They've survived for more than thirty days on…whatever the hell they're getting from her. We've been ordered to sit back and see how long they hold out."

Talbot said, "I don't suppose I can just say no and not expect to end up in a bomb shelter, can I?"

The engineer pushed Talbot back in his chair. "We need programs that will put the intellect to sleep and massage the emotional centers of the brain—weepy, soft-boiled sob stories—so the conditioning will stick without turning the audience into a pack of shit-flinging baboons when the duck-and-cover tone plays. You think you can do that?"

They both nodded, then looked at each other, then away. "I have to try," Talbot said, "but I don't even understand how you're…" He put his hand over his mouth, bit down on his fingers until his eyes bulged out and a droplet of blood streaked down his chin.

"You've had quite a shock," Tiverton said. "Why don't you take a minute… both of you." He and the engineer and Cooley and the stooge all left by separate doors, but locked them in perfect unison.

Corliss got up out of her chair. "Did you ever stop to think that maybe the hysteria over Communism might be…you know…a result of the conditioning they're putting into the water and over the airwaves? They've created an enemy to justify these experiments…"

He sprang out of his chair and crossed the room with his hand out to cover her mouth.

She turned away to fend him off, but then caught him by the arm and pulled him close. "I never gave politics a second thought when I wrote scripts, did you?"

He couldn't look her in the eye. For a moment, they looked past each other and their lips almost met. "I just tried to remind people how humans are supposed to treat each other, so maybe…"

She pulled away. "I think about it now, and it seems so silly, but I guess I was just playing with dolls. I used to play all day with my paper dolls and make up elaborate scenarios for them, with mistaken identities and lovers separated by cruel and fickle fate… And I suppose it just seemed like coming to Hollywood and writing for the movies would be like playing with the prettiest, most beloved paper dolls of all…"

The speaker above her head gave a keening noise for fifteen seconds, but he heard it in his bones, he will always hear it until the day he dies.

He already likes working here, he'd live here, if they'd let him, if only they'd turn down that noise—

Lila didn't like it. She knelt on the floor, hyperventilating. "Don't touch me…don't…"

Sliding his tie off his collar, he wound the narrow end round his knuckles and snapped the double-stitched silk like a garrote between his fists.

"Lila," he said, straining not to look for the cameras, "I think I figured out why they invited you…"

***

Talbot pounded on the door until it opened. He stumbled into an office even darker than the screening room, but for the cadaverous blue-white light from a wall of television sets. The engineer got up from a drafting table with an elaborate circuit diagram on it.

Talbot held a handkerchief to his cheek but failed to staunch the stream of blood that trickled down his neck to stain his collar.

The engineer led him to a chair then sat on the corner of his desk, tamping a charnel-smelling tobacco blend into his pipe. "Boy, when you want a job, you don't mess around."

"I didn't mean to… I mean, I didn't…" He shivered and looked at his hands, then he laughed. "For a minute there, I thought I…"

"Oh, but you did. I can show you the replay…the lighting is terrible, but it'll play well enough for a jury."

"Why? Why did you…you made me do it!"

"We told you the tone was buggy."

Wiping his hands on his legs, he let out a whipped, whimpering scream. "You'd better kill me too, or I'll—"

"You'll what, son? Tell them whatever you want, somebody might even listen. But it'll be a lot easier for a jury to understand that a convicted radical former screenwriter strangled the woman who fed him to the Committee."

"But why? I was going to cooperate. We both were…"

"You 'show business' people never can be trustworthy unless your own necks are in the noose. I'm sorry, but it's true. You think you're an exception to every rule. Well, now you're one of us. Now, we have your undivided loyalty."

Talbot slumped in his chair. For a long minute, the only sound was the patter of flop sweat and blood hitting the concrete floor.

"You don't realize how close we are to Terminal Midnight, son. Even clowns like Cooley, they don't get the big picture. A full-fledged atomic war would be a blessing, next to what we face. Without a real solution, America is going to be besieged on every front within the next ten years and totally overrun by hostile aliens, and I don't mean wetbacks. Something has to be done. Our brains and bodies need to be immunized, or we will go insane. As a nation, as a race, as a species, we'll become violent psychopaths or simply shut down in the face of the changes…"

"And you need me to make propaganda films…"

"No, we just need you to script and direct the same melodramatic crap you always did. We'll even let you direct your own shows, if you don't foul it up. We'll get your name off all the lists. Lila Corliss will disappear on a cruise in the Caribbean."

"So…you're already putting this programming out on the air-waves?"

"Of course, didn't our little demonstration get through to you? The program is going out over all radio and TV channels. Has been since last summer. We have to do it, or we'll be left behind… You must've soaked up enough of it, yourself, obviously."

"Oh, if the other side is doing it, that's the best reason to do it to ourselves, too? Why don't we just find another way? There's got to be a way to preserve order without turning people into…into…"

"This isn't anything. It's a toy. If the signal were boosted and the audience synchronized… Well, then, that would be something."

"Yeah?"

"If an army walks across a bridge in perfect lockstep, their syn-chronized footfalls will set up vibrations, which will potentially shake the bridge to bits. The Chinese are working with similar technology even now, which will utilize the observer effect… If an entire popu-lation observes a single object simultaneously, with their perceptive judgment yoked to a single influencing source, then their combined, unified perception could become an energy weapon like a gigantic magnifying glass, focusing the sun's rays upon and utterly destroying or even fundamentally altering anything they behold."

"Sure, all they need is eight hundred million TVs. You've got me, you can quit shoveling that shit, now."

The engineer showed Talbot to the restroom, boxed him in when he tried to go wash his hands. "I know what you're thinking. Just nod and smile and back out of the room, all the way to the car and run for your life. Don't. We need you to do this for us."

"For Mr. and Mrs. America and all the ships at sea." Sidling past the engineer, Talbot bent over the sink and splashed cold water on his face. "I don't know. How many innocent maidens can the hero tie to the railroad tracks, and still wear a white hat? Is it really better than whatever you're fighting?"

"Listen…I've been out here since '51, but before, I was in New Mexico, when the…when it crashed, and I followed it to Nevada. The stories they let out that it was a spaceship from another planet were easier to swallow than the truth. The truth was, we still don't know what the fuck we found. It's not from another planet, it's from another dimension. And it's not a machine, as we know them. It's alive, and we can't kill it.

"Those atomic tests out in the desert? They're not really tests. There's something down there that we've dropped a couple dozen H-bombs on, and so far, we're just spitting in its eye."

Talbot looked around. Nobody was watching, unless there were cameras. There were always cameras. "So…you don't get out much…"

"They probably told you this was temporary, didn't they? Don't get me wrong, this is no gulag. They take pretty good care of us, heh… And you can leave.

"This one fellow, he came from Naval Intelligence, they took him because he wrote that sci-fi potboiler stuff, so they thought he could handle it. He started spreading around the idea that the UFO was a message like the Ten Commandments. A call to worship, see? And he was the new Moses. They let him go, couldn't afford to just kill him, it'd be bad for morale, but they stirred his brains up with the stress test tone. That's one of the only useful things we've learned from this shit, see? The eggheads call it a 'remote lobotomy.' Us working stiffs call it the 'fire drill,' because that's what it feels like. Already a paranoid schizophrenic from studying the fucking thing, they turned him into some kind of broken robot. He's out there preaching his daffy zombie gospel, but it's dressed up as some new kind of self-improvement grift. Looks like a loose cannon, but if they wanted him gone, he'd be gone, so cui bono, you know? Just another brainwashing machine. We're all working for them."

"Who the hell is 'them?'"

The engineer leaned in close and put a hand on his shoulder. Talbot shrank from his touch. The gray-haired man was hardly older than himself. "You ever find out, do me a favor. Don't tell me, okay pal?"

Talbot turned to leave, but then snapped back as something dinged his brainpan. "These things...we're up against... What do they look like?"

The engineer shivered as he packed his pipe. "You don't want to know."

"But I'm supposed to believe—"

"Words don't contain them, never mind describe them. They're outside everything we know. You can't be sure what you're seeing is even real, or if your mind just threw a rod trying to perceive it. That's what they're like...not evil or bad in any sense like Communists or Nazis...just *wrong*."

The engineer busily stuffed his briarwood pipe. He didn't look up as Talbot leaned across the desk. "You know, we had a saying around the old typewriter pool at Warner's. The producers drill it into you before they let you pitch."

"What's that?" Patting himself down for matches, the engineer looked up into a weird silver-green glow he thought was a proffered lighter.

"Spare me the labor pains," Talbot said. "Just show me the baby."

***

Cooley leaned against the DeSoto and blew smoke rings at the moon. Talbot came out of the bunker and wandered over like a sleep-walker on a dance floor. His cheek was taped up, but blood soaked through the gauze. Sleepily, he slouched against the grill and covered his face. His shoulders shook, but no sound escaped the trap of his hands.

"Look," Cooley said, "I didn't pick you out, see? I was just following orders. But you people...you live up in the clouds feasting on nectar and ambrosia, but your whole kingdom is bullshit. Look how quick your life fell apart as soon as we dragged it out into the light. That's what'll happen to all of you, if you don't open your eyes and recognize what we're up against."

Talbot moaned and pounded the hood of the car, then looked up and lurched closer to Cooley. "No hard feelings, Cooley. I just—I just wanted you to know..."

He leaned in close enough to kiss. Cooley looked at the screenwriter's hands, hanging slack at his sides. He grinned, but his hand went into his raincoat.

Talbot's eyebrows waggled and he smiled, rueful like he'd just forgotten the punch line to a joke. Then he clenched his teeth and spit in Cooley's face as he twisted in some kind of spasm. Cooley reflexively threw out his arms to catch him, but something like a radium-glowing winged worm seemed to appear out of nowhere and fly in his face.

He ducked and covered his head, but it was gone. A cold, leaden weight like tumbling shrapnel in the center of his skull crushed him to the ground. Talbot leaned over him. Blood flowed freely from both his nostrils, but he was smiling.

A big stupid grin, just like Talbot's. "The thing in my head, it's been sleeping in there ever since I stayed with my friends in the Severn Valley Circle. That was where I got them…my 'foreign ideas.' Funny thing, before they found me, I couldn't write a decent sentence. It is like an idea, an idea is like a sickness, the way it spreads, makes you sick at first, and what causes sickness? Tiny bugs… They think of themselves as insects, the Shans do… 'Bug' doesn't begin to describe what they really are, because on an intellectual scale, we're the real insects."

Circling Cooley, he took a cigarette out of his pocket and lit it.

"We all became hosts, but they just slept inside us. For years, we've carried them around. Some of us you got on your lists, but most of us are still out there."

He blew smoke in Cooley's eyes.

"They feed on electromagnetic radiation, see? The subtle electrochemical energy of the human brain is like a drug to them. With time, they learn to run the show, to feed ideas and emotions like pulling puppet strings, or just to take over and drive the body like a car, to force more thrills to run up a bigger charge. But they were tired… jaded… Their idea of pleasure used up a lot of people, so they were only looking to hide."

Spinning and bending over, he ground his cigarette out on Cooley's neck. Cooley made no move to stop him. A sound escaped his trembling, riveted lips—something like a whinnying laugh that was also a wordless prayer.

"Oh, what kind of scenarist am I, anyway? I forgot the best part. See, they went to sleep inside us after our group had a little party, where the un-American principle of free love was studied at length. It inspired them, and for the first time in centuries, they engaged in the physical act, themselves. Their courtship rites are most…complicated, and many human hosts were used up in the process. They went to sleep to wait for their eggs to hatch. But that noise…that EBS stress test? You woke it up."

Cooley brought out his gun, but his hand shook so badly that he found himself staring down his own barrel. "Make it…please…make it stop."

"I wish I could, really," Talbot grinned, "but you see…I'm following orders, too."

Lila Corliss appeared behind him. Her neck was blotchy with grievous bruises from the tie still wound carelessly round her neck. She smiled like a stroke patient, watching with wonder and dread as her hand reached out to caress Talbot's wounded cheek, then to drive her nails into it until he hissed.

The alien thing behind his eyes squirmed and barely restrained itself from retaliating. "Something screwy about its atomic structure allows them to pass through solid matter, but as you can obviously testify, they are anything but imaginary."

Cooley moved his mouth, but no words came out. No shrill commands, no screams for help. An MP passed along the inner perimeter fence with a German shepherd. Talbot looked and smiled even as a sudden migraine sent him into convulsions. "It hurts so much less if you…don't fight it. Just…tell them what they want to know…"

Turning and struggling out of the soft gray matter of Talbot's brain, an insect the size of a game hen emerged, iridescent exoskeleton wriggling with feathery tentacles, metallic black wings thrashing like a wounded vampire bat. Three beaked mouths keened a tripartite chorus like steel on dry ice. Its teeming, intangible offspring writhed and clutched and slithered in and out of Talbot's twitching face.

Out of a monstrous cavity in its bloated, glowing abdomen that was equal parts birth canal and oozing wound came a swarm of winged larvae. The night swallowed them up just as Cooley found himself able to holster his gun and climb up off the ground.

The sentry fell to his knees and dropped his rifle. His dog barked and leapt at him, trying to bite his face. The sentry was laughing as he drove his bayonet into the dog's throat.

"What happens now?" Cooley asked. His legs still didn't know how to hold him up. He slumped against Corliss, who bit clean through the cartilage in his ear.

"Yours are both in the larval stage," Talbot said, "but they know their role. And yours. I don't think they're going to need to change anything here, really...at first."

"They can't make us do this," Cooley growled.

"You'll get used to it," Talbot said. "Now, I have in my head a list of names..."

FALLOUT

BY SAM STONE

Chris pulled the ribbon from the windshield of his brand new 1953 Chrysler New Yorker. The car was polished shiny red with a canvas soft-top that dropped back into the trunk space. A matching leather protector clipped over the back of the vehicle and the dash was real mahogany. It shone with the newness of recently varnished wood and Chris could smell the soothing aroma of the leather as he opened the door and climbed into the driver's seat.

"What do you think?" asked his Dad.

"I can't believe it. Really? This is for me?"

"Sure, son. Happy birthday it's not every day that my first born turns sixteen. Why don't you take it for a spin?"

The engine was excitingly loud as it burst into life. Chris released the brake and pulled out of the driveway, taking the car carefully out onto the street. Chris loved the car. It cruised smoothly, almost as though it was driving itself. He knew he would be the talk of the high school and—even better—he was now certain to get the girl of his dreams.

Ever since his father had started a new job at the base, out in the Nevada desert, they had seemed to have money to burn. In recent months his mother had completely redecorated the whole house, changed the furniture, and she was also driving a new car. Chris wanted for nothing and now he had friends and a social life that he had never believed possible.

Sometimes it seemed as though overnight he had gone from spotty geek to Mr. Popular: all because they had money. And Chris was generous with it too. Buying cokes at the local diner, handing out dimes for the jukebox, and even on occasion passing out cans of beer he had taken from his father's stash in the ice-box in the garage. No one questioned what he did, least of all his folks. They were all glad that the dark days had ended.

After touring his neighborhood, Chris drove the car back into the drive, locked the door and headed to the house. There, his father was talking about his favorite subject. He was obsessed with the Russians and the potential threat they posed. Chris supposed it was because he worked for the government.

"Almost a decade since the War," Dad said, "and the country is thriving again. But I wouldn't trust those Reds. That's why my work is so important."

"What do you do at the base, Dad?" Chris asked.

"That's classified, son. But maybe one day you'll find out. Maybe one day you'll join the team."

Chris's mother frowned, but he barely noticed it as he walked past her to switch on the new television set. He loved watching the evening programmes, that and the fact that they were the only people in their street to actually own a TV. He settled down on the couch as the news started.

Mom and Dad went out on the veranda, sat down on the wicker two-seater and looked out at the new car as it stood, gleaming in the drive-way.

"Well, at least he's happy," said Mom.

"Gotta keep your kids happy," said Dad.

It was a warm evening and Mom sipped homemade lemonade while Dad chugged a cold beer. After a while Chris came outside and admired his car too. The sight of it brought him joy, but also an odd feeling: a kind of worry that burrowed deep into his stomach.

"Dad?"

"Yes, son?"

"You know all this talk about another war? That the 'A' bomb could be dropped on us at any time? Do you think that will really happen?"

Dad was quiet for a time, then he looked up at Chris over his beer can. "I don't really think so. But just in case, that's why we have the shelter."

Chris cast a glance over his shoulder at the house. From the front he couldn't see the lead-lined shutters that covered the entrance down into a blast shelter, but his mind's eye visualized it. He imagined the shutters opening as the family raced across the lawn. He saw them all cramming inside: Mom, Dad and his sister Myra. The weeks, months, or even years might have to pass before it was safe to emerge because Dad said that radiation was something to fear even after the devastation of an explosion. Chris didn't know what worried him more, the concept of a nuclear explosion or the thought of passing through the fallout shelter doors and heading down into the deep, dark bowels of the earth.

"I'm going to the drive-in tomorrow," Chris told them, trying to take his mind off his morbid thoughts. "I'm taking a date. I'll need some money."

Dad reached into his pocket and pulled out a roll of notes. He peeled off five twenties and held them out.

A *hundred bucks*, Chris thought. That was enough for several dates.

"You have to treat the ladies right," said Dad.

Mum said nothing. She sipped her lemonade. Chris noted that she never drank beer but sometimes, when they had a dinner party, she would like to drink fancy wine that made her giggle like a teenager. At those times he would go to his room and play his 45's on his Victrola because he didn't like to see her like that.

"Thanks, Dad," he said as he took the money, but his heart hurt a little: it almost felt like he was losing a piece of his soul. He stuffed it quickly into his trouser pocket and tried to ignore the burn that seeped through the fabric into his leg. He couldn't explain the odd-ness of the moment or the feeling of anxiety that accompanied every gift. It was as if he felt that he would have to pay some awful price for their current happiness.

"Who's the lucky girl?" asked Myra.

Chris turned around to see his sister lurking in the doorway. She barely surfaced from her room these days. She was younger than him by a year, but Chris always felt as though Myra knew more about the world than he did. He didn't know why.

"Elizabeth Penrose," Chris said.

"Fancy," said Myra.

"Yeah. She is."

"I'm so proud. My boy courting a Penrose," said Mom. "This is worth celebrating, don't you think, Charles?"

Dad nodded. "Sure, Lucy. Whatever you want."

"We'll have a dinner party. Maybe we can invite the Penroses…"

Chris went back inside the house and left them planning his fu-ture. He didn't point out to them that this was only one date. Nothing more might come of it. Although he did like Elizabeth. A lot. And he was hoping that the new car would impress her tomorrow.

"Chris, don't you find it odd sometimes?" asked Myra following him into the kitchen.

"Find what odd?"

"How good things have become. Why I remember only last year Dad could barely pay the bills and now suddenly…"

Chris felt that knot in his stomach again. A sick, dark fear scurried around the recesses of his subconscious. The answer to a riddle that he just couldn't find but knew all the same, hid somewhere there. He tried to shake the feeling away. He opened the fridge and took out a beer, snapping open the top.

"You know that's illegal, right?" said Myra.

Chris couldn't even bring himself to tell her to shut up. He was rapidly learning he could do as he pleased. No one stopped him. In fact his father encouraged him by indulging his every wish. His new car was proof of that. But still.

The thought of the car made his heart lurch and not in a good way. It was the sinking feeling of the drowning man who is waiting for the final moment to take away the screaming pain in his lungs. It was the inconsolable cry of a frightened infant in the night. It was the dread of death that faces the dying.

Chris shook his head, sipped the beer and the fear receded but Myra didn't leave him.

"I just feel…" she said.

"What?"

"Scared somehow," Myra shrugged. "I guess you think I'm crazy."

Chris said nothing but his eyes fell on the kitchen window. The yard was lit up all night with security lights and they illuminated the shelter. Chris shuddered.

Myra moved next to him and looked out. "You feel it too. I know you do."

"We have everything to be grateful for, and nothing to fear," Chris said, but he didn't believe his own words.

Myra didn't answer and the two of them stood there looking out the window until the lights suddenly went off in the yard. Their trance broke. Dad was standing at the door, his hand on the outdoor light switch.

"Myra, don't you think you ought to go to bed?" Dad said. "School tomorrow."

Myra slunk away, but not before she cast another glance at the window. It was too dark to see the shelter but somehow Chris knew she felt its presence there. Just as he did.

Chris and Myra had never seen inside the shelter. All they knew was that one day, soon after Dad started his new job, a team of workmen arrived and began to dig up the ground at the back of the yard.

"It's a fallout shelter," Dad had explained. "When this is done we'll have enough space and supplies down there to last for months if the Reds jump the gun and send out the 'A' Bomb."

Chris had been excited at first; he saw the shelter as a new place where he could hang out. Maybe he would be able to use it as a den when his friends came over. But as the structure began to take shape, he started to feel odd.

One time he went out into the garden as the workmen laid the foundations. A deep hole had been dug into the ground at least thirty feet down, and Chris could see a pattern that resembled a spider or octopus taking shape. Most of the yard was exposed, but he had heard his father say that once the shelter was built the lawn would be laid again on top of it.

"Why's it like that?" he had asked one of the men.

The men all turned their heads in unison and stared at him. They had blank, empty, expressions on their faces.

"Come away from there, Chris," his mother called from the back door. "You shouldn't bother the men while they are working."

Chris stayed long enough to see the men return to work. He never heard them chatter or laugh and joke. He thought they were the oddest construction workers he had ever seen. Of course they were all probably military and sworn not to talk to anyone during the work. After all the fallout shelter had to be some perk of Dad's job, didn't it?

Sometimes in his dreams he found himself in the garden looking down into the foundations. He would be standing swaying at the edge, a terrible vertigo sweeping up like an invisible claw that wanted to pull him down into the dust. He would try to back away but his ankles felt as though they were held by some imperceptible force. He felt that he had lead feet and knew somehow that this always happened in dreams when you tried to escape something horrible, or run from some imagined terror. So he rarely fought the feeling. All he could do was gaze down into the pit.

Sometimes in the dreams he would see something slowly moving down there, a dark shape that was more shadow than it was form. At those times he would half close his eyes, squinting down into the gloom. He saw…he saw…

After he woke up screaming Chris couldn't bring the creature's image up into his mind, but he knew it was monstrous. He stayed away from the workmen after that, but the dreams still haunted him.

Chris had felt ill and sick during most of the construction. He even noted how pale his mother looked, how Myra began to stay out more at her girlfriend's house, and how his dad, usually patient, had become snappy and irritable. It was as though a thick fog of misery floated around the house and land. The open hole held such terror for him that he couldn't even bear to go into the yard anymore.

There was a palpable change in the atmosphere when the iron doors were fitted on the shelter. Dad turned the key, locking the doors before the workmen had finished packing up their equipment and tools.

After that life returned to some semblance of normality, but Chris didn't get any permanent relief. The discomfort was always there. The fear of some unknown bogeyman sat permanently in the pit of his stomach, and choked him while he slept. His Dad and Mom returned to normal, but Myra didn't: she distanced herself still further from the family.

The strange thing was, Chris had never seen his parents open the door again. He even wondered if they had bothered to put emergency supplies down there. He sure hadn't seen them do it. But of course he didn't know what his mother did when he was out all day at school.

It was easy to forget his fears though because the benefits of their new position outweighed any of the strangeness he felt. The money was a big issue. They quite literally wanted for nothing and this did seem to make his parents happier.

"You okay, son?" asked Dad.

Chris snapped out of his reverie only to find Dad standing by the fridge, beer in hand.

"Yes," said Chris because this was the expected answer.

"You happy?"

Chris nodded. He couldn't choke out another 'yes' no matter how hard he tried.

Dad frowned, then turned and walked away.

***

The next day, on his official birthday, Chris drove his new car to school. As his friends gathered around the convertible in the car park, he briefly forgot his worries and fears and enjoyed the feeling of owning the vehicle.

"That's a cool car," said Elizabeth sliding up to him. "I'm looking forward to our date later. And I have a birthday present for you too, but that can wait until this evening."

"You're a lucky guy," said Eugene, one of his new friends who happened to be the captain of the football team. "Here you go buddy. Happy birthday."

Chris took the gift from Eugene. He opened it up to find a football shirt.

"You're our new quarterback," said Eugene, patting him on the shoulder.

Chris felt on top of the world for the whole day. He shook away the craziness that had followed him for the last six months. His life was changing so rapidly that he could barely keep up. No sooner had he done the try-outs and he was in the team, in the favored position. He had always thought he was no good at sports, but the try-out day proved him wrong. When he had gone out onto the pitch he could just play. It was easy. He just couldn't believe his luck.

He thought back to the night before and realized that today he would have no trouble saying yes if his dad asked if he was happy. He was. All that he had ever wanted was miraculously coming true for him.

It's ridiculous to be worried by our good fortune, he thought. *Things happen because they are meant to.*

He went into history class and sat down to take the test. As he turned the page, and glanced down at the first question, Chris knew the answer. In fact the test went extremely well. He knew ALL the answers and he finished long before everyone else. As the bell sounded, he packed up and the thought crossed his mind that his paper would be graded an 'A'.

I feel that lucky today.

In his next class his math teacher took him aside. "Chris, I've noticed how hard you've been working lately. You seem to have natural talent with figures."

It was all so easy. Maybe he did have talent and had only just realized it. Everything he did that day just went right, without any apparent real effort. So, when he got into his car and drove home, he was on a high that he had never experienced before.

***

"So what's this movie about?" asked Elizabeth.

"It's called *The Beast from 20,000 Fathoms*," Chris said.

"Sounds scary."

Chris put his arm around Elizabeth's shoulder, "Hey…I'm here if you get scared."

The movie started after twenty minutes of adverts. During this time Chris bought popcorn and soda for them both and they were settled and ready when the credits began to roll.

He noticed how Elizabeth tensed silently when the creature first emerged from the sea but other than that she wasn't really scared. Chris, however, found the concept to be utterly terrifying. He couldn't quite place why, but the idea of a government experiment creating a monster seemed to be such a possibility.

Chris's mind drifted away from the film for a while. An idea formed in his mind, a terrifying thought about his father's job. What exactly did they *do* out there in the desert? His mind's eye imagined the base even though he had never seen it and his father working in some sterile lab, experimenting on a large creature in a huge tank.

A surge of panic rushed into his face and cheeks. His heart began to pound and he had a brief flash of memory of the monster in his nightmares: it was a large tentacled being of grotesque shape and size.

"You okay?" asked Elizabeth.

Chris snapped back into the now and realized that he had fallen asleep during the film. He hoped he hadn't been snoring.

"Sure," he said sitting upright.

Elizabeth smiled at him and turned her eyes back to the screen.

After the film finished, Elizabeth let Chris kiss her lightly on the lips before they followed the other cars out of the drive-in.

"Do you think our government would be capable of that?" Chris asked her as they drove back through town.

"No, of course not. I wouldn't put it past the Russians though," she said.

Chris noted that she spoke like his parents when discussing the government. They all felt that President Eisenhower could do no wrong and that the enemy still lived overseas. Since the war, patriotism was the norm. The movie showed a different view though, one that made him think that their world may not be so perfect and it had fed somehow into those ridiculous dreams he was having.

"We're so lucky," Elizabeth said. "We live in a great country that cares about its people. My dad says times are better now than they have ever been. He thinks we're going to 'prosper'."

"What do you mean?" Chris asked.

"Well I heard him say something to my Mom, about how almost all the sacrifices have been made. Now we're all going to reap the rewards."

Chris felt that odd prickle that irritated his nerves and sent a shudder up his spine. He didn't like the way she had used the word 'sacrifice'.

"Did your folks mind that you were coming out with me?" he asked changing the subject.

"No. Dad said that somehow it was fitting," Elizabeth said.

He parked up at the Penrose house and walked Elizabeth to the door. It was ten pm, the time her father had said he wanted her home and Chris didn't want to make the mistake of upsetting him on their first date. He wanted to be the perfect boyfriend. Elizabeth deserved that.

"Goodnight," Elizabeth said as she opened the door. Then she was gone and Chris was left standing on their porch looking at the screen door.

He felt somewhat deflated as he climbed back in his car. It was only a short journey home but he noted how quiet the streets were. He had never seen them this empty before.

His mind flashed back to the movie, his short sleep, and the dream creature. The image of it hadn't faded like it usually did. Chris could see it clearer the more he focused on it. He tried not to think about it, but failed.

As he turned the car into his street he felt a strange and irrational terror. *I should turn around now. Drive right out of this place and never come back.*

He pulled the car over to the curb and looked down the street at his house. He could see a light on in the lounge as he might expect at this time. His folks weren't on the porch though and the rest of the house was in darkness. Even Myra's window was in full darkness and she often stayed up late reading.

Palpitations, anxiety and total panic rushed through him in a matter of seconds. *What's wrong with me? Am I losing my mind?* He knew his fear was irrational but he couldn't shake it.

He waited for a few minutes longer. The street was eerily quiet. He turned his head to look at the house beside him. It was in total darkness and it was only ten fifteen.

Mentally shaking himself, Chris put the car in gear and slowly moved forward towards his drive, but again an unreasonable panic consumed him. Sweat poured from his brow as he parked the car. He felt paralyzed with terror as he looked up at the porch screen. He couldn't understand why the thought of being home frightened him so much. Surely he had nothing to fear here? Despite his rational thoughts he was incapable of getting out of the car and walking inside the house and he just didn't know why.

He placed his head in his hands and wept.

"Come on son," said Dad from the door.

Chris looked up, but his eyes were misty and the shape in the dark didn't quite look like his Dad.

"Come on, Chris," said his mother.

"Don't fight this," said another voice and Chris turned his head to find Abraham Penrose at the side of his car.

They were wearing strange clothing. Long black robes that had hoods and as Chris looked around he found he was surrounded by all of his neighbors.

Penrose opened the car door and took his arm. Chris didn't have the strength to fight, even though he didn't understand what was happening on some level he still realized that this whole thing was wrong, unfair. He hadn't done anything to deserve it.

They didn't go inside the house as he expected, Penrose led him round the side and Chris came face to face with his mother as she opened the gate.

"Mom...?" he pleaded but she turned away and said nothing.

They walked over the lawn. Chris thought he could feel something under the earth, a vibration. His anxiety increased to brain snapping levels. He was surrounded now by all of his neighbors and as they entered the yard they spread out into a crescent around the front of the fallout shelter.

Chris tried to resist when he realized that Penrose was taking him towards the heavy lead doors; he didn't want to see inside the shelter. That curiosity had long since passed. But Penrose wasn't letting him go. He tugged and pulled, bruising the skin on Chris's arm as he all but dragged him over to the doors.

"Brethren. We are gathered here to honor our god and to make good the promise we gave," said Penrose as they reached the doors, he turned around making Chris face the rest of the neighborhood.

Chris could see that his neighbors were all wearing black robes, some of them had pulled up the hoods, but most hadn't bothered and they stared at Chris with eager expressions, their eyes gleaming with something akin to madness. He recognized the old widow from number three, the newly-weds from number twelve and an array of other people who he had known for most of his life.

"This night is an important night for us," Penrose continued. "It is the start of the next phase and a completion of the old one. All of you will reap the rewards for your efforts."

"Dad?" said Chris as his father joined the row in front. "What's going on? Is this some kind of joke?"

"Sorry, son," said Dad. "You've had your fun and now we have to pay the price."

"I didn't...I haven't done anything wrong..."

Chris turned his head and looked at Penrose. He had never noticed the insanity in the man's gray eyes before and it was reflected in all of the faces that watched the proceedings.

"Time to go into the shelter," said Penrose.

Penrose pulled Chris round once more. This time they were facing the doors and, as if by magic, they were opening up on their own. *I'm dreaming*, thought Chris. *I'm still at the drive-in.*

There was a dull grayish-green light shining from the depths of the shelter and a sickly stench floated out on a thick miasma of mist.

"What is this?" Chris cried. "I'm not going in there."

A fanatic's smile widened on Penrose's euphoric face. "But you have to Chris, you belong to the god."

"What are you talking about?"

"We entered into a pact with a new and powerful god. He will give us everything. We are safe from war, will have unending prosperity for as long as we uphold our part of the bargain. We give him our first born, on their sixteenth birthday."

"What?" Chris gasped.

"*Alomoth rehath elimore dyseth.* I call on the god to come to us and accept our sacrifice," said Penrose.

"D…Dad?" Chris said trying to look back over his shoulder. He was shaking now. His legs buckled beneath him but he felt himself lifted back up by Penrose and another robed figure that he didn't recognise. They pulled him towards the door.

The stench was worse than ever. It stank of stale sweat and rotten fish tinged with sulphur. Chris gagged on the fog that rushed up into his face. It was as though an invisible hand was exploring his features. He felt cold fingers prod and poke his cheeks like an adoring grandparent.

The smell was all over him now. He felt that he had become one with the fog, dissolved into the rot and he noticed that Penrose and the other man were no longer holding him. They had backed away as though they were afraid of the mist.

The strange, foul gas pulled back and away into the depths of the earth, and Chris found life returning to his limbs. He turned around slowly to face the people. They were laughing and smiling now, the insanity seemed to be gone and Chris felt a tremendous relief.

It's all some kind of joke. Any minute Myra will come out and start laughing at me for being taken in. Sacrifice indeed!

A smile broke out on his face. He wouldn't let them win. He would pretend he hadn't been scared but had guessed all along.

"Very amusing, Dad. I didn't realize you had such a peculiar sense of humor."

Dad's sad eyes turned to him at the same moment that Chris tried to step away from the fallout shelter doors. Then the nightmare began again. He felt the mist rush up at him again. It surrounded him, grabbing at his ankles, his arms, his neatly trimmed hair. He saw the slight frown on his father's face, the guilt that danced in his eyes and then his Dad turned away and walked back to the house.

Chris tried to scream but the sound strangled in his throat. His eyes bulged as the air was squeezed out of his lungs. Blood pounded into his ears. He thought he heard his mother crying but the sound was lost in a rush as his eardrums burst. Red moisture poured from his eyes, nose and mouth and his internal organs exploded. His stomach seemed to be forced up into his mouth. White bile, mixed with blood seeped out between his lips. His teeth crumbled in his mouth and then, mercifully, he was pulled back into the shelter, his body too crushed to fight anymore, and the doors slammed shut with a sonorous crash.

***

The robed figures stared at the doors as Penrose hurried forward and turned the key in the lock. They were shocked into silence. They had expected it to be more symbolic and less horrible, but the creature from the other world had clearly wanted them to see what they had done. It was a message. No—it was a warning.

"Prosperity will be ours," said Penrose, raising his arms to the sky but he was afraid.

The creature would be satisfied, for now. But more sacrifices would have to be made or each one of them would pay the price. And his daughter Elisabeth. His own first born. She turned sixteen next month.

ELDRITCH LUNCH

BY ADAM BOLIVAR

October 15, 1951
Mexico City

Dear Allen,
 Time to get out of Dodge. Joan and I were doing the old William Tell routine and I put a bullet right between her eyes. You should have seen the look on her face. She was out like a light. Not a bad way to go. Dope on a rope. Nine bag a day habit. Did her a favor if you ask me.

Remember that professor of anthropology I told you about? Barlow? We met for drinks one night and he ended up blowing me in the bathroom. Then we went back to his place and did it again. He offed himself last New Year's. Overdose of goof balls. Vomit all over the bed. I can't see this suicide kick. Left me a clay figurine. Obscene little thing. Half man, half octopus. Looks like it's shitting tentacles out of its mouth. He'd showed it to me the night we spent together. I hated it the minute I saw it. Said he'd made it for a friend, some hack writer named H.P. Lovecraft. Guess they had a thing back in the thirties. H.P. Lovecock, more like.

That statue was bad news. Weird shit started happening the day I got it. I started having nightmares about a city. Like what Barlow told me in bed that night. The Black City. Some kind of Mayan legend. Barlow had come to Mexico looking for it. Never found it, but he dreamt about it every night. Now I dream about it too. Sometimes I see it in the daytime when I close my eyes. Junk is the only thing that gives me a respite, an island of heaven in an ocean of hell. But the junk always runs out and then it's back to the city.

I wish I'd never met Barlow, never laid eyes on that damn statue. I'd break it into a million pieces if I could. Throw it in the lake. But it's become a part of me now. I couldn't get rid of it anymore than I could get rid of my own cock. Speaking of which, it's time to head down to El Sapo, the local dive. The only thing I found lurking in the men's room last night was some day-old shit floating in the crapper. But maybe tonight I'll get lucky.

Bill

October 16

Joaquin said he knows the way to the Black City. I met him at the bar last night. He said he'd take me. I wasn't sure what to bring. A pith helmet? In the end, I just brought myself wearing a gray suit and fedora. Joaquin smiled when he saw me back at the bar.

"Are you ready, Bill?" he said.

"*Un memento.*" I ordered a shot of tequila to steady my nerves. "Okay. Let's go."

Joaquin offered me his hand. That surprised me. Every imaginable perversion happened in Mexico City. But it was always behind closed doors, in the shadows. As we walked down the street holding hands, nobody took any notice of us. No, that's not true. They noticed all right. But they looked away. Street vendors frying animal parts not fit for consumption by man or beast turned their heads as we passed. Two peso whores with lips the color of a baboon's ass went inside and locked the doors. We were shunned by the lowest of the low, outcasts among the outcast. It was a good feeling, a feeling of power.

It wasn't long before we reached our destination: a crumbling old church at the end of a narrow alley. I didn't see the alley until Joaquin jerked my arm and pulled me into it. I don't think anyone else saw the alley either. My skin turned clammy with fear. I had started down a path from which there was no return.

The church had been abandoned for years, maybe centuries. What little light that shone through the grimy stained glass windows did little to relieve the ancient gloom. Ancient pews so rotten they wouldn't have supported a skeleton's weight faced an empty nave. There was no Jesus nailed to a slab of wood looking down on us, no Mary weeping tears of blood. This was another kind of church. It was here before the Spaniards came with their crosses and guns, before the Aztecs had come to rip out the still-beating hearts of men in the name of their vile deities.

"This is not a young land," Joaquin said. "It is old and dirty and evil. Before the Spaniards came. Before the Indians and the serpent-men of Valusia. The Old Ones were. The Old Ones are. And the Old Ones shall be. They wait dreaming, locked in the in-between places, waiting for someone to turn the key."

He released a catch in the lectern, which slid aside to reveal a flight of stone steps that led beneath the pulpit. Lighting a half-guttered candle in a rusty lantern lying upturned on the floor, he beckoned me to follow him down the steps into the darkness. By all rights I should have fled. Run screaming out of that den of blasphemy, back into the company of the living. But I was a marked man. I was like him now, an agent of the Old Ones.

At the bottom of the steps was an underground chamber. There was an altar here, an oblong slab of smooth onyx. I wondered briefly if Joaquin intended to lay me out on it and plunge a dagger into my chest. Instead, he felt along the altar's edge with his fingers and found a secret chamber inside the black stone. He withdrew a wooden box, whose lid was engraved with strange hieroglyphs.

"Take it," he said.

I looked into his black eyes, which were filled with stars and galaxies. This was no man, no member of the human race.

"Who are you?" I asked.

He threw back his head and crowed. "I am Nyarlathotep, the Crawling Chaos. Begone and ask no more."

I was pushed by an invisible force, back up the steps and out of the ruined church. I stumbled from the invisible alley and back into the thrum and bustle of humanity once more. I didn't stop running until I was back in my room, where I opened the box. Inside was a little glass vial, which was filled with a powder the exact color of the moon. The fabled hypnosium mentioned in *De Vermiis Mysteriis*. I'll send you a report when I get back.

Bill

October 19? 20? 21?

I started the ritual. The ritual is like tea. You got your spoon—that's for mixing the junk with water until it dissolves into a clear solution. You got your cup—that's to hold the water to put in the spoon. And you got your needle—the needle's got a thousand and one uses—it's your ace in the hole, your secret weapon and your skeleton key all rolled up into one.

I held the vial up to the light, peering at the silvery dust piled up inside. Then I pulled out the stopper, breaking the seal made by a nameless alchemist who'd lived when Atlantis was young. Carefully, I tap-tap-tapped powder into my spoon. Just a little of it, just enough to try 'er out. Flake by flake, I measured it. Each one of those miniscule flakes was worth more than a gold brick to a Conquistador. I scrupulously replaced the stopper and set the vial on the windowsill, out of reach of accidents. I drew 10 cc's of water into the needle from the cup and squirted it into the spoon, where it pooled at the bottom of the concavity. Then I pulled the plunger out of the needle—it's like a Swiss army knife, I tell you—and used the rubber end to mix the flakes into the water. It glittered like stardust for a second then turned clear as crystal. I popped the plunger back and drew the solution into the pointy tip of the needle through a tiny wad of cotton to filter out any impurities. I forced the air out of the top of the needle—carefully, so as not to lose a single drop of that dream-juice, and tap-tap-tapped the side to dislodge the tiny bubbles. I took off my necktie and tied it around my arm, real tight so the throbbing blue veins stood out. My favorite one is a mighty leviathan that runs straight down the middle. But it was all crusted over, so I settled for the next biggest, a tributary just to the right of it. I thrust the needle into my arm and hit it on the first try. I knew I hit the vein by the unmistakable popping sensation it made. I drew the plunger back and was rewarded by the flood of blood rushing in and alchemically combining with the solution of hypnosium. I mustered my courage and kicked it. I only had moments to pull the needle out. In a matter of seconds, the nod set in. And the dish ran away with the spoon.

At first I thought I'd gotten a hot shot. That's when someone substitutes poison—usually strychnine—for your junk. But no, this was the real McCoy. I wasn't in a shabby hotel room in Mexico City anymore. I was in a perfumed garden, an Arabian palace. A fountain bubbled in a courtyard and veiled houris roamed ready to perform acts of exquisite pleasure. They had whatever equipment you needed—penises, vaginas, assholes, the gamut. And when you were done with them, they evaporated in a puff of sweet-smelling smoke, leaving you on a feather bed with a hookah on the side table and an unlimited supply of opium, hashish and tobacco. Too soon I'd wake back in my dingy room in Mexico City, and quickly fill the needle again with hypnosium, my beloved hypnosium.

I don't know how long I lingered in this garden of unearthly delights. It was beyond space and time. It could have been a few minutes; it could have been a thousand years. I don't know how many of the houris I consumed. It might have been an infinite number. But there came a time when I was approached by cold-eyed guards with bare, muscular chests and scimitars dangling from their waists. They took me to an audience with their master, a nervous man wearing a frayed tweed suit and greasy wire-rimmed glasses. He was sitting on an embroidered silk pillow, the stem of a hookah in his hand. It took me a minute, but then I recognized him.

"Barlow?"

He smiled, revealing blackened teeth. "Hi, Bill," he said, taking a hit from his pipe. He exhaled a cloud of fragrant smoke. "Where are my manners?" he added, gesturing to one of the other stems of the hookah. I took a hit myself. The hashish in the bowl crackled as it burned.

"What the hell is going on?" I said. "I thought you were dead."

"I am dead. In the waking world, at least. But it seems I merely traded one realm for another."

An old man wearing a turban sat slumped in one corner. He looked like shit. His eyes were red-rimmed and sunken into their sockets, but still they darted back and forth as he read a strange, mildewed book in his lap, his long-nailed fingers obsessively turning the pages back and forth and back and forth.

"That is not dead which can eternal lie," he crooned madly. "And with strange aeons, even death may die."

I'd met my share of repulsive characters, but these two took the cake. Just being in their presence made me queasy. I started to back away, but the guard grabbed my arm and held me in place.

"Look, I don't want to seem ungrateful," I said. "But I'd like to get back to smoking opium and screwing houris, if that's all right."

The Mad Arab took a hit from another one of the stems of the hookah and started coughing convulsively. He spat a gray-green globule of what could have been part of one of his lungs onto the floor and fixed me with a stare that made my blood run cold with horror. "In his house in R'lyeh, dead Cthulhu waits dreaming."

Barlow's skin turned yellow and then green and his flesh melted into viscous rivulets of transparent jelly, revealing a monstrous black centipede that gibbered and writhed on the silk pillow, which was now covered with mucous slime that pooled on the floor nauseatingly. Waves of fecal stench filled the room and I vomited a colorful mush onto my shoes. The centipede looked at me with Barlow's icy blue eyes, although they were now as lifeless as a crab's eye on the end of a stalk.

"You are an agent of the Old Ones now. You will be receiving your instructions soon. Remember: nothing is true. Everything is permitted."

Then I awoke on my piss-soaked mattress, shivering and sweaty. The Atlantean vial was empty. Shrill, discordant piping carried into my open window. I didn't have the strength to get up and close it. The habit had fixed on me. I would have to score another fix, and soon.

***

I set out to find the church that Joaquin or Nyarlathotep or whatever his name was had taken me to. Maybe there was more hypnosium in the basement. I walked up and down the street where the alley had been, but try as I might I couldn't find it. On the sidewalk, someone had set up an altar filled with flickering candles, flowers and Virgin Marys. Christ, how the Mexicans loved the Virgin Mary. Do what you mother tells you, boys.

"Hello, Beel," came a weary, disdainful voice. "Enchoying the night air?" I turned around to see Detective Muñoz standing behind me wearing a cheap suit that was too small for him and a sweat-stained fedora. He had been hassling me since arriving in Mexico City, trying to get the drop on me. "I have a few questions to ask you about the death of your wife, down at the station."

I considered making a run for it. I'd have had a good chance of outrunning this lard-ass flatfoot. But then I saw a couple of *Federales* coming towards me from the other end of the street. *La policia.* I was trapped like a rat. I decided to be gracious about it.

"By all means, detective. Let's you and me have a little chat."

The interrogation room was windowless and empty but for a plain wooden desk. Puke green walls with peeling paint. Hot as hell. All police interrogation rooms were the same. Muñoz sat on one side of the desk and I sat on the other. He offered me a cigarette and I took it, inserting it in my mouth and lighting it in one deft motion. Muñoz produced a .38 Special—the one I'd used to kill my wife—and the hideous statue of the octopus man I'd inherited from Barlow. He placed them on the table. Then the detective opened a manila file folder and flipped through its considerable contents.

"Some tasty stuff in here, amigo," he said. "You sure done a lot of drugs. Morphine, Dilaudid, heroin. Like to ride the horse, eh?"

"I've cleaned up my act," I said. "I'm a married man now."

Muñoz slammed a meaty fist down on the desk. "You *were* a married man. Before you put a bullet in your wife's head. Whatchoo got to say about that, *amigo*?"

He didn't sound like my *amigo*, and I had nothing to say.

"Nothing would give me more pleasure than to put a gringo junkie like you in jail. Throw away the key, you know what I mean?"

I did know what he meant, but I kept my mouth shut.

"But it looks like you got some friends in high places." He slammed the file shut. Then he stood up and opened the door, admitted a tall gaunt man in a trench coat and snap brim fedora. Muñoz made a gun shape with two fingers and a thumb and mimed shooting me in the head. Then he left the interrogation room, leaving me alone with the newcomer.

"Special Agent Armitage, FBI," he said, extending a hand, which I shook. It closed around mine like a steel vise. What was it with these all-American types and their death-grip handshakes? Armitage sat in the chair Muñoz had vacated and leafed through the file the detective had left on the desk.

"You've been a naughty boy, Bill," he said. "But I think you're just the man for the job." He pulled a new file from inside his coat and laid it on the desk on top of mine. This file was labeled TOP SECRET. He opened it. There was a photograph of a man wearing a dark suit. His jaw was abnormally elongated and he had a constipated expression.

"Ever hear of a man named Howard Phillips Lovecraft?"

"Sure. Pulp fiction writer, right? Never read his stuff myself. Heard it's pretty trashy."

"That was his cover story. We have a big file on him back at the Bureau. This is just the tip of the iceberg. He's been involved in subversive, anti-American activities. Old J. Edgar himself is interested in him."

"Didn't he die back in the thirties?"

"We've looked into it. We believe his death in '37 was faked and that he's hiding out somewhere in the South Pacific. He's the leader of a vast conspiracy whose sole purpose is to bring down the United States government and pave the way for an extraterrestrial invasion. Probably in cahoots with the commies, although we can't prove that yet."

"What's all this got to do with me?"

Special Agent Armitage offered me a Lucky Strike. I took it. He took one himself and we lit up together. "We need a deep cover operative. Someone who can infiltrate Lovecraft's organization. I think your writing background makes you ideally suited for the job."

He reached into his briefcase and pulled out a wooden box. Placing the box on the table, he opened it. Inside was a sight more beautiful to me than diamonds: another vial of hypnosium and a syringe. He pushed the box towards me.

"What do you say, Bill?" he said, baring his canines. "Are you ready to serve your country?"

I was already rolling back my sleeve. I'd do anything to protect the right to bare arms. In a matter of seconds, I had prepared the solution in a dirty coffee spoon and the needle was poised above a vein.

"One last thing," Armitage said. He walked around the desk and slipped the .38 Special in my pocket. "No American should venture into a foreign land unarmed."

The cold point of the needle punctured my vein—a vampire's kiss. The blood spurted into the glass tube with all the urgency of a sexual release. I rammed the plunger home. The last thing I saw was the octopus idol staring at me with bulging fishy eyes.

November 3, 1951
47° 9'S 126° 43'W

It was arranged for me to book passage on a Norwegian freighter, en route from Mexico to Australia. That it be a ship flying the flag of a neutral country was essential to my cover. The FBI must have paid the captain a pretty penny to make a detour to the required co-ordinates: 47° 9'S 126° 43'W. R'lyeh. The Black City. It was my assignment to infiltrate Miskatonic, Inc., a subversive un-American organization based on a tiny island in the South Pacific.

The Black City was a dream place, a ruin of impossible angles and grotesque carvings of abominable gods. The captain nervously agreed to meet me back at the landing spot in twenty-four hours. But as I watched the rusty tub steam away, I wondered if he'd come back. Why would he? He'd gotten his money. He could always claim I'd been lost at sea. Fucking lutefisk-eating Norwegian.

I sat down on a toppled column and tapped out the last of the hypnosium into my spoon. I had a kit in my coat pocket. Every junkie does. It had everything I needed: spoon, needle, a bottle of water. I rolled back my sleeve and tied off. That's when things started getting weird.

At the center of the city, a vast black monolith rose from the ground like an erect penis. Bestriding its tip was the big brother of my figurine, that revolting octopus thing. At the base of the monolith was an aperture that yawned open like a starving maw. A fetid, anal stench wafted from the interior. Looks like it was my job to crawl into it. The things a man does for his country. I shimmied up the slimy glistening rectum into the bowels of R'lyeh.

I found myself in a cavernous cathedral of black onyx. Echoing around the vaulted chamber was a cacophony of clacking typewriters, punctuated by little dings and the occasional fart. Along the wall were hexagonal chambers like the cells of a vast honeycomb.

I peered into one of the chambers, and saw an emaciated man in the tattered remnants of a tweed suit chained to a typewriter, which he was pounding furiously. It was Barlow. A pulsing tentacle dangled above him, and he greedily sucked it like a teat. I looked over his shoulder at the sheet of paper scrolled through the pincers of his insect-like typewriter. The words typed on the sheet were a tangled briar of obscure adjectives: rugose, gibbous, eldritch, squamous. Barlow popped the tentacle out of his mouth and a translucent white jelly ran down his chin.

"Hello, Bill," he smiled, offering the tentacle to me like it was a reefer. "Would you care to try some elder jism?"

I shook my head no. Shrugging, Barlow went back to sucking and typing, his expression slack with bliss. "Iä Cthulhu," he droned through his puckered lips. "Iä Yog-Sothoth. Iä Shub-Niggurath." I left him to his work.

Making my way past the row of chambers occupied by chained-up writers rat-tat-tatting their keys and suck-suck-sucking jism from tentacles like it was fucking ice cream soda, I came to the heart of the operation, where a giant bat-winged octopus squatted on an onyx throne. This was no statue. This was the thing itself, a living monstrosity, its tentacles winding through the cavern, feeding a thousand junkies like a goat suckling her young.

The creature turned to look at me, and I saw what looked like a human face covered by a murky layer of green jelly. Using the razor-sharp talon at the end of one its bat wings, the creature sliced a seam down the front of its gelatinous skin from the top of its head to its pulsating asshole. Human hands poked out from the inside of the skin and peeled it away with a horrible schlupping sound. Shedding the now-flaccid octopus skin, a man wearing an immaculately pressed black suit stepped out. He looked perfectly ordinary, except for a queerly protruding jaw, and chuckled at my expression of revulsion.

"Greetings, Mr. Burroughs," he said in an old-timey New England accent. "I've so been looking forward to meeting you. My name is Howard Phillips Lovecraft. But please, call me H.P."

"H.P.," I repeated.

"I understand you are interested in joining my little circle of Cthulhu Mythos writers."

"Thinking about it."

"You come very highly recommended by young Barlow. I knew immediately that we could use a writer of your caliber."

The word caliber reminded me to check my pocket. Yes, it was still there. Right where Armitage had put it. Good old American steel.

"And the elder jism?" I asked. "Would I have access to that?"

Lovecraft winced at the word. "Oh my. I really detest such vulgar talk, you know. References to amatory phenomena make me so... uncomfortable." I noticed the tentacles of his split-open octopus skin were still writhing. The thing was scampering across the floor towards him like a faithful dog.

"Oh come on, Howard," I needled him. "Homosexuality is the best all-around cover an agent can have."

"Please, Mr. Burroughs," he said. "I will not have such talk in my house."

"I can dig it. In his house at R'lyeh, dead Cthulhu waits dreaming, right?"

Lovecraft clapped his hands together like a kid who had just gotten a bicycle for his birthday. "Quite so! Quite so! So what do you say, Mr.

Burroughs? Do you accept my offer? I'm thinking you'll fit in nicely in the Carcosa department. The Lake of Hali is lovely this time of year."

I cocked my pistol. "Sure. Just one thing though. It's about time for our William Tell routine."

"Our what?"

There was nothing on his head. Oh well. It didn't matter. Nothing is true. Everything is permitted. I put a bullet right between his eyes. You should have seen the look on his face.

LITTLE CURLY

BY NEIL BAKER

The three knocks at the door were so loud, so evenly spaced, that only one person could be standing outside the door of Apartment 719.

Fedor sighed loudly and placed the ladle on the stovetop next to a simmering pot of soup; soup he would not be eating that day. He turned off the hob and moved the pot, then wiped his hands on his pajamas as he strode across his tiny apartment and opened the door. The large man filling the door frame sported a bushy face the same color as his salt and pepper suit and the small exposed patches of skin on his cheeks and nose were as red as the beetroot in Fedor's supper.

The man glared at Fedor's dishevelment, his wild eyebrows clashing like angry storm clouds, and he spoke in a voice so low it sounded like a tractor on gravel. "Comrade Demidov, you are required."

"Hello again, Lev. How long has it been, four months?"

"Six. We need to leave now."

Fedor Demidov smiled and plucked at the top of his cotton pants. "As you can see, I am not quite ready to travel. Besides, I don't think I work for them any more."

Lev Ovseenko glanced at his watch. "That is of no consequence. When I am instructed to bring you in, that is what I do. Get dressed, Comrade."

Fedor gave his waistband one last twang and then turned back toward his bedroom. "Then we shouldn't keep them waiting. Take a seat, Lev, I won't be long." He padded into the room, noting that the big Ukrainian hadn't moved from the hallway. Nothing changes, he thought as he rooted through the drawer beneath his mattress for something to wear. Something that didn't smell of neglect.

***

Ninety minutes later the squat domiciles of Astana had faded and merged to resemble dirty hillocks behind them, as Lev Ovseenko and his passenger drove away from the capital city toward southern Kazakhstan. This was how Fedor referred to his adopted home, even though government workers were encouraged to use Kazakh SSR on official documents. They were still one hundred kilometers out from Zhezkazgan, a well-developed town that Ovseenko had decided would be their next rest spot, but Fedor's legs were cramping in the rear seat of Lev's Moskvich 410 and he insisted that Lev pull over, finally convincing the driver that he needed to relieve himself. As Fedor faked a piss behind a scrubby bush, Lev took the opportunity to stretch his own long legs and light a cigarette. He had been mute for the drive thus far, determined to maintain an air of professionalism, but Fedor suspected the tedious journey and innumerable potholes had loosened his tongue and so decided to test the waters.

"Just like old times eh, Lev?" It was the smallest of small talk, but his gambit paid off.

Lev reduced his cigarette to ash with three long draws and flicked the butt into a large hole at his feet. "Indeed, Comrade Demidov. I am not surprised to see that this miserable road has been untouched since we traveled it last November."

Last November. How exciting that time had been. The west had watched with envious eyes as the Soviet space program sent *Sputnik 2* into orbit with its delicate, yapping payload. As a junior engineer with the life support system team, Fedor had done his job to the best of his ability on November third and had been sent home one day later, his bonus secure and his apartment paid for. Then he had waited. Waited for the call that would bring him back into the regulated warmth of the Cosmodrome's corridors; a chance to work on *Luna 1* and to share in the glory of space exploration. But the call never came. Evidently *the best of his ability* wasn't good enough. And now here was Lev Ovseenko, Tyuratam's facilitator, the man the agency trusted to drive their scientists to and from the Cosmodrome; a man who could be everywhere at once.

"Who will I be reporting to, Lev?"

The big man picked a strand of tobacco from his teeth, "I was told to bring you to General Kozlov."

Fedor quickly rounded the bush and strode back to the car, pulling his own cigarette case from his breast pocket and offering it to the Ukrainian who did not decline. "The general? This is a military matter?"

Ovseenko shrugged as he tossed the cigarette onto the dash before squeezing back behind the wheel. "I know this much, Fedor, the Cosmodrome is locked down tighter than I have ever seen."

Fedor resumed his position behind the driver and attempted to get comfortable on the over-sprung seat, "The Americans?"

"We will know soon enough, Comrade," answered Lev, crunching the car into gear, "perhaps our nuclear testing at Novaya Zemlya makes them nervous." He laughed, loud and long, and then coughed up a great globule of phlegm, which he spat through the tiny car window into the dust that blurred beside their wheels.

* * *

Several hours later the crosshatched towers and bulky hangers of Tyuratam Cosmodrome slowly ascended from the foothills of the Urals, breaking the crisp line that separated the vast steppe from a powder-blue sky thick with salty clouds from the Aral Sea. Antelope and roe deer scattered before Lev's angry-looking car as it roared onto the strip of concrete that would lead them to the perimeter fence. The steel bars of the main gate slowly parted like alfalfa in the breeze as they approached but this was not to accommodate their entry, instead, a fleet of silver buses streamed out through the maw and flew past them, rocking Lev's car in the process. At the rear of the convoy was a black GAZ-12, chasing the buses like a panther and escorted by a swarm of military motorbikes.

As the limousine brushed past, Fedor caught sight of the passenger in the rear and tapped his driver on the shoulder. "Lev, that was Lieutenant Gagarin."

"We have to keep our future secure, Comrade," growled the big man as he drove up to the guards on the gate, his security pass in hand, "it appears to me the lockdown has become an evacuation."

"Then I think we are traveling in the wrong direction," said Fedor, shrinking back into his seat as the car sped across a vast runway to hanger number four.

* * *

68

Three separate inspections welcomed Fedor, the final one being more intrusive than he had previously recalled, before he was allowed into a makeshift meeting room in the center of the cavernous hanger. The room had been hastily erected using three canvas sheets strung between scaffolding and sentinel floodlights; its rear wall comprised of the skeletal frame of *Vostok 1*. Several workbenches had been dragged into the center of the space forming one large table and an ill-matching assortment of chairs were scattered about, three of which were filled by gray-coated technicians while one was occupied by Kozlov himself. A quartet of soldiers stood rigidly to attention on either side of the flap purporting to be a door and two more stood at the shoulder of their superior officer. Lev Ovseenko sidled in and planted himself in a far corner while Fedor recognized one of his colleagues and strode over to him, grasping him firmly by the hand.

"Comrade Reznik! It is good to see you again, my friend." He looked at the other two scientists, vaguely recognizing them from other divisions. "Where's Kaplan?"

Nikita Reznik stared back at Fedor with dark-ringed eyes and then a flicker of recognition. He shook Fedor's hand firmly but briefly, and then indicated to a chair opposite the general. "Sit, Fedor. We must speak with you."

Fedor pulled out a wooden chair, not relishing the thought of subjecting his already numb nether-regions to another uncomfortable seat, and gingerly sat down across from the general. He had met Kozlov once before and had found him unpleasantly brusque.

From the look on the old soldier's face it was business as usual as Kozlov stood and placed both hands on the workbench, leaning in toward Fedor. "Fedor Demidov, you were part of the life support system team on Sputnik 2, correct?"

"Correct, General."

"Dr. Reznik here was your superior, and your project manager was Dr. Kaplan, correct?"

"Yes, sir," Fedor didn't like the general's tone which seemed to be unnecessarily angry, but the sudden recollection that he was no longer in the employ of the Cosmodrome emboldened him and he dared to venture his own query, "what is all this about, General?"

General Kozlov continued as if Fedor's voice had been a whisper. "How well did you know Laika?"

"Excuse me?"

"The dog, comrade. Laika. *Muttnik*, as our American friends dubbed her."

"You mean Kudryavka. Laika was the name given to her by the west."

"Yes, Kudryavka, *Little Curly*, the bitch you sent into orbit. You were friendly with her, no?"

Fedor thought back to the first time he had been introduced to Kudryavka; how he had fallen under the spell of that tiny mongrel, along with everyone else that had been instructed not to form emotional attachments to her. The ridiculous moniker given her by the foreign press translated to *Barker* but this couldn't be further from the truth; the little terrier mix was the gentlest dog on the program, and she had responded with enthusiasm and uncanny intelligence to the brutal training the agency had inflicted on her and her canine companions. He recalled the day before the launch, when Dr. Kaplan had brought his nieces onto the base for an impromptu playtime with Kudryavka; one last moment of joy for the little dog. She had danced and skipped with the girls, licking their faces until they were both drenched, performing tricks for tiny gelatinous treats. It was to be her last full day as a dog. As a living being. The next day Kaplan, Fedor and Reznik had shaved her, festooned her with sensors, chained her into a tiny capsule and then boiled her from the inside out.

Fedor looked back into the face of Kozlov: a face turning steadily redder as the general lost patience. "Yes, I knew her well," Fedor answered quietly, "I looked after her when Dr. Kaplan was unavailable, I exercised her, fed her. I wept when she died."

The general curled his thin lips in disgust, not bothering to hide his contempt for Fedor's weakness, "You were responsible for her death, correct?"

Fedor grimaced. It *had* been his fault. His main responsibility on the team was to ensure the thermal control system operated efficiently, but a series of mechanical errors upon launch, compounded by the failure of the Block-A core to separate correctly, had resulted in several rips in the thermal insulation. This meant their whimpering passenger was already exposed to infernal temperatures before she left Earth's atmosphere and was roasted before the fourth orbit had been completed. The thought of her suffering sickened him, and he had refused to take part in the post-mission celebrations. That wasn't to say Fedor wanted no further employment with the agency, however it had taken him the past six months to convince himself that, at the end of the day, *she was just a dog.*

"Yes, General. I assume full responsibility for her death."

Reznik quickly leaned across the table and placed his hand on Fedor's arm. "Now wait, Fedor, we were all to blame. It was a combination of system failures that led to..."

"Enough!" The general cut Reznik off with a bellow that made one of the guards flinch, "You may wallow in your communal guilt when the current situation is resolved." He stared at Reznik who slumped back in his seat, and then turned his attention back to Fedor. "As far as the rest of the world is concerned, everything went according to plan. They think the dog was euthanized before her oxygen depleted. As we know, this was not the case."

"I don't need reminding, General."

Reznik removed his hand from Fedor's forearm, "There is more, Fedor. These men," he indicated to the other scientists sitting across the table, "Sidorov and Andreev, they spotted an anomaly as the capsule entered the exosphere, by which time the dog was already dying."

The younger of the two scientists clasped his hands around his coffee cup and looked at Fedor as he spoke. "We ran the long-range trackers, Andreev monitored the capsule and I supervised the life support feed. Our reports have since been buried," he glanced at Kozlov who quickly stared him down, "but I can tell you that we observed a simultaneous discrepancy. Firstly Kudryavka's heart reached 280 beats per minute as the internal temperature reached 164 F and she died. A moment later Sputnik 2 vanished from all visual and audio monitors for two seconds and then appeared again; only it reappeared thirty kilometers *within* the thermosphere that it had already departed. Not only that, but we now detected a life sign coming from the capsule."

"She had been dead seconds before..." added Andreev shaking his head, still in denial.

Fedor was unable to subdue an impulsive laugh and instead turned it into a spluttering cough as he looked around the table and then back to the young scientist. "What do you mean, vanished? Surely your readings were incorrect."

"The readings were accurate, Comrade," whispered Sidorov, and the seriousness in his eyes chilled Fedor's blood, "besides, the events have been confirmed by Dr. Kaplan."

"Where is Kaplan?" said Fedor, his voice rising, his anger percolating. He suddenly felt he was the butt of an elaborate and inexplicable prank.

The general slapped his palm on the bench surface and half of the group visibly jumped in their seats. He then waited to see that he had Fedor's full attention before commencing in slow and measured tones. "Comrade Demidov, did you ever converse with the dog?"

"Converse...?"

"*Talk* to the dog, Junior Technician Demidov! Did you ever talk to... Little Curly?"

Fedor looked around the canvas chamber, trying to find support in his colleagues' faces, but Lev seemed more interested in the welding on the rocket frame behind him, Andreev and Sidorov were focused on their feet and Reznik was staring at the bench surface, his neck veins popping as he ground his back teeth. Confused, Fedor gave a slight shake of his head and answered the best he could. "I'm not sure, general. Perhaps a few words here and there, but..."

"Nothing substantial?" interrupted the military man.

"Not that I am aware of, general. Why do you ask?"

Kozlov stood and gestured with pistol fingers to his soldiers who quickly went to the exit and held open the flap. He then fixed Fedor with a gaze that would crack granite and extended one hand, inviting the junior technician to leave with him. "Because, Comrade Demidov, the dog has asked to speak to you."

***

Green-tinted overhead strip lights merged into one long ribbon as Fedor was led dazed through twisting corridors and out into the harsh twilight air as the group marched across crumbling tarmac garnished with unsupervised weeds toward the central training building. He had tried to listen as Reznik buzzed in his ear, bringing him up to speed, but the man's words were so fantastic that Fedor could only absorb some of what he was being told. The general's men held open a pair of large double doors as their leader shepherded the group into the building, their boots echoing in the deserted hallways, thin clouds of blue cigarette smoke still lingering above, testament to the sudden evacuation.

Fedor could smell fresh coffee as they marched past the recreation room, down a wide corridor and directly into the water chamber, a room used for weightlessness orientation training but which was now dry as a desert and being used for something quite different. Kozlov led the group to the observation wall of the vast pool and tapped on the glass. Immediately a row of lights stuttered on and Fedor could see three figures, two of them clad head to toe in HAZMAT suits, the third strapped to a gurney, seemingly asleep.

The general picked up a radio and turned it on as one of the protected figures did likewise.

One of the suited men approached the glass to better see the general and held up a clip chart, which displayed multiple line graphs and rows of numbers. "He's clean, General. We've been monitoring him at twenty-minute intervals for the past six hours and his readings are perfectly normal. I recommend moving him to the medical wing."

"That won't be happening. I need him to come with us."

The suited man did not even begin to protest; instead he nodded and returned to the gurney, waving at his colleague to release the patient.

Fedor held his hands to the glass to cut down the reflections and strained to see the prone person's face. "Is that Dr. Kaplan?"

"Yes," whispered Reznik at his shoulder, "Kaplan was the first person she spoke to."

"What happened to him?"

"We don't know. He's broken, mentally, we can't get a sensible word out of him."

"We don't know?" Sidorov's outburst was high-pitched and laced with incredulousness, "she was in his head!"

Kozlov spun and hissed at the scientist, "That's enough, comrade," he then indicated to one of the guards, "escort this man back to the main hanger. He is of no further use to us."

Sidorov's squirming and protestations were in vain as he was frog-marched from the pool room, and the General fixed the remaining party with a steely eye as a barely conscious Kaplan, slumped in a wheelchair, was pushed out through a side door and handed over to one of the remaining guards. "Come," ordered the general, "let's not keep it waiting."

Fedor glanced at Lev, but his old friend merely shook his head, equally bewildered, and fell into step behind the exiting soldiers. As the group left, the remaining two men slowly peeled off their suits then sat on the tiled floor of the empty pool and silently stared at their reflections in the plate-glass wall.

***

Their trip took no longer than thirty seconds, and the general drew them to a halt outside the giant shuttered door of the inspection hall; a vast housing where the remnants of satellites, space craft and other testing machines were analyzed and catalogued. Fedor had been in this section of the building only once before, as part of the team that attempted to piece together an earlier version of the life-support module that would eventually contain Little Curly, but had disintegrated upon test launch.

General Kozlov turned to face the party. "As of this moment, those of you who have not yet encountered the entity are now sworn to the utmost secrecy," he stared specifically at Fedor and Lev, both of whom were breathing quickly in nervous anticipation. "Divulgence of anything you see or hear in this room will result in execution without trial, am I understood?"

"Clearly," growled the big Ukrainian, while Fedor merely nodded.

The general knocked twice on the corrugated entrance and the squeal of multiple sliding bolts pierced the air before the door slowly rolled up accompanied by the rattle of chains and the hum of overhead motors. As the contents of the room were exposed, Fedor reeled, his senses assaulted by a crystal white light that seemed to burn into his eyes, a high-pitched whine that might have been that of a dog, but now sounded mechanical such was its pitch and longevity, and a smell that could only be described as raw meat tinged with the acrid sting of electrical discharge. As his eyes grew accustomed to the brightness in the room, he began to make out arc lamps, whirring film cameras and microphone stands surrounding a large shape; a shape that heaved and writhed but was ultimately wholly recognizable to him. The general waved one hand at the attending technicians and they immediately darted around the room, turning off the giant lamps until the only light source came from the object itself. This was still enough to reveal the monstrous object in all its unholy glory.

"It prefers to generate its own light," said Kozlov, marching up to the mass, his hands clasped behind his back, "we only illuminate it for recording purposes."

Noting with little amusement that Lev was frozen to the spot behind him, Fedor took a step closer. The object that pulsated and glistened before him was undeniably the conical shape of Sputnik 2 standing on its circular base, its tip pointed to the roof of the building. However, this capsule was twice as large as the one they had launched. Fedor estimated the base had to be at least ten feet across, an estimation that was hard to confirm as the object constantly changed shape, swelling and retracting like the muscular foot of a limpet, its gelatinous bulk rippling as fresh mucus seeped from the apex of the cone and solidified against the surface like a form of ghastly magma. The whole mass was in a constant state of agitation; polyps formed and broke free, rolling down the sticky slope for a few seconds before being absorbed back into the main 'body'. Thick, stubby limbs extended at random points, testing the air with their fern-like tips before retracting. The surface color was a muddied gray tinged with an oily iridescence that swirled and glowed, intensifying with each rhythmic pulse from the bulk.

Fedor turned to look at the others, and suddenly understood what had been gnawing away at his perception; there was no color in the room. Ruddy faces and dark green uniforms had been reduced to pale grays. Men merged with furniture, their forms rendered indistinguishable through lack of hue and contrast.

Reznik noticed Fedor's gaze and spoke loudly above the whining din coming from the thing before them. "Remarkable, isn't it? The creature appears to be absorbing all reflected light from its surroundings, we are illuminated only by its luminescence."

Fedor stared at his own hand, marveling at the lack of textural detail caused by the object's absorption of his skin tone. Suddenly he looked back at Reznik. "This is how she would see."

"Who?"

"Kudryavka. This must be how she saw the world."

Kozlov stepped between the scientists and brought his face uncomfortably close to Fedor's. "Why don't you ask her, comrade Demidov?"

His breath was stale and cold and Fedor turned back to the gelatinous capsule, favoring this view than that of the general who now resembled something that might be found squatting over a cemetery gate. Fedor could see the missing colors from the people and objects in the room dancing in the rainbow film that coated its quivering flesh.

A sudden cry from the corner of the room announced the full awakening of Dr. Kaplan and the distraught patient tried to stand, causing the wheelchair to spin backwards and sending him crashing to the floor. One of the guards grabbed the broken scientist under his arms and hauled him to his feet.

"Fedor! Oh, my boy. She has so much to show you."

"Dr. Kaplan," began Fedor, extending an arm to steady the older man, "what happened to you? How does she speak to you?"

"You'll see, young Fedor, she has asked for you by name. She wants to show you what she has seen, what she now knows, things we should not know," his grip on Fedor's arm tightened until it hurt, "The darkness, the colors! We are ants! Lower than ants! Protozoa tower over us!" He laughed, but it was devoid of any mirth.

General Kozlov snatched the older scientist's hand away from Fedor's arm and pushed him back toward the guard who grabbed Kaplan, forcing him back into the wheelchair. "Secure this fool!" shouted the general. He then turned back to Fedor. "Enough of this. Time is short. Find out what this thing wants!"

Fedor glanced at Lev who appeared to still be dumbstruck along with a subdued Andreev, and then to Reznik. "Nikita, what does he mean 'time is short'?"

His colleague looked as if he was about to reply but the words never escaped his lips. Instead, his eyes were trained on the service revolver that Kozlov was now waving in their direction.

The general's face contorted in fury as he hissed at them. "Dr. Reznik, get away from Demidov." Reznik did as the general said, slowly side-stepping away toward the other two men.

"Now, Fedor Demidov, speak with it."

"How do I...?" began Fedor, suddenly silenced as a finger-thin tendril emerged from the center of the pulsating, conical mound and snaked toward him. Fedor froze, mesmerized by the waving limb that grew closer by the second, then instinctively twitched when the tip of the appendage burst apart into four thin digits that quickly spread until it resembled a grasping hand. He began to step away as the limb reached his face but his retreat was cut short by the cold touch of gun metal against the back of his neck. He wanted to protest, but it was already too late and the tentacles were upon him, two burrowing into his ears and two into the inner corners of his eyes. A brief moment of absolute terror was instantly replaced by a sense of enormous well-being, warmth and security, and then Fedor was in his mother's arms. He was wrapped in black furs and could hear damp wood chips sputtering in the hearth as his mother rocked him back and forth, humming softly, her breath heavy with warm milk. Fedor wanted to gaze upon her beautiful round face, feel her kisses on his cheek, but when he craned his head to look at her, all he saw was the same gray room and its frightened occupants. He felt loving arms squeezing him tightly, and then he was falling, sinking into sweet, viscous fluids.

Darkness, then points of light that danced and merged to form an image. It was the room again, only this time he was sitting in a wheelchair. He glanced down at his hands, ashen, folded across his lap, then up at the tableau before him. His friends were pressed against the back wall, the general's gun keeping them in check. He could see himself, Fedor, floating in the air before the living capsule, his body stiff and horizontal, connected to the thing by the serpentine appendage that enveloped his face.

Get out.

The voice in his head was that of his old mentor.

"Dr. Kaplan?"

Get out. There is no refuge here. Speak to her.

Fedor wanted to address the voice but he felt bony digits pushing and prodding upon his back until he was forced from the chair and flew across the room, spinning, spinning.

Darkness.

Fedor opened his eyes. He immediately felt extreme claustrophobia, his knees were pushed up into his chest and he was hunched over in a crouched position. His arms were stretched out before him, tethered to metal walls on either side that were veined with brass pipes while a rubber mask smothered his mouth and he felt pinpricks of pain all down his spine. He realized he was naked and started to struggle.

Rest.

Fedor began to speak, but his words were already resonating in the cramped compartment before he had finished thinking them.

"Who are you?"

I am good dog.

"Kudryavka? I am so sorry."

You are good man.

"No, I failed. You should not have suffered."

Fedor was aware of great forces pushing against his physical body. Internally he was drifting in a balmy sea, but externally his skin was rippling and his muscles were compressing.

Come with me.

Live with me.

See with me.

Die with me.

The walls of his new prison shimmered and undulated and in a moment were no more. Thin cloud structures streamed all around him as he hurtled through a sky that became the most glorious blue he had ever seen as violet ribbons of atmosphere cocooned him, turning white as an intense heat blasted his body. Fedor could actually feel his blood boiling in his organs and looked down at his outstretched arms, marveling at the way his flesh blistered and split before curling away from his bones and melting into pink mist. He felt nothing.

"This happened to you?"

Fear. Great pain.

Fedor wanted to cry, but no tears would come. He was dimly aware of something blocking his eyes, burrowing into his tear ducts.

"I, I should have checked more thoroughly. I needed more time, I…"

See.

Fedor felt himself blinking; a phantom sensation layered onto his exposed and rapidly disintegrating skull. Then he saw it. The pitch black of the limitless void beyond his home was blemished by a shifting patch of golden light that swayed like a broken reed in a stream. The radiant slit grew larger and then opened like a jagged mouth to swallow him whole.

***

Lev Ovseenko looked on in silent terror as the body of his old friend, Fedor, bobbed gently at the end of the obscene limb extended from the former shell of Sputnik 2. Andreev had collapsed into a chair, wanting to leave but prevented by Kozlov's soldiers who were having a hard time maintaining their own composures.

In the corner, Kaplan cackled, "He's seeing what I saw."

"Explain yourself!" barked the general, still waving his revolver around like a protective talisman, "What is he seeing?"

"Our place in the universe," answered the old scientist, smiling, "…the truth."

"I asked you this yesterday, and I'll ask you again," the general stepped closer to him, "is this thing a threat?"

"And you still do not understand, General Kozlov, that our friend here has no interest in us. We are motes of dust, stirred by the currents of its passage through our space. It can only threaten our understanding of ourselves, of our importance. It serves to remind us that no achievement, however glorious, is of any significance."

Kozlov waved his free hand as if batting away the scientist's words and growled, angrily. "Enough of your meaningless prattle. Is it telling Demidov the same thing?"

"I expect so. Little Curly always liked Fedor, so I imagine she is telling him a lot more than she told me."

"We shall see. I am under orders to take any appropriate action to protect the space program. If I do not like what Comrade Demidov has to say, then we shall see how this invader likes the consequences." The general turned to face the levitating man and flipped the safety on his revolver before picking up a long-range radio mike. Lev felt his stomach tighten. This would not end well.

***

"Where am I?" Fedor's words barely resonated; such was the vastness of the barren, stone plain he now stood upon. He had already inspected his arms and torso and had been relieved to find he was whole once more and clad in his work clothes.

You are here.

Fedor felt himself lift into the air, rising vertically for what seemed like miles. He looked down and saw that the plain he had been standing on was, in fact, one of thousands of square faces that coated an immense sphere upon which the horizon barely curved. Above him, the sky seemed to be a giant golden mirror, reflecting an infinite swarm of similar, grid-scarred balls. He touched a finger to the lustrous surface and it rippled as if he had dropped a pebble into a pond. In the troughs of the circular waves he caught glimpses of infinite pitch studded with billions of stars.

You are there.

Fedor was floating above the gelatinous cone in the inspection room. He called out to his companions, but they did not respond. A blink, and then he was back on the smooth, silver plain. A snuffling sound behind him caused him to spin around and he smiled as the familiar brown and white shape of Little Curly padded over to him. The little dog was overjoyed to see him and she wagged her tail furiously, jumping up and licking his hands. Fedor laughed and scratched the excited terrier behind her left ear causing her to yap and roll over for more.

I love you.

Fedor continued to stroke Kudryavka, poking and tickling the dog until she writhed helplessly on the hard ground, her back legs kicking the air.

"Is this heaven?" thought Fedor aloud, immediately regretting his immature question.

This is life.

Little Curly suddenly stood and looked directly into his eyes.

They brought me here when I died.

"Who? Who brought you here?"

Before the question left his lips Fedor became aware of a bubbling sound that grew steadily louder. The ground beneath his feet began to throb and bulge and as he was thrown to the floor he grabbed the dog by her scruff and held her tightly. The plain shattered where the bulges peaked and giant forms rose into the space all around them. The shapes were solid, geometric and straight-edged, but their faces were not uniform and this caused organic bends and twists in their forms as they grew like bean sprouts, twisting up toward the mirrored dome. As soon as the thunderous event had begun it was over, and specks of debris dissolved back into the available portions of smooth plain left undeveloped. Fedor gazed upon these mighty monuments in astonishment as Kudryavka squirmed in his arms and he dropped her to the floor. She immediately ran over to the closest multi-faceted structure and stood on her hind legs, scratching at the base and wagging her tail. A crack appeared at the base of the shape, widening and growing as it defaced the lower third of the structure. Then the crack opened fully, peeling the face back like an orange, and Fedor felt every last drop of moisture evaporate from his mouth as a creature the size of his apartment block oozed out of the opening. The color of the foul thing was astonishingly vivid, pinks and reds flecked with rusty spots like leopard-print, and contrasted against the sterile landscape like a rose petal on a corpse. Fedor gagged as the true composition of the creature suddenly became clear; it was a conglomeration of hundreds of giant tongues, all of them writhing, coiling around and into each other like mating slugs. Toward the base of the monster, smaller muscles detached and wriggled on the ground as if blindly seeking sustenance, before merging back into their host. From deep within this heaving mass a steady stream of saliva oozed, running sticky rivulets down the center of each flapping tongue, dripping to the ground in pools of milky fluid. Fedor watched in horror as Kudryavka reached the foot of the creature, barking excitedly and licking at the drool. Fedor wanted to call her back, but no sound would come. Suddenly the little dog slumped to the floor and began to shake. She gave one last yap, and then she folded in on herself, turning inside out like a latex glove and flopping about on the ground. She now resembled one of the obscene tongue-muscles and quickly wriggled into the undulating mass, disappearing between glistening lumps.

I am here.

Fedor finally found his voice and wailed in terror, dropping to his knees. The mountain of tongues squeezed its entire bulk out of its angular tomb and rolled around him, forming a looping wall of quivering flesh. He wanted to run, but every direction was blocked by a twitching, magenta mass and he spun on his heels, his heart pounding so hard that he could barely draw a breath. Suddenly his fleshy prison lifted from the ground, exposing multiple escape routes, and Fedor took the opportunity to put some distance between him and the nightmare, but skidded to a halt almost as soon as he had begun his flight. He stared up into the air, where another ghastly behemoth swayed before him, stretching toward the golden sky. Inconceivably this creature was more horrendous than the first. The glistening orbs were not of uniform size; some were the size of a car, others the size of his fist. They were squashed together, bonded by sclerotic jelly and freely rotating with tendrils of optic nerves poking out from between cracks to quiver in the air. As Fedor stumbled back every eye swiveled to look at him, their pupils dilating, diminishing the brown irises streaked with gray. Blood vessels throbbed and snaked across alabaster sclera as the obscene lumps tracked his every move. He cried, a dry, pathetic sound, and slumped once more to the ground. The feeling of helplessness was so absolute, so crushing, that Fedor began to cry, silently yearning for the comfort he had felt wrapped moments before in his mother's furs.

You will leave soon.

He continued to sob, wiping his face with his hands and wrists as he watched the nightmares shift toward each other. Then they were joined by more giant monstrosities; one made up of meaty flaps layered around a central twisting core like a pine cone, another comprised entirely of coiled lengths of sinew that strode forward on limbs of fibrous muscle leaving moist prints in its wake, a third seemingly made of blood, bile and urine, the fluids held in place by the thinnest of membranes, bubbling and merging as they bounced together with each forward thrust of their combined bulk. Fedor was acutely aware of the moment his mind finally snapped. It was when the creatures fused together, drawing themselves up into one vast entity that filled the space between the silver plains and the golden roof, twisting, shifting until it was sitting on vast haunches, looking down as the speck of a man between its front paws, and wagging a tail as long as any cruiser in the Soviet Navy.

Know then, your place in the cosmos.

Fedor nodded, silent.

Share what you have seen.

"I will." His voice was thin, barely a whisper.

Speak for us.

"The capsule. The capsule is your emissary."

Tell your world. Tell them they need not strive for the heavens. You will all be among the stars soon enough.

"I will tell them. But they will not listen."

We will make them listen.

Fedor lifted off the plain, pulled up on invisible marionette strings to dangle before the monstrous dogface in the sky, its tongue lolling out of a gaping maw of muscle and teeth. Fedor could smell hot blood on its breath.

Then it will be time to play.

∗∗∗

Darkness. White light. Shouting.

As Fedor regained consciousness he was aware of several raised voices. Through watery eyes he could make out Lev and the general, standing nose to nose, neither man prepared to stand down as they stated their cases at the top of their lungs.

Lev was an inch taller, and drew himself up further to stare down the old soldier. "You will kill us all, man!"

"I said move back!" yelled Kozlov, pushing the nose of his revolver further into the Ukrainian's belly, "The program will not be jeopardized."

"Who did you just call?" Lev stretched an arm out for the radio, but the general held it back, out of the big man's reach.

"He called in the bomber." The voice came from the corner of the room, from one of the soldiers who had already set his rifle against the back of a chair and was rolling a cigarette. "He called in the Yak-26."

Lev pushed himself away from general Kozlov and turned to the door. "Then we need to get out of here!"

"Pointless," the dry voice came from Fedor who stood, swaying, the tendrils still attached to his head, "you cannot outrun what is to come."

"Watch me!" yelled Lev Ovseenko. He grasped the door winch as the guard stood aside, and promptly buckled as the general's gun cracked once, twice, felling him in an ashen heap against the corrugated metal.

Kozlov swung the weapon around to bear upon Fedor. "What did it say?"

"Does it matter?" replied Fedor quietly, "you have already chosen our fate. What happens after today is of little consequence"

"Tell me!" The general turned a darker shade of gray, which Fedor took to be beet-red.

He smiled and looked at Dr. Kaplan. "I suspect some of us will be playing with Little Curly again," he looked back at the general, "and then she will be playing with the rest of you soon enough."

General Kozlov started to sputter impatiently, but was cut short by a deep thunderclap that shook the room. He turned his eyes upward and murmured, "Sonic boom…"

Fedor closed his eyes, feeling the tips of the creature against his eyelids, and thought of his tiny apartment. He was vaguely aware of his eardrums bursting as the room collapsed in a bubble of light and heat and then he could taste turnips, horseradish root and onions. It would have been good soup.

THE DAY THE MUSIC DIED
BY CHARLES CHRISTIAN

-1-

They say a young Negro boy by the name of Robert Johnston was the first to die in the current war. Found dead at a lonely crossroads way down in the Mississippi Delta. Long before my time. I'd have just been a little-bitty kid growing up in Beaumont, Texas, at the time of his death. Still, I did hear some of his recordings much later. That sure was one talented bluesman we lost to the enemy.

As for the circumstances of his death? Surrounded in mystery, confusion and conflicting claims. Hey, we don't even know where he's buried. Last I heard there were at least three different graveyards claiming they held his remains.

Then there was Glenn Miller. Another great musician who died prematurely in mysterious and never adequately explained circumstances. His body also conveniently vanished from the surface of God's Good Earth as if it had never existed.

And finally there's Hank Williams. I used to listen to him on The *Grand Ole Opry*. If he was still alive today, he'd be giving us all a run for our money in the charts. But, the same old, same old. He also died prematurely and in mysterious circumstances. Of course there are some explanations for Hank's death. Trouble is there are too many of them. It's like people are trying to cover up the real reason for his death. Why? Well maybe there are some secrets people just aren't ready to hear yet. I think Hank knew his days were numbered, why else would he pen that final single of his *I'll Never Get Out of This World Alive.*

"Hey J-P, what you doing? You writing another song?"

I look up, it's just Waylon. I relax, he's standing too far away to be able to read what I'm writing in my journal.

"I sure am sir," I reply. "As I keep telling you, the only way you'll ever get rich in this game is to write your own material. You'll make far more from songwriting royalties than you'll ever earn from record sales or even your share of the ticket sales here. Wherever here is, that is!"

Waylon laughs. "Here happens to be The Surf Ballroom in Clear Lake, Iowa and you'd better remember that when you go on stage in thirty minutes time."

"With this darned influenza, all I'm going to focus on remembering is that I'll have finished my act and be off stage again in seventy-five minutes time!"

"Flu or no flu, you know you'll knock 'em dead in the aisles once you start your *Oh Baby you know what I like* routine with the telephone. Catch you later. Gotta go, Dion wants to discuss something with me."

As he heads off down the corridor, I shake my head. *This Winter Dance Party* is turning into a winter nightmare. If I have to spend another night on that freezing tour bus, I think I'll throw it all in and be going back to Texas.

Ed Murrow was on the radio the other night, talking about the late and much unlamented junior senator for Wisconsin. Murrow described Joe McCarthy as a bully and a charlatan. He was all that but he was also a darned fool. A dangerous darned fool.

He accused the Army of disloyalty and blamed them for aiding our enemies, the Russian commies. Little did he know the Army is our one remaining hope against an enemy far worse and more powerful than the Reds. In fact from what I hear, the Russkies have their own hands full right now, fighting our mutual enemy out in the snow-covered tundras of Siberia. You know those deep-frozen mammoth remains they keep digging up in Russia? Well it seems they also dug up something else that should never have been allowed to see the clear light of day.

I also remember hearing McCarthy ranting on during the last year of his life about the danger of teenage culture. How American youth was being corrupted by Rock 'n' Roll music and why movies like *Godzilla, The Creature from the Black Lagoon, Them!* and *It Came from Beneath the Sea* were slandering our attempts to protect this great country of ours from the commies.

The way McCarthy tried to tell it, these movies were nothing more than malicious left-wing propaganda because they suggested our atomic bomb tests were creating mutant monsters that were a danger to mankind. He also said the movies were intended to frighten the American people into such a state of hysteria, that it would sap morale and leave us believing we could never win a war against Russia.

That man got it so wrong. There are monsters out there but they are not the product of nuclear radiation from our tests on Bikini Atoll. No siree, we now know these are ancient monsters our bombs accidentally woke from hibernating deep down in the Mariana Trench beneath the Pacific Ocean.

As for rock music? God gave Rock 'n' Roll to us and it may be our only salvation in the years to come.

I notice Tommy Allsup coming my way. There's a decidedly jaunty look to the way he walks.

"Another change of plan," he says. "Only this time it could be good news. Buddy's looking to charter a plane to take us to our next gig."

"That's Moorhead, Minnesota. Right?" I ask.

"Man, it sure beats traveling all night in that freezing cold old bus. Soon as I hear more, I'll let you know," he adds, as he wanders off.

I know what you are thinking. Things from the deep! Monsters! Get outta here. I'd have thought the same thing five years ago. But that was before I was drafted into the US Army and did my time serving Uncle Sam. Now, here's the story of how I found out the truth...

As some of you may know, I started out as a disc jokey at Radio KTRM about ten years ago. In '53 I got a pay raise and promotion. Perfect timing as it happens. My wife Adrianne was pregnant with our daughter Debra Joy. Adrianne's pregnant again now and we're hoping for a boy. Anyhow, along with the extra dollars, I also took on some management for KTRM dealing with our advertisers and sponsors.

Sometime later, it must have been in the fall of '54, I got a call from one of our advertisers, the owner of a department store in Beaumont, who said he'd heard some terrible stories about Procter & Gamble and was concerned about continuing to advertise with us when we were also broadcasting Procter & Gamble-sponsored soap operas. Of course if he was concerned then so was I so I asked him to tell me more.

He explained that one of his oldest customers and friends, a much-respected God-fearing Southern Baptist gentleman, had told him he'd heard for a fact, from one of the gentlemen he played golf with, that Procter & Gamble was in league with Satan and their cor-porate logo was proof of this. Apparently, so the story went, the face on the logo was Old Nick himself and the stars in the sky referred to a passage in *The Book of Revelations* that foretells of a woman wearing a crown of twelve stars on her head.

I confess it all sounded a little cockamamie to me but I know better than to question other folks' religious convictions, particularly when they might also be commercial convictions, so I contacted Procter & Gamble up at their head office in Cincinnati and asked for an explanation. Two days later I get a personal visit by the head of their advertising agency, who has flown all the way down from New York City. He was one of those sharp-suited, button-down collar Madison Avenue types who liked his scotch and his cigarettes and, from the way he was checking out the talent in the bar, his women. Don Draper was his name and despite his no-nonsense, bristly outward appearance, beneath the surface he had a good down-home way about him. He also brought with him a thick file of papers that answered all my questions.

Seems these rumors were all started by P&G's competitors. And then he pointed out that not only is the face on the logo quite clearly the Man in the Moon, rather than a horned devil, but also there are in fact thirteen stars, not twelve in the logo, representing The Thirteen Colonies that founded this great country of ours back in the days of the Revolutionary War.

Draper went back to New York and I went back to the radio station. The explanation convinced me and it also convinced our advertiser, so that was the end of the matter as far as I was concerned.

Less than six months later, I got my call-up papers and was drafted into the United States Army to do my patriotic chore.

I wasn't expecting much to happen. Well there wasn't a war going on, apart from the stalemate in Korea that is. But then, one day during basic training at Fort Ord in California, I get called into the base commander's office and there waiting to see me is a special agent from the CIA. Can you imagine it, the Central Intelligence Agency wanting to speak to a Texas DJ!

The agent is a good ol' boy, who asks me a lot of far-out questions that seem to take longer than a country mile but then suddenly he pulls out a file containing a transcript of the meeting I'd had with Don Draper! He says he likes my attitude. He calls me "skeptical, pragmatic and willing to think outside the box" whatever that means. He also says he's going to have me assigned to Majestic 12, a special operations team based out of Fort Bliss in El Paso, Texas, where my cover will be that of a radar instructor. Then, just as I've been dismissed and am about to walk back out of the door, he adds "And if you think our conversation today was weird, just wait until you get to Fort Bliss."

That CIA man sure didn't lie as I spent the next three months in Texas being lectured by the Army, more CIA agents, radio and sound engineers and a trio of guys who looked like they might be more at home in a Three Stooges movie. Except instead of Moe, Larry and Curly, we had Willy, Ivan and Robbie.

Willy Ley was a little German who'd once supervised deliveries of the US Mail using rockets in Upper New York state, was friends with Herr Doktor Wernher von Braun and now wrote popular science magazine articles about space flight and mythical creatures like dragons, sea serpents and giant squid.

Then there was Ivan Sanderson, a former Naval Intelligence officer with a heavy Scotch accent. He could have been the role model for that James Bond character whose books are now so popular. Ivan ran a private zoo at his home on the New Jersey shore. I'd already heard him on the radio before I joined the Army and knew he was interested in the paranormal but there in El Paso he was given free rein to ride his pet hobby-horse. Cryptozoology is what he called it: the study of mysterious animals that people thought were either extinct or the stuff of folklore.

He and Willy Ley were close buddies but Ivan wasn't just a theoretician as he'd also gone out on field trips to investigate reported sightings of cryptids - that's the technical term for these critters - including the Jersey Devil, or Shantak, which Ivan said was a hoax.

Finally, there was Robertson Lancaster, an archaeology professor from Indiana who seemed more like a treasure hunter than any university lecturer I'd ever met before. Lancaster (Willy and Ivan inevitably called him Robbie) used to bring to his lectures copies of pages from an ancient manuscript he called the *Al Azif Grimoire*. They were xerographic copies of a manuscript kept hidden away in the library of the British Museum in London, England. Robbie said the original was too dangerous to touch because the text was written in human blood on parchment made from the skins of murdered infants.

Anyhow, after I'd been at Fort Bliss about a month, they felt it was safe to reveal Majestic 12's Big Secret. Humanity, they said, was engaged in war for survival with what they called the *Alter Kinder*, which translates as *Earth's Other Children*. Willy coined the phrase after World War Two, while he was researching his way through some secret files liberated from the Nazis. Seems the entire Third Reich was obsessed with the occult and weird science and had a whole SS division, *Das SS Ahnenerbe Brigade*, searching the world for monsters, magical talismans and lost passages deep in the Earth leading to the original homeland of the Aryan Race.

According to Ivan, the *Alter Kinder* could be divided neatly into three categories. There were the mythical beings from legends and folk stories, such as ogres, trolls, wights, djinn, gnomes, demons, goblins, vampires, werewolves, ghouls, and all the other denizens of the Faerie realm. There were the cryptids that had been reported living in remote parts of the world for generations, such as Bigfoot, the Yeti, the Chupacabras, the Thunderbirds and all those lake monsters, including the famous Loch Ness Monster. But, there was also a third group of creatures that had been hibernating at the bottom of deep ocean trenches for millennia but were now rising up again, having been woken by our A-bomb testing.

This third category were code-named the GO2 - or the Great Old Ones to give them their full moniker. Professor Lancaster said (and last I heard of him, he was down in Peru trying to get hold of some ancient extraterrestrial crystal skulls before the Russkies could get their hands on them) the best way to describe the GO2 was as a race of super-intelligent dinosaurs or dragons from somewhere in Outer Space beyond the Oort Cloud.

Of course one month previously, all of us recruits at Fort Bliss would have laughed out loud at these ideas but, thanks to our sessions with The Three Stooges, it had begun to seem distinctly plausible. Not least because it provided an explanation to some of the mysterious things that happen in this world.

"Hey Señor Big Bopper. I'm flying on an airplane tonight!"

I look up, again. This time it's the little Mexican kid Ritchie Valens. Young, good looking, great voice, plays a mean guitar and he can take over the drums when push comes to shove, as it did the other week when Carl Bunch was hospitalized with frostbite. Oh, I am seriously not looking forward to traveling on that cold old tour bus again.

"What do you mean you are flying on an airplane tonight? And you can save that cute Mexican accent for the girls, we all know you grew up in LA!" I reply.

"It's true. You know that plane Buddy has hired? Well he was planning to just go with Waylon and Tommy but when I get to hear of it, I persuade Tommy to let me have his place."

"Persuade?" I ask.

"Okay, we decided it on the toss of a coin and I won."

Now one part of me is pleased to hear this because I know Ritchie used to have a fear of flying and I'm glad he's conquered it. But another part of me is just a teeny-weeny bit envious as I'm dying of flu here and I could really do with being on that plane as well.

"Listen," I say, trying to disguise the eagerness in my voice, "did Dion say anything about wanting to go on that plane?" By the way, I reckon Dion's next single release *Teenager in Love* is going to be a huge hit.

"He did mention about it in the dressing room," Ritchie replies, "but then he went all awkward when it came to the thirty-six dollar air ticket price. Something about thirty-six dollars being the monthly rent his folks had to pay for their apartment when he was growing up in the Bronx and he couldn't justify the indulgence." Ritchie shrugs his shoulders. "Funny people eh! You are on in ten minutes, go break a leg!"

"And you," I reply although what I'm actually thinking is where's Waylon Jennings got to, I need a word with him.

Right, I need to prepare for going on stage but before I do, there's just a couple more notes I want to jot down in my journal.

I suppose the sixty-four thousand dollar question anyone would want to ask about the GO2 is: what happened after Fort Bliss? Where to begin? I got shipped out to a place called Area 51, in the middle of the Nevada Desert, to be shown some dead GO2s they had in storage. These included a couple of fish-like creatures found swimming in the Miskatonic River estuary, near Innsmouth in Massachusetts, and the pickled remains of a winged octopus thing. And 'thing' is the only word to describe this abomination against nature, recovered about ten years' previously from a UFO crash site near Roswell, New Mexico.

I also had more briefings from the Three Stooges. Studied more sections of the *Al Azif Grimoire* or *The Necronomicon* as it is also called. And I went on a couple of 'monster' hunts with Ivan and Willy. Both expeditions were out on the Great Lakes, up in Canada looking for the Ogopogo, the Manipogo, the Winnipogo and any other of their Pogo cousins who are meant to swim in those deep waters. But we found nothing, despite having the finest sonar equipment Uncle Sam could provide.

"All very interesting," as I said to Lancaster one evening over a beer in a downtown El Paso bar, "but what does all this have to do with me? Why do the United States Army special forces need a radio DJ, who'll be back on civvy street in eighteen months' time."

It was then, well probably about the time we were onto our third round of Buds, that Professor Lancaster let me in on the secret. "It's all to do with rock 'n' roll music, well at least the sound waves created by the music. You know how dogs can react to sounds we can't hear? Those are ultrasonic high frequency sounds that they can hear but are outside the audible range of the human ear. Then, at the other end of the acoustic scale, literally, are infrasonic sounds. Because of their ultra-low frequency, they are also inaudible to us but sometimes you can feel that sound."

"Like when you are standing too close to the speakers at a hop and the bass player has one of those new Fender electric bass guitars and is playing the rhythm line way down low?" I suggest.

"My point exactly," says Robbie. "And that's why Majestic 12 is interested in not just you but a whole stack of other young people in the rock 'n' roll music industry. You see exposure to ultrasound and infrasound may not hurt us human beings but these GO2s, because their origins are extraterrestrial, they have an entirely different reaction to sound waves. The noise can actually disable and kill them. The sound waves resonate within their body cavities in such a way that it mashes up their internal organs and turns them into jelly!"

"No way, Jose," is all I can bring myself to say.

Robbie takes another drink from his bottle and nods. "Oh yes my friend, sound waves can kill. Majestic 12 have been working on sonic weapons for a number of years. One of Willy Ley's friends tipped us off that the Nazis, led by a crazy Austrian called Zippermeyer, had been experimenting with a sonic cannon called a *Luftkanone* and that kind of jump-started our research. There's also a Doctor Vladimir Gavreau over in France who is working on sonic guns although so far he has inflicted more harm on his own research team than on any GO2s!

"Now simultaneously to all this," says Robbie, staring into my eyes to hold my attention, "we also knew some types of music could have a similar devastating impact. The potential harmful effects have been known for at least a couple of hundred years. For example there was an Italian violinist called Paganini whose virtuoso playing and the notes he could create were so radical for his day that everyone was convinced he must have sold his soul to the Devil to be that good. They said the same thing about Robert Johnson. And why do you think Hank Williams was killed? Because he could naturally sing ultrasonic notes.

"Music is a weapon and rock 'n' roll has made it a whole heap more potent thanks to electric amplification. Thanks to it being broadcast into every home and car by radio. Thanks to every platter the record companies press creating another copy of those killer tracks, the GO2s can be defeated. The Pentagon is developing sonic cannon to tackle these monsters head on but in Majestic 12 we now realize pop music offers an alternative approach. Through people like you and your involvement in the music industry, we can mobilize a whole generation of young Americans to fight for our cause. To wage a guerilla war! Every time a teenager plays a Buddy Holly, Gene Vincent or Everly Brothers disc on the jukebox at their local diner or the record player in their den, they are striking a blow for freedom."

"So basically," I said, "Uncle Sam doesn't want me for what I can do while I'm in the Army but for what I will be able do when I'm discharged?"

"Got it in one," said Robbie, nodding. Then he looked at his watch and said he had to be going. As he stood up to leave, he leaned over to me and whispered "Have you ever thought about the *Old Testament* story of Joshua and the Siege of Jericho?"

"You mean how the walls came tumbling down when his priests blew their trumpets? Oh my, I get it now...the Israelites attacked Jericho with a sonic weapon!"

"Right on the button, that Ark of the Covenant was also some sort of weapon. But did you ever think about the enemy Joshua was fighting?"

"They were the Canaanites," I replied, those Bible readings I listened to at Sunday school were not wasted on me!

"And who did they worship? I'll tell you who: the fish-god Dagon!"

"But isn't he one of The Great Old Ones mentioned in *The Necronomicon*!" I replied.

"There you go," said Robbie, "So now you can see we have not been making up this *Alter Kinder* stuff as we go along. Congratulations soldier, you are now part of a cause that has been fighting evil since Biblical times. Oh man, I hate these GO2s even more that I hate snakes." Then he tipped his fedora at me and headed out of the bar. I never saw him again.

"Five minutes to curtain up Mister Richardson," I hear one of the stagehands call out to me. Time for me to focus on the present...

- 2 -

Well, I survived tonight's show. Just goes to show that what doesn't kill you can only make you stronger. As soon as I walked on stage and felt the vibe from the audience, I forgot about how sick I felt. I performed all my favorites: *Bopper's Boogie Woogie*, *Little Red Riding Hood*, *You Made a Monkey Out of Me*, *Walking Through My Dreams*, *Pink Petticoats*, the slow one *Beggar to a King*, *Big Bopper's Wedding*, a couple of the songs I originally wrote for other people: *Running Bear* and *White Lightnin'* and then I finished off my set with *Chantilly Lace*. Oh yeah, and I also sang my *Purple People Eater* novelty number, which is my own personal way of making fun of the GO2s! As Robertson Lancaster once said "People don't fear something that makes them laugh."

After that, I came off stage on a natural high and bumped into Waylon Jennings. My luck was in as I somehow convinced him to swap his seat on the plane with me. Well, he's young and tough and can survive another night on the bus. Me, I'm from Texas and I don't do cold. Besides, if I don't shake off this flu, I won't be doing much of anything tomorrow.

Now we're in the car on the way to the airport. Apparently Buddy hadn't realized I'd swapped places with Waylon, so as we drove away from the Surf Ballroom, Buddy jokingly called out of the window "Well, I hope your ol' bus freezes up."

And Waylon shouted back "Well, I hope your ol' plane crashes!"

We all laughed, even little Ritchie who is no fan of flying.

By coincidence, Buddy and I had been discussing Ritchie earlier in the week and whether he might make a suitable recruit to the Majestic 12 project. We both feel his Latino background might make him more receptive, whereas Dion is much too much of a street-wise New York City boy to believe in alien monsters crawling up from the depths of the ocean, like that giant octopus in the movie *It Came from Beneath the Sea.*

Too right we want more recruits, like Ritchie, for Majestic. We've already got young Eddie Cochran signed up, we have high hopes for him. And Elvis too, why else do you think he made no effort to dodge the draft? Elvis is over in Germany now, helping the Army clear out some GO2s the Nazis inadvertently unleashed in the Harz Mountains. As for Buddy, of course he's involved. In fact he's been in league with Robbie and the rest of the guys at Majestic far longer than me. He even travels with a little .22 caliber pistol "just in case" he runs into a GO2 on his travels. Me? I can't help think I'd feel a whole lot happier with something with a little more stopping power, like maybe a Smith & Wesson .357 Magnum or even the Colt .45 Peacemaker my grand-daddy used to own.

We reach the Mason City airfield a little after midnight. I notice it's starting to snow and that the pilot, Roger Peterson, seems to be just a kid. Okay, maybe not as young as Ritchie but still a little green for my liking. Buddy doesn't seem to care, in fact he seems more interested in my idea for short television clips (music videos is the name I've coined for them) we were discussing on the way to the airport. Believe you me, video will be the future of music television.

Anyway, the three of us settle down in the cabin of the little red and white Beechcraft Bonanza, the pilot opens the throttle and we start taxiing down the runway. We don't speak during the take-off, much too noisy to make ourselves heard, but once we are in the air, the weather starts to close in and I begin to get a bad feeling about this flight. What worries me is we look to be heading into a whiteout yet the pilot is staring intently at the instrument panels in the cockpit as if to try to make sense of their readings. That's all we need, a disoriented pilot flying us blind into a blizzard.

I don't mention this to Richie, who has his eyes closed. I'm not sure if he is asleep or merely trying to blot out all sensations and conquer his fear of flying but I try to draw Buddy's attention to our situation, as I'm wondering whether it might be safer to return to the airfield. To my surprise, Buddy is taking no notice of what is happening inside the cabin but instead is peering out through one of the side windows into the gloom.

"There's something out there to our left," he says. It's big and it's heading towards us."

"Is it another plane?" I ask, leaning over in my seat to share his view.

"I'm not sure. It has to be, I can make out the wings but it's showing no lights. Oh, man, I can see those wings more clearly now and they are flapping. Whatever it is, it's alive. Either a giant bird or flying lizard, maybe even a dragon? Something like those pterodactyl dinosaurs you read about in books."

The creature is a lot closer now and I can see its features a little better. It is huge and its wings are like those of a giant bat. But then I catch sight of its head. It is not the beaked head of a bird or even the snapping jaws of a lizard I see. Instead it is an abomination, a nightmare. The front of its head, its face, is a tangle of writhing, twisting tendrils and tentacles.

Aghast, I look at Buddy and he returns my look of horror. We've both seen pictures of this creature before in the pages of *The Necronomicon*.

Buddy pulls out his little .22 pistol from his pocket and slides open the cockpit's side window. "If I can hit it in the eyes, we may have a chance," he tells me.

I nod encouragingly but I have my doubts. Then fate deals us a cruel hand as our pilot also catches sight of the creature. Peterson cries out in shock and instinctively hauls on the control column to roll the plane away from the monster. Only then does he realize that, distracted by the snowstorm and the poor visibility, he has allowed the plane to descend too far.

From where I'm sitting I can see the airspeed indicator. We're flying at one-hundred-and-seventy knots. From where I'm sitting I can also see the ground rushing towards us.

So can the pilot and, heedless of the blasphemous horror flying straight towards us through the blizzard, he now pulls hard on the control column to correct our pitch.

Oh My Sweet Lord he's too late! He's lost control of the plane.

There is an awful tearing sound as the tip of the right wing hits the ground. Then the plane flips over and we begin to tumble and skid, for what seems like an eternity of pain and nausea, in a jumble of debris and screaming, flailing bodies across the snow-covered landscape. In the final moment before everything goes black, the thought enters my head that I sure hope that flying monstrosity ain't going to be waiting for me when I wake up.

THE TERROR THAT CAME TO DOUNREAY

BY WILLIAM MEIKLE

I didn't know what to expect. All they'd said was that it was a *matter of national security*. Just what they wanted with a fifty-year-old doctor of biology with a gammy leg and a drink problem I wasn't told. I was given a train ticket and a contact name and sent off on an interminably slow train to Thurso.

Once there I was met by a sergeant and a truck—both of them well past their best. We rattled along an unpaved road for what seemed like hours, coming to a sudden halt at an manned checkpoint. A large sign at the side proclaimed the place to be Dounreay Site, AEC. That didn't help me much. There was also lettering underneath, but that was mostly covered by a strange construction of leaf and twig that had been hung over it.

An attendant waved a flashlight and a gun in my face, I showed him my paperwork and we were allowed through to a cordoned off area of Nissen huts with a towering concrete structure beyond.

The whole site lay along the top of what looked to be a raised beach, with the largest building clustered closest to the sea. A fogbank hung a mile offshore and moonlight danced in rocky coves. In other circumstances I might have found the spot calming, but I was not in the best of moods after my journey.

Without further ado I was marched inside one of the huts to meet the commander of the base. I'm afraid the Colonel, a stiff little man with a stiffer little moustache, didn't take to me. From what I understood of my short briefing, I was seconded to this unit to '*do my bit against the Soviets*'. But by the time his orderly led me, via a warren of corridors through and between the maze of Nissen huts, into a lab that butted onto the concrete block, I was still none the wiser. It was only when I was introduced to the head of the team that I began to have some inkling as to why I had been summoned.

I knew Professor Rankin by reputation as an iconoclast, a vision-ary…and as mad as a bag of badgers. We'd worked together for a brief period during the war, and last I'd heard he had gone over to the Yanks for a huge stipend at one of the West Coast think tanks. I never expected to meet him here on a remote Scottish shoreline. His unruly mop of white hair shook as he grasped my hand. He was as thin as a rake, but his grip was as hard as cold steel.

"Ballantine. And not a minute too soon. Come over here, man. You need to see this."

He dragged me over to a long trestle covered with electronic gear; all lights, switches, meters and dials.

"You know this isn't my thing," I started, but he was insistent.

"Just look."

He flicked a switch. Lights started to flash, meters started to swing.

"What am I looking for?" I said after several minutes.

"Look closer."

I was at a loss. Clearly there was something important here I was meant to understand, but for the life of me it just looked like a series of lights and meters. It was only when I gave up looking for an answer that one came to me. I had to squint to see it, but it was there, a per-sistent flickering shadow that played over the instruments. As elusive as smoke in wind.

Rankin leaned over and switched off the equipment. Now that I knew what I was looking for I could see it as it dispersed, rising away from the electronic gear.

"What the hell was that?"

Rankin smiled, but there was no humor in it. He looked to be more angry than anything else.

"That's what I'm hoping you'll tell us," he said. "Come on, I've got some Scotch in my hut. Let's see what we can do about getting some of it inside us."

***

First of all I had to get myself settled. I was given a bunk in a dormitory-sized hut occupied mostly by squaddies who were already either bedding down for the night or preparing for night shift guard duty.

"What are they guarding against?" I asked Rankin once I had joined him in his quarters. He had a small hut to himself, and had done his best to make it appear homely. Shelves filled with technical books filled the walls, and a pair of armchairs had been arranged beside a cast iron stove that filled the room with heat. Rankin poured two generous measures of Scotch, handed me one and waited until I got a pipe lit before starting.

"I don't suppose you know anything about what we're doing here?" he said in reply to my question

I shook my head.

"Top secret stuff, I'm afraid," he continued. "And the Colonel will have me shot if I say too much. But let's just say that inside all that concrete there's an atomic facility. We're testing the effect of different doses of radiation on a variety of materials."

"Why?" I asked.

He raised an eyebrow.

"You're not *that* naive, Ballantine. You've seen the guards and the guns. This is, first and foremost, a military operation."

I thought about that for a while as I got some of his, admittedly excellent, Scotch inside me.

"So, why me? And what did I just see?"

"One answers the other," he said, somewhat cryptically. "You specialize in exotic forms of life, don't you? Well this one seems to be as exotic as it gets."

"That wasn't life," I said, but stopped when I saw the look in his eyes.

"It grows, it moves under its own volition and it shows signs of intelligence. You tell me what it is, Ballantine."

He got up and poured more Scotch for the two of us. I wasn't about to complain. He sighed deeply when he sat down again.

"It started when we got the reactor going," he said. "My design, my baby, I had to be here for the big day, had to be the one hitting the switch. And so it was that I was the one who first noticed it...the only one that first time. I put it down to stress, but soon after that the night watch started to get twitchy and reports filtered through of badly scared men and *ghoulies* in the lab. I took to keeping watch myself, monitoring its behavior.

"Oh yes, Ballantine. It has behavior. I study it, and it studies us. It never strays far from the reactor core, and seems most interested in the control board. It has never done any damage, as far as can be seen. But, and here's the thing that has the Top Brass worried, Ballantine… it is growing."

***

So began the strangest week of my life. I spent most of it on the night shift in the lab, and my days on the hard dormitory bed, trying to grab some sleep while the installation worked on around me. The only booze to be had was what I could scrounge from Rankin and after several days of no progress in my *investigation* he cut me off.

It was on the first Saturday following my arrival that I decided to take a walk into town; I needed to clear my head after some peculiar events the previous night, and a long walk on the sea cliffs seemed the best solution. The guard at the gate refused to let me leave, showing me instead to the Colonel's hut.

There I had to listen to a long lecture about the importance of secrecy, and I was left in no doubt that the Colonel believed our *intruder* to be a device of Russian origin.

"And I will have no hesitation of blowing it to Kingdom Come if it comes to that."

With one final admonishment against talking to the locals, he gave me a daily pass, told me to be back by seven p.m., and I was finally allowed to leave.

It was one of those typically Scottish days where the sun only comes out sporadically between long periods of fog and drizzle. But I scarcely noticed. My mind was still reeling over the events of the night watch, and I let my feet follow the road while I tried to make sense of what I had seen.

I have said that Rankin was not pleased with the *progress*. That is because there had been none. I had *observed* the behavior of what we were now calling *the entity*, but had gleaned no new information.

Last night that had all changed.

As before I stood in front of the control panel and flicked the switch. And as before, the thing seemed to seep out of the concrete wall that housed the reactor core. What was different this time was the size. It had more than doubled, and seemed somehow more solid. Two long tendrils, like spectral arms, reached out towards me from the main mass and a chill seized the length of my spine. The squaddie who, until now, had stood quietly at the door let out a shriek and left at a run, but I was unable to move, frozen into immobility as *something* rifled through my mind as if it were little more than a filing cabinet. Memories I thought were long forgotten bubbled unbidden to the surface only to be tossed aside and discarded.

And so it went, for what seemed to be an eternity. Until we came to my holiday experiences in the Mediterranean. I relived hot days on the ocean in a succession of small boats, but when we came to my time spent snorkeling among tumbled ruins the rifling through my brain stopped, and I experienced, all over again, almost in slow motion, my descents into blue deeps.

Then, as quickly as it had come, the thing seemed to leave me. A thin mist hovered above the instrument board for several seconds then drifted off, once again soaking through the concrete until I was left quite alone. It was long minutes before I could bring myself to move, and even then all I could manage was to light a cigarette with a very shaky hand.

Now, out on the road in the cold light of day, I started to wonder whether I had imagined the whole thing…whether it was merely a spot of *Delirium Tremens* brought on by my relative abstinence of the past week.

I knew one thing for sure though.

I needed a drink.

***

It was a longish walk into Thurso, and my bad knee flared in pain with each step towards the end of it, but it was well worth it, as I immediately stumbled upon an open pub, and made myself comfortable on a tall stool at the bar.

For the first hour or so I managed to stick to some of their strong, malty beer, but the siren call of the Scotch was not long escaped. By mid afternoon I felt comfortably numb and finally started to forget the events of the night before.

That was all to change again when the singing started.

I hadn't been aware that the place had filled up around me, being too preoccupied with my own thoughts and the booze. I was therefore rather surprised to turn around and find a busy bar, with a band setting up in the corner. Surprise turned to cold fear when they launched without preamble into their first song.

She sleeps in the spaces to be found in between,
She sleeps, and she dreams, of the sights she has seen.

I felt the cold chill seize my spine, and the *entity* was there again, looking out of my eyes, listening to what I was hearing. It wasn't in control of me, for I was able to lift my glass and drain a stiff measure of Scotch. But this was no case of the DTs. It watched through me as the band continued, and the whole audience in the bar sang along.

She dreams of the lands she has ruled as a queen,
And the sleeping god is dreaming where she lies.

I felt a *surge* of emotion well up in me, something I might have described as joy if I'd had any experience of it. As the song reached its climax it became almost overwhelming in intensity.

She dreams of her lord in the space in between,
And the sleeping god is dreaming where she lies.

The bar fell silent, and I remembered to breathe. An old man turned and spoke to me.

"You've seen her, haven't you?"

"Who?" I managed to say.

"The *Cailleach*, the old queen. Whatever it is you lot are doing up there, don't stop. You're bringing her back to us."

He turned back in rapt attention as the band started up again.

In the fire, the queen will come.

The chill threatened to grip me again. I downed what was left of my Scotch in one hasty gulp and staggered out into the growing dusk.

***

I woke lying face up at the side of the road, staring at a star-filled sky overhead, with no memory of anything after leaving the bar. I will admit that, in itself, it wasn't an unusual occurrence for me to have a blackout after drinking. But what was unusual was the sense of *doubling* I still felt in my mind, as if something squatted in there, watching my every move.

I got up, checked my bearings, and started a long trudge back to the installation. I knew I was in trouble. I had obviously passed the extent of the time covered by my pass, and I suspected that the Colonel was not a man given to leniency. It was with some surprise that I passed through the barricade at the gate with no further fuss, although I saw by a clock on the gatehouse wall that it was already past nine.

"Away in you go, sir," the Scottish squaddie said. "There's a big fuss on up at the block. I dinna think they'll notice you're a wee bit late."

I fully intended to creep quietly into my billet and sleep the rest of the night away, but as I got closer I heard that there was indeed a *fuss* up at the block. An alarm sounded loud and clear in the seaside air. Soldiers stood, guns raised, in a jagged line near the front of the building. I checked myself for sobriety, decided I was just about okay, and headed for the lab.

Inside, the place was in turmoil. The Colonel and Rankin stood over three soldiers who lay on the floor, staring sightlessly upward; obviously alive, yet obviously somewhere else. I started to have an inkling of what might have happened. It quickly turned to understanding as the thing inside me *surged* again. It left me in a wave of cold and sudden sadness that felt like mourning. At the same time a white smoke rose from the three men on the ground and rose upward to join whatever it was that had been inside me. The men started to move, as if coming out of a dream, but my gaze was taken with what was going on overhead.

Rankin went white, and the Colonel let out a yelp that he managed to quell just before it turned into a scream. A gray-white mist, almost solid now, hung in the air above us. Once again it drifted over the instrument panel.

"Get away from there," the Colonel shouted. He un-holstered his pistol, and fired three shots into the thickest part of *the entity*. The bullets had no effect, passing straight through and *pinging* off the corrugated iron roof above. The officer went to fire again, but Rankin put a hand on his arm.

"Wait," he said.

As it happened, there was nothing to wait for. The thick mist rose up and away, drifted towards the concrete wall of the reactor chamber, and again sank through it.

"After it," the Colonel shouted, but once again Rankin stayed his hand.

"You know as well as I do that we can't get in there without suiting up. Proper procedure must be followed."

"But that takes at least an hour," the Colonel said. "Who knows what it might be up to in there?"

"Indeed," Rankin replied. "And who knows what we might learn from it, given the chance?"

"Learn? There'll be no more *learning* here. I think we've had quite enough of that."

For once, I was in agreement with the Colonel, but that scarcely mattered, for several minutes later I found myself placed in handcuffs.

"Put him in a cell," the Colonel said. "I'll speak to him when he's sober."

"No sense in arguing," Rankin said softly as they led me away. "We all saw where that thing came from. Now he'll need to know where it has been."

***

I spent the remainder of that night in a cold, draughty cell that sat perched on the cliff by the shore. Waves crashed on rocks, gulls cried...but no one came to talk to me. I ran out of tobacco sometime around midnight, and managed two hours of fitful sleep between then and dawn. My head hurt, I felt sick to my stomach, and my theory as to what happened the night before was threatening to throw me into the depths of despair. When the Colonel finally called on me the next morning, I was not in the best of moods.

And things did not improve when they led me to the interrogation room. At least they fed and watered me before the questioning started, but after that it was a long day of answering the same things, over and over as they attempted to pry a lie from me. I tried to tell them that I didn't remember anything, but they were having none of it.

It was late afternoon before they relented. Over my first, most welcome, smoke of the day I tried to explain the theory I was forming to the Colonel, but he was too angry to even listen.

"The ravings of a drunk do not concern me," he said. "You, sir, are a threat to National Security, and will be off this base as soon as we get to the bottom of whatever is going on."

"Let me speak to Rankin," I said finally. "I'll tell him what I know."

The Colonel was suspicious at that, but he had seen that his own tactics were getting him nowhere. Finally, just as dusk was settling in again, Rankin was allowed in to see me.

***

The Professor seemed almost embarrassed as he sat opposite me. He took out a hip flask and handed it across the table. Despite the fact that I wanted a drink more than I ever had before, I let it sit there. My first statement confused him further.

"Tell me about atomic theory," I said. "Is it true that we're mostly made up of empty space?"

"That's a bit of a gross simplification of a lot of very complex science…" he started.

"But, in essence, I'm right?"

"In essence," he agreed, grudgingly.

"And this reactor you have built here…it manipulates basic atomic structure at the lowest levels to get its results."

"Again, that's…"

"I know," I said, and managed a smile, although I felt far from any sense of good humor. "A gross simplification. But still, essentially true?"

"Where is all this leading?" Rankin said. "The Colonel wants you on the next train out of Thurso, and I'm afraid I can't help you unless you tell me what you know."

So I told him everything, from the time the *entity* started rifling through my brain until I woke, face up in the ditch.

"I think it has to do with the line in the song," I said softly. '*She sleeps in the spaces to be found in between.*' I think that's where this thing is from…the spaces between atoms; the part of the Universe we cannot see. Somehow, your experiments here have released it, woken it up from its long sleep."

To his credit, Rankin took me seriously, at least partially.

"I can understand that we *might* be releasing some form of *energy* we haven't seen before," he said. "But I cannot countenance anything resembling *intelligence* arising from that source. As for all this guff about the folk song and a myth of a *dreaming* god? Really, Ballantine, I expected better of you."

"And I expect the culture from where that folk song originally spread was rather more technically advanced than we have ever given them credit for," I said. "I will stand by my hypothesis until it is proven false. It fits the facts as we currently understand them."

"Let us say you are right," Rankin replied. "What does this entity want?"

"I doubt it *wants* anything, not in the way we think in any case. It lives, it feeds, it grows, and it doesn't give a damn about us. That's what I believe."

Rankin had a far away look in his eye.

"And if you are right, and it is indeed a form of intelligent life," he said. "Think what we might learn from it. We could unlock the secrets of the Universe itself."

I laughed, and I'm afraid I might have allowed some sarcasm to show through.

"As I said already…I don't think it gives a damn."

Rankin got no chance to answer.

Shots rang out across the installation, followed quickly by screams.

"Come on, Ballantine," Rankin said. "If you're right, you might be of some use."

I paused only long enough to lift the hip flask from the table.

We left the room at a run. Nobody tried to stop me.

***

Once again the area around the reactor block was a scene of chaos. A dozen men lay on their backs, staring at the sky. The remainder of the guard seemed unsure where to aim their weapons, and the younger ones looked almost as pale as those stricken on the ground. The Colonel's bellow could be heard at some distance as he shouted into a radio handset.

"I don't care if he's in bed with the Archbishop of bloody Canterbury. Get him up. I need a bomber, and I need it now."

Rankin strode up and reached for the handset, but the Colonel swung to one side away from his grasp.

"You can't stop me, Rankin. I have jurisdiction here. I'm leveling this place to the ground from the sky. It's the only way to be sure."

Rankin looked as if he might punch the officer, but instead he turned back to me.

"I'm going in. We need to try to reason with it. Are you with me?"

Every fiber of my being told me to run. But Rankin was adamant, and I could not in all conscience allow him to face this thing alone.

I drained the contents of the hip flask in one gulp, much to the Colonel's disgust, and followed Rankin on the path towards the reactor.

"You've got ten minutes," the Colonel shouted. "Then this place will be nothing but rubble."

"Won't that just spread radiation across the countryside?" I asked.

This time it was Rankin's turn to laugh sarcastically, and echo my own words back to me.

"I don't think he gives a damn."

***

As we approached the door to the lab I heard singing waft in the air. I looked over to my right to see a crowd of townspeople gathered at the main gate. Three squaddies had stopped them entering. But they couldn't stop them from singing. The song rang around us, echoing and seeming to amplify as it bounced off the concrete wall of the reactor building.

She sleeps in the spaces to be found in between,
She sleeps, and she dreams, of the sights she has seen.

The white mist seeped out of the wall; the first time I had seen it emerge anywhere other than the laboratory. It was larger now, and much denser. Discrete structures could be seen in its form, a slug-shaped body with long tentacle-like appendages that hung below the bulk, wafting in time with the singing, trailing almost to the ground.

She dreams of the lands she has ruled as a queen,
And the sleeping god is dreaming where she lies.

Rankin strode forward until he was close enough to the tentacles to touch them if he wished. I was more circumspect, standing further back and ready to flee at the slightest provocation.

"We mean you no harm," Rankin shouted.

I don't think it gives a damn.

The *entity* moved forward again.

Rankin shouted.

"I want to know you, to help you. Believe that." The tentacles moved closer, wafting across Rankin's shoulder, almost in a caress. "I'm not your enemy. I'm a scientist who's trying..."

The tentacles folded around him. He screamed, just once, and began to fade, becoming thin, like the creature that had him in its grasp. Outside the guardhouse the song rose to a climax.

She dreams of her lord in the space in between,
And the sleeping god is dreaming where she lies.

The creature started to drift towards me. I stepped back out of reach of the tentacles then stopped as a chill ran down my spine and it rifled through my mind again. This time it knew what it was looking for.

I descend through deep turquoise, feeling the cold water around me, at the same time hearing the song in my head; the song that now seems more like the forlorn call of a lost love. And, from somewhere far, far, below, the call is answered. A wash of pure joy runs through me.

My link to the entity was cut off by the rat-a-tat of automatic rifle fire. Six squaddies had come to my assistance, and although their shots did not appear to damage the entity at all, it at least paused in any attack, either physical or mental.

"Fall back," the Colonel shouted. "The bomber's on its approach."

That gave me impetus to move. I turned and fled, beating the re-treating squaddies to the line of Nissen huts. I stood beside the Colonel, guessing that he would know what was a safe distance if anyone did.

The singing rose again from outside the gate, until the noise of the approaching bomber drowned it out. It was another song; the one I had heard the first line of on my exit from the bar.

In the fire, the queen will come.

"No!" I shouted. "Call it off."

But I was far too late. The reactor building exploded in a roaring flame. The blast wave knocked off my feet and down into a deep darkness.

It felt welcoming. I let it take me.

***

I woke in a hospital in Inverness two days later, and was home in Glasgow within the week. Of course the Army chaps declared the matter over. The site was secured and no further Russian infiltration would be allowed.

But I have strange sores on my body, wounds that refuse to heal. The booze helps dull the pain of course, but I cannot quash the memories, of descending into deep turquoise waters, and hearing the call…and its reply. Two things prey on my mind.

The first is the line from the song sang by the townspeople.

She dreams of her lord in the space in between,
And the sleeping god is dreaming where she lies.

And the second is in today's newspaper. The Yanks are testing nuclear weapons in the Pacific Ocean. The water is deep and turquoise there. And that makes me wonder.

Who is the *Lord* mentioned in the song?

And what else may be sleeping, down in those depths, waiting to be woken, in fire?

THE ROMERO TRANSFERENCE
BY JOSH REYNOLDS

T *minus 24 hours, fifteen minutes, twelve seconds.*

"It's not a question of if, gentlemen, but of when," Freeman said. He leaned back in his chair and looked around the conference table. "Einstein said it best, 'mutually assured destruction.'" The other men in the room shifted uncomfortably in their chairs, to a man thinking thoughts full of fire and Hiroshima shadows on Heartland walls. Freeman let it sink in.

The clapboard office was hot, the window fan barely stirring the air. Outside, the Frenchman Flat facility was baked brown by the Nevada sun. Frenchman Flat was south of Yucca Flat. Officially, it was a dry lake bed. Unofficially it was a Federal landing strip. In reality, it was Freeman's personal fiefdom, thanks to a healthy blend of paranoia and preparedness on the part of the current administration.

He let his gaze drift out the window while his guests chewed over the imminent apocalypse. Freeman had designed the facility himself, and selected the staff personally. He didn't know their names. As far as he was concerned, they were all anonymous drones with similar high and tight haircuts and smooth faces, picked from a federally approved pool of potential candidates. But he knew every inch of the facility. He had gone over every foot of dry, cracked ground with a theodolite and a notebook. The layout was based on a theoretical geometric coil which limited the number of right angles and provided a dedicated hyperspatial run-off. It had only taken a year to finish construction; as far as Freeman was concerned, it had taken far too long. They were running too slow.

Two years earlier, the Russians had made their first successful atomic test. Things had escalated quickly and where before there had been one superpower, there were now two, both mutually hostile. The nuclear shadow had been cast and the world was out of time; rockets in Red Square and the almanacs predicting a decidedly nuclear winter.

The men in Freeman's office were a mix of bureaucrats and brass, military men and politicians. The men who thought they made things happen, as Peaslee had been fond of calling them back when Freeman had been on the tenure track at the university. Freeman glanced at the class ring on his finger. He hadn't seen Peaslee since Potsdam. Wingate wouldn't approve of what he was preparing to propose, he thought, but needs must when the devil drove. Necessity was not the mother of invention but the child of desperation.

Freeman cleared his throat. They had stewed long enough. "It's an ugly phrase, isn't it? It implies that we are locked on course. The future is immutable. Someone's finger will slip maybe today, maybe in ten years, and we will burn. Mutually assured destruction," he repeated. He tapped the top file on the pile in front of him and continued, "Or perhaps not."

"You'd do well to remember that you're not in a classroom, Doctor," one of the men grunted. "Are we finally going to get to see what this little money-sink of yours is for?"

Freeman frowned, stung. "Point taken," he said. "And this 'money-sink' of mine, as you call it, is going to save the lives of every American from nuclear annihilation."

"How?" one of the others said.

In reply, Freeman slid several files forward. "These are copies of the relevant portions of the Hoccleve texts, among others."

"What about—?" someone began.

Freeman spoke up quickly, re-evaluating. Someone had done their homework. "Those as well, and I've included reports from the subsequent Australian expedition by those involved, including myself."

"Have we had contact with them recently?" the quick study continued, "Einstein, Oppenheimer, or one of the others from Groves' old circus?"

"Nothing recorded," Freeman said. "Which is why we're due, according to—" his face twisted in a grimace, "—certain sources."

"Care to name these sources?" someone said. The quick study leaned forward, face pale.

"Was it Cold?" he asked softly.

He wasn't asking about the temperature. Freeman swallowed. "Agent Indrid Cold has been invaluable to this project, yes. Lieutenant

General Groves made the recommendation, as did the director of the Office of Scientific Intelligence. He has also pinpointed a potential subject zero for transference; a-ah-'first contact' scenario, if you will."

"You're going to kidnap one of them," the quick study grated.

"We are going to expedite a mutually beneficial arrangement, yes," Freeman said tersely. He leaned forward. "It will work gentlemen. It has worked, and it will work again. The American people will survive the coming storm."

"In one form or another," the quick study muttered.

No one thought the comment was in good taste.

***

T minus twelve hours, twenty minutes, ten seconds.

Romero gnawed on a knuckle as they read the charges. Freeman watched him from the back of the room and thought, *gotcha*. They almost hadn't. Romero, whatever his other faults, wasn't inobservant. When the MPs had come for him, he'd already been on the move, heading south, away from Nellis Air Force Base. They'd caught him quickly enough, thanks to Cold.

Freeman glanced towards where the spook stood, leaning against the wall and smiling. The name suited him. He was like an icicle dressed in Hoover's best, black on white, tie and shiny shoes, black gloves, but it looked *wrong*, like a wrapper on a rotten fish.

As if he'd heard Freeman's thoughts, Cold's ever-present grin widened unpleasantly. His face was like wax and he had eyes as dark and as black as the lenses of the sunglasses in his breast pocket. "Good things come to those who wait," he said. There was something about his voice...Freeman shuddered and looked away.

Cold worked for one of the alphabet agencies, or maybe all of them. Hell, he might have *started* half of them. Freeman, in contrast, was a consultant. And Romero...Romero was an asset. One acquired just in time. Time was a valuable commodity these days, the most precious resource on the planet, depending on how you thought about it. It was all about time, or the lack thereof. They had no time, and that made what they did next very crucial indeed.

Romero made a sound halfway between a groan and a snarl as the verdict was read out. His restraints clattered as he gripped at the air. Romero wasn't a brute; indeed, he was handsome enough, in Freeman's opinion. Too bad such a good looking package contained such a nasty surprise. He couldn't restrain a smile. It faltered when Cold pushed away from the wall and joined him in watching Romero being led out.

"He'll do nicely," Cold said.

"Yes," Freeman said. He couldn't help but stare at Cold's face, especially the spots where the pearlescent skin twitched and stretched. He swallowed a sudden rush of bile. They'd warned him about people like Cold, back at the university. There were stories about midnight festivals in out of the way houses and deep, dark tumors under American soil where things bred and squirmed that made the Commies look like Minnesotans on a bender.

"I'll have him brought to your patch at Frenchman Flat tonight, Mr. Freeman," Cold said, his smile threatening to split his face, "After he's been debriefed." Cold never stopped grinning, that was the word from on high.

"That's quicker than I expected."

"Soonest started is soonest done," Cold said. "The Red Chinese took Seoul last Wednesday, Mr. Freeman." He said it as if it were no more important than the weather. *What do we look like to you?* Freeman thought, and then wondered where the thought had come from. It clung to the surface of the mind like a stubborn mosquito. *Do you even care that we're facing Armageddon?* He didn't ask either question. He didn't think knowing the answer would make him feel any better.

Instead, he settled for protocol pedantry. "Doctor," Freeman said curtly.

Cold smiled benignly. "Doctor Freeman," he said. "Time waits for no man and the shadows lengthen."

"Very poetic," Freeman said.

Cold's smile didn't waver. "I'll see you at Frenchman Flat, Doctor."

Freeman watched Cold walk away and tried not to think about the things that seemed to be moving in the other man's coat. "Evil the mind that is held by no head," he muttered.

***

T minus five minutes, eight seconds.

It was hot.

Strange shapes swam through the waves of heat that coruscated across the space between his office and the Box. Lupine, feline, of no earthly genus, the shapes swelled and reached and then burst like clouds. Freeman ignored them as he strode through the dust and sunshine.

He'd gotten some sleep. Not much. His dreams had been bad; no, worse. They were always bad, but these had been horrific, full of empty cities, a hundred thousand Hiroshimas, coated in blankets of ash and shadow-shapes, with no more substance than the dust beneath his feet, hunting him through the ash fall of a nuclear winter.

He knew the Russians were working on their own plans, their own back-doors and fire-escapes and bolt-holes. Earth might be reduced to slag, but the great Soviet state would continue on, lurching towards oblivion on some vast and multi-angled, multi-dimensional plateau that could barely be seen, let alone colonized. Then, it could hardly be worse than Siberia, eh comrade?

Would they still be Russians then? Would America be America, when America had been pounded into atomic dust? They would be minds without bodies, minds with *new* bodies, thrown forward or backward into a chronal fallout shelter…would they thank him, or would they curse him?

Cold was waiting for him in the control booth, ever-present grin in place. "Ready, Doctor?" Cold said as Freeman entered the booth and someone handed him a cup of coffee.

Freeman didn't bother to answer him. Now that he was on the cusp of it, he wanted to say no. He wanted to take his time, to explore the ramifications of transference. But they didn't have time. Instead he leaned over a technician's shoulder and checked the control panel. The Box was part bunker and part temple. He had designed it himself, built it to call up and cage what came.

Freeman looked through the observation window. Romero was the only thing in the Box, strapped tight into a steel chair that looked as if it had been requisitioned from the base's dentist. He had been doped to the gills. There was no reason for him to be conscious for this. "You're looking green, Doctor," Cold said.

Freeman didn't look at him. "What we're doing is very close to human sacrifice," he said.

"Romero is a murderer, Doctor," Cold said. "And sacrifices must be made for the greater good."

"I didn't say I wasn't going to do it," Freeman said, stung. Who was Cold to lecture him on sacrifices? "I said I wasn't entirely comfortable with the implications." *The truth, if a bit hypocritical,* he thought, even as the words left his mouth.

Cold made a sound that might have been a chuckle, though whether because of Freeman's words or his thoughts, the latter couldn't say. Several of the drones seated in the booth shifted uncomfortably. Cold had that effect on them. In the spook's case, familiarity didn't breed contempt. The longer you were around Cold, the more frightened of him—of what he represented—you became.

Freeman took a sip from the cup of coffee in his hand and swallowed convulsively as his eyes slid up the observation window to fix on the man in the box. "Time?" he asked, breaking the tense silence of the control booth.

"Two 'til," someone murmured, checking a wrist watch.

Freeman licked his lips and looked around the booth, taking in the pale sweaty faces and nervous expressions. They had good reason to be nervous. There were a thousand ways that things could go wrong in such an operation.

"You're certain this is the time?" he said, looking at Cold.

"As one can be," Cold said lazily.

"That's not good enough," Freeman said, knowing it didn't matter.

"One minute," another technician, or maybe the same one as earlier, said.

"Too late now," Cold said.

Romero twitched, making the chair rattle. Freeman tensed and looked back at him. "Did we check those straps?" he murmured, more to himself than anyone else. Someone said yes and he relaxed.

"Nervous, are we?" Cold said from beside his elbow.

Freeman jumped, startled. Cold ignored his startled curse and leaned forward, his face nearly pressed to the glass of the observation window. "Of course I'm nervous. We've never tried this before," Freeman stuttered.

"The Russians have already made contact—" Cold began.

"I understand that," Freeman said, trying to control his revulsion as he watched Cold's face move as the agent spoke. "But this is not the same as that. We are—"

"Contact," someone said softly.

The air in the box went wet and heavy all at once, like the bottom falling out of a storm cloud. Water beaded on the observation glass and dark, damp patches grew on the reinforced concrete walls. Even in the control booth, the sudden change in temperature was obvious. Freeman dabbed at his forehead with a handkerchief, his eyes never leaving the man in the box.

He twisted and jerked as if he were dancing to some melody undetectable by those gathered in the booth. Froth built at the corners of his wide open mouth and his tongue waggled like a worm emerging from a red tunnel. His eyes bulged and the frame of the chair gave a groan as he jerked. The straps held.

"Is this normal?" Freeman asked, unable to look away.

"Define 'normal,'" Cold said and gave a wet chuckle that set Freeman's stomach to roiling. Romero screamed and slumped forward. "Transference complete," Cold said, stepping back from the window.

"How can you tell?" Freeman demanded.

"He's stopped screaming," Cold said.

Freeman swallowed and looked at Romero. "Status," he barked.

"Breathing normally," one of the drones said. "Vitals are good."

"As promised," Cold said, still grinning. "Well, Doctor? You wanted to question one of them. Here is your opportunity." He gestured to the door that led from the booth to the box.

Freeman licked his lips. "Will he—will *it*—understand me?"

"Yes," Cold said. He cocked his head. Freeman realized that he hadn't ever seen Cold blink.

"Are you sure?" Freeman said.

Cold said nothing. Freeman knew what he was thinking. He was stalling, and Cold knew it. The funny thing was that he'd volunteered for this. Hell, he'd *suggested* it. And now, on the rim of the gulf, he hesitated to take that last step. He closed his eyes and took a breath. Then he opened them and gestured to the door. "After you," he said.

***

T plus two minutes, five seconds.

His mouth was dry and he could feel the itchy tingle of a migraine building at the base of his skull. He'd been working too hard, not getting enough sleep. There wasn't any time for sleep, just naps, full of monsters and phantasms and clinging worries.

The box smelled like a swamp. The air was like syrup and his clothes were instantly damp. Cold didn't seem to be bothered, but then, he never was. This was old hat to Cold. He'd been doing this since before the first crate of tea had hit the waters of Boston Harbor, if you listened to scuttlebutt. Better the devil you know, that was what they'd told him after the first meeting. Better the devil that was as American as apple pie and Betsy Ross and witch-burning.

Romero moaned.

Freeman froze. There was nothing human in that sound. He'd known that might be the case, but knowing and seeing were two different things. "Are those straps secured?" he hissed. There was a chance, however slight, that their calculations had been off, that they had not gotten their target, but something else instead.

"He won't hurt you," Cold said, circling the chair and its twitching burden. "They are not a violent people, in my experience."

"They aren't people at all," Freeman said harshly. Cold's grin didn't waver. He simply looked at Freeman with what the latter assumed was patient disdain. Freeman grimaced and stepped forward, sinking to his haunches beside the chair. "Can you hear me?" he said.

Romero's eyes found his. They no longer bulged, but instead looked drowsy. His mouth opened and he gurgled something. It was English, but mangled into incoherence. Cold had said that might happen. After transference it took a few hours or even a few days for them to attain full control, which meant that they had plenty of time to isolate and restrain it, to question it and learn what they needed. To learn what they needed to know to save American lives in the event of a full-blown nuclear strike.

Freeman hesitated, overcome with the thought of millions of minds jumping from their bodies at the moment of destruction, hurtling to safety in new bodies, a new time. Oh, there'd be a few who'd go ahead of them, to prepare the way, in imitation of the thing that crouched in Romero's body, colonists to another time, readying the world for invasion-no, *migration.*

He stood and plucked at his shirt. The Box was still full of heat and tropical smells. "How long can we hold him?" he said, looking at Cold. The spook shrugged.

"Until you wish me to send him back," Cold said. There was a device, Freeman knew. He had seen it reproduced in certain diaries, but frankly, he had no idea how it worked. The visitors who were readying themselves to return to their own time constructed them with the help of men like Cold. Though a cursory attempt had been made at discovering the identities of the rest of those involved in such efforts, nothing conclusive had ever come of it. Cold had made sure of that.

"Will they come to look for him-it? Can they?" he said.

"You had best hope not," Cold said, tapping his brow. A chill coiled through Freeman. He had never even considered-

"Will this work?" he croaked, more to say something than because he expected an answer. Cold looked at him pityingly.

"It's a little late to be asking that now, isn't it?"

Freeman looked at Romero, at the thing in Romero and cleared his throat. He looked back at Cold. "Is it worth it, I mean?"

Cold cocked his head. For a moment, Freeman thought his grin faltered. Then the strap broke and Romero's hand grabbed his and then Freeman was screaming.

A kaleidoscope of images crashed into his head all at once. Not of the great towers and vessels described in the diaries, but of basalt vaults and windowless edifices and of the long darkness. He saw the cone shaped beings firing strange weapons at *him*, hurting *him*, driving *him* back into a crackling cage and he knew they'd got it wrong, that their calculations had been off, that they'd gotten something else and that it was *hungryohgoditwashungry—*

***

T plus ten hours, four seconds.

Operation Ranger proceeded as authorized and the world went white as Frenchman Flat was boiled down to glass, and Freeman's facility with it. Trapped inside the Box, the thing that had been Freeman and Romero and a half dozen others screamed and screamed and screamed as atomic fire reduced it to carbonized dust.

Freeman's hand had burst like an overripe fruit, wriggling and sloughing into Romero's, two limbs becoming one. Two mouths opened and one groan had rattled forth and the air in the Box had shifted at the sound, coalescing and surging like an incipient hurricane. Romero had torn his other arm free and swung it into Freeman, the two men had splashed together like clay, their clothes tearing and flapping as they bled into one another and became something else. Something monstrous that spat alien curses and tried to re-build its body from the materials at hand.

Cold had left it to it. Preparations had already been made. The records could be prettied up later, to show a scheduled test, as opposed to a containment effort.

He watched the mushroom cloud vomit upwards into the sky, his smile bland and unwavering. Someone behind him coughed. Cold didn't turn around. "Freeman's plan has been judged a failure and his notes classified," he said. "And the evidence has been tidied up."

If Freeman had been there, he would have been surprised to see the quick study from his briefing. The man shifted from one foot to the next, clearly uncomfortable, though whether with the situation or simply in general was unclear. "The warning was appreciated," the quick study said.

"Simply doing my part," Cold said. Which was true, as far as it went...the visitors required help in returning to the past and hiding the traces of their visit, and Cold had provided them that help for centuries without measure. Who better to render aid to time travelers than immortals, after all?

"I didn't know that the process would work on one of polypous race," Cold said, rolling a finger towards the expanding cloud. "Quite a trick that, I must say. Peaslee's texts implied—"

"Peaslee knew only what we told him," the man said.

Cold chuckled. "He was something of a double agent, wasn't he? Spilling your secrets, but only those you wanted them to know."

"Much like you," the quick study said. Cold's smile twitched.

"Yes. They could learn much from you..." Cold said.

"They have learned enough, despite our-*your*-best efforts," the other man said. "If they discovered the secret—"

"Which they will, inevitably," Cold said and laughed. The quick study swallowed.

"Yes, you are proof enough that they have the means and the tenacity." The quick study frowned. "They are dangerous. *You* are dangerous. You should be exterminated, like the star-headed cannibals and their servants."

Cold turned. "Never doubt it, my friend. But now that they have seen what wolves await them on this path, they will choose another. Your great plan is safe, and humanity will remain trapped in its moment, for the moment. You are safe from them and them from you."

"It is better that way."

"Debatable, but pithy," Cold said, his grin stretched tight. He looked back at the cloud and thought of the screaming thing and what had likely been its last moments and then of Freeman's last question. He looked at his gloved hand, and the slight squirming of the things beneath the leather.

Cold made a fist and murmured, "Things are learning to walk that ought to crawl." Then his smile stretched to its full length. The quick study stepped back, looking nervous. Cold thought he had good reason to be.

"It's not a matter of if, you see, but when," Cold said. And he laughed.

IT CAME TO MODESTO

BY EDWARD M. ERDELAC

"I never see you around after school."

"I work late at my dad's garage. I get off early on Saturday though. Wanna see me then? Maybe catch a flick at the State?"

Georgie Calato saw the punch coming in the reflection of the big glass window of Burge's.

Debbie Lomax had put down her copy of *Look* and giggled to her two friends as they smiled around their milkshake straws at his approach, which was the sign that had emboldened him to ask her out. Debbie was in his biology class. Even though he was a new kid, she'd been easy with the smiles for him. She was a beauty, long necked and blonde, with big doe brown eyes and creamy skin that flashed between the hem of her poodle skirt and the cuffs of her pink bobby socks, and on the slender, hairless arms that slipped out from under her angora sweater.

Georgie took the punch on his shoulder. It was a glance, but it stung, coming from a guy like Jimmy Lucas, wide receiver for the Downey football team.

Jimmy and his cronies, that asthmatic toadie of a towel boy Babe Wilkes and the big shouldered tackle, Dombrowski, had formed a semi-circle around him and the girls, blocking the way to the parking lot, looking like a gang in their blue and silver Knights jackets.

Jimmy had one of those pasty faces you could see the blood move through. His cheeks were flushed like somebody had slapped him.

"I told you not to talk to my girl, paisano," Jimmy snarled.

That was only partly true. Georgie wasn't really a paisano. There was no Indian in him that he knew of, though his mom had been part Mexican and his dad was Italian. But Jimmy had slammed him against a locker after gym and told him plainly to keep his garlicky hands off his girl.

"We were just talking, Jimmy," Debbie said, annoyed.

"Yeah well now you can say goodbye," said Jimmy.

"Cool out, man," Georgie warned.

"Or what?"

"Big tough guy when you got your friends with you," Georgie muttered.

"Least I got friends, Pancho."

"You got a car?"

"Yeah I got a car," Jimmy said, folding his big arms. "So what? You writin' a book?"

Georgie knew Jimmy had a car. He had seen it in his dad's shop when it had come in for an oil change. A spanking new Studebaker Golden Hawk, cherry red with white fins and a big 352 bent eight under the hood.

"Cut the gas, man. What do I gotta do, spell it out for you?" Georgie said coolly.

"This feeb wants to race!" Babe exclaimed, smacking his gum like a tough guy in a gangster movie.

"What d'you got, greaser? Your grandma's old Plymouth or something?"

"That's my car," Georgie said, pointing over Dombrowski's shoulder to the silver Rambler Rebel with the copper stripe, catching and smearing the pink neon glow of the Burge's sign in the parking lot.

Again, this was only partly true. The car had been left at his dad's shop by a guy who had skipped town. Georgie's dad had kept the thing covered in the back parking lot in case the guy showed up, but it had been a week and a half. Georgie had started taking the car out for a spin late at night. He hadn't bugged his dad yet about claiming it. A four door, it didn't look like much compared to Jimmy's Golden Hawk, but it was still a beauty. 327 V-8 engine, Holley 4 Barrel, stainless steel dual exhaust (he had flipped the mufflers backwards himself for an extra kick), it had 6-ply Goodyears that cornered like nobody's business. He'd got it up to one hundred and thirty out on Route 99.

He was pretty confident that despite the smaller engine, he could beat Jimmy's Golden Hawk. His car, fast as it was, was as-is. Jimmy was a cruiser, not one of these motor heads that raced out at Laguna Seca. He didn't even change the oil himself. The car was probably a birthday present from his daddy, who owned a chain of shoe stores in the valley, chosen for the look, not what was in the guts. Like most things in Modesto.

"I don't know Jimmy," Dombrowski said in his friend's ear. "These Mexicans are all crazy reefer addicts. You don't wanna race no reefer addict."

"I ain't no Mexican," Georgie hissed, which wasn't entirely true, "and I ain't no reefer addict." Which was.

Jimmy's five cent blue eyes stared into Georgie's penny browns.

"What're we racin' for?"

Georgie had no money. He had the car…sort of. But if he lost it and his old man found out, he was dead.

"Tell you what, paisano," Jimmy said. "I win, you stay away from Debbie."

That made Georgie grin, because he knew now Debbie had something for him. Probably Jimmy had noticed. That's why he'd put him up against the locker.

Behind him, Debbie played outraged.

"Hey! I'm not some kind of piece of meat you two Neanderthals can just fight over!"

But she was fighting to keep the excitement out of her voice.

"Crazy, man. Whatever you say," said Georgie, shrugging, like it was no big thing.

But it was.

A couple of the carhops that had skated over during the to-do flitted from car to car spreading the word, until every kid in the Burge's lot knew Jimmy Lucas was gonna race that new kid over Debbie Lomax. The chicks were swooning 'cause wasn't it so romantic and the nerds were rooting to see that asshole Jimmy get blown off. The gear heads were flipping to see that cherry of a Studebaker lay a patch. All the Knights piled into Babe's blue DeVille and passed a jack of whiskey between them, talking about how they couldn't wait to see Jimmy give that dirty Mexican kid what was coming to him.

They all left at separate times so as not to tip the heat off as to what was shakin,' but everybody knew to be at the 99 crossing outside of town in an hour.

Georgie thought about how things might finally turn around for him if he beat this kid and the whole school was there to see it.

He'd had it tougher than most kids, dark as he was. He knew he was good looking. He'd figured what the long stares of girls meant early on, just as he'd figured out what the looks of the white boys on their arms meant. They didn't know what he was. He was too dark to be one of them, but he didn't talk like a Mexican. All they knew was they hated him.

He didn't speak a lick of Spanish, so the Mexicans didn't have anything to do with him either. Not that he was worried about fitting in with them anyway.

Georgie and his old man had moved to Modesto to get away from that whole scene back in El Paso. His dad was dark haired, but pretty fair. His parents couldn't hold hands in public without getting spit on. Then a year ago this redneck and his buddies had been settling a bill in the front office of the old man's garage. When they saw Georgie's mom come in and give his dad a peck on the cheek, they went right out to their truck and pealed out of the parking lot, swinging by to pitch a cinder block through the front window. Georgie's mom had been straightening out the magazines in the waiting area. Dad had told him late one night, in between sobs of hard, kerosene-smelling breath, that she had looked up just as the block came through the glass and hit her in the face.

Now clinking bottles lay in Georgie's mom's spot in the old man's bed.

There was a line of cars waiting on either side of the road when Georgie pulled up. They flicked on their headlights, illuminating the dark country road like some kind of Hollywood premiere.

Georgie's Rebel growled its way up to the starting point. Jimmy was already waiting in the Studebaker. Georgie could see the glint of spectacles and the shine of the kids' eyes in the dark spaces between the parked cars, like hungry animals looking out. He tried to keep cool and disinterested, running his comb through his greased hair and glancing out the open window, hoping to catch sight of Debbie. He did grab an eyeful of a dark haired china skinned girl with blood red lipstick, a motorcycle jacket and tight green cigarette pants. She was wearing sunglasses, despite the night. He'd never seen her around.

Georgie pulled up alongside Jimmy, who was chewing his gum furiously, looking bug-eyed at him under the brim of a Reds cap.

Georgie revved the engine a couple times to let the kid know what he was up against. The mechanical gargling of the unmuffled V-8 seemed to fill up the empty countryside, drowning out the crickets like a steel lion groaning to be fed asphalt.

Jimmy turned up his car radio. Chuck Berry was lighting into 'Roll Over Beethoven'.

Georgie grinned across the gap at him and turn up his own radio to the same station. The onlookers mistook it as some kind of ritual, and soon a dozen or more car radios were blasting in the night.

Babe Wilkes stepped into the road between the two revving cars and shouted to be heard.

"You race to the big house on the hill out past the bend and back! Got it?"

Georgie nodded, but watched Jimmy the whole time. Jimmy looked nervous. He nodded emphatically.

Babe slapped the roof of his friend's car and jogged backwards till he was in the beams of their headlamps. He took a Buck Rogers pistol out of his pocket and held it in the air.

Georgie spun the Rebel's tires with a piercing squeal. Jimmy pulled the brim of his hat low.

Babe pumped the tin trigger, little red and yellow sparks spouting up into the sky.

The drivers popped their clutches and screamed past Babe, swiftly leaving him waving his raygun in their taillights.

The two cars sped down the gauntlet of onlookers, Chuck Berry wailing in their ears, early in the morning, giving them his warning not to step on his blue suede shoes.

Georgie squeezed the wheel and watched the needle climb on the speedometer. In six seconds it inched past the sixty mark, two hundred fifty five horsepower vibrating beneath his All-Stars as he urged the pedal to the thrumming floor.

The Golden Hawk flew like a red rocket on the fourth of July, Jimmy leaning over the wheel, eyes bugging.

The Rebel was a spurt of mercury that slipped ahead inch by inch, devouring the black road ahead.

They blew free of the gauntlet of cars and in the rearview Georgie saw the kids pour into the road, shadow people jumping in the beams like excited cannibals that quickly receded into a far off spot of light.

It was just George, Jimmy and Chuck Berry in the dark, the wind tearing through the car, blowing in his ears.

He *had* this.

When he skidded to a stop in front of all those kids there'd be no more paisano, no more cockroach jokes. Everybody'd know he'd whupped Jimmy Lucas and won his girl. Maybe he'd even have the gumption to talk his old man into letting him have the Rebel, take it out to Laguna Seca on the weekends, get the garage to sponsor him. Sure, him and his old man, they'd slap some big magnet signs on the doors—CALATO'S AUTO REPAIR. Debbie'd be there to cheer him from the stands.

Georgie saw the lights of the old house up on the hill and knew the bend was coming, so he slowed for the turn. It was just enough to let Jimmy catch up.

Georgie spared a glance at Jimmy. He saw what the asshole meant to do right off. He wondered if his mother had felt the same way when she saw the cinder block coming through the window.

Jimmy wrenched his wheel to the left.

Their front quarter panels met with a flat, hollow sound, like a pair of trashcan lids coming together.

The Rebel was doing one hundred and twenty five.

The impact spun the front end of the car violently around. The tires left the road, spraying gravel as they scrabbled for traction. The whole car tipped suddenly over the embankment.

Georgie latched onto the outside of the driver's side door as the wheel jerked out of his hands.

The car flipped and landed on its left side with a smash that blew out the green tinted Solex windshield and crushed his left arm between the ground and door. He felt his stomach churn as the car continued to roll. He actually saw his forearm tear loose from his elbow in a shocking burst of blood. Before the pain hit he struck the top of his head hard on the roof. His consciousness was clubbed down into the pit of his stomach. Bereft of vision and hearing, it succumbed to total darkness.

***

Gale Storm was cooing 'Dark Moon' somewhere, a siren urging his mind to the shore of reason.

There was a bad smell in the air. Faint. Like rotten fish.

Georgie opened his eyes. His ears rang from the bright light shining from the green ceiling. His head felt like somebody had strapped a hot iron to the top of his skull.

Jesus, I totaled, he thought. His dad was gonna murder him for wrecking that car.

Then he remembered his arm.

But he must have imagined that, because he could feel the arm still there, move it even. When his swimmy eyes cleared, he saw it there on the metal table beside him, and lifted it to be sure.

He figured he must be at a hospital, but when he turned his throbbing head to take in his space, he saw he wasn't. The floors were poured concrete, gray. The walls were unadorned. The only windows were high on the walls, making him feel like he was below ground.

Of all the various machines, the only one Georgie could identify was a meat freezer in one corner. The rest was all Dr. Frankenstein stuff; banks of controls and switches, blinking lights, gauges, spiraling copper coils and tubes of bubbling liquid. He almost laughed.

He tried to turn on his side, and realized he was strapped firmly to the table by a pair of broad black leather restraints over the white sheet that covered him up to his chest.

"Hey! Hey what gives?"

The music snapped off. There was no sound but the bubbling and droning of the weird machines.

Then Georgie heard a squeaking noise.

From out of the dark emerged a bag of a man, pale skinned, with a sagging face and wiry gray hair springing out from beneath a black hat pulled low, almost to the bushy brows that sprouted over drooping, bloodhound eyes.

He was dressed in a rumpled suit and white lab coat, and seated in an old wheelchair.

Pushing him was the black haired girl with the deep red lipstick and the green cigarette pants, in motion ten times the Venus that had distracted him at the start of the race.

In the old man's lap was a blue Dictaphone. As the girl pushed him, he keyed the mic and whispered into it, through a pea souper of a foreign accent.

"Twelve midnight. Subject, George Calato, aged seventeen years. Awake. Lucid."

As he said the last, the girl wheeled him to a stop beside Georgie.

"Hello, George."

His face had no expression. Not even the great eyebrows twitched.

"How do you know my name, man?"

"Your driver's license was in your pocket," the old man said, a little testily.

"So who're you? What the hell am I doing here?"

"My name is Dr. Golovkin. You were in an automobile accident in front of my house. Do you remember?"

"Yeah sure I remember."

"My granddaughter extracted you from the wreck and brought you to my home. She saved your life."

He looked up at the girl. She was expressionless as her grandfather, but beautiful, like one of those Greek statues. She still had on the dark sunglasses.

"Thanks."

"She doesn't speak English."

"What are you? A Russkie?"

"Something like that, yes," said Golovkin.

"How come you didn't call an ambulance?"

"The nearest hospital is an hour away. Your needs were immediate. The car that struck you did not remain behind."

That rat Jimmy had left him to die. He'd get his. Georgie opened his lips to ask why they hadn't called an ambulance for him now, but the doctor cut him off.

"Do you remember anything about the accident?" Golovkin asked.

He remembered his arm ripping off, but he said nothing. His glance down at his arm seemed to be all the answer the doctor wanted.

"Yes. Your arm. It was damaged, but not irreparably. I had to administer an anesthetic gas to sedate you. Do you feel any pain now?"

"Just a little in my head."

"You may be suffering from a concussion. With your permission, I'd like to administer an additional dose. It may help you sleep. Then when you awake, you'll feel better."

"I ought to get going."

"But of course, my granddaughter will drive you home. But first."

He raised one weak, wrinkled hand. The girl stepped out from behind his wheelchair, went around to the other side of Georgie, and began to fiddle with something under the table.

Golovkin put the Dictaphone mic to his lips again.

"Twelve oh five. Administering second Liao dosage."

"Really, I'm okay, man," Georgie protested weakly.

The girl was looming over him. One cool smooth hand clamped down with surprising strength on his forehead. She slapped some kind of mask over his mouth and nose. There was a hiss and he smelled something sweet and serene that reminded him of his mother's lilac water. He felt the cool wind of the anesthetic blowing down his throat and sucked it in. The effect was immediate. The ache in his head subsided to a pleasant warmth.

He almost protested when she took it away.

Her hair dangled down. She was lovely.

"Twelve oh six. Subject appears tranquil."

"You bet, pops," George agreed.

"No sign of rejection."

The walls of the room expanded and contracted like a living thing, in tune to the chugging of the machines. It was like he was inside a heart made of concrete and metal.

He felt sleepy. He laid his cheek on the cool metal and blinked. There was a metal tray on a wheeled cart next to him, and he noticed on the floor, a trail of water leading to the freezer, as if something had been taken out of there and defrosted.

He closed his eyes.

***

The next thing he knew, it was morning. He was sitting on his front lawn.

A yellow Pontiac was pulling away from the curb, The Great Pretender wafting out of the open window.

He stood slowly, and groggily stumbled up the walk to his house, his mind a waking mind, still trying to separate faintly recalled dreams from memories, and all of that from the present reality.

The screen door banged open.

His father was looming there, red faced in his grimy coveralls.

"What the hell you stayin' out all night for when you got school in the morning?" his father roared, the smell of Schlitz blanketing Georgie in an invisible cloud.

"Ain't going," Georgie managed. "Sick."

"I oughta box your damn ears! Get in here!"

He stepped aside and Georgie plodded into the kitchen. The cat, his mother's orange cat, Gloria, rubbed against his leg, then stiffening, hissed at him, and scampered off.

"I'm late openin' up the garage on account of you."

"I was out. With friends."

"All night on a Thursday? Where's your coat?"

Georgie realized he was just in his t-shirt and jeans.

"What the hell's gotten into you?" he sniffed at him. "Phew. You stink. You hung over?"

"That's a laugh comin' from you," Georgie snapped, before he'd thought about it.

"You watch your mouth!"

"Or what? Are you pissed 'cause I didn't come home or 'cause you're losin' business? Maybe if you let me have a goddamn life of my own instead of makin' me go there after school everyday, I wouldn't—!"

He stopped short then, as a weird sensation came over him. His left arm was shaking uncontrollably. He clapped a hand to it. The flesh seemed to run between his fingers like wax. It threw him into a panic. He needed to get away from his dad.

"Aw the hell with this!" he shrieked, and turning, he ran out of the kitchen for the stairs up to his room.

"Don't you try and turn this around on me!" his father yelled after him. "You're grounded, you hear? I'm goin' to work, but don't think we ain't gonna have this out when I get back tonight!"

Georgie ran into his room and put his back to the wall. He was scared to look at his arm, but he wasn't sure why.

He caught a glimpse of himself in the mirror on his dresser. He was a wreck. He rolled up the sleeve of his t-shirt to his shoulder. He turned his arm over. There was a slight discoloration about midway up past his elbow. Not a scar exactly, just a subtle difference in color.

He thought hard about the accident again.

The wreck, Golovkin, that chick. And what had he felt in the kitchen? That weird spasm? Was it some side effect of the gas Golovkin had given him? He ran his hand through his mussed hair.

He guessed it was only a matter of time before the cops came knocking, probably at the garage about the wrecked Rebel out on Highway 99. No doubt Golovkin or one of the kids had reported it. His dad hadn't been at work, didn't know it was missing yet. He was going to catch holy hell tonight.

Georgie went to his bed and sat down. His head felt like it weighed fifty pounds. He dug in his jeans pocket and took out his crumpled pack of cigarettes. At least he still had them. He pulled one, lit a match, took a drag. It tasted funny, but familiar. Before he knew it, he was at the filter. He set the end on the nightstand and let his head fall back on the pillow.

Once his dad learned about the wreck, the cops would find out about Golovkin.

What the hell was Golovkin about anyway? All that weird stuff in the basement? Maybe the guy was some kind of commie spy or something. What was he doing in Modesto, though? Well, you don't stay secret in someplace like Washington DC or New York City. Actually Modesto wasn't a bad place to hide, except for the fact that there was nothing here important to spy on.

Maybe the girl was a spy too. Did they have girl spies? Sure. They probably made the best ones. Maybe she wasn't his granddaughter at all. They sure didn't look alike.

He was thinking of her when he dozed off.

***

Georgie couldn't help staring at the girl's swaying backside as she crossed the room to the wheeled cart sitting in a puddle of water next to the freezer.

She pushed it back to the table. When she stopped beside Golovkin, she reached into the tray and lifted a plastic bag about the size of a pillow. Sloshing inside it was a shifting mass of what looked like something shoveled off the floor of a slaughterhouse. It was pinkish and gray, and changed whenever Georgie tried to focus on it, all nipples and knuckle bones and a sudden bloom like an ear or a black animal eye popping open, rolling in between a pair of lids and then disappearing. The whole mixture was swimming in some bloody liquid, like the drippings of defrosted chicken, and seemed to be constantly moving, though the girl wasn't shaking the bag. Maybe it was the gas again, playing tricks on his eyes.

He laid his head back and closed his eyes to stop the spinning world.

Golovkin's voice droned into his Dictaphone.

"The Freygan method was an unwieldy undertaking, and made no considerations for the psychological effect of symbiosis. The end result was oft-times uncontrollable, savage. Working from the recovered Greenwood notes, I have streamlined the treatment considerably, substituting the use of parabolic reflectors with an infusion of vita-rays and a catalytic compound developed by the Mi-go. Combined with the regular introduction of Liao-gas to encourage psychic adaptation, the first stage of the process is for the most part, quite painless."

Georgie looked from the old man to the girl. She was leaning over, upending the bag. The weird stuff was sliding slowly from it, plopping wetly, like a quaking afterbirth into the tray. With it came an awful, fishy stink.

Somehow his bandages had been unwrapped. It was shocking to see the point where his left arm simply ended in a ragged stump. He couldn't see the wound well, but the lack of his left arm was enough to make him whimper.

The girl slapped the gas mask over his face. He breathed deep reflexively.

His eyes went to the girl, lingered tantalizingly on her form. She was older than him. Maybe a college girl. He could see the white mounds of cleavage through her open jacket, straining against the black top she wore beneath. Her lips were so red.

When the mask came away, his head slumped to the table, no will in him to lift it.

His eyes went to the silver tray.

Something dragged itself ponderously over the lip. It bubbled and boiled. The bubbles sprouted a dozen tiny human eyes that rolled and blinked. It flopped down onto the table and oozed towards his stump. He wanted to scream but he couldn't summon any effort.

He felt a sharp tug at his shoulder then. A vertical fissure had opened in the mound of fleshy ooze, wide enough to fit around his stump. The edges of the opening changed multiple times. At one point it sprouted shaggy hairs, and mimicked a pair of giant lips, and then it rippled and diminished.

He felt nauseous. Then something was in his mind. Not the voice of Golovkin, not his own confused thoughts.

Something *new*.

***

He was startled awake by a frenzy of hissing and yowling coming from the open doorway of his room. Gloria the cat was agitated to the point of hysteria. He sat up. Something huge moved rapidly in the corner of his eye, snapping back from the doorway like a rubber band toward the bed. The cat skidded off, feet padding quickly down the stairs.

His left palm was full of clumps of Gloria's orange hair, stuck together with some snotty fluid. He wiped the hand on his jeans in disgust.

There was a trail of the same sticky slime leading from the bed to the doorway.

He gasped, pulled himself to his feet. His hair was in his face. He blew at it, whimpering, thinking of the nightmare. It was a nightmare, right?

He was ravenously hungry. But it was a strange hunger. It didn't emanate from his belly. Somehow, he felt it as a pervading ache in his left arm.

His eyes went to the cigarette butt on his nightstand. He picked it up. Smelled it. This wasn't one of his Marlboros. It smelled…funny. He dug out the pack and opened it. None of them were his. What was this? Marijuana? He flung the carton in his wastebasket.

He brushed the hair angrily from his face. Was he losing it? What was happening? Why? The answer popped into his head. Because of that chickenshit sonofabitch Jimmy Lucas. Georgie could still see the scared look in Jimmy's eyes as he sideswiped him off the highway. Over Debbie Lomax. No, it wasn't even over her. That'd be too noble for that chickenshit. It was just so he wouldn't lose in front of the kids at school. To a Mexican.

He slammed his hand down on the dresser.

To his surprise, the entire thing broke down the middle, collapsing in a heap of busted wood and seven years' bad luck.

He stared at his arm. The skin was shiny, as if sweating. It looked plastic. He touched it. It was covered in that slime.

He looked down at the rubble of his dresser. He had smashed it with one hit. God, what had happened to him? Then he got the thought in his head. This wasn't his arm. He'd lost his arm in the wreck. And that nightmare about that bag of moving goop…had that really happened?

He grabbed his own wrist and shook it.

The arm did nothing out of the ordinary. It stank a little though.

He went to the bathroom to change his shirt and wash away the coat of slime. It was early evening already. His dad would be back soon. He was surprised he wasn't back already with the cops.

He peeled off his shirt and ran the sink water; splashed his face and pits.

He couldn't find his comb anywhere. Looking in the medicine cabinet mirror, he tried to smooth his hair and nearly jumped through the ceiling when his left hand came eye level. There was no hand at the end of his wrist, but a black comb, just like the one he'd been looking for. He shrieked in surprise.

Instantly the comb seemed to melt and reform into his hand.

He stared at his hand. He wanted to run screaming. But what the hell? He couldn't escape a piece of himself.

The hand became a comb.

He thought about his hand.

It changed back.

A comb.

Actually, it was kind of cool.

He ran it through his hair, gingerly at first, then styled it into the usual DA and pompadour. He didn't even need to hunt up his hair grease. The comb hand seemed to provide it.

Then it was just his hand again.

It didn't even hurt. All it took was a thought.

Crazy.

He stared at himself in the mirror, made a fist with the hand, flicked his finger out. It became a switchblade. Even made the click sound.

But all this playing around made the arm ache.

Hungry, he thought, remembering the mouth that had latched onto his stump on the table in the dream.

What did it eat? He didn't know.

Anger boiled up over that Jimmy Lucas. He was a freak now, and it was all his fault.

Something in his head, that new something he'd felt in the dream, said *yes!*

Georgie threw on a shirt and skipped down the staircase two at a time.

***

It took Georgie a half an hour to hike to Burge's, and by the time he got there the sun was going down.

Friday night. The joint was hopping, cruisers pulling in and out.

The car he was looking for, that cherry red two tone Golden Hawk with the brand new dent on the front left quarter, was in the lot. He boogied over and tried the door. Locked. He thought about the keys. Didn't even matter that he'd never seen them before. His finger fit right into the keyhole and with a twist of his wrist the door locks popped up. He sank into the cushioned driver's seat.

Oh she was a hottie, alright. Sweet as pie. He stuck his finger in the ignition and heard that V-8 engine turn over. She wasn't as loud as the Rebel, but she was loud enough. He revved the engine and watched the glass door of Burge's kick open. Three kids in blue Knights jackets poured out, with that Reds cap marking Jimmy Lucas out front.

He cranked the radio. Little Richard was yelling his head off about Saturday night. Georgie laid on the horn as he peeled out of the parking lot, Jimmy running full tilt on those wide receiver legs, almost catching hold of the right tail fin till Georgie kicked the gas and left him coughing in a cloud of exhaust.

He tore onto 9th, but he didn't open her up until Babe Wilkes' DeVille bottomed out in its haste to catch up.

Georgie roared all the way to O Street, the whine of the McCullough supercharger kicking in as he passed under the big arch that read WA-TER-WEALTH-CONTENTMENT-HEALTH. He didn't keep them much more than a dot in his mirror, all the way out to 99.

When he neared the bend where the Rebel had wrecked, he slowed, but not much. He wanted Jimmy to see what he was gonna do.

He wrenched open the door and jumped out, hit the shoulder rolling.

The Golden Hawk hit a telephone pole at somewhere around sixty, and the pole split that beautiful raised hood right down the middle like it was butter.

Georgie picked himself up and walked over to the hissing wreck. Not a piece of it was unbent but the trunk. He jumped up on it and sat there, waiting.

Soon the DeVille screeched to a stop and her doors popped open. There was Dombrowski and Babe. Jimmy nearly dropped the bat he was carrying when he saw the wreck.

"What the hell did you do to my car?" he wailed.

"Jesus, Jimmy," said Dombrowski. "It's that Mexican kid."

Georgie hopped down off the trunk and walked brazenly down the middle of the road.

The three of them looked nervous now.

"Hey," Babe wheezed. "Hey kid, we all knew you were gonna be okay."

And Georgie knew. None of the kids had called the cops or an ambulance. They'd all split. Every last one of 'em. Split and left him to die.

"Shut it, square," Georgie snapped.

Jimmy continued to advance, staring only at his twisted car.

"You sonofabitch, you're gonna wish you never crawled outta that wreck."

Jimmy brought the bat up, and that was the last thing he did.

Georgie had thought about turning the arm into a knife or something, but it leapt up without any prompting from him. It grew immense, like a python, and flowed straight at Jimmy's face. Every finger on the big hand at the end of it sprouted a jagged tooth. By the time it reached him, it was a huge mouth that clamped down on Jimmy's head and shoulders.

Georgie tried to jerk the arm back in surprise, but the motion tore off Jimmy's head completely, like he was picking the head off a daisy. The arm arced up whip-like through the air, trailing Jimmy's dancing, bloody vertebrae, slurping it up like a noodle, blanketing Dombrowski and Babe in blood and slime.

Jimmy's body took a few steps, swung the bat half-heartedly, and collapsed on its belly in the road.

Dombrowski and Babe turned to run.

The arm splashed down on Dombrowski's head, lifting him into the air.

Babe tumbled back into the Coupe. Georgie could hear him wheezing uncontrollably as the ignition whined, the engine stubbornly refusing to turn over, as if paralyzed by what the ogling headlights on either side of the DeVille's grill had seen.

Georgie felt a pleasant shiver travel the length of the arm and down his own spine.

Dombrowski crumpled to the ground headless.

The arm undulated. Georgie could feel and hear the crunching of their skulls. It was like rock candy. Even tasted something like it somehow.

The DeVille's engine spluttered to life and the car lurched onto the shoulder. Babe threw the thing into reverse. His face was beet red in the mirror.

Georgie threw his arm at the back window. It smashed through the glass. He didn't see exactly what it did, but he felt that same pleasurable sensation, like a taste of candy, and the car rocked on its chassis. Babe's foot kicked through the windshield and stayed there, ankle bleeding.

The arm slid from the shattered window and snaked back to Georgie, like a tape measure returning. A minute later it was just an arm again.

Georgie felt bloated and sick.

He stumbled over Jimmy's headless body and puked into the road. He pulled up the sleeve of his shirt. The discoloration on his arm had moved. It was over his shoulder now. He found it under the collar of his shirt. Sweat broke out on his scalp.

What the hell had he done?

It was getting dark. He knew where he had to go and it wasn't home.

***

Georgie pounded frantically on the door to the house on the hill with the yellow Pontiac in the driveway.

"Doc! Lemme in! You gotta take it off! I'm sick! I'm real sick!"

The light in the window came on. There was a rattling of the handle. The door swung open.

It was her. She still had those damned sunglasses on. Her hair was perfect, the color of starless space, and her lips were red as the hood of that Golden Hawk.

"I gotta see your grandfather," he stammered. "I'm sick. He did something to me. This arm…"

She put one white finger to those full red lips.

The next minute she had taken him by the hand. The left hand. Her touch was cold.

She led him inside, down the basement steps.

The machines were silent.

She pulled a chain and the light over the steel table came on.

Roaches scurried for the shadowy corners.

She took a cigarette pack out of her pocket, Black Lotus brand. He'd never heard of it. He was afraid for her. Afraid what the arm might do.

She flipped open the pack and bit a cigarette. He didn't see her strike a match, but he smelled it. In a minute it was lit. She took it from her lips and blew a cloud of sweet smelling smoke into his face.

He took it into his lungs. It was the same stuff that had been in his smokes. The smell…it reminded him of her.

He floated up with it, to the low ceiling, then through it, passing up into the sky, through the clouds. Way up there he exploded. But it was a good kind of an explosion, like on the fourth of July. He drifted down to earth in fiery fragments.

"To understand Stage Two, the most radical deviation from the Freygan method, but the one which garners the most appealing results, we must consider the Chalden word 'shaggathai,' and its implied relation to the root word 'shoggoth.' 'Shaggathai' is thought to mean 'fornication.'"

It was Dr. Golovkin's voice, whispering through his head. What was going on?

"The shoggoth itself is asexual, but when created from the merging of sentient flesh and proto-shoggoth, it is necessary to achieve the final obliteration of the base humanoid physique willingly. This ultimately renders a creature which is obedient and yet capable of some rational thought. A potentially powerful weapon. With a generous application of Liao to once more stimulate psychic symbiosis, a physical joining with an earlier generation subject is encouraged to awaken and foster the mental union of host and parasite."

He didn't remember getting undressed, but he was entwined with the girl on the cold table. She still gripped his hand tightly as he lathered her icy chest and tried to push himself ever deeper into her. He was like a pup nuzzling at feeding time, but what she fed him was more intense than any nourishment he'd ever had.

Her lips never parted except to accept his probing kisses. She made no sound, no expression. It was infuriating to him. She still had the glasses on.

He released his grip on her hip and reached up, yanking the sunglasses off.

Her eyes were black holes, pink rimmed, and from their depths sprang a pair of slithering proboscises, tipped with tiny gaping, gummy mouths that sucked the air like dying eels. Her hand was full of writhing tendrils, the curling 'fingers' lined with suction cups that drew at the animate flesh of his strange hand, both of them slick with an oozing slime like the feel of spoiled ham. He could not tell where his fingers merged with hers. They were one.

Over her shoulder he saw the shadowed shape of Golovkin in his chair, the edge of the light glinting off his Dictaphone mic.

The eyestalks reared back and elicited shrill, inhuman piping sounds that raised Georgie's short hairs.

"*Tekeli-li! Tekeli-li!*"

Then they plunged towards his own eyes, the puckering little mouths sealing over his eyeballs and sucking, drawing them out.

He screamed. Something thick filled his mouth.

"Stage Two ends. The subject host is consumed because it wants to be," droned Golovkin. "The requested large scale demonstration will commence Saturday evening."

***

Georgie dreamed strange, subpolar dreams.

He awoke in his bed.

His arm hung to the floor, a tremendous thing now, pulsing. It wound lazily around the corner, like something engorged.

He got up and followed it, retracting it slowly as he went.

Down the hall, to his father's room. It had slipped under the closed door.

He heard the crackling, the wet sucking noise.

He yawned.

***

Across the street from the theater, he finished a Black Lotus cigarette and watched Debbie and the other kids from school file past the box office into some schlocky horror movie.

When they were all inside, he went to the man at the counter.

"One for *The Blob*."

The show was about to start.

WITHIN THE IMAGE OF THE DIVINE
BY BEAR WEITER

With smooth chubby cheeks, two working eyes that mirrored each other, and a full head of blonde hair, the young girl was an abomination, a freak. She was younger than Mirabel by several years, though Mirabel had no way of really knowing—the girl did not look like anyone she knew now. *Before*, yes—but those days were gone, as were the Damned.

And yet here one was, clutching a doll to her chest.

It was the tattered Raggedy Ann doll that tugged at Mirabel's heart first. The doll—one eye missing, hair torn out, an arm shredded to fluff, burn marks across its surface—was like herself; it was one of her kind, one of the blessed.

The girl can't be all bad if she has a doll like that, Mirabel thought.

Mirabel had found the girl in the loft of her family's barn, hiding behind a stack of hay bales. She had heard crying first—a good sound, a *normal* sound, but unusual to come from there. *Maybe Timmy or Carl is hiding inside,* she had thought. It would have been fine if it were one of them, even if they shouldn't be playing here alone.

This, though—finding one of the Damned, one who should no longer be—this was big. Mirabel should report her to the priests, and the girl should be offered to the Angels. It was the right thing to do. Plus, everyone would know how she had done a good deed—like her friend, Timmy. She would be treated differently, with honor and respect.

But the girl held that doll. And through her sobs she spoke. "Can you help me?"

Her voice was strong, even though she spoke just above a whisper. Most of the people Mirabel knew sounded thin, taut, wheezy, or gurgly—each different, like their looks. Mirabel herself spoke with an airy voice, and a lisp where the left side of her mouth pinched up and her lips never met.

Mirabel worked up the courage to respond. As different as she was, the girl did not look threatening. "You should not be here," she said finally.

The girl's lower lip quivered, and she started crying harder. "I'm lost," she said.

Report her, Mirabel thought. *It's the best thing you can do for everyone.* "Where did you come from?" she asked instead.

"We lived in a cave in the woods. Me, my brother, and my dad. There were a few others, like Uncle Billy—who wasn't really my uncle."

"How long did you live there?" Mirabel asked. *Stop asking her questions. Report her!*

"I've always lived there, I think. My brother said we used to live in a house, but I don't remember it."

Mirabel only had vague memories from before the time of Angels—gathering around the radio, riding in the back of her Pa's old '39 truck, and seeing her first and only movie: *Cinderella*. She could not picture what Cinderella looked like any more, though she suspected she would be as horrid as this girl.

"But then it rained so much, and wouldn't stop, and everything flooded. It was night when the waters poured in. My brother and dad couldn't get out..." Her voice broke from the sobs. "I couldn't find the rest." Her talking sped up. "I had been told to follow the river and I would find more people, but the river kept getting smaller and it became a creek and that led me to here." She gestured behind her, toward the stream between this land and the farm beyond.

"I saw people last night and started to go to them, but then I saw... they looked..."

"Like me," Mirabel said, finishing her sentence.

The girl looked down. She hugged the doll tight, the doll that was so unlike its owner.

"What's your name?" Mirabel asked.

"I'm Ginny," she said, looking up again.

"I'm Mirabel." She extended her hand.

Ginny looked at it briefly before shaking it. Ginny's hands were odd, with each finger completely separate from each other. Mirabel's right hand had the last two fingers growing together, and on both hands extra skin between each digit. Her friend Carl said the webbing made her swim faster, but he had one arm partially fused to his body and she thought that was the reason he was slower.

"Are you hungry, Ginny?"

Ginny's eyes grew big and she nodded furiously.

"I'll bring you something to eat, and some water, too." Mirabel started down the ladder. "Stay there, and don't make any sounds." She thought she heard a quiet "okay" in response but wasn't certain.

The house sat a little ways off and Mirabel's thoughts weighed heavy on her as she walked. She knew what was right—the Damned had started their wars and nearly destroyed the world—certainly they had got what they deserved. The Angels didn't save them. But Ginny—she was just a kid, even younger than herself; how did she cause any of these problems?

Ginny was different. And she acted as if Mirabel's people were the strange ones. *She just doesn't know any better.* Mirabel's mom had said the same thing many times about Timmy's parents, often with a *tsk tsk* sound. She, too, supported their sacrifice but not, as she called it, their *vilification*. Mom was patient and understanding—Mirabel could be, too.

Maybe the Angels had overlooked Ginny, and others like her. *But if she was overlooked, how can I help her?*

That was a tough one. She pondered it as she worked—making a beef-scrape sandwich and filling a thermos with water. She had no more of an answer by the time she returned to the barn.

Once inside, however, amongst all of the equipment her Pa had on the ground floor, a small idea sparked in the back of her mind.

It's not possible, she thought, climbing back up the ladder. Still, the idea clung.

Back up on the top level, Mirabel handed Ginny the sandwich first. Ginny had held a few pieces of paper but tossed those to the side and snatched the food.

"Oh, thank you!" she said. With food in her mouth, she sounded much more like people Mirabel knew.

"Is it good?" Mirabel asked. Ginny nodded quickly. Mirabel already knew it was good—her cow, Bess, grew the best meat. She could have fed Ginny some scrapings from Hoss, the bull, and she would have been satisfied—even though they only used him for stews. The girl ate too fast to really appreciate the food. She placed the thermos by the papers Ginny had dropped.

The papers were small, white, and almost stacked. The bottom sheet, though—the corner of a black and white photo peaking out—hinted at something interesting. Mirabel knew of photos but had only seen a few in her time. She picked up the sheets.

Each one contained a picture of people—*before* people, like Ginny—unmarked, unscarred, standing aggressively straight, and smiling fiendish grins. Her hands trembled as she looked through them.

Ginny saw her looking and smiled herself.

Mirabel gasped. "You should not have these!" She shook the photos in the air. "These are forbidden. Sacrilegious. We should burn them!"

"No!" Ginny shot up, trying to grab them back but Mirabel stood, holding them high. The girl jumped in the air, but just couldn't reach. She sat back down, sniffing. "That's my family! Those are all I have left."

"They're dead now, as they should be. They were damned anyway."

"Don't say that," Ginny yelled.

"It's true—"

"It's not!"

"The Angels have told us this. They came down to—"

"There are no angels! They're from another world!"

There it was. Mirabel froze, one hand cocked back ready to strike. First Timmy's parents, and now...this. "Don't you say that. What would you know about it?"

Ginny glanced at the fist, but carried on in a quieter voice. "It's what my dad told me. He said that the war was so bad it opened something, or called them here. And the things, the aliens, they made it even worse. He used to be a scientist, he—"

Mirabel slapped her. Her hand left a bright red mark across Ginny's otherwise smooth skin, and Ginny scrunched her face up in response.

"He was a fool. He knew nothing, and he's dead now. God sent the Angels to look over the chosen, those of us who did not cause or aid the horrible war. Do you not see how we have been remade in their image?" *How could she not see it?*

Ginny's head tilted to the floorboards, and she mumbled something too quiet to hear. "What was that?" Mirabel asked.

"It's because of the radiation," Ginny said.

Mirabel swung back to strike the girl again, this time with a closed fist. As she did, Ginny pulled her doll close, turning the Raggedy Ann's one good eye up to Mirabel. She hesitated. *Report her!* rang out in her mind, as loud as the town bell. But there, within the darkness of the doll's button-eye, innocence reflected back, a glint of need.

Ginny, too, had the same look of innocence, the same obvious need—except her eyes were blue, close to the color of Mirabel's. And while Ginny had a lot of hair, its color was not much lighter than the thin patches on Mirabel's head. Sure she looked different than everyone else, but the similarities were there, too. Remove the surface differences, the way the eyelids folded, or how they mirrored each other—perhaps deep down she was the same as her kind. The girl's ideas were wrong, certainly, but she had not been taught properly—that could be addressed. And if those could change...

Maybe we can change her looks, too.

"Your father was wrong," Mirabel said as patiently as possible. She relaxed her hand and sat next to Ginny. "Maybe at first the radiation changed us, but we are the way we are because of the Angels. And they *are* Angels—they came to us in our hour of greatest need and saved us. We owe our lives to them. We are the reflections of our saviors, and we live to serve them."

Mirabel stroked Ginny's hair. Dirt clumped it together in spots, but there was so much more than what her people had, and it was *soft.* "I can understand that none of this makes sense. You will learn in time. I can help you." Mirabel picked up the photos, avoiding the horrible people portrayed in them. "I am sorry your family was not blessed. It is best to forget them anyway." Ginny's head remained hanging down. "Would you want to live here with us, among the Angels' chosen? Would you want my help?" Mirabel felt like her mother just then, how she could be patient and understanding no matter the issue.

Ginny did not respond right away, sobbing quietly. After a while, she wiped the snot from her nose and looked up at Mirabel. Great pools of tears welled in her lids, cascading down through her lashes in fat drops. "I want help," she said at last.

Pride filled Mirabel's heart. She had reached the girl. There was a great amount of work to be done if she was going to help her, but it was a start.

She spoke before knowing she had come to a decision. "If I can help you, you'll have to be brave. Can you do that?"

Ginny nodded vigorously.

Mirabel would need help, and had only two options.

Timmy lived nearby, and was a kind boy. He could help keep Ginny calm. But he also talked. His parents had once told him a tale much like what Ginny had said—that the Angels were not really divine, but instead were aliens from the skies, drawn here by the nuclear wars. Timmy told some of his classmates before telling his teacher. Within a day the town had come together to stamp out this sacrilege. His parents were offered to—and consumed by—the Angels, while Timmy was given a new home with a family who would raise him right. And while Mirabel knew they were wrong and deserved to be sacrificed, it still seemed harsh coming from their own son.

She could not trust Timmy with this.

Carl, on the other hand, lived just one field further away. He had a deep respect for the Angels, just like the rest of the town, but Carl could keep his mouth shut. When the two of them had started a field fire north of town—Mirabel had actually started it, but Carl was there—they both had played dumb, even when many were blaming Carl. He did have a mean streak, but Mirabel could get him to do things for her. He did just about anything she asked.

He was also big for his age. With what she was thinking, size might come in handy.

Mirabel left Ginny back in the loft once more and headed out across the stunted fields. Buoyed by the thought of helping another, she skipped much of the way. She had always been a helper, but this was the first time she had acted on her own, without direction from her mother or father. She was especially prideful for living the Teachings, specifically the commandment to look out for those less than you. *I could make a great Angel.*

She found Carl throwing rocks at his family's pit of legless swine. She didn't tell him about Ginny directly, only that she had found something big and needed his help. He readily agreed, but pestered her the entire way back.

"What is it?"

"I told you I can't tell you. But you'll see soon enough."

"Did you dig something up?"

They both enjoyed digging in the fields, hoping to find some treasure buried from *before*. They never did, but their failures only encouraged them. "It's nothing like that. You'll see."

"Well you can't stop smiling. It must be something good."

"Oh, it is. But you have to promise—you can't tell anyone about this."

"I don't tattle, you know that."

She stopped. "I know, but I need you to promise."

"Okay, okay. I promise. May the Angels take me if I ever tell another living soul."

"They might at that," she said.

This only renewed his efforts at guessing.

"Another three-headed dog?"

"Another nest of spider-mice?"

"Something start growing out of Bess like our pig, George?"

They continued on back to the barn, with Mirabel only smiling at Carl's attempts.

She entered the barn first. She did not expect Ginny to have come down, and she had not, so she waved Carl in. His eyes darted to every dark corner, searching for Mirabel's secret. After several seconds he leaned against the shaving stand, staring at Mirabel.

"So?" he asked.

"You remember your promise, right?" she asked quietly.

He nodded in his spastic, Carl way.

"I mean it. This is really important."

"Yeah, of course I remember it," he said.

"And you'll help me with whatever I ask?" She knew the answer, but needed him to say it.

"I'll help. I won't talk. Now show me already!"

Mirabel smiled at him before looking up to the top of the ladder. She spoke in a loud voice. "Ginny, you can come down. My friend is here, he's going to help me help you."

Carl followed her gaze. His eyes grew large and his mouth fell open further as Ginny appeared over the edge. She came down slowly, still holding her doll crooked in one arm.

"What is it?" Carl said in whisper.

Ginny made it to the bottom, but held on to the ladder. Her eyes stayed on Carl, and Mirabel could tell she was ready to bolt back up.

"Carl, this is Ginny. Ginny, this is my friend, Carl."

"She's a *Pre*!" Carl said, loud enough to be heard outside of the barn.

Ginny flinched, but did not scurry away. Mirabel, though, took two large strides toward Carl and swatted him on his shorter arm.

"Hush!" she said. "What's the point of swearing you to secrecy if you're just going to yell it out to everyone?"

He looked away from Ginny to her. "I'm sorry, it's just...I mean she's—"

"I've already been through all of this with her. She's different, yes, but she's not bad. And she needs our help."

Carl whispered this time, his face bent down to Mirabel's. "But how? Everyone will see right away that she's not one of us. You can't hide her here forever."

"You're right," Mirabel said. She still wasn't sure they could really help, and with Carl's reaction her confidence dipped. "I don't want to hide her, I want to help her. I think we can make her one of us."

Carl's eyes stretched open in surprise. "Only the Angels can do that!"

"Well, today we're Angels then." She had not meant to say it, and seeing Carl's face she regretted it immediately, but she knew she couldn't take it back. "Just think, we can help someone lesser become more. To be better. There is no greater blessing than this."

His face twisted into one of thought as he looked between Ginny, clinging to the ladder, and Mirabel, standing as upright as she could. She knew he could report her for what she had said. She would be sacrificed, just like Timmy's parents, and Carl would be celebrated throughout the town. Carl was not well liked and this would be a big boost for him. But Mirabel had been one of his few friends, even with his mean streak. *Does he like me enough to not say anything?*

He finally spoke. "So how do we do this?"

She noted the *we* immediately and smiled, the right side of her face pulling up to match the pinch in the other. "We start with that." She pointed to the shaving stand next to Carl. There were all kinds of straps and ropes to secure their cattle, as well as a wide board that lifted up into a low table-like support for those beasts with fewer legs.

Mirabel walked over to Ginny. She brushed the girl's hair with her hand. "Are you ready to be brave?"

She glanced at Carl, then back up at Mirabel. "Will it hurt?"

Their cattle rarely cried out once strapped in, and Mirabel assumed the same for Ginny. She had seen the animals always walk away afterward, so it shouldn't be too bad. Even if it did hurt a little, it should be a quick pain, like yanking off a band-aid. "It might, a bit," she said, feeling better about not lying. "But we'll only do what we have to, and it will be quick. Okay?"

Ginny nodded lightly, and squeezed her doll tight.

Mirabel guided her over to the stand. "We have to strap you to this table. They won't hurt or pinch, just hold you tight so you don't hurt yourself." Pa had said how the straps were there to keep Bess from hurting herself, and Mirabel knew it to be true. She had Ginny lean back against the tilted board and slipped a strap across Ginny's chest. Next, she secured another strap around her feet.

"Carl, can I get you to lift the stand?" Mirabel asked.

Carl came over and Ginny, with her arms still free, pulled the doll close to her face.

"He's okay," Mirabel whispered as Carl lifted the board into a flat table and secured the support.

"Can I keep Ann with me?" Ginny asked.

Mirabel had already thought of that and realized Ginny's arms needed tying down, too. "Let's put her over here instead, so she can watch." She took the doll from Ginny—it required a bit of a tug—and placed it on a shelf next to them. The doll slouched forward, its one black button eye looking down upon its owner.

Ginny sniffled a bit when Mirabel secured her arms but didn't complain, or say anything at all. She did keep glancing at Carl, but he stayed a couple of steps away unless Mirabel asked for his help.

"That doesn't hurt, right?" Mirabel asked.

"No," Ginny said. She had tried shaking her head at the same time, but Mirabel had a strap across her forehead. Head to foot, Ginny was secured tightly and completely immobile.

There were many tools spread across the barn. Carl helped her gather them up, suggesting the biggest scraper or the largest-toothed saw, but Mirabel already had an idea of what they needed and kept telling Carl no.

"What about this?" he asked, holding up a low-heat torch.

She was about to say no once again, but saw the block of wax next to it—what they used to seal the larger scrapings—and pointed at it. "Grab that, too."

They arranged the tools around the base of the stand—a bucket of water, a pair of rusty shears, a couple of different sized knives, a small scraper, rags, the torch, and the block of wax. Mirabel kept finding Ginny's eyes on hers, big, fearful, and shiny with unfallen tears—but also full of trust.

Please let this work.

"Where do we start?" Carl asked.

We're doing the Angel's work. Where should we begin? "With prayer," she said.

Mirabel took Ginny's right hand in one of hers and gestured to Carl to take the other. Carl offered his smaller hand, contorted into a hook and connected to his fused arm. Ginny hesitated, but after seeing Mirabel nod, she took it gingerly. Mirabel closed the loop by grabbing Carl's large fist.

"Let us pray," Mirabel said, like her father did before the start of each prayer. She closed her eyes and bowed her head, hoping Ginny would follow her example. "Our Angels, come from heaven, hallowed be thy gifts, thy kingdom brought, through war hard fought, on earth as it is in heaven. Give us this day our daily pain, and cleanse us of our flaws, as we cleanse those who trespass against us." Mirabel took a quick peek: Carl had his head bowed, and Ginny—who could not bend her head—had her eyes squeezed tight.

"Accept the will of Ginny, the sacrifices she's about to make in order to be one of your chosen, and allow our hands to work your miracles, making her into one of us, in your names, for your worship. Amen."

Both Ginny and Carl repeated the "amen" in unison.

With a squeeze of Ginny's hand, Mirabel asked, "Are you ready?"

Ginny's eyes had dried, and she beamed at Mirabel. Happiness filled her smile. "Yes," she said. "And thank you."

Mirabel started with Ginny's hair. She used the shears and hacked through a large chunk, close to the scalp. She had to work the blades to cut instead of pull, and Ginny winced through it.

"That just looks like a bad hair cut," Carl said, standing beside her.

He was right. *This is going to be harder than I thought.* "What do you suggest?" she asked.

Carl grabbed a small handful of Ginny's hair in his meaty hand and bunched it up tight. With a quick tug, he yanked the hair free.

The girl screamed. It was a good sound, like how the rest of her own kind sounded at times. It was the sound of thanks, of worship of their saviors. Tears poured from her eyes.

Where the hair had been a bald patch now gleamed bright red and dotted with blood. *Once it stops bleeding, it'll look like my head.*

She knew they were on the right track.

"More," she told Carl.

He worked her hair in small batches, plucking her head like a chicken. The results were patchy, and one chunk of her scalp hung in a flap from where he grabbed too much.

"Let's try the wax," Mirabel said.

Carl started the torch—something her Pa would kill her for lighting here in the barn—and she cut a hunk of wax into a bowl. All the while, Ginny continued to cry out in near-panicked gasps. Mirabel patted the girl's arm. "It's okay, honey," she said. "This is going to work great."

They heated the wax together, and Mirabel set to pouring it across the girl's head. Ginny screamed again. It required a steady hand to hold the flap of skin down, have the wax cover it, and avoid having it burn Mirabel's hand, but she worked with care. The wax formed a bubbly, ripply surface across Ginny's skin—an impressive mimicry of the skin over Mirabel's left ear.

We could be sisters. This idea warmed Mirabel's heart. *I want her to be my sister.* She kissed Ginny's forehead just above the eyes, a place reddened by the crying but otherwise untouched.

Ginny screamed out.

Mirabel looked at her, confused. Then, out of the corner of her eye she caught a flash of light.

Carl held the torch at Ginny's feet, waving it back and forth.

"Carl!" With two large steps she jumped between the two and yanked the torch away. "What are you doing? We're not trying to hurt her, damn it!"

He slouched down, bending away from her fury. "I'm sorry," he said. "I wasn't thinking."

She wanted to strike him, harder than she had slapped Ginny, but she knew it wouldn't help. Instead, she killed the flame and set the torch on the shelf, near the doll. She returned to Ginny's side.

The girl continued to cry in loud spasms.

"I'm sorry, Ginny. I won't let him hurt you again." She smoothed down the patches of hair that remained on her head as she talked to her, like her mother did when Mirabel was upset. "We'll try to finish quickly so it can all be over."

Ginny's cries remained loud, noisy things. While the sound might be good, Mirabel feared it could also become too much—and she didn't want anyone surprising them. She grabbed one of the rags, soaked it in water, and shoved it into Ginny's mouth.

It helped considerably.

From that point onward Carl remained attentive and helpful, never straying from Mirabel's side.

They opened wounds, removed skin, and sealed it up again. They carefully poured wax over one eye, just enough pinch it down to a slit, and across her ear, flattening it to her head.

It was tedious work, but they altered as much as they could while trying to keep the pain minimized. Mirabel already thought of herself as a big sister to Ginny, taking care of the younger girl, comforting her frequently, and overall making sure she would belong. It was a good feeling, clean and pure.

Mirabel guessed it was later afternoon. *The prayer bell will ring in an hour or so.* She knew she could not bring Ginny today, she would need at least a few days of healing before she could introduce the girl to the rest of the village. That would be the real test. There, in the presence of the Angels, Ginny would officially become one of them.

If we're successful.

Yes, but Mirabel was confident now. Ginny was bloody, but altered significantly. With just a little healing, she should look right.

But can I control what she says?

Somehow reading her mind, Carl raised the point more succinctly. "Should we take her tongue?"

It was a good question, and not one Mirabel had considered. Even through all of the crying, Ginny had heard it too and her one normal eye locked on Mirabel's, as large as could be. A subtle side-to-side shaking of Ginny's head was all she could do to plead for them not to do it.

"Do you know how to read or write?" Mirabel asked her.

Ginny wiggled her head again—*no.*

Without her tongue, she would not be able to communicate at all.

"Take it," Mirabel said.

Carl did most of the work, forcing Ginny's jaws open and holding onto the tongue. It bothered Mirabel how much Ginny struggled, and her own eyes teared up as she sliced through the meaty appendage. Once removed, she tossed the tongue to the side for later feeding to the animals.

"I'm so sorry," she said. But something still bothered Mirabel. Perhaps they weren't being smart about this. She looked hard at the girl—beaten, bloodied, and so close to looking like one of her own kind. Ginny also looked much closer to her doll, sitting above her in silence—only one button eye, and a hand torn away. She held Ginny's hand in her own, giving it a light squeeze to comfort the girl.

"Do you think she could draw?" she asked Carl.

"Not very well. She's just a kid."

"No, I mean to communicate."

Carl looked at the girl. It took a second for realization to dawn on his face. "We should take her fingers, shouldn't we?"

"Let's remove her whole right hand," Mirabel said.

Ginny screamed anew, a warbling, gurgling sound now without her tongue.

Mirabel swelled with pride. *She sounds like one of us. We're almost there.*

YELLOW IS THE COLOR OF THE FUTURE
BY JASON ANDREW

And remember, my friends, future events such as these will affect you in the future!

— Criswell narrating for *Plan 9 from Outer Space*

Sickly yellow light washed through the chain-linked gate casting long spider web shadows over the lot. Ed cupped the rusty padlock in his hand, and awkwardly poked the borrowed key into the slot. He jiggled it until it finally opened smooth as sandpaper. He glanced back through the headlights to his friends waiting in the pearl-white 1955 Chevy Convertible.

The driver, a thin man with dark hair, groaned then honked the horn wearily. "It's almost midnight, Ed! Can't we save the showmanship for later? I gotta work a double-shift tomorrow!"

"There's always time for a bit of showmanship, Pauly!" Ed wrapped the chain around his hand then bowed as though suddenly caught in a spotlight on stage. With a grand flourish, he jerked the chain as though he were a magician pulling a white table cloth out from under a full dining set. He flashed his patented Wood smile known for dazzling friends, actors, and debt collectors alike. The gates slowly swung open anticlimactically with a loud creak. "Destiny awaits us, friends!"

"Bravo! Bravo!" The gray-haired gentleman in the backseat of the Convertible stood and clapped loudly. "Quite right, Edward. Quite right! Never let the soulless minions of banality deter you from eloquence."

Paul rolled his eyes and reluctantly clapped. "The great and powerful Bunny Breckinridge doesn't deign to rise from his bed until well past noon. I'm a working stiff."

"Pauly, the world can be a wonderful exotic and beautifully bizarre place if you know just how to look at it." Ed opened the side door of the Convertible, slid into the passenger seat, and gestured forward. "We have the opportunity of a lifetime here. Let's not diminish that by focusing too much on the details and lost sleep. Kelton the Cop managed to survive the *Bride of the Monster* and *Plan 9 from Outer Space*. I promise that he shall appear on the big screen once more!"

The mention of his most notable screen role, such as it was, brought a much needed dose of cheer to Paul. "You really think that there's going to be undiscovered treasures here just lying around an old studio warehouse?"

Bunny sat back in his seat, adjusted his cravat, and nodded enthusiastically. "Oh yes, the studios hoard uncanny stores of costumes, props, and even old scripts. When I performed the Scottish play a few years ago with Rock Hudson, we scavenged a number of sets and prop swords from Ivanhoe. Incidentally, that's also how James Whale furnished the laboratory set for Frankenstein."

Ed grinned as wide as a kid waiting to sit on Santa's lap. He loved listening to Bunny's stories of the glory days of Hollywood, especially when said tales included a healthy sprinkle of sordid details. "Whale stole that set?"

"He found the Tesla coils from one of the lost studio warehouses," Bunny explained with great flare. "The rumor is that he found a number of broken sets from a proposed remake of Metropolis. No one knows exactly where the instruments came from. Records for such things aren't always well kept as you know."

"We don't even have a script for our next movie," Paul complained. He started the Convertible then drove through the vacant parking area to the freight entrance of the warehouse. "How will we even know what we're looking for?"

Ed laughed confidently. "Why don't you see? That's the perfect time to start looking for props. We can't afford a big studio budget, but what we do have is limitless imagination and vision. We'll look for things that might appear visually interesting on camera and I'll write a script around it. It'll save us a ton of money budget-wise without sacrificing a penny on the screen."

"If this is all perfectly legal, then why do we have to come here at night?" Paul complained.

Ed waved away his friend's valid concerns. It wouldn't be the first time that they had engaged in a freelance guerilla film production. "We're just getting the jump on the rest of the bargain-hunters tomorrow morning. I had to hand over one of my last autographed Bela as Dracula posters for the privilege so let's make the most of it. I'm not going to lie to you, times are hard all around. And if this doesn't work out, I might have to go back to making teenage delinquent movies."

"Perish the thought!" Bunny reached over and patted Ed on the arm gently. His friend always reminded Ed of a cat just dignified enough to treat you well, but haughty enough to still remain aloof and mysterious. "I'm sure Bela would have wanted it that way. In a way, he's still making movies with us."

***

The warehouse stank of mold, dank fabric, and rotted wood. Years of neglect combined with a broken window and damaged roof ruined much of the western wing of the warehouse. Ed now understood why his friend had given him such a good deal for the Bela poster, but he had a good feeling about this place and refused to let the obvious flaw in the bargain drain his enthusiasm. He found himself lost amongst the stacks of crates and only found Paul by his continual sneezes.

Ed jabbed the crowbar just under the lid of the wooden crate, coughing from the dust and the mold. He used the leverage of his body to pry it open. It finally popped open like a Champaign cork. He flipped it open, careful to avoid the nails, and fished through the straw until his hand felt coarse fabric. He produced a set of dark robes with a long hood and presented it to Bunny Breckinridge. "This is the second crate I've found with these creepy robes. I'm thinking this would be perfect for some sort of evil cult. They would go perfect with that crazy box of curved daggers we found."

Bunny turned from the crate he was exploring and reached over to feel the fabric. "This is pure wool, Edward. It'll be quite warm under studio lights, but perfect for an outdoor shoot. I wonder what production company paid for such quality."

Ed shrugged, not about to look a gift horse in the mouth, even if it did have wobbly legs. "The manifest for all of these crates mentioned someplace called Innsmouth. I've never heard of it, but it looks like the whole lot was bought at a government surplus auction. I'll mark this crate and we can claim it later."

Paul sniffed and peaked over the wall of crates. "What would the government be doing with creepy cult robes and leather books filled with old yellow news clippings?"

"What sort of news clippings?" Ed asked.

Paul lifted his hand revealing a leather-bound folder over the crates. "I can't read them. I think they might be in French."

Ed took it and started glancing through the pages. He couldn't read the text, but Paul's guess seemed spot on. He recognized the structure of the language, a few cognates, and the word Paris that appeared in almost every article. There were a number of old theater ads featuring a golden crown on top of a horrific death mask. Were these Parisian Theater reviews? "We might be able to use this as a prop of some sort."

Bunny tilted his head sardonically and wiped his brow. "May I?"

"You read French, Bunny?" Paul asked.

"I was born in Paris. She has forever left her mark upon my soul." Ed passed the folder to Bunny, who immediately started skimming the articles. His friend might have stopped performing Shakespeare on a regular basis, but you would never know by listening to him. "Why these are clippings of Le Canard Enchaîné; one the best Parisian newspapers still in print! I used to read these pages as a child." His voice grew somber, quiet as the grave. "Oh yes, I remember hearing stories about this. Very tragic!"

"About what?" Paul asked, his curiosity peaked.

"Murder most foul!" Bunny explained with his usual flare. "These articles detail a horrible massacre that occurred during the performance of a play in the '20s, just after the war. When I danced the burlesque in my youth, we used to drink absinthe after hours and frighten each other with stories about this play."

"What play?" Ed asked, imagining the free publicity such a ghoulish backstory could generate for even the tired Hollywood rags. "Have I heard of it?"

"Doubtful. *Le Roi en Jeune* it was called. The King in Yellow. It was written by a man named Castaigne. They say he gouged his own eyes out after writing it." Bunny glanced through the pages a bit more. "The King in Yellow was only performed the once and then it was banned forever. All of the copies were burned in a public bonfire." Bunny held the book tightly to his chest and then spoke barely above a whisper. "They say the entire audience went mad and killed each other. Tore the flesh from their bodies with their bare fingers and teeth. This article says that there was a strange poison in the grain of the meal before the show that caused hallucinations. The director was hanged. None of the actors were ever found."

"Why haven't I heard of this play?" Ed asked credulously. "You'd think that there would already be a movie starring Bela or Karloff."

"Alas, it was lost. There is only one mention of it at the Revue Biblique in Paris. It is only a legend whispered amongst actors in the theater. It would be a miracle to discover a lost copy of the play akin to the discovery of a new Shakespeare play."

Ed shook his head wistfully. "Too bad! We'd rake in the cash with a ghoulish tale like this for the publicity. We couldn't keep the teens away with a cattle prod and a ten foot fence."

Paul tilted his head and then ducked down amongst the crates and produced a thick leather-bound book with golden-yellow lettering that read *Le Roi en Jeune* over an arcane looking sigil pressed in the center of the cover. "You mean like this?"

Ed's eyes widened as he accepted the book gingerly. It had a solid weight to it and more importantly the skin of the leather cover looked downright creepy as though it had been bound with human skin. It would look amazing on screen with the proper angle. Ed could almost believe that he was holding the sacred tome of the devil himself.

He studied the strange yellow sign; it looked to be three interlocked spirals that resembled a horrible tentacled creature. Strange, he hadn't felt so shaky since the Battle of Guadalcanal. He pressed his fingers against the flesh of his arm and wished desperately that he felt the soft comfort of his angora sweater. Ed shook his head, feeling silly. "That couldn't be what I think it is, could it?"

"Le Roi en Jeune! The King in Yellow. Could this be a surviving manuscript of that play?" Bunny snatched it greedily and flipped open the thick tome and started scanning the page. "Let me see if I can translate any of this. *Strange is the night where black stars rise, but stranger still is lost Carcosa.*"

"It sounds almost Shakespearean," Paul retorted skeptically.

"Yes, yes, but we can clean up the language a little, if Bunny will help translate!" Ed interjected.

"Surely you don't mean to film this play?" Bunny asked. "What about the alleged fate of the first audience?"

"You said it yourself that it was likely dangerous hallucinogens. Why I once saw a grown man try to eat his own hand once after smoking some reefer." Ed turned his hands into an imaginary screen and held it before him with rapt reverence. "Imagine it! *The King in Yellow*, an Ed Wood Jr. production. See the major motion picture based on a play so insidious that an entire French audience committed mass suicide after watching it."

"What about the censors?" Bunny asked concerned.

"Why we'll rewrite it with an anti-communist slant," Ed explained. "They love that stuff!"

"Won't it be hard to film yellow in black and white?" Paul asked, scratching his head. "I mean the title suggests that there's a lot of yellow in the play. Isn't that hard to see on the screen?"

"We'll use special lighting and sepia tinting to give off that eerie yellow perfect for the movie." Ed snapped his fingers at the thought of it. "The process is actually very cheap these days since most movies have turned to Technicolor. Will you do it Bunny? Will you help me translate it?"

Bunny barely glanced up from the page. When he finally spoke, it was slow and stilted as though he was forced to wake from a splendid dream. "Yes. These words must be heard by the public."

Ed smoothed his mustache and then smiled. "Looks like you were worried for nothing, Paul. If you have the right attitude, fate just has a way of making sure everything works out in the end."

***

"*Song of my soul, my voice is dead.*" Bunny paused a moment letting the words germinate as he scanned the page for the next line. The overhead lamp illuminated his head as though Bunny was crowned with a golden halo. "*Die thou, unsung, as tears unshed shall dry and die in lost Carcosa.*"

Ed typed furiously, listening to the words of the play dreaming of this lost city of ancient gods. Later he would run through rewrites as needed, but for the moment he wanted to experience the chilling vibe of the play. "That's just swell Bunny! Can you give me a moment to catch-up?"

Bunny wiped his brow with his handkerchief and glanced around the director's makeshift office. He seemed paler than normal like he had not slept in nights. "The words seem to haunt me even when I close the book, Edward."

"Imagine how it will go on-screen, Bunny. Why this could be the part you'll be remembered for!" Ed stopped typing just a moment and gestured to the Technicolor Dracula poster that hung over his writing desk like an altar. "You could be as famous as Bela after this."

Bunny closed the manuscript with a loud thump and reluctantly set it next to Ed. "I think I am spent for tonight. I've given some thought as to the costume for the role of the King in Yellow. Tattered golden lamé fabric! It will glitter on the screen!"

"Bunny Breckinridge, you are playing a legendary god-king of an ancient city with unfathomable secrets and pleasures both subtle and gross. You can't play the King in Yellow in golden lamé fabric. Show some taste!"

Bunny huffed and then closed his eyes, holding his face in his hands. "You're right, of course. I'm just so tired."

"Do you want to take a snooze on the couch?" Ed asked concerned. "Kathy won't mind. She adores you."

"Perhaps just a nap to collect my strength." Bunny loosened his cravat then flopped backwards on the comfortable couch. "I've never had a role burrow into my brain before. Perhaps I should take a valium."

"Just don't lose yourself. I need you tomorrow to help convince the Hollywood Shakespeare company to lend us those Julius Caesar columns. With the right lighting and sepia tinting, we can capture the feel of the Carcosa palace throne room and film everything in extended long shots like a play."

Bunny waved away Ed's concerns. "I have given my life's blood to that company. They will lend us what we need, especially for the chance to play roles in the movie. There's quite a buzz starting to form in the underground."

Ed stopped typing and tilted his head. Never had such a thing been said about one of his movies. "Really?"

Bunny sniffed and wiped his brow again. Droplets of sweat formed at his gray temples. "They say the play is cursed and that only you would dare to try to film it. Half of them expect you to fail miserably."

"And the other half?"

"Well, they think you are the only director deranged enough to capture the essence," Bunny admitted.

"This is some kooky stuff." Ed started typing once more. "I had a nightmare about a winged man in tattered robes chasing me last night. Kathy had to shake me to wake me."

As if on cue, a blond slim woman with a sweet smile entered the room. Bunny roused himself and politely nodded. "Speak of the horns and the devil appears."

Kathy laughed. "I'm not the devil, I hope."

Ed stood and kissed his girlfriend. "Only an angel as far as I am concerned.

"Are you boys going to work late in the office?" Kathy asked. "I could make sandwiches."

Ed smoothed his mustache and smiled. "That would be swell, honey. I think we're making good progress. This script is giving me the willies." His hands were shaking. Why should they be shaking? "I don't think I've felt such dread in my stomach since the Battle of Guadalcanal."

Kathy patted Ed. "How did you handle it then?"

"I fought every battle with a brassiere and panties under my uniform." Ed laughed at the memory. "Somehow that soft feeling next to my body gave me the confidence to keep fighting."

"Sometimes, my friend, I think whatever gets you through the night is helpful," Bunny added. "I was a little bit wild when I was young, darling, but I lived my life grandly and didn't let fear stop me."

"Was Paul disappointed that he can't play Kelton?" Kathy asked, concerned.

"He was at first, of course." Ed stood from his desk and then hugged her. She cared deeply about their friends and that was partially why he loved her. "However, I think he warmed up to the idea of playing the lustful Prince Thale seeking the hand of beautiful Princess Camilla to secure the throne of lost Carcosa."

Kathy shook her head. "Listening to you two talk about these characters, I imagine that they are real somewhere."

Bunny stared off into space listlessly. He answered without realizing it. "Perhaps they are."

***

The white pillars of the fabled city of Carcosa cast long shadows on the marbled floor of the ballroom. Banners embroidered with the yellow sigil, three interlocked jagged spirals, adorned the walls. The soft waltz faded slowly as the assembled guests removed their masks, one by one as dictated by imperial custom, at the end of the masquerade ball. The lone dissenter stood in the center of the court and watched as the guests herded closer to the ivory throne huddling together for protection.

The Stranger stood motionless, defiant. He kept his back towards the camera allowing only the flowing, tattered yellow robes that seemed to ripple with power to be seen. Slowly the shot panned up towards that back of his head hidden by the hood shaped in the form of a lonely crown. When he nodded slightly, the frightening edges of the ivory mask teased barely into frame. Ed never imagined that Bunny could project such fearsome menace. He almost believed that the Stranger would snap the neck of the first interloper to dare confront him.

Paul Marco, standing as brave Thule, strutted between the princess Camilla and the Stranger. "Beware the price of standing too close to those above your station without the courtesy of identification."

Ed noted with some satisfaction that Paul performed his role brilliantly. Valda Hansen didn't have as much to do as Camilla except fill out her sheer white dress magnificently and that she did in spades. "He does not speak. Who would dare to refuse such an order?"

Naotalba, the high-priest of Yhtill and adviser to the queen, pointed accusingly toward the Stranger. He leaned forward and stage-whispered in his booming stentorian voice. "See how this stranger dares to mock our tradition? What does that say of the power of the throne?"

Ed shifted the camera's perspective over the Stranger's shoulder towards Queen Cassilda to capture Griswell's daunting performance. His friend dropped his usual stoic mannerisms and disappeared into the role.

Queen Cassilda grimaced, tightening her lips angrily. Her hands were held firmly upon her hips. Ed hadn't been certain of casting Dolores Fuller, as their breakup hadn't been completely without rancor, but he knew from experience that the actress could project anger better than any woman outside of his mother. She breathed slowly, trying to catch the last of her bravery. "You fail to play the game, sir? Will you not identify yourself?"

The Stranger did not deign to answer. He stood before the crowd motionless while silently judging them. Cassilda turned to her guard, the mighty Castellan, and nodded.

The bald giant with white eyes snarled. Ed knew that Tor would be perfect in the role and was not disappointed. The wrestler had been a mainstay in his movies for years and knew exactly how to growl at the screen to make the audience shriek with fear. "I would know the name of a man that I must kill."

The Castellan opened his meaty hands and reached for his enemy. The giant took a menacing step towards the Stranger and froze. He opened his mouth to scream, but his face spasmed and his throat constricted and quivered in a fashion Ed never imagined possible. Tor flipped onto his back with a loud thud. His hands shaking as blood dripped from his nose and mouth.

It was only when the Castellan collapsed onto the floor dead that the Stranger decided to speak. "If you must place a name upon the terror before you, I name myself the Phantom of Truth."

Queen Cassilda stepped forward grandly, offering her own neck in place of her court. "What truth do you speak of?"

"I speak of the truth at the end of all light. The terror of knowing the secret ways of the world where black stars hang in the heavens and the shadows of men's thoughts lengthen in the afternoon when the twin suns sink into the lake of Hali."

Cassilda gestured to the rest of the guests. His fingers were little more than bones with sickly flesh pulled over them. "You, sir, should unmask."

The Stranger, the so-called Phantom of Truth, refused to move. The camera slowly shifted to catch a glimpse of the pallid mask in shadow. The ivory bone seemed to snarl hungrily as black veins snaked down the hood. "Indeed?"

Cassilda shook her head eagerly. "Indeed it's time. We all have laid aside our disguises but you."

The Stranger merely shrugged. His eyes bore down upon her. "I wear no mask."

Camilla, terrified, turned aside to Cassilda. "No mask? No mask!"

"How might this be possible?" Queen Cassilda asked.

The Phantom of Truth stepped closer as though he were a lost lover returning to embrace her. "There is much about the truth that you do not know." His robes extended like bat wings and then enveloped Cassilda. "We will experience this truth together."

Queen Cassilda opened her mouth to scream. A horrible high-pitch screech of terror assailed their ears. It seemed to linger in the air as though it would last forever. Ed waited several beats and then yelled into the megaphone. "CUT!"

Dolores continued to scream as though her very soul burned. It was no longer a role she played as Cassilda. Ed yelled again. "CUT! Who the Hell do you think you are?"

"The King in Yellow." He stood slowly allowing the terror to properly escalate and then turned towards the director. Dolores wept softly to herself on the floor. There was no sign of Bunny Breckinridge in the figure that stood before him. He pointed towards Ed with a skeletal hand. The ivory mask had melded into his face with a hideous deathly grin. "You are but my catspawn in this play. You will obey my will in this. This film will be my new avatar, my new window to your world. You will ensure that this happens."

Ed clutched at his chest. It was as though cold fingers gripped onto his heart. He gritted his teeth and smiled as best he could sensing that supplication was the only route to survival. "Yes, sir! I understand completely. I just need to set the next scene. You want to continue the movie right?"

The eyes of the King in Yellow glowed yellow like fire from Hell. "This is my will."

"Sir, I need to breathe to make the movie," Ed protested weakly.

"Continue."

Ed felt the release of his heart and breathed a great sigh of relief. "Actors prepare for the next scene." Tor was slowly starting to stir on the floor. A number of the extras helped drag him to the side of the stage. Paul quickly swept Dolores into his arms and whisked her away from the King in Yellow. "Prepare for the next scene! I'm going to my office to grab some notes."

"Ed! We can't keep at this!" Paul protested as he handed Dolores a cup of water.

Ed waved off his concern before the King in Yellow could zap him into submission with hoary magic from beyond the grave. "You think this is the first time a star threw a fit on a Hollywood set?"

"You saw how he dropped Tor!" That guy's a big time wrestler and I've never seen him knocked out cold," Paul protested. "Something evil's possessed Bunny!"

"I'm pretty sure it wouldn't be the first time that was the case in Hollywood," Ed said through gritted teeth and a forced smile. "Everything will turn out alright! Everyone just set the next scene!"

The King in Yellow nodded approvingly then spoke in a booming voice. "Do as the director says if you wish to live."

Ed nodded thankfully, retreating quickly to his makeshift office.

**

Ed paced the length of the office smoking a cigarette. Kathy opened the door quietly and slipped in. "What are we going to do Ed? Bunny is keeping everyone hostage!"

"We can't call the cops! They'd never believe us."

"Can't we snap Bunny out of it?"

"I could barely get myself out of there. I can't help them. He can look into everything I'm afraid of."

Kathy kissed him on the forehead and opened the closet. "You need something to give you confidence." She pointed to his beloved Angora sweater. "A knight needs his armor."

Ed quickly did as she suggested and instantly felt better. He knew it wouldn't last, but he would take the respite. "How can we fight this thing? It's like it isn't even real. It's a story."

"Can you tell a better story?"

Ed looked up over his writing desk at the poster of Bela Lugosi as Dracula. "What would Bela do?"

"If only he were here."

Ed smiled. "I think I have a better end for Act Three." He leaned close and whispered, "This is what I need you to do."

**

Ed stood before the trembling cast proudly in his sharp pencil skirt and wonderfully comfortable Angora sweater. It felt like fuzzy heaven at the edge of hell. "There are things undreamt of in the shadows that defy the imagination and tempt the soul. I've seen the worst of the world in the muck and the blood and still managed to find the gumption to spit right in the eye of despair. I fought the Battle of Guadalcanal while secretly wearing a lace brassiere and panties beneath my Marine uniform. I lost most of my teeth and a good chunk of my leg fighting for my country so I figured I deserved to take what comfort I could." Ed cringed at the fear in their eyes, desperately wishing he could signal to them that he had a plan. "Okay gang, we're going to skip ahead to Act Three!"

Paul Marco raised his hand trembling. "That's the mass death scene!"

"Yes, yes! The mood is right and we can use that as actors." Ed nodded to Kathy who was fiddling with a projector at the end of the room behind the cameras. "We'll cover the seduction and terror of Act Two later."

"The movie will continue!" The King in Yellow commanded.

"That's right!" Ed agreed. "We're shooting out of sequence so we'll need all of the actors tomorrow. Living. You understand?"

"Blood must be spilled!"

"And that will show on the screen, but we need the actors for the scene tomorrow." Ed urged. "We want to make sure we get all of the shots so the movie sparkles. You need it to be perfect, right? Or it won't be your avatar, right!"

"Proceed."

"Places everyone! Remember to act as though your life depends on it. It just might!"

The King in Yellow pointed to Dolores. She tried to pull on the mask of Queen Cassilda but failed due to her trembling hands. "Do you feel the pull of the black stars in your soul?"

Dolores quivered. Her throat constricted. Ed signaled and Kathy turned on the projector.

Bela Lugosi flickered on the wall twelve feet tall, mighty and young. He hissed towards the camera. "It turns out the role you want was already taken by a man with more class that you could ever imagine! He's the star of many nightmares and beloved the world over."

The King in Yellow turned towards the image and roared. "A dead man that died alone."

"And beloved by children of all ages across the world. Something stronger than you can imagine."

The King of Yellow laughed, a hollow mocking sound of broken dreams. "You think this can frighten me?"

"Works as a diversion."

"What?" The King turned back towards Ed. The film dailies were on fire in the trash can. He screamed and rushed forward. "You dare to burn the great work!"

"People always forget that I was a marine. Diversions kill. You said yourself that the play was your entry into this world. No movie, no entrance."

"You will suffer for this."

"I might be a hack, but I'm my own man." Ed pulled on his sweater. "Now get out of my friend you sick son of a bitch!"

The mask dropped to the ground, shattering into dust. The robes billowed wildly until the hood dropped revealing a tired Bunny Breckinridge. He stumbled a bit before lowering himself against one of the marble pillars.

Ed and the crew crowded around him checking each other to ensure that they had survived intact. "What happened?" Bunny asked after a long time.

"Well, Bunny, it's a little complicated but I think you were possessed by the spirit of the King in Yellow and I forced it to leave this plane of existence by setting fire to the film."

Bunny blinked. "But you shot my best side, yes?"

"You fought him. I think that's why he couldn't kill any of us." Ed knelt down and hugged Bunny close. "We caught the best of you."

The wrestler Tor blinked and pointed at the burned footage. "What will we do now?"

"The play's too dangerous. We'll have to destroy it all," Ed sighed, thinking of his pile of unpaid bills.

"We have the warehouse for the next month and we've already paid for everything," Paul protested. "This could ruin us."

"You know, I do have a script that I've been saving. Night of the Ghouls, what do you think?"

"You never do give up, do you?" Paul asked.

"That's why I love him," Kathy said, kissing him.

FEARS REALIZED
BY TOM LYNCH

Bill Thomas cracked himself on the head climbing up the stairs out of the bomb shelter. "Sweet Jesus!" he yelled, clutching his throbbing skull. It was times like this that he got really angry stocking it for an attack that would never come. Fitting his six foot five inch frame through the low doorway of a ten-by-twenty paranoia space was never easy, and he almost never remembered to duck far enough.

"Honey!" he growled, walking through the back door to the freezer for the ice pack. "Do we really need that thing out there? If something were coming, don't you think the university'd know? My department keeps tabs on stuff like this."

"The university, Bill?" began his wife from the pantry. "If even the *government* knew about all the attacks then they'd have known about Pearl Harbor! But nobody did! Nobody was prepared! My brother is *dead* because they weren't prepared. They *didn't* know. I'm going to make sure we are prepared, and that my children have a future."

He knew once that argument came out, he'd already lost. He should have learned by now, but he always shot his mouth off when he'd gotten hurt. He sighed. "Sorry, honey. I just wish they came in extra-tall."

"Oh, no, Bill! Not again," she said, rushing into the kitchen. "Let me see."

Bill ducked down so his five-foot-two-inch wife could see the top of his head. "No broken skin. Just keep icing it. Sit down, while I get the rest of the cans in from the garage."

Nora, Bill's wife, was a nurse. She'd served in that capacity during the war, while Bill stayed stateside in the lab. He was currently assigned to a top secret facility in the Nevada desert, but his wife was under the impression that he taught college physics. They were far enough from the coast that a bombing run was unlikely, and he was *reasonably* sure the Soviets didn't know anything specific about his particular lab.

He leaned back and stretched out his legs, pulling a cigarette out of the pack in his shirt pocket, and lighting it with his engraved Zippo. The lighter had been a birthday gift from Nora. It read 'To the Light of my Life.' Corny, yes, but he liked it. He chuckled, took deep drag, and dropped his head back, closing his eyes. The ice and nicotine helped to ease the pain of his injury, and the rest helped his bruised ego.

He heard a thud from outside. Opening his eyes and knitting his eyebrows, he turned toward the window. He couldn't see out into the night, so he tossed the bag of ice into the sink and peered out the back door.

Bill couldn't see clearly past the pool of light on the patio into the yard. There was movement out there. "Hello?" he called. He reached into the cabinet drawer and grabbed the flashlight, and shone it out into the night. There looked to be someone lying on the ground by the back fence. Bill stepped forward slowly, calling with every other step. No response.

Finally, he got to the form lying on the ground. There was a man, lying in the grass, and he appeared to have steam rising from him. Bill shone the flashlight all around, scanning the area, but he saw no one else, or any signs of a scuffle. The back of his yard was surrounded by a six foot wooden stockade fence. Bill could easily see over it, but most could not. The ground beyond the fence didn't show footprints. The morning's thunderstorm would have left the ground wet enough for tracks to be obvious, so where did this fellow come from?

Bill looked back to the man lying in his yard.

"Bill?" Nora called from the back door.

"Out here, Hon."

"What's the matter?" she asked, hearing the tension in his voice.

"Can you grab your bag?"

"What? Are you hurt?"

"It's not for me...please come quickly."

A few moments later, his wife bustled over and gasped, almost dropping her medical bag when she saw the stranger lying in the grass. She recovered in a flash, and went into medical emergency mode. "Bill, put hot water on, and bring me a bowl of clean, fresh water."

"Right." And Bill hustled inside.

By the time he got back, Nora was holding the flashlight in one hand and wiping grime off the stranger's face with the other. He had a slight build and appeared to be of Middle Eastern descent. While Nora cleaned him, Bill looked through his clothing for identification in his pockets.

Rather than find a wallet or billfold, all Bill found was oddly cut clothes. He realized this was no ordinary set of clothes. He didn't recognize the material or the cut. In fact, all he did recognize was the color: black. He found no pockets either. Puzzled, he continued to examine the stranger's clothing. It had no buttons, hooks, or zippers, but it closed and opened where needed. It was only after realizing this that Bill pulled on other sections of the fabric to see if pockets opened, but they did not.

"Okay, Hon, I've cleaned him up and dressed the knot on his head," Nora said. "Did you find anything?"

"Not a thing."

"What now?"

"I guess I carry him inside, and maybe call the cops. Might be that someone reported him missing?" Bill pondered.

They carried the unconscious form in and placed him on the couch. There, in the light Bill saw more details about the odd clothing. In addition to being oddly cut and closed, there was a glitter to the black fabric. Sparkles were visible as the material moved.

Bill was moving toward the phone when he heard a low moan. He spun and looked back at the couch. Nora, still standing next to the couch, was staring, wide-eyed. The stranger was waking up.

"Where am I?" asked a rich, melodious voice.

For a few moments, Bill and Nora only stared, taking in the eyes that were now open. They were a glossy, reflective black. No irises or corneas were visible...just pure black.

"I'm sorry...my research indicated that most in my target area spoke English. *Comprende?*" the stranger asked.

"No, no," stuttered Bill. "We speak English but...well..."

"I'm sorry. I did my best to match your appearance, but some details were bound to be different. I am sorry."

"Don't...well...no, that's not it," Bill eventually stuttered. "It's just that..."

"You're not..." Nora whispered.

"No," the stranger said. "I'm not human."

"That's..." Bill started, and then he let out all the air in his lungs with explosive force.

"Yes, it's a major milestone. This visit proves that humankind is not alone in the universe." Nora dropped onto the arm of the couch.

"...Okay," Bill finally said after a long silence. "But how did you get here? And why was this your 'target area'?"

"How, meaning my method of travel?"

"Yeah! And where—"

"Before we discuss such heady topics, let me move on to your second question."

"Oh?"

"Yes, it was quite deliberate, I assure you. I came to meet you, William, and to speak with your team and your superiors."

"Me? My superiors? But why?" He glanced nervously back at his wife.

"You work in the Advanced Propulsion Division in the Theoretical Physics Laboratory at Area 51, do you not?"

Nora's face went white. "William Hayes Thomas! You told me you were teaching physics!"

"I'm sorry to have upset you Mrs. Thomas," began the stranger. "But could you get me a glass of water?"

"O-oh. Of...of course." Nora rose and walked into the kitchen. Bill stared after her, his head still spinning from all that was happening. His head was suddenly wrenched back by the hair, and before he could cry out the stranger's face filled his vision, black eyes burning with hell's fury.

"William!" he hissed. "Listen to me very closely. I carry with me the secrets of survival and prevention of the annihilation of the universe, and very much need to get to your air base as soon as possible. I can no longer afford to be gentle."

With that, images flooded Bill's mind. Pictures, he somehow knew, of the apocalyptic future: seas of people, fighting, war, genocide, fire, burning, pain, suffering, vista-blurring agony, RAPE, MURDER, DEATH, STARS FALLING, METEORS COLLIDING, **EARTH IMPLODING!**

Bill came to lying on his back on the living room carpet, the shag rug tickling his left ear. His hands had been pulling on his face, and his eyes still watered. Nora came back in at that moment.

"What happened? I heard a thump...Oh my Lord! Bill! Are you okay?" Nora stopped and spun. "What did you do to him?" she spat at the visitor.

William. We have no time. She has to go.

Bill heard the stranger's voice boring into his already-tender brain. But he stood, as if he were watching a horror movie while strapped to a chair. He wrapped one arm around Nora's shoulders, and the other around her head. Then, Bill Thomas broke his wife's neck with a vicious twist.

He heard the cracking, popping sound from far away as if he were dreaming. As her body hit the floor, he knew it was real, but he was still numb. Still outside.

We need to go, William. To the base. There has to be no trace here.

"But...my children."

No trace, William. Fire.

The strange numb, separated feeling clawed at his connection to his children. "But...they're so young...surely..."

An iron wall slammed down between his body and his emotion, with his mind vaguely aware of both, but fully aware of neither. He felt a pushing against his body, separating his emotion further from the rest of him.

Robotic movements took over. His body jerked its way over to the door to the garage. His hands reached down and picked up the five gallon gas can. He lumbered back into the house and up the stairs. He went to his infant daughter's room, all decked out in pink, complete with pony wallpaper. He stalked into the room and doused the carpeting in the room with gasoline, splashed fuel onto the crib bedding, and walked out again. Then he went next door to his son's room. He looked, but did not see the cowboy motif to the room that he and little Danny had worked on over the four years of his life. He soaked the carpet and bed in here as well.

Danny stirred as the bed got wet. The little boy's eyes opened still glassy with sleep, but when he saw his father, he smiled, rolled over, and drifted off again. Bill was at war with himself, pushing, pulling, *trying* to fight, but the outside control clamped down, and did not allow him to react or stop what he was doing.

Leaving the can upended, he walked down the steps and back into the living room, splashing fuel along the stairs, onto the living room carpet and couch, and finally emptying the final sloshes onto his wife's corpse.

The stranger stood by the door to the garage, waiting. He nodded. Bill took out his lighter, flipped and lit it, and dropped it onto Nora's body. Flames immediately bloomed to life, and flowed outward, running along the floor, over the couch and out of sight up the stairs.

As he walked to the garage to get into his car and drive his visitor to the base, he heard faint coughing and a baby wailing. His body kept moving, but his eyes filled with tears.

He dropped into the driver's seat of his Studebaker Land Cruiser, and his visitor sat in the navigator's seat. *Don't worry. No one will be able to see me.*

They pulled out of the garage and into the night, and as he pulled away from his house, he heard his neighbors cry out the alarm as his house burned. Minutes later, he heard multiple fire engines, their sirens crying out into the night. Bill glanced over his shoulder and saw orange flames licking at the sky and red, white, and blue lights of fire and police vehicles nearby as they fought to get the blaze under control. And he drove away.

Suddenly, out of nowhere, a police car swerved in front of them and screeched to a halt. The police officer stepped out and shouted at Bill. "Out of the car! Now!"

The cop reached into his patrol car and pulled out the CB. "This is car fifty-five. I've got the suspect the neighbor phoned in. I'm holding him on the corner of Angell and Phillips streets." The officer turned back to Bill in the car. "Sir, please. Get out of the car. Now."

Try as he might, Bill could not move or speak. He struggled and pushed, but his hands remained clamped on the steering wheel and his body remained rigid. He felt sweat rolling down the small of his back. His eyes glued to the agitated policeman, Bill watched in horror as the policeman drew his gun and pointed it through the driver's side window right at his head, clearly oblivious to the man seated next to him in the car. Bill wanted to close his eyes, but he just couldn't. As he watched his certain death unfold, the policeman's body seemed to lock up. The gun started the move. The stranger next to Bill had gone very still, but was breathing as if lifting something very heavy. The policeman's gun arm was shaking now...quivering with tension. Fighting his own arm, the officer turned the gun with aching slowness, and pressed the barrel to his own temple. His eyes filled with horror.

Bill jumped as the gun went off, and the policeman's form crumpled to the ground.

Drive on, William. Others will follow. We must hurry.

Colored lights flashed from behind as Bill mashed the pedal down and the big sedan lurched forward. The fallen police officer's comrades had arrived moments too late, but the damage had been done. Bill was now fleeing the murder of a police officer. Sweat poured freely down his body, and the tension shot from his shoulders to his jaw in painful spasms.

Just pull onto the highway, William.

Bill raced up the ramp, his car's engine roaring. He glanced into his rearview mirror in time to see the lead police car suddenly swerve into the barrier at the side of the road, spin out of control, and whip its tail end into the following car. The second car then smashed into the opposite barrier. The driver of the third car hadn't had time to respond yet, and slammed into the two cars in front of him. Three more cars, all in pursuit of the car fleeing a deadly fire and police shootout, smashed into the piled cars in front of them, piling up and blocking the on-ramp to the highway.

Bill sped away. Before long, the flickering lights from the sirens faded behind them, and they drove in silence until they approached the base.

Bill pulled up to the security gate. He and the guard knew each other. Vinny was his name.

"Working late tonight, Dr. Thomas?"

All Bill could manage was a mute shrug. Vinny smirked and handed him the clipboard to sign in. Shortly, Bill had parked the Studebaker in the lot by the back entrance away from the areas regularly patrolled by the MPs. He got out of the car, and his guest leapt out of his seat and gestured for him to lead the way into the building.

Bill led him in and down a quiet hallway and into a small window-less office.

"William," said the stranger, speaking for the first time since they were at his house. "Call a meeting."

"But..."

"An urgent one. Bring everybody in, and have them meet us by the vessel. Give them thirty minutes." *No questions, William. Do it.*

The psychic push at the end spurred Bill into action. He spun his rolodex, picked up his phone, and started dialing all seventeen members of the team.

Forty tense minutes later, the last person filed into the enormous hanger. Bill stood under the alien spacecraft found in the desert at the crash site eight years earlier. Looking up it, bolted to multiple levels of scaffolding, one thing was very clear: this was no weather balloon.

Bill had been quieting many a cantankerous coworker as they entered, assuring them that answers would be forthcoming. The last person to enter was Major Roger Mullady, the highest ranking Air Force officer in Bill's division. He was not happy to be called in this late, no matter the reason. "Dammit, Thomas, what in hell is going on here? You called me away from an evening with my wife."

"Actually, Major, you were in bed with your secretary," called a voice from behind Bill under the scaffolding. "Your wife is visiting her sister in Tahoe."

"Who the fuck said that?" shouted the Major, drawing his .45 from under his suit jacket.

"I the fuck said that, Major Mullady," said the stranger stepping out. "Kindly holster your weapon." The eyes of everyone gathered locked onto this newcomer with impossible eyes. Everyone was too terrified to do more than breathe.

Major Mullady's breath was heaving, his eyes wide. He continued to point his gun at the stranger. Suddenly, it looked like he was fighting an invisible tug of war over his pistol, with his unseen opponent trying to push the gun to the floor.

"Your will is strong, Major, but really you have no chance."

The officer's nose suddenly started to bleed, heavily. Still the major fought. He then started to cough, his mouth spluttering blood as well. Finally, he lowered his gun and fell to the floor on all fours. Everyone else pulled back from the fallen officer, staring in horror at the new-comer.

"I trust I now have everyone's full attention," the stranger said.

There was a murmur of yes's from the crowd of physicists and military strategists.

"Good. Dr. Thomas was good enough to bring me here tonight and to call this meeting as you know. These next few minutes will be the most important of your short lives."

There was more fidgeting from his audience, and many stared daggers at Bill, who merely stood as if locked in position, his head drooping forward and his shoulders sagging.

"This craft behind me showed you that you were not alone in the universe. Some of the greatest minds of humankind, therefore, sought to use the mysterious technology herein, rather than develop their own. They, and you, want to leapfrog evolution, and I am afraid it does not work that way."

With that, the stranger turned and waved his arm casually at the most incredible find in human history, and with screeches of metal and crumpling of bulkheads, the craft slowly, deliberately folded in on itself, over and over again until it winked out of existence with a sound of sucking air.

The assembled officers and scientists gasped, too dumbfounded to be enraged. They just gaped at this newcomer who, without the aid of technology or weaponry, destroyed their lives' work.

He started again. "My brief stay here is almost at an end. I will, therefore, be direct so minds as small as yours will be able to grasp my meaning. The universe is a harsh, uncaring place. In some ways, my actions may be seen as a mercy. In others, a warning. We who travel the stars do not wish to be bothered by primitive pests such as yourselves. When you have proven your *own* ability, without the use of borrowed technology, we will see how you do. If you proceed beyond this planet as you have overrun it: without respect to greater powers, then you will have proven your questionable nature." He paused, letting the people in the room absorb the challenge.

"There is a pecking order," the stranger continued. "And you are at the bottom of the pile. Know that we may destroy you; humanity pursues distant horizons at its own risk."

The stranger glanced out at his audience, letting the gravity of his statement sink in. "Now I must leave. You have heard my warning and seen what I can do, and I am not the greatest of beings in the cosmos," he said, and knit his eyebrows, looking off over the group's heads. He exhaled. "And now, we wipe the slate clean."

A red plastic phone mounted to the wall suddenly rang, and the light bulb on it flickered and flashed. Major Mullady dashed over, and identified himself. He stopped and stood stock still; his face drained of color as he listened. "I understand," he said finally, and hung up the phone in slow motion. "Area radar has multiple signals, and they appeared out of nowhere," he told the assembled team.

No sooner had he finished addressing the stunned group then he cocked his head, but they could all hear the droning buzz of propeller engines. "Dear God," Major Mullady said. "Those are Tu-95s! How could our radar have missed planes that big?"

"Anything's possible, Major, if you know how. And now, fulfilling the worst fears of your Senator McCarthy, this place will be consumed by Russian fire! I wonder which of you will be labeled a 'commie bastard' and shamed throughout history."

At last the situation seemed to sink in and panic filled the room. Everyone on the team scrambled for the door. "THERE'S NO POINT," Major Mullady yelled. "The Russians have H-bombs. Now that we can hear the bombers, they'll drop their payload before we can get beyond the blast radius."

A chorus of whimpers and cries rose in response. "My only solace," Major Mullady began and he turned to the stranger, "is that you'll be burning with us."

The stranger chuckled. "No, I'm afraid not. My work here is done. I now must leave you to face your fate on your own." With that, he made a swift elaborate gesture, and disappeared.

"Dammit, Thomas, what have you DONE?" Major Mullady growled.

"Death..." whispered Bill, finally released of the iron hold on his will. "Death will be a mercy."

The next sound the assembled group heard was the scream of bombs tearing through the air. And there wasn't a damn thing they could do about it.

PROFESSOR PATRIOT AND THE DOOM THAT CAME TO NICEVILLE

BY CHRISTINE MORGAN

In dark-shadowed dimness, a pallid light flickered and tinny voices spoke.

The hush was classroom-quiet, a surface listening attentiveness underlain by the swinging of feet and shifting of bodies, the soft scritch of a pencil, the rustle of paper as notes were passed or comicbook pages surreptitiously turned, the occasional whisper.

The projector continued its rattling hum. The educational film played on, showing a cartoon family in a cartoon dining room.

Dad sits at the head of the table, Big Sister Susie to his left, Little Brother Jimmy to his right. Mom, smiling, carries in a steaming pot roast from the kitchen.

Ding-bong!

"What's that?" says the narrator. "Someone at the door?"

Susie hops up, all poodle skirt and ponytail. She goes to answer it. "Hi, Uncle Bud!"

"It's Uncle Bud," the narrator says. "And he's brought someone with him. Who could it be? Why, it's his new fiancée!"

Cartoon introductions and small-talk follow, during which only Jimmy seems uneasy, frowning and suspicious.

With a *pthoo!* sound, a spitwad flew through the air and pasted itself to the blackboard beside the pull-down screen. Muffled snickers and giggles erupted around the room.

"Eddie," Miss Chambers said, using one of her milder but serious warning tones.

He immediately adopted perfect posture and an expression of angelic innocence. The other children followed suit.

By then, of course, they'd missed the dramatic moment in which cartoon Jimmy exposed Uncle Bud's new fiancée for the batrachian monstrosity she truly was.

"Golly, Jim, thanks!" Uncle Bud ruffles Jimmy's cartoon cowlick hair. "Good thing for me you knew what to do!"

"Aw, shucks," says Jimmy, freckled and grinning a wide gap-toothed grin. "I just pay attention in school, is all."

The rest of the family crowds around them, lavishing congratulations on Jimmy before Dad suggests they go out for ice cream sodas.

"Looks like it worked out all right..." The narrator trails off into an ominous pause. "...this time. But would *you* know what to do? Would *you* recognize the signs? Let's go over them again. Read along with me."

Bold lettering appears on the screen.

THE INNSMOUTH 'LOOK':
1. BULGING EYES
2. CLAMMY SKIN
3. WEBBED FINGERS
4. MUSHY VOICE
5. SEA-SMELL
6. GILL FLAPS

"Now that you know what to watch for," the narrator says, "it's up to you to stay alert. If you notice anyone with some of these tell-tale signs, report it at once. Remember, the safety of your family, friends, and fellow Americans could be depending on *you*."

The closing-credits came up—"This has been a civil defense production from the Department of Eldritch Emergency Preparedness." Then the 3-2-1, and then a blank white square filled the screen. The loose end of the film strip made its familiar whap-flutter-whap noise.

Mikey, puffed with self-importance at being one of this week's Class Helpers, switched off the projector and began the process of re-threading the reel to rewind it. Georgina turned the overhead lights on and raised the blinds, letting spring sunshine spill through the windows.

Miss Chambers glanced at the clock above the door and saw that they still had time to go over some fractions before the readiness drill. The students groaned when she instructed them to open their math workbooks, but complied.

They did eight problems before a click and a chime issued from the PA speaker on the wall. Principal Ross read the noon announcements—Open House next week, sixth grade field trip permission slips due, Arkham Care Brigade was collecting letters for injured servicemen, the cast list for the school play would be posted after lunch.

There followed a pause, another click, and a brief scratchy hiss. Then the speakers jingled out a bouncy tune and a chorus of perky singers:

> *What do you do when the sirens sound?*
> *And the sky goes strange for miles around?*
> *Well the first thing you do is to hit the ground!*
> *You DUCK (do-dee-do) and COVER*
> *Just DUCK (do-dee-do) and COVER*
> *What if there's a color from out of space?*
> *And cyclopean horrors all over the place?*
> *Well better make sure that you hide your face!*
> *Just DUCK (do-dee-do) and COVER*
> *Yes DUCK (do-dee-do) and COVER*
> *(do-dah!)*

The song finished with a brassy flourish and cymbal clash. The alarm whooped a shrill triple-blast.

The children, on cue, in a flurry of motion, pushed back their chairs, scooted beneath their desks, squeezed their eyes shut, tucked their foreheads down by their knees, and laced their fingers at the napes of their necks.

Miss Chambers walked among the rows, checking, nodding, and making occasional corrections. "Head lower, Marcie. Billy, your left foot's sticking out. Mary-Lou, are you chewing gum? That had better not be a comicbook, Charlie."

Mary-Lou was able to get rid of the evidence with a guilty gulp, but Charlie did not have that option.

"It's Professor Patriot, though!"

She tapped her foot, snapped her fingers, and reached down.

"Awwww…" He snaked up his arm to hand over the comic.

"Thank you," said Miss Chambers crisply. She rolled it into a tube and proceeded toward the rear of the classroom, smacking the cylindrical roll of colored newsprint into her palm.

When the all-clear and then the lunch bell sounded, the orderliness broke into a genial chaos. Students scrambled out from under their desks, girls fussing at their clothes, boys jostling each other. They raced for the row of lunchboxes and brown bags on the shelf beside the door.

Moments later, the last echoing footsteps faded from the hall, and the room was quiet again.

Miss Chambers smiled, shook her head, put down the confiscated comic, and went about tidying up in preparation for the afternoon lessons. She straightened askew desks, pushed in chairs, erased the fractions from the blackboard, and listed a dozen new vocabulary words:

Squamous
Rugose
Cyclopean
Amorphous
Stygian
Unutterable
Loathsome
Tenebrous
Foetid
Ichor
Monolithic
Lambent

Satisfied with the state of the classroom, she sat down and slid open the drawer where she kept her own sack lunch. As she arranged the sandwich, carrot sticks, hard-boiled egg and oatmeal-raisin cookies, she noticed that Charlie's comicbook had relaxed into a mostly-unrolled curl.

Professor Patriot...

She smiled and shook her head again.

There he was on the cover, in a dramatic action pose, wielding a glowing yellow-white stick of chalk that reflected in the lenses of his hornrim glasses. Professor Patriot always managed to look both respectable and rumpled in his tweed jacket with the elbow patches, slacks, flag pin, and sneakers. His brown hair was short enough to not alarm anybody's parents, but tousled and unruly enough that the kids found it 'cool' as well as vaguely rock-and-roll. Young but not too young, old but not too old, he gave every impression of the dedicated teacher...but quirky, the kind that made learning fun.

Also on the cover were hideous half-reptilian/half-canine creatures, fanged and gaunt, boiling out of an unearthly rift in reality, raging as they came up short against a brilliant flare of light issuing from the equations Professor Patriot had etched in mid-air.

Bold comicbook lettering splashed jagged and excited across the page: WILL THE POWER OF EUCLIDIAN GEOMETRY DRIVE BACK THE HOUNDS OF TINDALOS???

She'd brought a paperback to read while she ate her lunch, but found herself leafing through the comic instead. It was silly, without a doubt. It made light of the everpresent threats under which they all now lived, turning horror into mockery. It was absurd and over-the-top in its heroics.

And yet...

Reading it somehow made her feel better. More hopeful, more in control, more confident that the world they knew and loved would survive this, would emerge stronger than ever.

That was the entire purpose. Like the daily drills, and the civil defense films put out by the Department of Eldritch Emergency Preparedness. Yesterday, it had been Big Sister Susie who had the problem...her best friend Ronette had fallen in with a Bad Crowd.

"Aw, come on, Susie, don't be a square! We're just going down to the lake to drink some beer and do the Dance of Dagon. *All* the cool kids will be there!"

Or like the jingles, which, yesterday had been about what to do if you found a suspicious tome of ancient evil sitting around:

Just don't LOOK
(do-dee-do, do-dee-do)
In the BOOK
(do-dee-do, do-dee-do)
JUUUUUUUSSSSST
DOOOOONNNNN'T
LOOK!!!
(dah-dah!)

So, they had their Fungus-Free Victory Gardens, and the Arkham Care Brigade delivering letters to the hospitals and asylums. They had cartoons in which various Warner Brothers characters carried out wacky hijinks against the Mythos Menace, and the MovieReel clips celebrating the brave scholars and scientists of this great nation's military fighting the good fight to protect the American way of life. They had comedy sketch shows like Miskatonic 6-5000 on television, and radio serial dramas like *The Rats in the Walls*.

And they had Professor Patriot. There was even a stage show that toured the country, with puppets, comedians, and an actor in a tweed jacket and hornrims. The chorus girls were the Patriettes, leggy beauties in short pleated skirts and tight tweed vests. The highlight of the performance was said to involve the Professor punching Cthulhu in the face.

The comic's last page was an advertisement in which the Professor rescued an innocent family, closed the Thirteen Gates, and saved the day, all because:

"Even evil cultists can't resist the wholesome fruity goodness of Mostest Snack Pies! Mmm, they're the Mmmostest!"

The back cover sported a mail-in offer to sign up for the Professor Patriot Fan Club, complete with certificate, flag-pin badge, Patrioteer membership card, and Omniglot Decoder Ring. The ring in the picture—an antiquarian sort of relic, corroded with verdigris—bore little resemblance to the plastic baubles she'd seen several students wearing to school.

Done with her lunch, Miss Chambers stepped outside for a breath of fresh air before venturing over to the teachers' lounge to get a cup of coffee.

She'd walked to school through another perfect Niceville morning of clear blue skies, warm sunshine, butterflies dancing above the flowerbeds, birds twittering in the trees. Now, the day had warmed and gone slightly muggy. The breeze had stilled. The cars motoring up and down Main Street, chrome glinting, fins gleaming, looked dreamlike and faraway in the haze.

In the lounge, the talk was of Senator McCarthy's latest committee findings, the relative merits of Oldsmobiles versus Buicks, the unfortunate Ladies' Garden Club incident regarding Mrs. Mallory's debut of her 'Sweet Yuggoth' orchid, Mr. Jenkins' new color television, and the subversive musical and literary influences of juvenile delinquents possibly creeping toward their very own town.

"Here?" Mr. Benson scoffed as he filled his pipe. "In Niceville?"

"Preposterous," said Mrs. Andrews, with the imperious declaratory tones worthy of the seniormost member of Ashton-Smith Elementary's faculty.

"I did hear that they caught a group of teenagers over in Fairview," Nurse Harper said. "Reading…reading *The King in Yellow.*"

Gasps arose, but Mrs. Andrews withered them all with her gaze. "Well, that is Fairview for you. Ever since they put in that roller-rink, what do you expect?"

Mr. Evans, the vice-principal, nodded. "Heard they were talking about having one of those drive-in movie theaters put in, too."

More gasps, and a round of tutting disapproval, greeted this. They moved on to a discussion of Niceville's own movie theater, the Paradise, which normally showed decent, family films like *Singin' in the Rain* and *Cinderella*. The latest poster in the 'Coming Soon' display case, however, was for Marlon Brando and James Dean in *The Thousand Young*.

Jill Chambers, sipping her coffee, listened and said nothing. Her status in the school hierarchy—newest, youngest, unmarried, pretty, a hometown girl who'd been in many of these very teachers' own classes not so long ago—didn't lend itself well to speaking out.

Besides, she'd been on dates to roller-rinks and drive-ins…she'd read part of The King in Yellow herself in college, though it had frightened her so badly she'd thrown the book away long before reaching Act II…and she might go see *The Thousand Young*, despite the leather jackets and sullen pouts that made both stars look like Bad Boys of the worst sort.

It wasn't as if she had her family's reputation to worry about, either. She was the only Chambers left in Niceville now. When her parents were mentioned, it was usually in tones of sidelong sympathy flavored with delicious hints of gossip, tragedy and scandal.

"You heard about Frank Chambers, of course," they'd say. "Poor Vera. It's no wonder she…" This would be accompanied by a significant, knowing lift of the eyebrows and a pantomime gesture of tilting a glass.

"All because of what happened to their son, you know."

"Surprising the daughter stayed, don't you think? Oh, she's a nice enough girl and all, but…"

Danny Chambers had been the ideal clean-cut all-American boy—good-looking, popular, athletic, class president as well as captain of the football team. Everyone adored and admired him. When he'd enlisted, it seemed like the whole town turned out to see him off at the train station, waving from the platform as he waved back from the window, on his way to San Diego.

Jill, who'd adored and admired him more than anyone, had even planned to join the Army Nurse Corps when she finished high school. She'd follow in his footsteps, do her part, serve her country, make them proud.

But then, Danny died in the South Pacific, along with all of his shipmates aboard the *USS Derleth* at the Battle of R'lyeh. Their father... well, they'd found him in the garage, the military notification telegram still in his hand, as if he'd figured no further note was needed.

After the funerals, their grief-stricken mother had gone to Des Moines to live with Aunt Rose, leaving Jill on her own.

She did have to admit it was lonely sometimes. The house, small though it was, often felt too big with just her in it. She'd given up on the nursing idea, becoming a teacher instead...and though she liked it, and was good at it, she still had the occasional pang of wondering what might have been, of feeling as if she'd taken the safe path rather than the right one.

From out on the playground came the distant trill of the recess monitor's whistle, signaling the students to gather up their jacks, jump ropes, basketballs and bubblegum cards. The faculty performed their own variation on this, rinsing cups, finishing crosswords, and stubbing out cigarettes.

The change in the weather sapped the sass out of even the most rambunctious of her students. They went through the Presidential Health-and-Fitness regime with limp dispiritedness, barely complained at all when Miss Chambers sprang a math quiz on them, and wrote listlessly in their journals without the usual giggling and whispering.

The afternoon dragged by, each tick of the clock more and more sluggish as the hands crept endlessly around.

The alarm whooped.

Miss Chambers, who'd been fanning herself—with what turned out to be Charlie's comic—nearly sprang out of her skin.

The familiar triple-blast was followed by a series of shriek-pause-shriek-pause siren wails that went on and on.

The students, startled but well-trained, obediently shoved back their chairs and ducked under their desks.

"We already *had* the drill," said one of the girls in an indignant fussbudget *that's-so-unfair!* tone.

"Heads down," Miss Chambers said, recovering herself as she got to her feet.

In the pauses between the shrieks, she heard protests from neighboring classrooms and annoyed outbursts from her fellow faculty. She was sure there'd be a good deal of discussion in the lounge about *this.*

Her own training took over with the comfort of routine, despite the ongoing sirens. She moved down the aisle between two rows of desks.

Another more distant but ear-splitting screech joined the din.

"Is that the town whistle?" someone shouted.

"That's the town whistle!" shouted someone else.

Anxiety rose in Miss Chambers' throat like bitter acid.

"The fire bell, too!" a third someone cried, and yes, there was a persistent jangling clangor adding to the cacophony.

Several of her students chimed in:

"What's wrong?"

"What is it?"

"I want to go home!"

"Make it stop!"

"Miss Chaaaaaaambers!"

"Stay where you are!" she barked, in her most authoritarian teacher-voice. "*Heads down!*"

The classroom door burst open and Tommy stumbled in, clutching the restroom pass. He lunged at her, tripped, fell to his knees, and grabbed her skirt.

"The sky!" he howled. Then he dove under his desk.

The other children screamed.

"Stay *put!*" Miss Chambers ordered.

She rushed to the nearest window, and immediately wished she hadn't.

The sky over Niceville was green.

A terrible, churning, bilious green...the western horizon choked with clouds that were not clouds but undulant, amorphous, spongelike masses...from which dropped a rain that was not rain but something else, some sort of writhing, dark specks...

Townspeople ran, frantic, in all directions. Cars sped down streets, tires screeching. They sideswiped mailboxes, hopped curbs, plowed headlong into storefronts or collided with each other in snarls of chrome and gleaming metal.

"The bunker! The basement! Hurry!" It sounded like Mr. Evans, the vice-principal, his voice a hectic urgency mixed with the maniacal laughter of impending insanity. "Get the students to the bunker!"

The school hall filled with a mad stampede of footsteps, voices raised in cries of fear, cries of pain.

Some of Miss Chambers' class began sliding out from under their desks but she knew if they went out there it'd be a packed mob of bodies, a throng, pushing and jostling. They'd be trampling each other in their panic. She raced to the door and banged it shut.

"Stay *put!*" she ordered again.

It halted their surge toward the exit, but they did not all return to their duck-and-cover positions. They gathered in the aisles, the girls clutching hands, the boys trying to act brave.

They'd propped the windows open in vain hopes of catching a sluggish breeze. Now a hard wind gusted. It stank of mold and spoiled coleslaw. The half-lowered blinds snapped and flapped, whipping about, some rattle-rolling back up. Papers blew everywhere.

The hideous green sky filtered the daylight to a swamp-sickly hue. The black, spongelike masses dipped lower, toward the buildings, shedding their weird rain of writhing specks. Closer now, they resembled burrs or jellyfish, something both prickly and tendriled. There was purpose in their descent, as if targeting in on anyone or anything that moved.

As Miss Chambers and her students stared in horror, one of the writhing things divebombed a fleeing man. Its myriad whip-thin tentacles lashed around his head and neck. He tried to yank it off, went into flailing, jerking spasms, and landed in a flowerbed amid a flurry of tattered petals…but, mercifully, blocked from view.

"Class Helpers, shut the windows!"

She hadn't known she was going to speak, but Mikey and Georgina were on it like a flash. They slammed and latched all the windows.

Aircraft swooped in from the northeast, fighter jets with engines roaring and machine guns firing in peppering staccato. All the boys cheered and some of the girls did too as the jets engaged the clouds-that-weren't-clouds in an aerial battle. The enemy fired back with some kind of organic javelins, long and twisted, glistening, tipped with barbed points.

The machine guns riddled the not-clouds, pierced and perforated them, blew off large irregular chunks that hailed down in a grisly shower of ichor and dark, spongy matter.

A helicopter appeared next, buzzing in low and heavy like a bumblebee. It was apparently heading for the Niceville Town Hall when the plummeting shredded mass of one of the not-clouds struck it with a wet, indescribable noise of rotors chugging and chopping and clogging. The helicopter veered out of control. A man either jumped or was hurled from it as it wobbled, wallowed, and plunged drunkenly toward the school.

"Get down!" Miss Chambers cried, seizing as many students as were within reach and pulling them to the floor.

DUCK (do-dee-do) and COVER jingled in her mind, perky and inane. It was drowned out seconds later by an enormous thudding crunch, the shrill shearing of metal, and the fiery thunder of an explosion. The building shook. A window broke, showering them with fragments.

Half-deafened, shaking glass from her hair, Miss Chambers raised her head and did a frantic count-check. Some of the children had sustained scratches, bumps and scrapes, but none of them were seriously hurt and she almost sobbed with relief.

The stink of mold and spoiled coleslaw was not improved by the smoke from burning fuel. They picked themselves up, coughing, waving at the thick and foetid air.

*Foetid…amorphous…ichor…*Miss Chambers wondered how many more of this week's vocabulary words they were going to need before this was done.

The helicopter had missed the school, leaving a scorched crater and a smoldering track as its mangled wreckage skidded to a stop just outside the front doors. Burning debris and bubbling clots of sludge littered the lawn. If anybody had still been in it when it hit, the fireball blaze was too bright to see.

"Hey, look!" Mikey pointed. "There, in Home-Safe Tree!"

Miss Chambers looked where he pointed. The name had been bestowed on the grand old oak long before her parents' time here; it was a landmark in its own right as well as being the centerpiece of many recess games, and a shady place to sit on sunny days when the teachers decided to take some of the lessons outside.

Now, a figure struggled amid the leafy branches. It was the man who'd jumped or been flung from the stricken helicopter. He seemed to be trying to clamber the rest of the way down, making a precarious job of it. Whether this was due to him being injured or just dazed was impossible to tell, but, even as they watched, he lost his grip, tumbled to the ground and collapsed.

Several of the children spoke:

"I see him!"

"Is it the pilot?"

"Is he dead?"

"He's not moving."

"He's dead."

"Maybe not!"

Charlie, who'd been staring out with a stunned expression, said, "It's Professor Patriot."

Eddie elbowed him. "Don't be a dumbo."

"It *is*! See the jacket?"

"Professor Patriot's not real," sneered Eddie. "He's a made-up thing for babies, like Superman, Mickey Mouse and Santa."

"You take that back, Eddie Parker!" Marcie faced him with imperious foreboding, arms crossed, jaw set, glowering with such wrath that Eddie, class bully and troublemaker though he was, cowed.

"Whoever he is," said Miss Chambers, "he needs help."

"I'll go!" Charlie said at once, starting for the broken window.

She caught him by the collar before he could climb out. "No. I'll get…"

…the principal, she'd been about to say, or one of the other male teachers, or Mr. Savinsky the janitor.

But the hall, previously packed, was empty when she opened the door.

The rest of them must have reached the basement survival bunker. They'd be huddled in there, adults doing their best to keep everyone calm, waiting for the all-clear, for the government radio announcement, or for rescue to arrive.

Another glance outside told her those might be a while. The aerial battle had shifted north, over Mr. Prescott's fields instead of the town, but Niceville remained awash under that turbulent green sky, downtown swarming with the monstrous burr-jellyfish creatures that writhed and flailed over Main Street's tidy shops.

Her mind wavered.

This wasn't supposed to be happening.

The final bell should have rung by now. She should have been walking home, skirt swishing demurely around her shins, looking forward to a quiet evening grading papers while *I Love Lucy* and *The Dark Door* were on.

An urge seized her to just go, just run for it, get to her little house—

But she couldn't abandon her students. And she couldn't just leave that man out there by Home-Safe Tree, whoever he was.

Danny wouldn't have done it.

"Wait here," she said.

She used a science workbook to brush away the glass, scrambled through the windowframe with no regard for teacherly dignity, and ran with both arms waving above her head like someone trying to fend off bats. It would do no good if one of those things divebombed her, she knew, but she did it anyway.

He certainly *dressed* like Professor Patriot, she noticed as she neared the groaning, stirring man. Charlie had been right about that.

Tweed jacket, slacks, sneakers...respectable but rumpled—though he *had* also just fallen from a crashing helicopter into a tree, which would rumple a person.

Closer yet, she had to admit the resemblance to the comicbook character was striking, even as battered as he was from the fall. All he lacked were the hornrims.

Miss Chambers knelt beside him. "Sir?"

He groaned again, mumbling something incomprehensible.

"Sir?" She grasped his shoulder, shook it, hesitated, and said, feeling not un-foolish, "Professor?"

His eyelids twitched open. The eyes beneath were also brown. He squinted up at her, clearly confused, if not stunned or concussed. "Hello?"

"Are you all right?"

"Ahhh...where am I?"

"Niceville—"

"Niceville!" He bolted to a sitting position, winced, and doubled over with a hiss of breath through his teeth, cradling his left arm to his ribs. "And you are...Miss—?"

"Chambers. Jill Chambers."

He touched his face, then groped about in the grass. "Miss Chambers, I don't suppose you see a pair of glasses anywhere?"

She found them. Hornrims. Of course. She saw that he even had a flag-pin in his lapel. Suddenly it made partial sense. The stage show, the stage show was playing up in State City.

"Thank you," he said when she gave them to him. He settled them into place and looked around. "That's better." When he looked again at her, the corner of his mouth tilted up in a half-smile and he added, "*Much* better."

Miss Chambers, caught off-guard, blushed and hoped her curls hadn't gone too frizzy from the humidity.

Yells from the direction of the school made her glance back, almost glad of the distraction. Her students were crammed against the windows, Charlie and Eddie both trying to lean out of the broken one. When she shifted her glance in the direction of their urgent gestures, a chill of horror, like some loathsome trickle of cold, gelid fluid, shivered the length of her spine. It was very effective in quashing her flustered reaction.

A cluster of the burr-things, floating somehow, propelling themselves by whipping their tendrils, advanced from downtown. Though they diverted and paused to examine various objects, their meandering course brought them slowly but steadily toward Home-Safe Tree.

The man, following her gaze, uttered something that sounded like, "Nyeeth," and shuddered. It summed up her own opinion of the creatures fairly well.

"We have to get indoors," Miss Chambers said. "Can you walk?"

"I…" He got most of the way to his feet, swayed, and grimaced.

"Here, let me help you." She put her arm around his waist.

"Miss Chambers—"

"I know, we've only just met, this is highly irregular…" She swept her free hand to encompass the scene. "But then, what of this isn't?"

"Good point." He leaned on her and together they made their awkward way at a quick hobble back to the building.

They detoured around the places where helicopter-chopped lumps of the spongy matter appeared to be slowly sinking in on themselves, deflating like ruined soufflés.

Youthful voices clamored:

"Hurry up, Miss Chambers, hurry!"

"The monsters are coming!"

"It's okay, everybody, Professor Patriot's here now! He'll save us!"

Miss Chambers cast an anxious look at the man. "Please play along. For the children's sake?"

"Play along?"

"They need something to believe in. They need hope. Please."

"Miss—"

Squeals in terrified unison came from most of the girls and some of the boys.

"Look out! Eeeeeee! Look out!"

One of the creatures swept toward them. Miss Chambers saw it all too well—the round body nothing but a cluster of chitinous pincers, flexing around tiny tooth-ringed orifices…the dozens of thin, scaled, pustule-covered tendrils lashing…the nightmarish noises it made, a sharp clicking and slithery rustling…

"Move, dumbo!" At the window, Eddie elbowed Charlie aside. He held a slingshot, and regardless of everything else, Miss Chambers noticed it was not the same one she'd confiscated from him only last week. That one's handle had been yellow; this one's was black.

He drew back, took aim, and let fly. Something whizzed through the air, passing not a foot over their heads. It scored a bullseye on the creature with a sharp crack that sounded strangely like the break-shot in a game of pool.

"Gotcha!" crowed Eddie. "Take that!"

Then they were at the window. Again, regularity and teacherly dignity were cast aside; she gave the man a boost by the seat of his pants as Mikey and Charlie pulled on his jacket, then hoisted herself up and through with such fear-inspired strength that they all ended up on the floor in a heap.

"Cover the window!" Miss Chambers said, panting for breath. "Desks…pile them on the art shelf…barricade…"

Four of the boys did as instructed, while Georgina and Peggy pulled down all the blinds. Gloom filled the classroom, tinged swampy-green at the edges.

"Will it hold?" Billy asked.

Mary-Lou shushed him.

Everyone waited, tense.

…*click*…

…*scrape*…

…*rustle*…

...*click-scraaaaaaaape*...

Silence.

"Is it gone?" Katie whispered.

"I think it went away," Charlie said.

"Yeah." Eddie lowered his slingshot. "Did you see? I beaned that ugly bastard with my aggie!"

Betty raised her hand. "Miss Chambers, Eddie said—"

"Never mind," said Miss Chambers, deciding that if teacherly dignity could go on hiatus, so could teacherly discipline. "That was a very good shot, Eddie. Thank you."

"Saved our lives, sport." The man in the hornrims heaved himself into a chair, favoring his left side. "Well done."

"What are they, Professor?" asked Charlie.

Miss Chambers cast him another anxious, pleading look.

"Nyeeth," he said again, in reply to Charlie. "They're called the Nyeeth. And you, son, you must be one of my loyal Patrioteers, am I right?"

"Yes, sir!" He proudly showed off his plastic Omniglot Decoder Ring.

"That's swell!" The man clapped Charlie on the back, making the boy beam, and raised his eyebrows at the others. "Anyone else?"

Several eager hands went up. The children pressed around him, all chattering at once, bombarding him with questions. Tommy, shyly, offered up a Mostest Snack Pie he'd traded for at lunch but had been saving for later. At that, the Professor laughed and told them he'd put them in for commendations.

"Patrioteers First Class, how does that sound?"

Their delighted smiles said it sounded great. Miss Chambers even found herself smiling at their excitement. How the day had gone from normal to horrific to *this*...

He really was good, this 'Professor.'

Not to mention handsome...

"I am very glad to meet you all," he said. "Right now, though, I think we need to get to someplace a little safer, don't you?"

Heads nodded in vigorous agreement.

"Miss Chambers? The school must have a bunker."

"In the basement," she said. "Though they'll have locked it, and closed the Seal, by now. They won't just open it until the all-clear, not without notification from the government, the Office of Civil Defense or the Department of—"

"Oh, absolutely," he said, brown eyes twinkling. "Nor would I expect them to, under normal circumstances. But, as you mentioned earlier, these aren't. Shall we?"

She studied him a moment, lips pursed. There *was* such a thing as *too* good, when it came to acting.

On the other hand, if they couldn't get into the bunker proper, the basement would be better shelter than a classroom with a broken window.

Miss Chambers clapped twice. "Line up, assembly order, please."

The students scurried into place, two lines, boys and girls, the Class Helpers at the front.

"One more thing, Miss Chambers?"

"Yes…Professor?"

He grinned disarmingly. "May I borrow a fresh stick of chalk?"

"I'll get it!" Charlie bounded to the supply cupboard.

"Are we ready?" Miss Chambers asked, standing by the door. "Good. Calmly, patiently, staying together."

Their little procession made its way into the hall, Miss Chambers at the lead and Professor Patriot bringing up the rear. Evidence of the earlier stampede was everywhere—posters half torn from the walls, wastepaper baskets overturned, the Academic Excellence trophy case cracked, dropped pencils, someone's lost shoe—and the only light came from the EMERGENCY EXIT signs. Here and there on the tiles were spots and smears of what she thought might be blood, hopefully nothing more serious than a bloody nose or scraped knee.

The south stairwell had never seemed creepier. Their steps were loud on the industrial-gray metal stairs, echoing hollowly back from painted cinderblock walls. A yellowish bulb in a wire cage sputtered high overhead.

At the bunker door, she stopped.

"It's locked," she said. "The Seal is closed."

As she'd known it would be…so, why did she feel such a crushing weight of disappointment?

She stood there with her palm laid flat on the thick steel, letting her head slump forward. A ragged sigh escaped her. They would have to make do in the basement storage area after all.

"Pardon me, Patrioteers. Excuse me, Miss Chambers, may I?"

Shrugging indifferently, she moved aside.

He took out a stick of the chalk and began swiftly etching numbers and symbols on the door. Equations. Algebraic and geometric equations...which weren't on the door, she realized, but suspended in the air before it...as the chalk-stick took on a strange lambent glow.

Lambent, another of this week's vocabulary words...

The Seal released, the lock unlocked, and he pulled the bunker door open on its immense hinge-pins.

Miss Chambers stared at the man in the tweed jacket and hornrims. "I thought you were an actor," she said.

He flashed her a quick grin and a wink as he tucked the chalk into his pocket and ushered the children inside. The next few minutes were something of an uproar of exclamations, outbursts, demands for explanations, and assorted confusion. He ignored it all, his attention on her students.

"You'll be safe here," he said. "Re-lock the door, re-close the Seal, and keep everyone calm until rescue arrives. I'm counting on you, Patrioteers."

"Yes, sir," they chorused. Even Eddie, who'd scoffed before, was convinced.

Charlie added, "But aren't you staying, Professor?"

"I can't right now." He gripped Charlie's shoulder and gave it a firm squeeze. "The Nyeeth are still out there, and I have work to do."

"Will we see you again?"

"Of course you will," he said. "And, Miss Chambers, it's been a privilege. You are a very brave, cool-headed and capable young woman. Your brother would be proud."

"How do you know about Danny?"

"I was at R'lyeh, too," he said, and a haunted look shadowed his eyes. "Oh, yes. I was at R'lyeh."

"I..." she began, but did not know what to say.

"They were heroes," he said, shaking off the haunted look. "They all were. So are you." The corner of his mouth slanted up again in that half-smile. "If you ever want a job as an Assistant Professor, look me up."

With that, he stepped out of the bunker. He saluted. The children saluted in return. The huge, heavy door began to swing shut.

The safe path...the right path...

"Professor!" Miss Chambers darted through the narrowing gap. "Wait! I'm going with you!"

And, together, off they went to save the town and their fellow Americans from the doom that had come to Niceville.

ROSE-COLORED GLASSES

BY MICHAEL G. SZYMANSKI

Billy Standish figured he must have the neatest job in the entire world. There sure wasn't much glamour in it, but as manager of the Sundown Drive-In he got to watch all the latest flicks every night during the summer, hang out in the snack bar as much as he wanted and, best of all, talk to all the cutest babes from school when they came in. And he was paid for it; almost $75 a week!

Sure, he had responsibilities but gosh, like his dad always said, that's why they called it work; if they called it play, you would be paying *them*! It was his task to open the snack bar each night to air out the swelter of the day, then fire up the fancy new air conditioner in Mr. Blodgett's office, because the Sundown's owner liked to have it crisp and cool in there whenever he came in. Beyond revving up the snack bar machines, that was pretty much all she wrote; well, that and accepting whatever deliveries showed up that day.

Mostly it was food stock and paper items plus the newest flicks that arrived every Friday from some wonderful far-off place where really cool things came from. He planned to go there someday, but for now he had to settle for running the double feature and dreaming.

Tonight would be a treat; it was "Fright Night", and Mr. Blodgett had booked two boss flicks, including *The Creature From Dimension X*, filmed in Pano-Rama and startling 3-D! A week-long agony had led to this moment, and it was with shaking hands that Billy applied his jackknife to the cardboard box which had accompanied the film canisters.

Inside were hundreds of 3-D glasses, banded together in bundles of 50. The blue and red cellophane lenses glowed in the fluorescent light of the snack bar, gleaming with the promise of worlds beyond imagining awaiting those brave enough to slip on a pair of those boss shades. How cool this would be, and Billy had a guaranteed front row seat for it!

He carried the glasses out to the ticket booth and stacked them on a shelf so Cindy Potillo would be ready to roll when she showed up for work that night. Cindy was a real doll; kind of kooky but never stuck up like most of the other popular girls. He would never admit that he had a crush on her but it was there, and it was a struggle to keep it under control whenever she was around.

He removed another bundle from the box and hesitated. There amidst the unpacked bundles lay a pair of completely different glasses. They were made of smooth, shiny plastic, the lenses nearly a quarter of an inch thick and both tinted a soft, rosy color. How they were supposed to work with 3-D was a mystery; one of the lenses had to be blue, he knew that much about the process. Maybe they were some kind of prototype, shipped to the Sundown by accident. Yeah, that must be it.

There was enough work on his plate to keep him busy till the movie started, so he filed the weird glasses in his shirt pocket for future examination and got back to it.

The first feature that night was a low-budget black-and-white flick that would satisfy the backseat bingo crowd until it was good and dark; then it was off to Dimension X! It was a good crowd, hipsters and their Sophies from three different high schools and a scattering of oldsters who'd come to actually watch the movies. Then there were the greasers; there were *always* greasers.

They were the troublemakers, the bane of Billy's existence. They were loud, rude and arrogant for no reason he could fathom, considering most had dropped out of school, didn't have a job and were responsible for most of the town's random acts of vandalism and petty crime. It fell to Billy to deal with these hoodlums; Mr. Blodgett would hide in his icebox office making excuses until Billy gave up and tried to do something about it himself. That usually got him laughed at and shoved around a lot, plus a couple of times he'd wound up with a bloody nose or a shiner that had given his mom a fit.

But he never backed down and always came back. This unwise stubbornness was eventually rewarded with the grudging respect of Joey Spadona, who everyone knew was the greasers' unofficial leader. Things rarely got out of hand, which pleased Mr. Blodgett because he wouldn't have to suffer the personal or professional embarrassment of having the cops show up at his place of business.

The first feature turned out to be kind of a snooze, so Billy pulled out the glasses for a better look. The stems felt rough against his fingers, and closer eyeballing revealed they were engraved with a line of weird symbols he'd never seen before. They looked like something out of one of those black magic flicks where a bunch of rejects call up some slimy demon to do their bidding and manage to screw it all up.

Those peepers were more than just a passion pit novelty, and it was a sure thing they were intended for more than viewing *The Creature from Dimension X*, but what? Only one way to find out; he slipped the glasses onto his head.

A flash of something washed through his brain and his eyes grew cold as though chilled by an arctic wind. Instinctively he moved to pull the glasses off, but the sensation abated before his fingers could reconnect with the plastic. That hadn't been too bad, but what had been done to him?

He focused on the movie screen; nothing there, the first feature wasn't in 3-D, but it now had a rosy glow to it thanks to the tinting of the lenses. Scanning the field of cars ranked in a gentle arc facing the screen revealed that the glasses did make things more visible in the gathering darkness. Cool, night vision glasses!

A figure passed the doorway in which he was standing, the motion drawing his eye. He froze, gripping the doorframe as a wave of sick fear coursed through his veins.

What he saw was a twisted combination of lizard and snake, a scaly, iridescently green creature that walked upright but in no other way bore resemblance to anything human. An abnormally long neck supported the overlarge head of some giant serpent who's forked tongue fluttered out to sample the night air as its yellow, ophidian eyes glared out on the world with cold cruelty and unutterably evil intent.

Stifling an outcry, Billy fell back into the storeroom behind him, yanking the glasses from his face. What was that, and what was it doing prowling around the Sundown in plain sight? Billy inched back to the doorway and took a cautious peek outside.

A figure was there, but it was only Mr. Harrington, who'd recently got a job as night janitor over at the nuclear power plant just outside town. A lot of people had been employed at the plant, and several new families had joined the community because of the place, so there were a lot of strangers around town these days, meaning more potential customers for the drive-in.

Mr. Harrington wasn't one of those; he'd been a resident for as long as Billy could remember. That was the thing about small towns;

everyone knew everyone and, it seemed, everyone ended up knowing everyone else's business.

Billy stepped back outside, keeping his eyes locked on the now plain old Mr. Harrington as he strolled to his car, popcorn in one hand, tube stake in the other. What could be more normal on a Friday night at the drive-in? Reluctantly he raised the glasses to his eyes.

The reptilian horror strolled unnoticed between the rows of parked cars, disappearing behind the fins of Tom Petri's Cadillac. It *had* to be some trick; had to be.

Billy swept his gaze around the lot, settling a moment later on Mr. Krupke, the high school principal, known to his students unaffectionately as Mr. Krupcake. Despite the glasses, he remained very Krupcake-like and entirely human, which came as a disappointment to Billy. So the glasses didn't turn *everyone* into lizards, but why just certain ones?

Next to fall under his enhanced vision was Mr. Hendricks, one of the newcomers. He was a lizard man. Billy continued his scan for the next twenty minutes, and by the time he'd had to switch reels he'd estimated that one out of every five of the Sundown's patrons that night were lizard people.

Billy's hands shook so badly he almost botched the switch. None of the patrons noticed anything, but it had been close. Were the glasses showing him the truth? Were these creatures real and living among them undetected? Where had they come from and, more importantly, what were they doing here?

He thought about all the people who weren't people he'd seen, struggling to find a shared connection, something they all had in common. Of course it was simple; they all worked at the nuclear plant.

If Billy hadn't been scared before, that realization put him over the top. If these things were truly as they appeared to be, then the plant and the town were in serious danger.

He knew he should tell someone but he couldn't think of who. Even with the evidence of the glasses he wasn't sure he'd be believed. Worse, the glasses might be taken from him and he would no longer be able to distinguish the real people from the lizards.

"Hey Clyde, what's with the shades?" The unexpected question threw an electrical jolt through Billy that made him jump nearly out of his socks. "If you're trying to be hip, you're still not making the scene."

By the time Billy recovered, Joey Spadona was strutting on towards the snack bar, a triumphant sneer on his mug. That sneer didn't last long, not after Billy dragged him into the storeroom by the collar of his jacket. By then his expression was purely murderous.

"You are *dead* Poindexter," the switchblade appeared in Joey's hand as if by magic, but Billy had better things to be afraid of.

"Kill me later," he said, thrusting the glasses at the outraged greaser. "After you take a look through these."

"I ain't puttin' on no lame shades, spaz, and get your dweeb hands off my threads."

"Put the glasses *on*, dammit!" Billy never swore; the fact that he had cut deep into Joey's anger, made him take notice of the fear in Billy's voice.

"All right, all *right*, just get off me!" He pushed Billy away as he plucked the glasses from his assailant's hand. "You don't have to flip out on me." He slipped the glasses on. "This better be good or you'll be eating a whole plate of knuckle sandwiches, and from what I'm seeing right now it's gonna be a double helping."

"Look at the people," Billy instructed. "Look at the *people*."

"Yeah, so what? I see a bunch of squares out on Friday night. It'll take a lot more... What the *hell*!"

Billy was relieved despite himself; he wasn't the only one who saw the lizards.

"You playing some kind of joke here, Poindexter?"

"No joke, Joey; it's the glasses. They make it so you can see the lizards. Question is..."

"Is it real?" Joey finished as he yanked off the glasses. "And if it is, what do we do about it?" Joey studied the glasses. "Why not drop a thin one and get on the horn to these people?"

He held out the glasses so that Billy could see what he'd previously missed: what looked like a telephone number etched into the inside of one of the stems, only visible if you held it to the light at just the right angle.

Billy thought about it. "We could use the phone in Mr. Blodgett's office; he left for the night about twenty minutes ago."

"Coolness. Let's go."

Billy did what little talking there was. "Won't catch me talking to The Man," Joey explained as he slouched into Mr. Blodgett's office chair. So Billy dialed, and waited.

Something was happening over the phone lines, but he wasn't sure what. A series of clicks, beeps and bursts of static poured into his ear in no pattern he could make sense of, culminating in a dead silence that made him suspect that the line had gone dead.

Then, into the silence: "Yes?"

"Uh, yeah... I got this pair of weird 3-D glasses, and when I put them on I see some really strange stuff."

"Like?"

"Well, like lizard people."

"Understood."

"What should I do?

"Nothing."

"But someone ought to..."

"Someone is being sent."

"Okay. I'm at..."

"We know where you are." There was a sharp click as the connection was broken.

"They said we should..." Billy began as he turned, only to find he was alone in the office. Rushing to the office door, he arrived in time to see Joey stalking toward the exit, slouching posture warning of trouble ahead. "Joey!" He hissed, uncomfortably aware of the patrons crowding the snack bar.

Joey of course ignored him, ducking through the doorway into the flickering gloom of the night. Billy scuttled after, catching up to the greaser just as he reached the door of the men's room.

"What are you doing? The guy on the phone said we should stay put."

"Forget him," Joey sneered. "I saw another one of them lizard guys go in here, and I'm thinking we should have a little chat."

"Are you *nuts*? Those things look dangerous, and they sure don't seem like the chatty type."

"I can be real persuasive. So cool it, or wait out here with the rest of the kiddies." Joey pushed into the restroom; after a brief moment's nervous hesitation Billy followed him in.

Not being the one wearing the glasses, all he saw as he slipped into the restroom was some guy at the sink splashing water on his face. He was a newcomer, Billy had seen him around town but didn't know his name. One thing he did know was that he'd moved into town because of his new job at the atomic plant.

Joey sauntered over to the next sink over and made a big show of combing his hair. "So, slick, you enjoyin' the show?"

The guy regarded the greaser a moment before nodding and pulling down another length of towel from the dispenser to dry his face. That done, he turned to leave, bearing down on the terrified Billy, who was frozen to the spot right in the doorway.

"Is that the kind of stuff you lizard guys watch at home, or do you even have movies?"

Billy would later recall the gist of what happened next, but the exact details eluded him. His one clear memory was of the man's face rippling, flesh sagging to accommodate a gaping mouth as it yawned wide, jaws distended far beyond human limitation. A forked tongue slithered from that maw as the lizard man whirled to face Joey. God alone knew what the greaser was seeing.

Joey only gave up a single step back before his usual belligerent attitude reasserted itself. "What's the matter, Daddy-O, cat got your forked tongue?"

The thing lunged, hissing its cold rage. The switchblade once more made its magical appearance in Joey's hand, arcing up in a lightning swing that embedded the blade to the hilt in the monster's ear, or ear hole, as it had now become.

A piercing squeal flooded the office as the lizard man vented its agony, malformed body spasming as the alien brain controlling it began to shut down. Billy clamped his hands over his own ears to shut out the sound, but just before the outcries were muffled he was certain he heard them answered from outside.

The creature fell to the floor, writhing in a disturbing, boneless manner as it pawed at its injury, it's cries choked to a thick gurgle by a stream of thick green bile oozing from its nose and mouth. With a final shudder it went rigid and still, ophidian eyes wide and fixed on infinity.

Joey, visibly shaken but struggling to cover it, bent to retrieve his knife, wiping the green gore off on the lizard man's shirt. "Uncool," was his only comment, most likely because he didn't trust his voice to any lengthy speech.

He needn't have worried. Billy ignored him, more concerned with the sounds he'd heard coming from outside the snack bar. Easing the restroom door open, he risked a cautious peek into the lot.

People were getting out of their cars; a lot of them, and all were converging on the snack bar.

"Joey, we got problems."

The greaser came to the door and checked out the view. "Whoa; they're all lizards."

"We can't stay here; we'll be trapped."

"We can take my chariot; she's packing a bent-eight that'll leave just about any other rod in the dust. We'll agitate the gravel before they can even get back to their own machines. Then we're home free."

"But they can see who we are. Won't they just hunt us down at home?"

"Cut the gas, will ya? First we get to the car, then we figure out the next step." Joey left no room for argument, bursting out of the restroom and laying tracks for his hot rod and leaving Billy with the choice of following or remaining to face a gang of lizard men on his own. He opted for the first choice.

The lizard men charged the moment Joey had taken off, and they were only steps behind Billy when the greaser fired up his glossy black hot rod and slammed it into reverse.

"Jump for it!" He shouted as he approached, forcing Billy to launch himself at the rod or be left behind. He landed face down in the passenger seat, struggling to get vertical as the car spun and lurched forward.

They were bearing down on the exit at almost forty miles an hour when Billy finally regained an upright position. Foster Road and safety were in sight when Joey suddenly pounded the brakes, skating the hot rod to a dusty halt.

"What are you doing?" Billy screamed. "They'll get to their cars and come after us!"

"Cool your jets, I'm thinking."

Billy wanted to comment that Joey had picked a fine time to start thinking, he really did. But just as his mouth opened to utter those potentially fatal words Joey arrived at a decision. Popping the clutch, he sent the rod down Foster Road at a pretty good clip, but not nearly as fast as the vehicle could have gone.

Billy was puzzled, and more than a little scared. The cars now pursuing them were gaining ground, though Joey didn't appear concerned. In fact, he seemed pretty satisfied with the situation. This was definitely not the way chase scenes played out in the movies, where the pursued actually made some attempt to get away.

He could just about read the license plate of the lead vehicle when Joey pulled up in front of Keller's service station out at the edge of town. The place was closed up and dark, Mr. Keller having left an hour before, most likely to pick up his family and take them to the drive in, as was his habit every Friday night in the summer.

While they were in front of the station they were also a long way from the pumps, so they couldn't have fueled up the rod even if the place had been open. Billy's curiosity finally got the upper hand.

"Why are you stopping here? They're gonna catch us."

"Less gab, more action, Poindexter. Follow me." Joey leapt from the rod and raced for the front office of the station. Alone and exposed, Bill elected to participate in whatever insane plan Joey had concocted.

The greaser paused briefly at one of the pumps to yank out the nozzle and toss it to the ground. A pool of odorous Hi-Test quickly formed and spread; Billy was forced to waste a few precious steps in a detour around the spill.

He caught up to Joey just as his leather-jacketed elbow smashed through a glass pane in the station's door, allowing him to reach in and trip the lock. He dove inside, Billy on his heels.

"We're gonna be caught in here for sure!" Billy protested, his sentiment emphasized by the slamming of multiple car doors out front.

"Only if we hang around, which we are not. C'mon."

Joey led Billy to the station's back door. No need to bust this one; it opened easily from the inside. Back out in the night, Joey turned right and slunk off around the side of the building, keeping low and taking advantage of the plentiful cover provided by the half dozen cars awaiting Mr. Keller's attention.

Crouched behind the front fender of a Studebaker, he whispered, "When I give you the go, beat feet to the rod. I'll be right behind you, so don't get in my way." Before Billy could ask any questions Joey hissed, "Okay, go!"

Billy ran for all he was worth. He caught a brief glimpse of a crowd of dark figures clustered around the station door, a few heads turning in his direction as he broke into the open. Joey's feet pounded out a frantic beat on the hard dry dirt behind, forcing him to focus on maintaining his forward momentum.

He reached the hot rod and vaulted into the seat, coming up in time to see Joey toss something over his shoulder. As it arced through the moonlight, Billy was able to identify the object: a cigarette lighter, and it was lit.

Billy had exactly enough time to realize what was about to happen before it did. As Joey leapt into the driver's seat the lighter touched down square in the center of the still-expanding gas pool.

There was a deathly silence as flame radiated out from the point of impact, followed by a soft concussive *whoosh* as the fumes ignited. Shortly after, the screams began.

Bearing not the remotest resemblance to human utterances, these outcries were high-pitched and piercing, the death knell of things that were unnatural and unwholesome. Then the pumps blew.

This was louder, more violent, and brighter, lighting up the country-side for two hundred feet around. Thankfully, the flames concealed the figures that had been trapped in and around the station. Oil cans, small tools and flaming debris peppered the road around them, though both the rod and its occupants somehow managed to avoid serious injury.

Joey fired up the rod and floored it, laying a patch away from the station. Billy figured the cops would be showing up soon and Joey didn't want to be making the scene when they showed up. To prove him wrong yet again, the gas storage tanks under the station blew.

A fireball of immense proportions erupted into existence, obliter-ating Keller's service station and everything near it, rolling over the road where the hot rod had been standing and melting the macadam to slag. The furnace heat of it slammed into Billy's face like a right cross, forcing him to turn away from the conflagration.

When next he risked another look back the receding fireball was ascending into the night sky, leaving behind a gaping, charred crater in the earth and very little else. As the fireball rose higher, the scene was consumed by gloom.

Joey took a roundabout route back to the other side of town, pulling up at the corner nearest the Sundown. "This is where you and I split up," he told Billy. "Nobody could've seen you in the dark but they sure got a good look at my machine, so it's a good bet The Man'll be after me real soon. You just go back in there, be cool, and you'll be out of it."

"What about you?" Billy asked as he climbed out of the car.

"I'm gonna fade. It was time I blew this burg anyway. I know a guy who'll give me a new paint job on the QT, and with a new set of plates I'll have it made in the shade."

"Well, okay then. But be careful."

Joey treated him to a lopsided grin. "Ain't I always? And hey, Poin-dexter? You're okay."

"Thanks Joey."

Joey revved his engine. "Well, it ain't like were getting married or anything." He floored the accelerator and, as Billy watched, faded swiftly away into the night.

There was a big investigation. Men in black suits who were not part of the local police force were seen all over town and at the nuclear plant for two weeks following that night. No one knew who they were, but they had absolute authority over the investigation. Billy was certain their appearance had a great deal to do with the phone call he'd placed from Mr. Blodgett's office.

A couple of those men even came to the Sundown, and for Billy the experience was more frightening than facing a dozen lizard men. They were taciturn, unsmiling men who observed the world through dark tinted sunglasses that never came off, even at night. A cold chill hit his spine when he realized that, aside from the colored lenses, those glasses looked exactly like the ones that had incited the entire nightmare.

Those rose-colored glasses had vanished into the night along with Joey Spadona, and Billy did not expect to see either of them again. For the moment, though, he had other things with which to occupy his mind.

They knew. Those men in black knew he'd been involved in everything that had happened, though they never brought it up, never even hinted at it. That made the torture all the worse.

Billy did indeed keep his cool and his silence for those two interminable weeks, and then the men in black were gone. Behind them they left the story of Communist saboteurs and a plot against the nuclear plant. Joey was painted as a kid who was in the wrong place at the wrong time and heard something he shouldn't have. In this version of the truth, Joey had been killed in the explosion at Keller's.

There were so many holes in that story you could have strained noodles with it, but only if you knew what had really happened, and Billy never spilled the beans, not even to Cindy Potillo, whom he later wooed and wed, nor to any of his four children, whom he considered his finest achievements.

He was wrong about one thing, though; he did see Joey Spadona again.

It was years later, and Bill was in Los Angeles living his Hollywood dream. The kids were at school and Cindy was shopping with friends, leaving him a quiet house in which to work on his next script.

The doorbell rang and Bill set aside his work, secretly grateful for the distraction. There was no one on the porch when he opened the door, just a small black case resting in the center of the welcome mat. He retrieved the case, eased it open and peered inside. He froze, instantly transported back to that nightmarish evening at the Sundown.

Inside the case rested a pair of rose-colored glasses. *The* pair of rose-colored glasses. How...?

An engine revved out on the street. A large black sedan hulked by the curb in front of his house, a vehicle almost identical to those driven by the mysterious men in black all those years ago. Almost the same.

Someone had worked on this car, customized it, souped it up. Bill's eyes found the driver, a black-suited figure sporting a black fedora and a pair of impenetrable black sunglasses. But unlike those other occasions, this time the figure reached up and removed the shades.

He looked older, but who didn't? There was wisdom in his eyes now, and experience was clearly written in the lines of his face. He didn't recognize him at first, but once that face brightened and shifted he found himself staring at the patented lopsided grin of Joey Spadona.

They never spoke a word but exchanged volumes. Together they forged a connection to another world, were alien beings walked amongst us to evil purposes, a world of men in black and strange 3-D glasses that offered glimpses of a horrifying reality.

It was Joey who broke the spell. Offering Bill an enthusiastic thumbs-up he gunned the engine, nearly popping a wheelie as he tore off down the street. Bill watched him go a second time, acutely aware of the case in his hand and those rose-colored glasses he knew he was destined to wear once again.

THE PRESERVED ONES

BY CHRISTOPHER M. GEESON

Day 44

I can hear it lurking outside again, the hideous screeching from its throat audible beyond the metal hatch. It knows Frank came from this shelter and it knows there are more of us.

Day 1

"It took God six days to create the Earth," I say. "It took us a matter of minutes to destroy it." Granted, events had been building up for some time, but most of us doubted anyone would actually press the button. "I can't believe we defeated fascism, only to destroy ourselves little more than a decade later."

"What do you mean—destroy ourselves?" Harve MacNeil says. In the dim lamplight, the shadows accentuate his sneer.

"You heard the siren; the explosions. What do you think I mean?"

"Sure," he says, puffing on a cigarette, "I heard the explosions from in here, *alive and well*, with four months' supply of food, water and a nice little generator."

"You think four months are enough?" I ask, smoothing my tie (we've got to have standards, even in here).

Harve laughs. "Course I do—and I'll bet the damned Soviets and Chinese ain't got shelters beneath every street." He smirks at his wife, Carol, who of course smiles back. "No sir, we'll have incinerated them—just like we did the Japs."

Up in their bunks, a few of the others laugh with him. Frank looks uncomfortable, though, and old Mrs. Henderson folds her arms. Carol continues to smile, as if her face is made of porcelain. Harve turns on the battery radio. Static, no matter which way he winds the button. His thick brow furrows over his small eyes.

"And we'll just crawl out of our cozy shelters in four months and pick up where we left off?" I ask. "Rebuild the American Dream all over again?"

"Sure we will, Doc," he says. I recognize that fanatical gleam in his eye, the one he had when he barred the shelter door before the black family from Number Twelve could join us.

Day 3

I'm already tired of canned pork and canned beans. "We should work together," I say, putting down the empty can, the fork leaning in it. "Make a meal on the stove instead of eating separately."

"Good idea," Ed Cassidy says. "The food will last longer." Dan Cassidy nods too. They're the kind of brothers you only see in movies—Ed is tall and dark with an Elvis quiff; Dan shorter, blond, like a boyish James Dean. It's like they're played by actors with no relation to one another, apart from their plaid shirts. "Dan's a pretty good cook," Ed says.

Harve MacNeil snorts at that and sits up. "This is turning into a goddamned commune."

"There's plenty of cold rubbery meat in those cans if you prefer," says Frank Finkelstein. "Or we can share resources. Think of it like the army canteen, *Colonel* MacNeil—I'm sure you can stomach that," he says with a smirk. Being a journalist, he has a way with words.

"All right, Finkelstein," Harve scowls, "if we're all gonna eat together, do you want ham or bacon with your eggs?"

"You know full well I don't eat pork."

"I know you're a goddamned communist!"

I'm still quick enough on my feet to insert myself between them before it gets violent. "It's alright Frank," I say. I turn to MacNeil. "You've had your say, Harve. Back off, please."

I wait for him to apologize to Frank, but no apology comes.

"I could cook us a nice stew." Mrs. Henderson breaks the silence. "A family recipe from the colonial days, tried and tested." Shuffling in her rocking chair, she turns to Mrs. O'Brien from Number Nine, who's lying on one of the bottom bunks. "You could help me, dear," she says with a sugary smile.

Mrs. O'Brien is smoking, her back to all of us, accentuating the curve of her hip.

"Now Marcy," Mrs. Henderson croons, "I know you're worried about Adam and the children, but I'm just *certain* they got to a shelter in time."

Mrs. O'Brien's shoulders quiver. "There aren't any shelters in the mountains."

Mrs. Henderson turns to me, eyebrows raised. "Tell her, Doctor Burroughs. Go on. *Please*."

I shrug, mumble something. I'm hardly the best choice to reassure anyone about a lost spouse. There was a time I was better at reassuring patients, but it's been a while. "Listen Marcy: the sirens came at around 4:30pm, yes? Well, Adam and the kids would've been up at dawn, out on the lake. By four, they would've had a full day's fishing. If I know Adam, he'd be thirsting for a cold beer by then."

Mrs. Henderson nods at me with encouragement.

"I could sure do with a beer," says Harve. He turns and stares at his wife. "Did you hear me?"

Carol trudges over to the small icebox—though it's probably not cold any more.

"So," I continue, "I'd be amazed if they didn't all get into your Plymouth Savoy and head for the store at Devil's View. That'd put them near a shelter at the precise moment."

"By Jove, the Doctor's right," Mrs. Henderson declares.

Marcy turns over. Tears have made her makeup run, but she looks younger than her years; still beautiful. "Thank you, Doctor," she says, stubbing out her cigarette. "That'll be what happened. Yes." She nods over and over, deluding herself.

"There," Mrs. Henderson says. "Now let's agree on a menu for the rest of the week. Everything's going to be just fine."

Day 43

I didn't sleep last night and I shan't tonight either. Even though he died yesterday, I can still hear Frank's terrible screams as he hammered on the outer hatch. "My God! There's something out here!" With a dreadful rending noise, his screams were silenced, but not until he yelled one more thing: "You're all trapped in there!"

Day 15

I never thought I'd say this, but I feel like we're safe down here, despite the deep rumbles outside. Sure, there are times this prefab shelter feels like a sealed can—when the re-circulated air gets stifling with the generator on, the stove cooking and only flushing the lavatory once a day to preserve water—but the air filter takes a quick gulp from outside, removes the radioactive particles and we're back in business.

I didn't like him one bit, but thank God President McCarthy was paranoid enough to build shelters on every street corner in all the nice areas. This place is starting to feel like home. The meal idea has taken off; we've stacked crates for a table between two bunks and we've even got a red and white checkered tablecloth that old Mrs. Henderson brought in the panic.

My skills—and the supplies I packed—are in demand, whether it's treating one of Marcy's headaches, Harve's old war wound, or reminding Mrs. Henderson to take her pills.

The Cassidy boys entertain us every night with a singsong—Elvis or Bill Haley—and the Glenvilles from Number Three are all musical. Clara, their nineteen-year-old daughter, brought her guitar, and their younger son, Paul, struts around like he's Elvis. Say, I wonder if Elvis is in a shelter someplace?

Finkelstein is a great storyteller, the sort of fellow who's swell with young kids. The Burtons from Number Twelve had two girls and two boys, until Harve shut them out. "There's a colored shelter downtown," Harve said. "I ain't sharing with any of their kind." And God forgive me, I helped him.

Day 16

I can't sleep. My wife's dead face, pale and serene, drifts into my mind. Her eyes snap open, accusing, as her body wracks with pain. She speaks, her voice wet with fluid: "*Let me die again.*"

Day 27

We finally got something on the radio. First, just an eerie buzzing noise, like a swarm of insects, but with a little tuning we found a broadcast repeating continuously:

"This is President McCarthy. I said I'd find a way to beat the communists and I have."

Frank sags against the wall when he hears that. No doubt he was hoping, like I was, that McCarthy hadn't survived; that his crazy rise to power had finally ended. Frank says nothing. We all have our little secrets.

The President's voice is a droning monotone—tired, weighed down by all that's happened, I guess: "The Soviets and the Chinese have surrendered. We are victorious. But I urge all citizens to stay in their shelters." Something about the message bothers me. "You are quite safe," he continues. "When the time is right you will hear the all-clear siren. God bless you all and God bless America."

Harve MacNeil holsters the pistol he's been cleaning and turns off the radio. "We should have ourselves a celebration tonight." He winks at Carol. "You know what'd make this day even more perfect?" Harve grabs her arm and takes her off to a bunk, where—hidden under the covers—he takes advantage of the only privacy they can get.

The rest of us gather around the Cassidy boys and sing *Rock Around the Clock*, trying to ignore what MacNeil is doing to his wife. Ed Cassidy can do a pretty good Bill Haley impersonation but it's not perfect. We're on the second chorus when I realize what's bothering me about the radio message: it sounds like President McCarthy but it's not perfect.

Day 38

I wake up in the middle of the night, heart pounding, breathless, my face only a foot or so from the cold ceiling. Another horrid dream about the Burtons from Number Twelve. I see their four children as Harve and I shut them out; hear them pounding on the outer hatch as we seal the inner door. I've been telling myself they made it to the segregated shelter downtown, but there aren't nearly enough places for every black family. There was a time when I tried to stop death—really tried.

I lie in the dark, taking deep breaths. A distant rumble vibrates the walls.

Harve doesn't seem to have nightmares—I'll bet he didn't lose sleep over what he did in Korea either. But every time I drift, my thoughts dwell on death. And now we've shut out Mrs. Henderson.

I'm just drifting again when I hear a gentle footfall below, across the aisle between the bunks and then a faint rustle of covers. I've been expecting that young hormones won't be able to contain themselves. One of the Cassidy boys, I reckon, with Clara Glenville, or perhaps even Marcy O'Brien. I inch towards the edge of my bunk and peer over, until my eyes adjust to the darkness. Well, I was nearly right.

Day 37

I stare at the dial; close my eyes; open them again. I cannot deny the evidence. Despite our miracles of technology, something has gone wrong. The human race created bombs to wipe out our fellow man, but we couldn't make a batch of air filtration units and guarantee that one of them won't be faulty.

I break the news at dinner, interrupting Ed Cassidy and Harve as they argue about whether John Wayne or Randolph Scott cowboy films are better. Personally, I don't think either has made a film as good as *High Noon*. And now, they probably never will.

"The shelter can no longer support this many people," I say.

They all look at me, as if I can save them.

"What do you mean?" Marcy cries. She points to the rack of unused bunks. "It's designed to support twice as many—the Burtons, Adam—" she breaks down before she can add her children to the list.

"It's not working properly. It's going to get hotter and harder to breathe. Unless somebody leaves the shelter," I say, "we'll all die from lack of oxygen."

Everyone is silent. MacNeil's fingertips brush against his holstered pistol.

"Then we have to decide who," says Frank, dropping his fork into the chicken stew Mrs. Henderson made.

"How?" asks Carol. "Draw lots?"

"You keep out of this," Harve tells his wife. "It's a decision for the men."

"Baloney!" says Frank. "Everyone should have a say."

The Cassidys and Mr Glenville agree with Frank.

"What about you, Doc?" Harve asks with a glare.

The women look at me. For a moment I see my wife's face instead of Marcy's.

"I agree with them," I say. "Everyone gets a vote."

"Jesus Christ," says Harve. "A real bunch of commies, aren't we? McCarthy should've weeded out our neighborhood first."

"MacNeil, you're an idiot," says Frank.

Before another argument can erupt, Ed says, "So, how do we decide?"

Old Mrs. Henderson stands. "No need," she says. "I'll go."

"What? Harve asks. I don't suppose he's ever seen a willing sacrifice before.

Mrs. Henderson looks down her nose at him. "Yes Mr MacNeil, I'm a woman and I can make a decision all by myself," she says. "Unless *you'd* like to volunteer, I suggest you keep quiet."

Harve folds his arms.

"Fine," says Mrs. Henderson. "Well, I'm the eldest here, by about thirty years; I've no family; I'm losing my memory and I only just survived cancer two years ago. I'm the obvious choice."

"And you've got more guts than anyone," says Frank.

She smiles. "Well, don't let that stew go cold."

Slowly, we see her to the hatch. She walks more upright than she has in years. We mutter our goodbyes, guilt weighing on all of us. She refuses any offers of food or warm clothes. "You'll be needing those," she tells us. I wind up being the one who seals the inner door; I operate the outer hatch from in here, knowing that she'll die out there to save the rest of us. And there's nothing I can do to bring her back.

Day 39

The ground rumbles again. Half-asleep, I imagine myself in the good old days, when Pa's generation was blasting in the mountains ten miles from town, mining and quarrying. Riding the streets on my bicycle, I'd duck, pretending I was a Confederate cavalryman dodging cannonballs at Gettysburg.

But now the rumbles get louder; the concrete walls shake; tins of food tumble from the shelves. We've never had earthquakes before, and I think we can rule out mining blasts. Bombs? But the President said the communists surrendered. So what is going on out there?

Day 42

Mrs. Henderson's death isn't enough. The needle on the air unit dial rose for a few days then sank back down. So we're all gathered again, struggling to breathe, fighting off headaches as we work out who else is going to die. This time there are no volunteers.

Harve lights a cigarette. "I fought at D-Day and Inchon in Korea. I'm a survivor and a hunter. When all this is over, the rest of you'll need me." He leans back so we can see the pistol on his belt—the only gun in the shelter. "It can't be me," he says, "or my wife."

For the first time, Carol looks glad to be with him.

"Well," says Dan Cassidy, glancing at his brother, "it was Mrs. Henderson last time. Her reasons made sense. Who's the oldest now?"

"We can't just get rid of the oldest!" Frank says. "We need to think about what skills we're going to need."

"I'm an engineer," butts in Glenville, "I'll be building bridges, repairing water pipes—there'll be a whole heap of things to do. My wife's a teacher. And whatever we decide about age, we can't be killing the kids first." He puts his arms around Clara and Paul.

"Well, Finkelstein," says Harve, smirking at Frank, "you're a journalist. Do we need your skills?"

The Cassidys laugh.

Frank glares at them, clasps his hands together. "As a matter of fact, you do. First, I'm an Editor, not a journalist—so that makes me a leader and a thinker. We'll need good leaders. And we need to preserve language and knowledge—I think I've got a better handle on those than any of you."

"What about Doctor Burroughs?" asks Marcy. "He's got those skills. *And* he's a Doctor."

Frank sighs. "Well if you want to look at who's the eldest, I believe the Doc beats me there."

"You just said we shouldn't go by age. Besides," I say with a smile to Marcy, "I *am* a Doctor."

"That settles it," says Harve, drawing his pistol and moving towards Frank. The Cassidys move to back up Harve. Glenville moves in from the side to block Frank. Just like High Noon, where the cowardly townsfolk turn against Gary Cooper, rather than standing up to the real enemy.

Frank backs away, shaking his head. "I didn't want to have to say this, but…"

"But what?" says Glenville.

Frank looks at me apologetically. "The Doc isn't what he seems to be."

A shot of fear courses down into my stomach. Everyone looks at me. I smile, trying to look innocent, but I fear what's coming. I take off my tie, finding it hard to breathe.

"The Doc was struck off eight years ago," Frank says. "The hospital tried to hush it up, but I heard things—awful things."

Suddenly it's me—not Frank—who feels the trap closing in. Harve's gun is on me now.

Frank gulps. "After the Doc's wife died, he tried to bring her back."

I close my eyes.

"Who wouldn't?" asks Marcy.

"He tried to bring her back *from the dead*," says Frank. "Tried to reanimate her corpse by injecting it with chemicals, after reading about some crackpot in Arkham who did the same thing, half a century ago. Does that sound like the actions of a sane man to you? Would you trust him with your lives?" He turns to the Glenvilles: "With the lives of your children?" Like I said, he has a way with words.

The verdict is as damning as it was at the hospital. They surround me. It's a matter of survival now and there's only one course of action left. I laugh. "Is that the best you can come up with, Frank? Jesus Christ, did you get that from *Weird Tales*? What a load of baloney!" I can tell I've already won Marcy back and Harve might be dumb, but he doesn't go in for anything that stretches his imagination. "You wanna hear another one? Finkelstein's paper was accused by McCarthy. Looked to be in deep trouble for a while there, didn't you, Frank?"

Harve points his gun at Frank. "I was right all along." Pure hatred erupts over Harve's face. "All this time, a goddamned commie living among us."

The Cassidys grab Frank and drag him to the hatch.

"You're making a mistake!" Frank wails, wrestling in their grasp. "It's all lies!"

Glenville operates the inner door. The Cassidys shove Frank; he twists, trying to force his way back in. Harve fires. The crack of the shot echoes around the shelter. Frank staggers, blood welling from his leg, but still he doesn't give up. He shoves the Cassidys aside and he's halfway back in before I slam my fist into his jaw. Frank reels and I shoulder the door shut. Pushing past the stunned Glenville, I take the controls of the outer hatch and seal Frank's fate. Harve grinds his cigarette end beneath his shoe.

We sit in silence. I wonder if any of them think there's a grain of truth in what Frank said. A grain? It was a sack-full of truth and there's no denying it. But even Frank didn't know the full story.

And then he's back, hammering on the outer hatch. "My God!" he screams. "There's something out here."

Harve leaps up, pistol drawn. The Cassidys gather behind him. Glenville holds his wife and daughter, their faces buried in his shirt-front. I close my eyes and pray it will be over quickly.

"You're all trapped in there!" Frank cries. He thuds against the steel hatch. There's a raucous squalling, as if a monstrous bird is flapping around him. With a dreadful rending noise, his screams are silenced.

Day 46

None of us mention the creature outside, as if by ignoring it, it will cease to exist. Frank's death brought us a temporary respite, but the air unit is still failing. And so, the process begins again, each justifying their usefulness to the rest of the group. Harve MacNeil presides over us, pistol within reach. The Cassidy boys tell how their childhood on a farm will be useful when we grow crops in the future. Glenville still counts on the fact we won't break up his family.

"I've got a family too," says Marcy, smoking, "and my husband's a scientist. We'll all be together again."

"Don't count on it," says Harve with a snort.

"Tell him, Doctor Burroughs," she says. "Remind him what you said about them going to the store at Devil's View."

It was all baloney, I want to say, but I don't think I can break that little heart of hers. She's too much like my wife. "Adam and the kids are in a bunker up there, alive and well," I say. "Don't let anyone tell you different."

My reasons for remaining must be looking shaky. Even if I've convinced the others Frank's story was wrong, there's still the fact I was struck off eight years ago.

"That leaves you then, Doc," Harve says, cigarette between his teeth. "What've you got to say this time?"

"You need a Doctor more than you need a couple of farmers."

Ed and Dan don't like that, of course.

Harve butts in: "You reckon, Doc? Cause all we really need is your medicines."

The Cassidys and the Glenvilles chirp in agreement.

This is it then. Either I go, or it's time for another secret. "What it comes down to, Harve," I say, "is this: do you really want to share this cozy little shelter with a pair of homosexuals?"

Harve's eyes narrow. "What do you mean?"

I point at the Cassidys. I don't want to do it, but it's them or me. "Look at their faces. They're no more like brothers than you and me, Harve."

"Why, you goddamn liar!" says Dan.

Harve's gun is already hovering in their direction.

"What are you talking about?" Ed blurts.

"I'm talking about one night last week," I say, "when you crept across the aisle into Dan's bunk. I saw the whole thing. Don't tell me *that* was brotherly love."

Ed goes as pale as a corpse. Dan looks to him, panic darting across his face.

"Three years you've been living on our street," I say, "and not once have either of you brought a girl back."

"Jesus Christ," Harve barks, pointing the gun at Ed's head. "Get the hell out of here—now!"

Ed and Dan back up to the hatch, then—darting forward—they jump Harve. The pistol goes off; with a strangled cry, Dan sinks to the floor. Ed kneels beside him, cradling Dan's head as blood wells from his neck. I open the inner door.

"Get out," Harve spits.

Ed drags Dan through. As I seal the door, Ed glares at me, anger and sorrow etched onto every crease of his face. Don't get me wrong, I've nothing against their type. It's just that I've seen death and I intend to avoid mine for as long as I can. Whatever it takes. I operate the controls for the outer hatch. Ed's screams are immediate, desperate and primal. There's a cacophony of leathery flapping; the sounds of flesh being shredded. Whatever is outside, there's more than one of them.

Day 47

I wake early as the shelter vibrates again. Even though we're not talking about it, we must all be asking ourselves what is going on out there: the strange creatures that sound like a flock of gigantic flesh-hungry bats; the subterranean rumbles. What has happened to the world while we've been underground?

"Dammit," Harve mumbles.

Leaning over the edge of my bunk, I peer down in the darkness. There's enough room now for me to have a bottom bunk, but I feel a little safer up here.

"You got anything to put us back to sleep, Doctor Burroughs?" Marcy asks.

"Sorry," I say, though I reckon I could put them all to sleep. For a very long time. Marcy last, of course.

I swing my legs over the side and clamber down the ladder. At the bottom, I step into my shoes and sit on the empty bunk to fasten the laces. "I'll make us some breakfast," I say. Putting my jacket on—over the clothes I've slept in for the past week—I head for the cooking area and turn on the lamp. The food we brought with us is almost half-gone. Some of our suppers have been a little extravagant. Squeezing the tin opener into a large can of beans, I begin to peel back the lid.

There's a deep thump, like someone banging on the outer hatch. A screeching sound—as of metal being cut by an industrial machine—sears through the shelter.

Harve dashes out of bed. "What the hell?" he cries. I've never seen him afraid before. I imagine him like this in Korea; his animal instinct breaking down his façade. Leaving the half-opened can of beans, I walk in a daze towards the inner door. An empty clunk sounds from right outside, as if—against all possibility—the outer hatch has fallen off.

"What was that?" Marcy says, wide-eyed.

Before I can answer, the buzzing restarts and a great pointed blade pierces through the inner door, cutting a vertical line downwards. The Glenville kids' screams have barely echoed around the chamber when the inner hatch curls back, as if it's no thicker than the lid on the can of beans. White dust swirls into the shelter, followed by the hideous squawking and leathery flapping of the creatures. Like eight-foot bats, they swarm in, with hooked claws and pronged beaks. One swoops on Harve's wife, pierces her and fastens its dark maw around her neck, making a nauseous sucking sound. Harve shoots; the thing flies off, releasing Carol. She drops to the floor, drained of color. Extreme blood loss.

A bat-creature swoops towards me. I turn, grab Clara Glenville's arm and swing her into its path. The creature thrusts her to the floor, beak clamped to her neck. Her little brother rushes at the creature; its claw whips out, slashing the boy's throat. As more creatures descend on the adult Glenvilles, I rush to the hole where the hatch used to be. Marcy joins me; we almost collide with Harve who lunges for the opening too. Elbowing me against the doorway, he forces his way through. I yell as the serrated metal gouges a line into my back. Stumbling, I race to catch up with Harve, as he scurries up the steps outside. With a screech, a bat-creature descends on him; Harve brings up his pistol and fires. Twisting in the air, the thing plunges into the white dust on the ground.

"Good shooting, Harve!"

He turns and looks at Marcy and I, as if deciding whether to shoot us too.

"Let's get away from here," I say, and then we're running down our street, kicking up a white mist. Behind, agonized screams burst from the shelter. Destroyed houses flash by as we run, their roofs caved in. Only a few partial walls stand, bearing gaping holes where the windows have melted. A line of black ash marks where Mrs. Henderson's picket fence was; the crumpled hulk of Harve's Chrysler Saratoga waits uselessly. I pass Harve, who seems more upset about the automobile than about his wife. On the corner, my house is a flattened wreck; one plantation-style pillar emerges as a reminder of the porch.

"Doctor!" Marcy shouts. "Don't stop!" She pulls at my arm. I take a deep breath and break into a jog again. Glancing back, I see Harve speeding to catch up.

"Wait for me, goddammit!" he shouts.

"Maple Drive," Marcy gasps. "There's another shelter here."

I hurry down the street with her, expecting one of the bat-creatures to bear down on us at any moment. If we can get to the end of Maple Drive, the folks holed up there might let us in. A picture of the Burtons flashes into my head for a moment; I hope the folks in Maple Drive prove to be more neighborly than we were. We dash past more flattened houses and skeletal, burned-out automobiles, until we reach the shelter.

Marcy collapses against me. "My God, it's horrible," she sobs.

The Maple Drive shelter is like ours, hatch ripped open by a metal cutter. In the debris and dust lies a femur. Tassels of gnawed flesh cling to it. A tremor shakes the ground. Hearing a distant screech from a bat creature, we set off again.

Near the next shelter we duck behind a collapsed wall, as two of the winged fiends suckle on the blood of an occupant. When the beasts go inside the bunker, we dash around the next corner and into the remains of a food store. We huddle inside, shaken and restless. Marcy shares a cigarette with Harve. Tearing a strip off my shirt, I bandage the deep cut in my back.

"Jesus Christ," Harve mutters, surveying the ashen mess of the store.

"It doesn't make sense," Marcy cries. "All those people survived the bombs, only to be killed by those creatures."

"I'm afraid it makes a warped kind of sense to me," I reply, tying up the bandage. "People are nothing more than preserved food for those creatures—like meat in a tin."

"What are you saying?" Marcy asks. "What are these creatures?"

As my wife's condition deteriorated month by month, I became fascinated with the ghoulish descriptions of those reanimation experiments in Arkham. And from there, my research led to other dark, unsavory works—the journals of mad cultists, some would say. But together, the connections in these works painted a hideous picture of life beyond our planet and beyond our understanding.

"They're from another world," I say, "that much is obvious. I think they've found a new home here and a ready supply of food."

"This is *our* planet," Harve growls. "The President built these shelters for *us*, so we could emerge into a new world without the damned communists."

"You still believe that?" I ask. It takes effort not to laugh—it's a new world alright.

Running his hands through his hair, Harve turns away. I wince as I put my jacket back on.

"Adam and the children are trapped," Marcy says, finishing the cigarette. "I've got to find them."

My little lie has come back to haunt me. "It's ten miles away," I say. "Uphill all the way. With those creatures circling—"

"You said yourself they'd be in the shelter at Devil's View," she snaps. "If I can find them, they're sure to let me in. Maybe these creatures aren't there yet. It's got to be safer than here."

After nightfall, we make for the edge of town, Marcy and I holding each other, Harve scouting a few yards ahead with his pistol. Patrols of the creatures fly overhead. If there are this many in every American town and city, there must be millions of them. Most of the shelters we pass have been opened, but some remain sealed. With the threat of the beasts, I daren't risk hammering on a shelter hatch, even if I thought anyone would believe our warnings. "Sorry folks," I mutter, "you're on your own."

Day 49

We trudge upwards, the town behind us. Progress is slow; less than five miles a day, by my reckoning. Harve is enjoying this, I'm sure, proving that he's a survivor and we need his skills. Apart from the tremors which shake the ground, the world is dead. There are no birds singing in the forested slopes around us; Harve might be a hunter, but there's nothing to hunt; nothing to eat.

The white dust we kick up leaves us gasping for breath. Marcy and Harve are both out of cigarettes. We've all got headaches and I'm certain that even if I had my medical supplies, I wouldn't be able to cure us. We had to drink the water, we were so thirsty. Marcy was dreadfully sick earlier and I'm barely holding it together.

Another rumble shakes the ground. Marcy falls to her knees.

"Hey, MacNeil!" I call, "wait for us."

He scowls, but stands there, watching the swaying trees and the skies above.

"Come on," I tell Marcy, "We can reach Devil's View by nightfall." I make the mistake of looking back: from this height, we can see for miles. A burned, gray wasteland, empty highways, flattened towns.

As dusk approaches, we round a bend in the road; five bat-creatures rocket towards us.

"Run!" I yell to Marcy, stooping as I charge for the trees. Harve fires, three shots in succession, attracting the attention of three of the beasts, though he doesn't seem to have hit any. Marcy runs behind me, but the other two creatures swoop quickly, healthier than us and not wearied by a two-day uphill trudge. She cries out as a creature lands on her. I turn and in a blur, the other one is on me, wrestling me to the ground, enveloping me in its leathery wings. If that beak gets around one of my arteries, it'll drain my blood in seconds. I kick and punch at the thick wings, but it holds me tighter and tighter. My breath comes in gasps. Images of my wife flash into my head: alive and smiling; dead and cold; resurrected, twisting in anguish.

An eerie voice brings me back to the present: a buzzing, static-filled voice, as if from a badly-tuned radio. The bat-creature releases its deadly grip, leaving me splayed on the ground, with a full view of where the sound has come from.

I have never seen anything so horrific in my life. A man-sized creature hovers over us, even more terrifying than the bat-beasts. It has a long insect-like abdomen of many sections, ending in a barbed tail that twitches near me. From its pinkish body sprout wide membranous wings and numerous pairs of clawed arms. Its head is a mass of quivering antenna as it addresses our captors in its strange language.

The bat-beast drags me to the road, where Marcy is held by another one. The other three surround Harve, who rolls on the ground, screaming. His severed arm lies a yard away, still holding the pistol, ripped off by one of the creatures. I rush to him, tearing off a strip of his shirt to bandage the stump. None of the creatures interfere. On the contrary, the hideous insect-like leader seems fascinated by what I'm doing. I think about plucking the pistol from Harve's severed arm, but daren't risk it with the creatures hovering around me.

The insect-monstrosity gives more orders and we're hustled up the road, the light dimming around us. The hairs on my neck prickle, as I wonder what horrid fate awaits us. Harve staggers, muttering curses, as one of the bat-beasts gorges on his severed arm, like a kid with a chicken drumstick. There's no sign of the pistol. I reach out to Marcy; she yelps.

"Relax," I tell her.

"Relax? Are you insane?"

"For the moment they want us alive," I say. "That's the best situation we've had for a long time. Even our fellow humans weren't that generous."

"You'll do anything to stay alive, won't you?" She laughs; it has a hysterical edge to it, but I know she's right.

Day 49: Devil's View

We reach an area of level ground nestling between the wooded ridges of Devil's View. Three massive cubes stand in the clearing, each about twenty feet wide, dotted with small portholes of a cloudy glass-like material. As one cube vibrates, shaking the ground about us, I get an idea: somehow these gigantic alien boxes are responsible for the earth tremors. Dozens of the bat-creatures flap around the cubes, while two insectoid leaders look on.

Marcy cries out when we reach the demolished remains of the store and the wooden tourist cabins. "Adam!" Lurching from the grip of her guard, she looks around wildly, as if she expects her husband to wander out of the store with a beer. Her guard swoops into the air with a shriek, but Marcy stops by the blackened remains of a Plymouth Savoy. She straightens from looking inside and lets the guard bring her back.

"Marcy?" I call out.

She looks up, tears streaming down her cheeks. "They weren't in there."

"Let's hope they're in the bunker," I say. I glare at Harve, daring him not to contradict me.

We are taken past the cubes; beyond them is the Devil's View bunker. Its hatch, like most of the others, has been crudely torn open. Marcy shudders and sobs.

"Great," Harve mutters as we are pushed forward, "we come all this damned way to find they were bat-food too. What great plan are you gonna come up with now, Doc? Because I'd sure like to hear it."

"We're still alive—against the odds—and that's all that matters."

"I'd rather die a hero," Harve says, "than live like a cripple, waiting to be eaten by a giant bat."

"Go ahead," I say, as we stop midway between the gigantic cubes and the bunker.

The hovering insectoid looks down at us. "You will wait," it crackles, its voice a distorted buzzing that pierces the inner ear. It takes a moment for me to register that it spoke English.

"You know our language," I say. "What are you doing here?"

"Yeah," Harve adds, "why don't you clear off back to where you came from? We've got enough damn foreigners and commies already."

"We were invited here," it replies, "by your own President, to eradicate the ones you call communists. In exchange, we use our cubes to mine for the substances in your mountains—chiefly, uranium ore. And your President saved a plentiful supply of human flesh in the bunkers, to feed our Byakhee workforce."

"What the hell?" Harve blurts.

I am too stunned to speak. President McCarthy sold out our world to these monsters? Surely, even he wouldn't go that far?

"Where is my family?" Marcy shrieks.

"You will have the answers," its voice hisses to me, "from your own President." It turns to Marcy. "As for your family: I believe they are with the President in the bunker."

Marcy surges forward. "I want to see them. Now!" She struggles against the creature's grip. "Adam! I'm out here!"

"Silence!" the insectoid hisses, its voice even more distorted when raised. "Silence, or our Byakhee servants will feast on your blood."

Two of the Byakhee bat-creatures emerge from the bunker, with a hovering platform between them. A cluster of strange equipment covers it: a squat metal cylinder about a foot in height, connected by cords, tubes and sockets to three other apparatuses far removed from our technology.

"What's all this junk?" Harve says, as they halt in front of us.

"I am your President," a voice intones from the cluster of equipment.

Harve stiffens to attention, like any good soldier.

President McCarthy's voice is the same lifeless monotone as his radio broadcast. Inside the cylinder, a human brain pulsates. "I said I'd find a way to beat the communists and I have."

Day 50

Join them or die. Become one of the select few whose skills can aid our new overlords from Yuggoth. There was really no alternative. Back when the air filter failed, we gave our reasons for staying alive. This time, we convinced ourselves to *go on living*. Harve is a survivor, eager to help his President reign over what is left of the Earth. For Marcy, it came down to family, and now she's finally reunited with her scientist husband and her two children—their brain cylinders are linked together in a corner of the bunker.

Even though their bodies were injured, ravaged by radiation, both Harve and Marcy struggled with the idea of having their brains preserved in a cylinder. As a doctor, I saw the benefits straightaway, as I'm sure McCarthy did, with the health problems he had. We are immortal now; we'll never feel pain, never need to sleep, eat or drink. Our masters from Yuggoth inform me we can even travel the galaxy in these cylinders. But the most important thing is I will never die. I've always tried to preserve life—for others first, but more recently, for myself—and now I have finally cheated death!

Day 57

I need to occupy my mind in this immortality. I am haunted by dread images: the Burtons, begging us not to close the hatch; Frank's face as I betray him; Clara Glenville with a Byakhee clamped to her neck; Ed Cassidy glaring at me as Dan bleeds in his arms; my wife, pleading with me to end her resurrected existence. They repeat over and over and over again. I have no eyes to close, no medication to take, no sleep to help me forget. If it carries on like this, I will lose my mind. An *eternity* of madness—there must be something I can do to stop it!

PUTNAM'S MONSTER
BY SCOTT T. GOUDSWARD

Walter looked back over his shoulder as he ran, eyes wild, mouth open, gasping for breath. He heard the hard heavy footfalls catching up from behind. They'd followed him from the street. He leapt at the security door, colliding full force, knocking out the guard on the other side. A damp red smear painted the wall, an obscene lithograph, where the guard's head collided with the painted cinderblock wall.

Walter jammed chairs under the handles like he'd seen in the spy films. The library door loomed ahead. The hallway seemed to elongate with each frantic step; his black wing-tip shoes squeaked on the tiles, marring the polished surface with black streaks. Walter hit the swinging door hard; he went into an uncontrolled slide on the thin carpeting, his arms flailing, looking for anything to grab onto.

The silent room resounded with a great rip as half of his suit coat tore and was left behind, clinging to the corner of a metal shelf. His thin black tie felt like a noose, and as Walter slid, foot pointed towards a display case like it was home plate, he finally started to slow. His breaths came hard and fast, spittle quivering on his bottom lip.

Walter stood up, looking at the glass topped display case. Three heavy steel locks hung in place, keeping the case closed. Walter struggled against the locks, grunting and groaning. At last, he ripped off his tie and the remains of his coat, dropping them on the floor. He heard the faint shouting approaching as he struggled with the case.

His glasses fogged as sweat rolled down his face and dripped onto the glass. He saw his own crazed expression, but still knew what had to happen. Beyond the well-insulated walls of Innsmouth University, the helicopters were coming, and the bombers, and by this point the army. Putnam's beast was destroying the ocean town.

What the University kept hidden and locked away was the only thing that would save them all. Walter balled his fist, prepared to smash the glass with his hand; after a second thought, he drove his elbow through it. The glass shattered; pain ripped up his arm as the jagged glass tore into his flesh. He grabbed them all, ignoring the display cards with the small typed warnings 'handle carefully with supervision.'

Walter hugged the tomes to his chest and ran for the small librarian's office. He locked and barricaded the door with the desk. There was one window with reinforced glass. His blood-slick hands flew across the pages, leaving crimson smears, seemingly absorbed into the pages. His fingers stopped on a passage; blood leaked down his hand to feed the book. Walter didn't know all the words, though some he'd seen in the professor's notes *Summoning Spell.*

***

Constance tittered as she spied the empty desk. Three rows, six desks in each, with one empty, last row, first desk. The typewriter sat quiet amongst the *clickety clack* of the other typists, or glorified secretaries, as Churchman called them. Her sweater was draped loose across her shoulders to show off her ample cleavage, and over the curve of her horn-rimmed glasses, she spied.

Walter stumbled in, twenty minutes late. All typing ceased for the few seconds it took for him to stagger to his desk and get his coat off. He unlocked the lower left drawer and dropped in a brown paper bag, and a copy of *Astounding Science Fiction.* The inbox on the narrow desk was crammed with banded bundles of papers and folders. Sometimes the 'girls' liked to drop their extra work on his desk. With a heavy sigh, he loaded the typewriter with a clean piece of paper and got to work.

Walter glanced at the open folder on his desk as his fingers flew across the keys. His system was infallible. Translate the notes, work them into the text already on the page, mark the page done and then drop it into an open desk drawer. The women were tidier in their storage of completed pages, but none of them had Walter's speed.

Walter was in the typing pool because he was fast and knew it. Walter could pound out over seventy words a minute; he was the fastest typist in the pool, thanks to his mother. His shorthand was the best, also thanks to his mother. It was at her urging that he took administrative courses in college instead of the sciences that he loved. "*You'll never get anywhere with the science,*" she'd chided while a Chesterfield burned between her fingers. "*It's only because of me you work at the university.*"

He dropped another empty folder into the desk drawer. The once-laden inbox was now half-full.

Walter smirked as he heard the others trying to keep up with him. He didn't worry about chipping a nail or smearing make-up, he pounded away until his work was done. In his mind he pictured Constance pleading with Churchman, as he escorted her from the office, faux-leather purse clutched tight to her chest, hands full of damp tissues and tears rolling down her face. While Walter imagined fancy ends to his co-workers; they dreamed of Kirk Douglas, James Dean and the latest Buddy Holly and Elvis Presley songs.

Walter drummed his fingers on the desk, trying to decipher some notations in the margins of a paper. The words were almost as strange as some hand-drawn doodles. He shrugged and dropped the paper into the drawer. His mind wandered to the newest episode of *The Adventures of Superman* as he glanced out the window. The college campus spread out before the slightly opened windows. A cool sea breeze rolled in, and Walter reveled in it. The girls liked it warm, sometimes too warm. The ocean was right there and the cooling winds that blew off of it were often lost.

The sun glinted off the other windows in the office buildings, administration, science and research; the dormitories were further towards the city as were the classrooms. What always seemed to steal his attention away was the reactor silo.

***

Churchman leaned against the little brown desk that held no other form or function. The small fans on either side of him did little to cut the stale office air. He looked over the desks at the bodies attached to their typewriters. He slid a finger under his collar, damp with the sweat rolling off his balding head, trying to ease the tension.

He watched them through his brown-rimmed Ronsurs. He found the clacking of the keys terribly relaxing, knowing they were working and he wasn't. Taking a deep breath, George Churchman clapped his hands lightly as if at a golf match. "Ladies and gentleman, please." He waited as fingers slowed on keys, until the typing stopped. George waited for the last typist to stop; it was Walter, always Walter. The last to work and the last one to stop. Walter's fingers hovered above the keys, the tips teasing the letters as they waited above the enameled surface.

"A new opportunity has been made available." Walter shifted his fingers on the keys, his eyes darting to the pile of papers in his desk tray. As Constance watched, a bead of sweat trickled down Churchman's cheek to be absorbed in his shirt collar. She loosened the top button on her shirt, exposing a tad more view.

"There's one new position, and our department has been chosen to fill it." Churchman's eyes swept the room, lingered on Constance's chest, a smiled playing at the corner of his mouth. "And our little office here will fill it." The excited chattering rose. "Please keep in mind that we took everything into consideration, from output to attendance and security clearance." George looked around the room, trying to read the expressions. "There's a pay increase and a transfer to the Marine Studies division of Innsmouth. You'll be leaving Miskatonic; you'll be working directly with their research staff." Churchman shrugged apologetically, "Walter, they chose you."

Walter's expression was blank; he looked from the typewriter to Churchman to the ladies next to him. He closed the folder on his desk and added it back to the stacks. He forced a smile and opened the desk drawers to remove his personal items.

"Anything to say to the ladies, Walter? You won't be seeing them any time soon." Walter stood, draped his sport-coat over his shoulder.

"I am going to miss the view," he said to Constance.

***

Walter struggled to keep up and write at the same time. The team powered on ahead of him, while he fought to get all their words down, pausing for a step to keep the dictation flowing. His shoes clicked off the black and white floor tiles as he ran to catch up.

"You get all that, Berman?"

"Yes, I believe so."

"Don't believe, be sure." Walter folded back the page on the pad and continued to write.

"You don't need to jot down our advice, Berman, just everything else." Walter nodded and flipped to a new page in the pad. The pack of scientists and assistants continued down the hallway while Walter scribbled everything down in shorthand, stopped to catch up and then jog-stepped to keep up. The lot of them stopped at the swinging door to the laboratory.

"Get that all deciphered, Berman. Type it up and I want it on my lab station in the morning." Walter nodded and looked at Doctor Putnam. "We'll need you in the library tomorrow morning first thing. There'll be a load of books to pick up." Putnam buttoned up his white lab coat; his eyes seemed to glaze with a flash of color. Putnam ran his fingers through his salt and pepper hair and pushed through the door of the lab. The others followed behind.

Walter took a deep breath and pushed up his glasses. There was a trail of black scuffs on the floor behind him. Looking at the scribbles on the pad, Walter headed back to the office, following the scuffs like a trail of breadcrumbs.

***

Walter stood in the library; Putnam had thrust a handful of requisition forms at him before his coat was off. His desk tray was stuffed with papers and folders, from a quick glance most of them looked to be hand-written.

"Fetch those books, Berman," was all Putnam said before charging off.

Walter tried for an itch with the tip of his shoe. A stern-looking woman came towards Walter wearing white cloth gloves, a clipboard held tight to her chest. She had a large mole on her jaw line, and when Walter looked at it, he swore the thick black hairs stirred and danced in an unknown breeze. She handed him the clipboard.

"Sign these forms, in triplicate." She turned her back while Walter scanned the form. With a shrug he signed and dated each page. The librarian wore a plain black skirt and plainer blue blouse. Thick heels *clumped* on the floor with each step.

From an unseen pocket she pulled a ring of keys and opened a locked cabinet. From inside she lifted an ancient book. She turned and cleared her throat. Walter placed the clipboard on top of the case and she rolled her eyes.

"There's a briefcase on the desk. Be a good boy, and go get it." He moved past and retrieved the case, opened it, the lid blocking his view of the book. Walter still hadn't seen a name or author printed on it. He felt the tome's weight as it was gently laid in and the lid was closed, the case locked.

"Twenty four hours, no more, no less." She picked up the clipboard and inspected the forms signed and dated in triplicate. "You tell Putnam, twenty four hours or we'll be after him." Walter stared, transfixed by the mole. The hairs weaved like snakes. The briefcase was warm in his hands, getting warmer.

Walter hurried back towards the lab. There was something sinister in the case, he sensed it, and he didn't want it near him any longer than needed.

***

Walter browsed over the paperwork. His wax-paper-wrapped sandwich sat untouched on the desk. Walter smiled and dropped another stack of papers into the trash bin. His fingers flew across the keys, punching them in a fevered pace. Slapping the carriage return, pretending the *ding* was his mother's pained cries. He didn't hear the footsteps coming up from behind.

The next batch of papers was hand-scrawled and barely discernible. The markings seemed to move on the paper, the blue ink morphing into new shapes. Walter took off his glasses and pressed his palms into his eyes until he saw stars. There were pictures, drawn in charcoal pencil. Strange beasts that looked like alien roaches. Walter shivered and almost shrieked when his shoulder was tapped. He closed the manila folder and saw the radiation symbol on the cover amongst the scribbles.

"Berman," Putnam said. "Bring the books back." He placed the locked case on the floor near Walter's desk; he felt the heat coming off it.

"You still have time left, Doctor. Lots of it." Putnam crossed his arms and stared at the wrapped sandwich.

"Take a break, Berman. Go to the quad, eat your lunch." He all but spat out the last word. "Bring the books back. You signed for them. You don't want the librarian to collect it." Walter pulled on his coat. The rolled-up copy of *Analog* slipped out and bounced on the floor. Walter stuffed it and his sandwich in his pocket. "You're a good worker, Berman." Putnam seemed uncomfortable speaking the compliment.

Walter eased himself from the office, walked to the building's cafeteria, and bought a bottle of Coca-Cola and potato chips. In the quad, students lounged on blankets on the neat grass, radios played Elvis and Walter sat alone on a bench reading his magazine and eating. He almost felt good, in the fresh salt air and the sun. Not too far off he heard the waves. And deeper beyond all that, Walter felt the thrum of the reactor and the image of the crab thing fill his mind.

***

"You're so late, every night." Agnes Berman said. "I hardly have anyone to talk to anymore." She tapped her Chesterfield ash into a full tray near the edge of the table.

"Go to Aunt Helen's; play cards." Walter answered.

"Helen is boring." She crushed out the cigarette and tapped out a fresh one. "You're doing this to me. I smoke all the time now because there's no one here to talk to." Walter pushed at the chicken wing on his plate with his fork. He loathed dinner time, but he had a responsibility to be the man of the house since his father died. His mother did put him through college.

"I can drive you to the harbor side, you can shop, eat at some nice restaurants."

"I suppose I can go look in on your father's grave, too."

"If you want, Mother."

"If you want, Mother," she answered back, mocking. Walter took the cloth napkin off his leg, wiped his mouth and stood up.

"Let me know before bed. I'll…"

"Be in your room." She finished his sentence. Agnes crushed out her new cigarette in the tray near her elbow and threw her arms in the air, dismissing her son.

***

Walter shrugged off his coat and hung it over the back of the chair. The office was empty; it was always empty. It seemed like everyone avoided this section of the university. As for the Marine division, the closest thing he'd done and seen related to the sea was the crab thing Putnam had been sketching. Or was it a roach? His mother had locked herself in her room, didn't answer his questions, never responded. Through the closed door he smelled the cigarette smoke, so at least he knew she wasn't dead. So much for her day out.

"Berman," Putnam barked. "You get those books back?"

"Yes, Doctor, right after I talked to you yesterday."

"Very good," he said nodding. Putnam handed Walter a brown-paper-wrapped package, tied with string. "Open it." Walter tore into the paper like a kid on Christmas, ignoring the string. Deep in the folds of the brown paper was a white lab coat and on top was a radiation badge.

"Thank you." Walter said.

"I need you at the silo today. You'll need the button." Putnam picked it up and clipped it to his collar. "Green is good, yellow you should think about leaving, red means you'll be in isolation at the hospital. You keep the coat on at all times when you're over there." Walter slid it on to test the size.

"What are we doing over there, sir?" Putnam walked around Berman's lonely desk. There were no windows in the office. The windows in the hallway overlooked the back half of the campus.

"We're going to test radiation levels and its effects on marine life. Specifically crabs. I want to see what happens if they're exposed to radiation should there ever be a leak at the silo. It's all water cooled, you know."

"Yes, sir."

"We'll be there all day. I'll have lunch called in." Walter looked at the stack of paper in the desk tray. "Ever get lonely in here, Berman?" Putnam asked.

"I prefer it."

"What do you want for lunch, then?"

"Anything will do," Walter answered. "My mother isn't talking to me and I didn't make anything today." Putnam rolled his eyes.

"Get your pads and pencils and follow me. We're going to be there all day, and I like to talk when I walk, helps me work out things." Walter pulled a handful of pencils out of the desk and a fresh pad. "Better bring more than one, Berman. Might want to call home, too. If you have a telephone and if its party line, call someone else."

***

Walter followed Putnam around the lab. His mind wandered to trying to get his elderly neighbor off the party line so he could get through to his mother, but it wasn't happening. He scribbled on the pad, watching over Putnam's shoulder, trying to see what was going on. On the exam table, Putnam had several dead crabs in various stages of dissection, which he poked and prodded with a scalpel and tweezers.

Walter didn't understand a word, but he jotted down everything the man said and did his best to document his studies on the table. The lab was cold; one wall devoted to aquarium tanks, some with insects, others with fish, and the last bank was crabs in different phases of radiation exposure. Some looked healthy, scrabbling along the sandy bottom of the tanks, others had drooping eye stalks, diseased pincers, others missing legs.

Walter found himself drawn to the insects, watching them burrow in sawdust and converge on twitching bodies as they fed; ants, roaches, crickets and spiders. Berman smiled, thinking of his mother screaming in her bed as a spider skittered over her face or seizing as she put her feet into a slipper packed with roaches.

He shook his head, already a few paces behind Putnam, and caught up in his note taking. Putnam never slowed or stopped to look over his shoulder. Walter wondered why he didn't have a reel to reel to record his words. Maybe he wanted a witness to his big breakthrough, or someone to pull him back should he go too far.

Walter stopped and gasped, looking at the last dissection tray on the cold metal table. It had a spotlight beaming down on it. On the tray was a hideous creature. Walter rubbed his eyes to make sure he wasn't imagining it. Whatever it was looked like something that had crawled from the pages of his science fiction magazines. A small smile curled at Putnam's lips.

"This is why, Mr. Berman, I had your security checked." Putnam poked the tray with the scalpel. "This is why we're here. To make this corpse history. Every word, Berman." Walter nodded absently and set pencil to paper as Putnam ran the sharp scalpel down the belly, or what he thought was the belly, of the creature.

"Does it have a name?" Walter asked.

"What? No of course not. Don't disturb me again." Putnam turned his back on Walter and, using tweezers, pulled apart the layers of hard exoskeleton. Walter gagged and struggled, breathing heavily through his mouth. "Problem?"

"I was never any good at seeing this in school."

"Do you need a glass of water?"

"No, Doctor Putnam, sorry." Berman heard every squish of flesh and crack of shell as if magnified a thousand times. He glanced away to the tanks. One of the crabs, still blue and soft had something growing from its body. Where the pincer should be, it looked like a small tentacle.

Putnam pushed the tray away and peeled off his rubber gloves. Walter put his full pad on the table and started a new one.

Putnam moved for a small door near the back of the lab that Walter hadn't noticed. He pulled a chain from under his coat, looped around his neck, from which a key hung. He unlocked the door and stepped in, waving Walter through as he did.

Walter bit his knuckle and did his best not to scream. Putnam was elbow-deep in an aquarium, partially filled with water and a slope of sand. In it he was reaching for the only inhabitant. Another thing, like from the table in the exam room. Long black antennae and eye stalks waved frantically as Putnam's hand got closer. The front of the creature had pincers like a crab; the back half was hard, dark exoskeleton and multiple legs like a cockroach.

"No, Berman, it has no name."

"What are they?"

"This is what happened when I bombarded the tanks with radiation." Walter glanced down at the badge on his collar, still in the green but leaning towards yellow. "Don't worry, you're still fine." Walter took a step back when Putnam got closer, holding his creation. "I put the crabs and roaches in the same tank and flooded it with radiation from the silo. Somehow they merged and became one." Putnam held the creature up, struggling in his grasp to get free. "They're terribly strong, and growing at an alarming rate."

Putnam pushed past Walter to the exam room. He set the insectoid down on the table and watched it scuttle away, stop, and go back to look at the dissected corpse on the tray. "Look Berman, it's showing intelligence, and stopping to look at the body of its 'brother.'"

"Maybe it's just hungry?"

Putnam turned, raising his eyebrows, and tapped Berman on the chest with the tweezers.

"Excellent conjecture. Maybe they're omnivores, parts of each creature with the more powerful instincts surfacing." As they watched, Walter scribbled shorthand onto the executive pad, while Putnam paced up and down the length of the table, poking the thing with a pen when it got close to the edge. With a strong pincer, it grabbed the plastic pen and snapped it in half.

"Flight or fight response! Are you getting this, Berman?" Walter nodded as his hand moved methodically across the page. He was staring at the thing, his hand moving out of instinct. He stopped and pointed at the table. Putnam turned his crazed gaze back; it was growing, slowly but definitely getting bigger as they watched.

"Should we put it back in the tank?" Walter asked with a tremor in his voice. Putnam pulled a small ruler from his pocket, took a measure and then stared at the minute hand on his watch. He looked at the bug thing and measured again.

"One minute, one half an inch, approximately." The whispers of Walter's pencil filled the lab. He tried not to think of the thing on the table, to focus on the bubbling fish filters, the tanks full of ocean fish swimming peacefully. Then the scuttling of the crab-roaches took over. "At this rate it will outgrow the tank in three hours. Do I kill it and examine it? Or see how big it gets?" Putnam turned to Walter, pale and wide-eyed, staring at the table. "What do you think?"

"Kill it. Kill it now." Walter spat out.

"That's what I thought you'd say. No imagination; you have no imagination." Putnam reached into his pocket and pulled out a library request form. "I need you to retrieve those books again from the library, the same two." He shook the paper in Walter's face, distracting him.

"You don't want me to stay and take notes?" Putnam tapped at his watch.

"I've kept you long enough. Besides, I want those notes translated and typed by morning. Get the books, leave them in my office." Walter nodded dumbly and reached for the pad on the table. The thing snapped at his fingers with its pincers. "Be careful, man. It could snap your finger off." Walter snatched at the pad and back-stepped through the lab, not stopping until he was through the lobby.

The security guards checked his radiation levels and then ran a Geiger counter over him. The guard nodded and unclipped the pin from his collar. Clutching the pads tight to his chest, Walter ran from the lab and stopped in the quad to catch his breath. The day was gone; night had blanketed the campus in inky darkness.

The buoys in the harbor clanged in boat wakes; strings of lights run mast-to-cabin lit up the boats as they left Innsmouth Harbor for deeper waters. Walter stopped in the quad to catch his breath. He dropped the pads on a bench and bent over, hands on knees, and greedily sucked in breaths of cool sea air. He wondered while he gasped if what he saw would get him back in Arkham, typing where he was safe amongst the gossiping biddies.

"The library," he wheezed. Walter stood up, unbuttoned his lab coat and picked up the pads. "The library will relax me." Walter took his pulse from his throat as he walked.

***

The library hadn't changed. Most of the lights were out, save for the librarian's office and the emergency lights over the door. Walter cleared his throat several times to get someone's attention. Finally he took the form out and placed it on the glass top of the display case. It was warm to the touch and a slight vibration raced across his fingertips. Walter laid his hands on the glass and images flashed through his mind. Deep space and deeper gods. Something inside cracked and his eye twitched.

"Can I help you?" came a high pitched voice. Walter turned, whisking the form off the case. He waved it in the air at the approaching person.

"Book retrieval for Dr. Putnam." She looked at the form then at Walter, sweat trickling down his cheeks. She ripped the form from his hand, tearing the corner off.

"Wait here." She pointed at some chairs in the corner. "Do you want some water?"

"Yes, please." Walter sat in the hard, straight-backed wooden chair. She returned with a paper cone filled with water. Walter grabbed it from her hand and gulped down the water. Some of it ran down his chin. Most of it made it into his mouth.

"I'll get your books." She walked away, glancing nervously over her shoulder. Walter remembered all the images burned into his mind. Holes the size of planets in space. Tears and rips through time. Jagged horrible cracks running the length and width through planets. Giant eyes staring; long reaching tendrils that dripped water and blood.

"Can you help me with this?" Walter nodded and stood. The librarian handed him the keys. Her hands were shaking. He held the case open and Walter unlocked the display. With trembling hands he reached in for the books, no titles, no text on the outside; no print on the covers. Each one brought horrible and wondrous images into his mind. He smiled, laughed a little and closed the case. Before she could lock it, Walter took the case from her, signed the forms and ran from the library.

Outside in the courtyard, someone screamed. The sharp crack of a gunshot rang out. Walter ran down the sidewalk; it was too late for a bus and too far to walk. He needed a taxi. When he saw the black pincer coming from the lab, Walter turned and ran for home.

***

Walter woke with a start. He was home, in his bed, covers splayed across his legs. He reached for the bedside table and his glasses. His fingers brushed across the warm surfaces of the books before touching his lenses. He fumbled with the thick black frames before slipping them into place. Walter cringed first at the books, then at the pounding on the door.

"Are you awake yet? You lazy piece of..." his mother's voice trailed off and he heard soft shuffles headed for the stairs. He slid the first book over and held it tight to his chest, smiling and rocking, just a little. The faint sigh of a siren getting louder drifted in through the window. Walter's eyes snapped open as sleep oozed its way from his brain. He crawled from under the covers, still clutching the book.

From somewhere in the house came Johnny Mathis crooning *chances are, your chances are awfully good*. Walter stepped into his slippers and headed downstairs, he didn't seem to notice the book was in his arms.

***

"I told you, Mother, I was working late."

"That's no reason not to call. I worry."

"You don't worry; you just want someone home to gossip to and insult."

"That fancy new job is making you brave." She lit a Chesterfield and blew the smoke at him. Walter moved on the couch, the plastic cover crinkling with each inch. Beyond the house a police car raced by, sirens blaring. His mother reached out a hand and switched off the radio. Walter stood without thinking and after laying the book down, wheeled the TV cart over.

"What's going on out there?" he asked as another car whizzed by.

"You really have been out of it." Walter retrieved the book and sat back down as the TV tube blinked to life. A concerned-looking man in a suit and slicked back hair appeared on the small screen.

"Ladies and gentlemen, again I emphasize this. Stay in your house and lock the doors. Close the curtains and keep the lights off."

"Are we at war?" Walter asked. His mother hissed at him and waved her hand for him to be quiet.

"A monstrous creature has been spotted near the harbor; it is destructive and working its way deeper into the city." Walter reached out and switched off the TV.

"What did you do that for?"

"I need to go to work, Mother."

***

Walter snuck into the library. The school hallways were all but deserted of faculty and students. The few people he did see were running past him. Walter kept one eye on the hallways and the other out of the window. Putnam's creature was out there; the glimpses of flashing red lights and blaring sirens were proof of it punctuated by the sounds of gunfire.

Walter slipped into the library and slid the keys from the display from his pocket. The books were warm and buzzing. He didn't attempt to fight at the visions anymore. The books had a place and until he figured it out, they would have to stay at the library. Walter locked the case and ran his fingers lovingly across the glass. A final image flashed into his brain, of fire and water erupting and reptilian wings larger than Innsmouth rising from the water.

Walter didn't have his lab coat or radiation badge; something told him he wouldn't need it. The doors to the silo were open. One hung from its hinges. The front lobby was clogged with debris, and beneath it laid the bodies of security guards. Walter bit his knuckle to keep from screaming and tasted blood. He carefully stepped over the piles and went into the lab.

The primary lab was destroyed. The metal surgical table was tipped on its side, the legs bent. All of the glass tanks smashed; nothing moved inside the shattered shells. The door to the specimen room was blown off the hinges; the smaller room was barely recognizable. A lab coat-clad arm stuck out of the debris, blood dripping from the fingers.

"Dr. Putnam? Is that you?" Walter whispered, inching forward. He leaned on the overturned table to get past a large pile of rubble. Walter picked up a piece of wood and poked the arm; it rolled and fell out of the pile of debris, missing its body. Walter let loose with a horror movie scream and back pedaled, stumbling over broken glass and chunks of cinderblock. He ran out of the lab towards the harbor—he had to see what he had helped unleash. And all of the shorthand notes in the world weren't going to stop it.

***

The police set up temporary barricades and blocked off the streets with their cars. The black and white Chevrolet Bel Airs were big and bulky, and stopped other vehicles from getting past. Not people though. The policemen were nowhere to seen. Walter followed the path of destruction past the grocery store, where he used to wait outside while mother bought cigarettes. The entire front of the building was smashed in. Walter did his best to walk slow and steady and keep from sight in case any police came by. He had to see Putnam's monster.

The movie theater was in ruins, the billboard broken, lying in front of the doors, still proclaiming 'Double Feature Saturday, Bridge over the River Kwai and Elvis Presley in Jailhouse Rock.' Walter skirted past to the corner and stopped. He could see the docks; the monstrosity seemed to be headed for the water, maybe following instincts to safety.

Police swarmed around it like angry bees firing revolvers and rifles, which had no effect at all on the armored exterior. The giant black pincers snapped and cracked at the attackers. The only good thing seemed to be that it was slow, still growing from the looks of it. Walter took off his glasses and rubbed his eyes. More images flashed into his mind, lit like gunfire; like he was connected to the books in the library. He grabbed his head and screamed, realizing too late that the noise was bad.

He heard shouting, then footsteps running towards him. Two strong hands grabbed his shoulders and shook him, the cure-all for all forms of hysteria.

"Are you okay, buddy?" The cop asked. He towered over Walter by a good six inches. "You shouldn't be here, it's dangerous; didn't you watch the news?"

"I need to go to the University." Walter stammered. The cop stuck two fingers in his mouth and whistled.

"I got a nut over here." More footsteps. Walter fought against the one-handed grasp, and failed. The more he struggled, the more the cop tightened his grip. "You need to settle down, buddy. What's your name?"

"What's going on, George?"

"Got a smart guy here, wants to go to the school."

"Put him in the car, lock him in." The second policeman took off his hat and wiped at his forehead with a meaty hand. "I wasn't made for all this running." They each grabbed an arm and started walking Walter back towards the police cars.

"Please you don't understand. Dr. Putnam and I…"

"Putnam? The loon from the school?"

"Yes, I'm his assistant." Walter spat.

"We found what was left of Putnam in three chunks near the docks."

"I need to…"

"You need nothing, pal. Now stop fighting, they're evacuating Innsmouth, calling in the army." The second cop said with a smile. "You know, George, I hear they might drop the bomb on that thing."

"They can't drop the bomb. My mother is home." Walter broke free and took off at a full-out run. He heard the police shouting behind him, followed by their footsteps, trying to catch up. Walter was never good at sports, but was always able to run fast, away from bullies, away from his brothers and today from the police.

***

Tears welled and spilled from Walter's eyes as he pushed the heavy wooden desk to block the door. There was no way those two policemen were going to get him. There was no way he would allow anyone to bomb Innsmouth and harm his mother, despite her nagging and pressuring.

Walter swept an arm across the desk, sending a small calendar, cat photo and a cactus crashing to the floor. He eased the books from his shirt and laid them on the desk. He was bleeding from the cut on his arm. The hole near the elbow of the sleeve showed ragged skin peppered with splinters of broken glass from the display case.

The blood oozed from the wounds, dribbling out of his sleeve onto the desk. He opened the first book, the cover alive and buzzing beneath his touch. Walter slid his clean hand among the pages, a whimper of fear and anger escaping his lips. The pages were all blank. He clenched a bloody fist and slammed it onto the page out of frustration. The blood spattered across the aged paper. Then it moved and changed, formed words and illustrations. Whatever formed soon faded.

Walter ripped the sleeve of his shirt, exposing the ragged flesh. He grimaced for a second, knowing what he had to do. He located the biggest piece of glass in his arm and pulled it free. A cascade of blood poured out onto the book. The blood was instantly absorbed and transformed into text and images. He flipped through the pages looking for the familiar text and runes he'd seen doodled on Putnam's papers.

The text started to fade; Walter grabbed the next piece of glass and, with a groan, tore it free. This one was deep. He dropped the glass onto the desk. More blood poured and pooled, but only for an instant. Walter pulled up the only chair, wooden, hard and straight-backed with no cushion. He was feeling faint from the wound, the loss of blood and the books blooming to life, fed by his blood in front of him.

He closed his eyes, took off his glasses and breathed deep. Just like the book told him to. He laid hands on the pages and his lips moved involuntarily, spewing words he didn't know nor had ever heard before. The pounding on the outer door broke him from his trance.

His hands were dry and vaguely clean. The pages were barren save a few flakes of dried blood. Walter closed the book and tried to stand, collapsing back into the chair; there was no strength left in him. Through the small window he watched the door shake and bow as it was repeatedly kicked and slammed. The furniture he slid in front of it was starting to move. They'd be in soon and then he'd be in jail.

Summoning the reserves of his strength, Walter pushed the desk enough to squeeze past into the library proper. He heard the muffled shouts of the policemen as he moved past the doors to the windows. He sat on a comfortable bench and looked out the window towards the bay.

Through the windows he saw the creature, grown even more immense since Walter last glimpsed it. The sun reflected off the monstrous head as the eye stalks moved and swayed, looking for the next target. Walter heard the helicopters and airplanes next, wondering if they carried missiles or 'the bomb' he same kind that flattened Hiroshima. He was too weak to worry.

Only one thing mattered, staying conscious long enough to see his job done. His mind wandered to his mother, sitting home alone, seething and fuming while watching the TV and chain smoking her Chesterfields. She'd make pale tea for herself and perhaps really indulge with a few cookies. Walter smiled and the harbor exploded.

Water and fire shot up into the sky. The water boiled and rolled; steam and smoke poured out. Putnam's monster moved away. The docks were torn apart from below. Men and wood flew into the water. The gunfire stopped and was replaced by screaming. Something was coming. Massive tentacled tendrils slithered up from under the water, indiscriminately killing and smashing everything in their path.

The library doors burst open, the two cops stumbling through the debris and spotting Walter. He smiled and pointed out the window. The tip of an immense wing broke the surface of the water, then the crown of a gigantic green head dotted with several hundred eyes.

It let loose with a scream that vaporized half of the bay and most of Putnam's abomination. Its next scream flattened the rest of the waterfront. The cops stood paralyzed and Walter tried to tighten his tie with pride at what he had done. When Walter looked outside again, it had raised a colossal hand from the depths. Its massive head swiveled and stopped, seemingly staring at Walter, knowing he had summoned the Old God.

Walter screamed as his mind melted away into the Abyss, and all the policemen could do was stare at the low afternoon moon low in the sky, with a jagged split running its width.

OPERATION SWITCH
BY PETE RAWLIK

December 8, 1953
The Bridge of No Return

I t was cold, the air was crisp, and a thick fog had rolled in and settled in the gully and around the bridge that spanned it. There was
a scent in the air, smoke tinged with gunpowder and exhaust. To
the north the enemy, North Koreans, were scurrying about, postur-
ing, flexing military muscles, making sure that the American troops
to the south knew what they were capable of. The Americans were
doing much the same, though in a slightly more organized and better
equipped manner. It was a scene the man on the hill had watched time
and time before, only the players had changed. At the designated hour,
trucks, one from each side, began unloading their human cargo, prisoners of war. The man on the hill, whom his subordinates thought of
as the Old Man, and occasionally referred to as the TOM, or Terrible
Old Man, lit a cigarette, picked up his field glasses and watched as the
prisoners moved from either side and across the bridge.

The two groups that passed each other in silence couldn't have
been more different. Those moving from south to north, were all
well dressed in clean uniforms, and well fed, Asian, either Chinese or
Korean; the TOM could tell the difference even when his others could
not. The prisoners moving in the opposite direction were in contrast
a sorry lot, dressed in what was left of their filthy uniforms, which in
some cases were little more than rags. They were a motley crew, some
Koreans and Turks, but mostly British, Australians, and Americans,
though to the untrained eye they all looked the same, tattered uniforms
covering gaunt, emaciated bodies. They shuffled across the bridge, in
single file, so slowly that their steps barely made a sound. The condition of the troops was a telling clue to how poorly the North Korean
army was supplied, for even the soldiers that guarded the prisoners
were only marginally better off. Still, amongst the waves of shuffling,

downtrodden prisoners of war, there were always a few who had not succumbed to the torture, starvation, and depression that was epidemic amongst former POWs. These men always had clean uniforms, good shoes, healthy bodies; even their minds were relatively unaffected. They walked faster and stood prouder than the others coming back across the bridge. They were easy to spot, and after interviewing dozens of them the TOM suspected something, something that he hoped to confirm as the exchange of prisoners drew to a close.

As the former POWs came to the base of the bridge they were loaded into waiting vehicles and whisked away. The Australians and the Brits were the first to leave. The TOM had no jurisdiction over these nationalities; he had to let them go. But when it came to Americans, they were his to do with as he pleased. It was a familiar position, one that he had enjoyed while working in Japan, and then after the war for the CIA in both America and Europe. His recruitment into the Joint Advisory Commission, Korea or JACK was merely a new variation on an old game, one that he had become very good at.

He lowered the field glasses and took a drag off of his cigarette, then handed a name to his assistant. "Lieutenant Hollister, have this man collected." Hollister nodded, and relayed his master's instructions into his radio. A half mile below as the prisoners made their way to the waiting trucks, one oddly healthy prisoner of war was removed from the others and loaded into a waiting jeep with armed guards on either side. The TOM smiled and muttered, "Now that we have collected our gift, let us see what we have been given."

December 12, 1953
JACK Base 3 Codename: Whitechapel

The TOM watched through the one way glass as Captain Marcus Troy fidgeted at the table in the interview room. Like the rest of the room the table was white, clean, and almost sterile. A blank slate on to which anything could be written and then if need be wiped clean, and forgotten forever. It had already witnessed the confessions of Lieutenants Marquand and Hodgson, weak willed men, both pilots on reconnaissance missions who had panicked and ejected from their planes when they came under enemy fire. They both had been captured, and held in Chicom camps far to the north. They were what the Chinese called progressives, and what the members of JACK thought of as indoctrinated. It would take some rehabilitation, time and effort, but the programming could be broken, the men returned to a semblance of their former selves, at least enough to pass for normal in society. Friends and relatives might have trouble; notice some behavioral issues, emotional outbursts and the like. But such symptoms could be, would be, attributed to the stress of war, and not to any shoddy psychological reconstruction work on the part of SHOP 3, the TOM's team of interrogators and therapists. Not that anybody back in the states would even know of the existence, let alone the function of such a group.

He watched Troy for a few more minutes, let the man sweat. It was part of the interrogation process. You leave a man alone with his thoughts for long enough and he might just tell you everything you need to know, and some things you might rather not. Give a man time, and he might give you the world without even needing to be asked. He finished his cigarette, nodded to Hollister to start the camera, picked up his equipment case and with a deep breath went into the room.

He flashed a smile as he introduced himself, his gold teeth catching the light, "Captain Troy, my name is Peaslee, Doctor Wingate Peaslee. I am a psychologist. I am here to ask you some questions, about your time as a prisoner, nothing serious, just a debriefing. Standard procedure I assure you."

Troy's response was impassionate, cold and little more than a whisper. "I understand. You have a job to do. We all have tasks we must perform."

Peaslee opened his equipment case to reveal a rather large array of tubes, valves, a roll of paper and some integrated pens. There was a cuff that went around Troy's arm, and another, quite a bit smaller that went over his finger. "This is a polygraph; it detects changes in blood pressure and temperature." He flipped the machine on and it began to hum. A bellows expanded and then collapsed with a puff, only to begin refilling once more. "We use it to detect stress, mistruths, and attempts at deceit. It's part of a test, one developed by the Germans, but still very functional. The Kampff test was originally used to detect traitors, now we use it to detect evidence of psychological tampering."

Troy nodded. "Do you think me a traitor Dr. Peaslee?" There was no emotion in his voice.

"We shall see." He settled down in the chair. "Do you mind if I smoke? I'm going to ask you a series of questions. Answer truthfully and this will all be over very quickly." Peaslee shuffled through some paperwork. "Your name is Marcus Troy. Born and raised in North Hills, Pennsylvania, a graduate of the University of Pennsylvania, Masters Degree in Engineering from Stanford. Last address 22C Lathe Ave, Oakland, California. Is that correct?"

"Is this part of the test?"

"No, no. Sorry, just getting my facts straight. You were assigned to the engineering corps, and captured July 22 1950 while working on fortifications at Outpost Harry?"

"Yes."

Peaslee circled an area on the paper that was slowly rolling through the machine. "Good. Where were you held prisoner?"

"Camp 12."

The interrogator dropped his pen. "Camp 12. Troy, I have to tell you that military intelligence has identified a number of Prisoner of War Camps, and until today none of us have ever heard of Camp 12."

"I'm sorry. They must not be very good."

"To whom are you referring Troy?"

"Your spies Dr. Peaslee, they must not be very good if they don't know about Camp 12. It is quite large, several thousand prisoners."

Peaslee picked up his pen in a huff. "Tell me about Doctor Hu."

The pen on the machine jumped as Troy asked "Who?"

"The Chinaman in charge of the re-education program at Camp 12, his name is Hu, H U. Your friends Marquand and Hodgson seemed to know who he was."

"Those men are not my friends."

"That is a strange thing to say. Do you know what they said about you?" He shuffled through some papers. "Here, 'Marcus Troy is the bravest human being I've ever known.' They both said it, the exact same phrase. Funny things to say from men who you say are not your friends." He shuffled more papers. "The same phrase. Very odd don't you think?"

"I've told you; those men are not my friends."

"But you do know Doctor Hu don't you?"

Troy stared at his interrogator. There was something in his eyes, something that made Peaslee suspicious. "Oh yes, I know the good Doctor Hu. I only met him once, but . . ."

Peaslee leaned in, 'But what Captain Troy?"

"I have dreams, vivid, horrible dreams. Hu is in them, he is always in them. He does strange things in my dreams; incomprehensible things; things that make no sense; horrible things."

"These things he did . . ."

"IN MY DREAMS!" interjected Troy.

The interrogator nodded, "These things that Doctor Hu did in your dreams, he did them to you?"

Troy shook his head sadly and his hands turned into fists. "No, never to me, Doctor Hu never hurt me. But he did strange things, horrible things, sometimes to buildings, sometimes to the landscape, sometimes with machinery, and sometimes to other men, but never to me, never to me." The officer paused and swallowed back tears.

"What is it you're not telling me? I can't help you Troy, unless you tell me everything."

"In my dreams when Hu did those things, I wasn't his victim. I was his assistant. GOD FORGIVE ME I WAS HELPING HIM!"

December 15, 1953
JACK Base 3 Codename: Whitechapel

"How are you feeling today?" Peaslee asked while rubbing the bruise on his cheek.

"Better," replied Troy. "I am sorry about the other day. I don't understand why I reacted like that."

Peaslee nodded. "It is hard to predict how we will react to stress. We've given you a sedative, it should help keep you calm." The man lit a cigarette. "I know that you don't want to, but we need to talk about your dreams, the ones with Doctor Hu in them."

The damaged man nodded, "Why do you want to know?"

The Terrible Old Man closed his eyes. "When I was a boy, my father suffered an attack. He lost his memory, became a different person. He left his wife and family, he didn't know us, we didn't know him. For years he traveled the world. Then one day he came home, and his memory came back. He tried to set things right, but he was haunted. Haunted by all that he had lost, and by dreams, horrible dreams in which he was not himself, and did things he did not understand."

Troy seemed to perk up. "Like my dreams."

"I think what happened to my father, something similar has happened to you. I want to understand it, help you to understand it, and perhaps find a way to heal you. But you have to tell me about your dreams."

The captain cleared his throat, leaned forward, and then began to speak. "In my dream, the one I have most often, we're getting off a plane, Doctor Hu and I. We're dressed oddly, a uniform of some sort, not Korean uniforms, or Chinese, yellow silk with black stripping. As Hu leaves the plane there are whole groups of bureaucrats, military officers, diplomats and they are all bowing as Hu approaches. When they don't rise up after he passes, I realize that they are bowing to me as well. We are escorted to a tented pavilion where we mingle with dignitaries from a number of countries. I recognize some of them, they are people of importance. There's a large man speaking Korean and laughing that I think is important. To his left is a wiry little Chinaman who could be Hu's brother, who introduces himself as Kang Sheng. It was only when Sheng spoke that I realized that none of the guests including myself were speaking English. Indeed, there were voices speaking not just Chinese and Korean, but Russian, Hungarian and even German, all of which I understood as easily as I understand you now."

"The gathering was not purely social. Hu and I were engaged in some great negotiations; the gist of which escapes me now, but it involved the purchase of great machines, great conglomerates of tubes and metallic spheres constructed piecemeal, but on a massive scale. For these components we traded information, secrets, designs and formulas that could devastate cities and lay waste to whole continents. We gave them such knowledge as if it were nothing, as if it could never be used. For in truth we thought of them as insignificant, useful but insignificant. They were like bees. You can give a hive the designs for a gun, but you should have no fear of them actually taking advantage of them."

"The negotiations take days, not because they are difficult, but because Hu and I are just two, and our needs are great, and they are a chattering unorganized horde desperate for our attentions and favor. We work non-stop. We do not sleep, we eat almost constantly, and Hu frequently dispenses for our consumption a strange yellow powder, heavy and granulated, like sugar but thicker. It is a stimulant, of that I am sure, but one that seems to have no deleterious side effects. It sustains us until we return to the plane. The flight takes hours. We are exhausted but content with our progress. We should be happy, ecstatic even, but I realize that during the course of our negotiations neither I nor Doctor Hu has shown any sign of emotion at all. The dream ends as I finally get comfortable and fall asleep in my seat."

Peaslee reached into his briefcase and pulls out a folder. "I would like to show you some pictures. They are grainy, but you should be able to make out some faces." He lays out the photos in front of Troy. They are of men of a variety of nationalities and cultures at a meeting; they appear relaxed, almost happy.

Troy pulled three photos out of the batch. "These men I recognize from my dreams."

The doctor nodded and held up one of the photos. "This is Kang Sheng. He is a confidant of Chairman Mao. We believe him to be the Minister of Security for the People's Republic of China." The second photo Peaslee holds up is of a rotund little Korean. "This is Kim Il-Sung the Prime Minister of North Korea." The third photo was of a soft looking but severe man in a suit and tie. "This is Lavrenti Beria, First Deputy Premier of the Soviet Union, and head of the NKVD, the Soviet Secret Police."

Troy seemed unphased by the revelations revealed by his interrogator. The little psychologist slid another photo across the table. "Do you recognize this man?"

The former POW stared at the image before him. The man was small, with a vaguely Asian look. Thin almost gaunt, with a shock of wild white hair surrounding a pair of knowing eyes. He pushed the photo back and nodded. "That is Doctor Hu."

"I see," there was a judgmental tone in Peaslee's voice, "One last picture, who is the man in-between Sheng and Beria, the one behind Hu?"

Troy looked at the photo. There were dozens of people, all posed for a formal photo. He recognized many of them from his dream, and yes there was the man Peaslee had identified as Beria, and the other he called Sheng, and between them was Hu. Behind them all was a man who seemed out of place, a man whose features were so familiar, but whose expression was entirely alien to him. There was something wrong with that face. It was slack, emotionless, and almost dead. There was no life in those eyes. Yet they were eyes that Troy recognized, and that recognition welled up inside him and brought him to his feet. He turned away from the table and stood there shaking.

"Who is that man?" demanded Peaslee. "Who is that standing behind Hu?"

A tear escaped from Troy's left eye as he fought to speak. "I don't understand! How is it possible? That man, it's me!"

December 20, 1953
JACK Base 3 Codename: Whitechapel

Hollister opened the large enamel box, connected up the battery, flipped a switch, and the machinery inside suddenly began to hum. He watched a few dials jump, adjusted them to a standard and then nodded to his superior. Doctor Peaslee nodded back and dismissed his junior with a subtle hand gesture. Then he turned back toward his subject. "Captain Troy, we are going to try an experiment today. You are going to tell me about another one of your dreams. Then I am going to ask you some questions, just like we did yesterday. The difference is this little piece of equipment. It's called a Voigt magnetometer, it detects subtle changes in magnetic fields. It can help us detect certain influences, aberrations in the brain that are too subtle for the Kampff Test."

Troy nodded slightly. "Do you still think I am a traitor Doctor Peaslee?"

"I think it might be more complicated than that Captain. I assure you that I am going to do everything to help you get back to normal." He watched Troy squirm a little. "Now, tell me about another one of your dreams."

The engineer took a deep breath, closed his eyes and began to speak in a strange, almost monotonic voice. "I'm on a train in a tunnel, I'm vaguely reminded of the subway in Philadelphia, but this tunnel is much larger, much older, and it isn't level. I'm going down, down into the earth. I'm not alone; the car is full of men, young men, all of whom are covered in dust, which makes determining their nationalities difficult. From the wide range of features they seem to be mostly Asian, but with some Europeans and a few Africans. They are dressed in single piece utilitarian suits that zip up the front like a flight suit. They don't talk to each other; they don't even look at each other, the only thing they do is sway and bounce to the jostling rhythm of the train.

"We slowly pull into a station, little more than a raised concrete slab, and the doors open with a hiss. I step out and the air is hot, stagnant and heavy with the stench of humanity. I recoil a little as it seeps into my sinuses. I am just one of hundreds who march out of the train and down the platform. We move as one, in a practiced pace that may be slow, but ensures that we can all keep up. As we pass through a great gate a whistle blows, and suddenly there is another great throng of humanity, identical to our own, but moving in the opposite direction. We pass them as they move up, and we follow the wide tunnel that gently slopes down toward the dimly lit area below. We round a curve and emerge onto a staging platform overlooking a vast cavern. I move in one direction, while the others move in another. The horde moves down into the vast chamber, while I move up along a still oddly wide spiral ramp. The ramp and the tunnel itself seem different than the material around them. The cavern walls are dark gray and pitted, like sandstone. The ramp and the tunnel are smooth and slightly reflective, almost nacreous, and I can see no evidence of striations or layers. The material is slick, and difficult to walk on, though not impossible. I reach the top and find myself in a turret-like structure that allows me to see the entirety of the vast cavern that stretches out below me.

"Vast is not sufficient to describe the scene that my eyes took in. The cavern was immense, Brobdingnagian, cyclopean, stretching as far as I could see, and disappearing into murky darkness with hints of dim lights moving about in the distance. The cavern was not empty, everywhere were men, hundreds of men, and their machines, moving earth and climbing the scaffolding that clung like strange metallic growths to the masses of rock and sediment that were being excavated. Beneath the diggings were more of the strange nacreous structures, glittering in the faint light. They emerged from their earthen tombs like spiraled and bejeweled shells, or an ancient and petrified species of gigantic fungi. All seemed to be adorned with strange rods of an odd metallic compound, that would suddenly bulge into a sphere or oblong joint. These branching groups of apparatus shared the queer organic feel of the structures that supported them, though as I said the matrix was definitely more metallic in appearance. The purpose of such equipment was known to me, but I cannot tell you what it was. It bore some resemblance to the forest of antennae one can see across the rooftops of major cities, and it reminded me of the materials I sought to commission from the attendees at the party in my other dream, though infinitely better crafted. In some ways I think that the parts I was intent on purchasing were mere crude analogs of the pieces that were being excavated; that I was asking a blacksmith to supply parts to help repair a Lockheed F-80 fighter jet. Still, despite reservations, there was an undeniable sense of pride concerning what was happening in the cavern before me, pride and an immense sense of satisfaction.

"That feeling was suddenly interrupted by a disturbance in the distance. There was a sound, an explosion of sorts, but also a great roaring, like a pump or engine suddenly tearing itself to pieces, but on a massive scale. A plume of dust, smoke and debris suddenly mushroomed into view, it was at least a mile away but even from that distance I could hear the screams of men as they ran for their lives from whatever it was that had happened. Doctor Hu appeared by my side, mumbling some strange words I did not understand. In his hand was a tool of some sort, not totally unlike a screwdriver but where the blade should have been, there was instead a small glass bead that glowed as Hu chanted. With each repetition the bead glowed brighter, and was soon joined by a high-pitched whistling that hurt my ears. As the infernal whine grew louder something large and amorphous reeled up into the sky, flailing amongst the smoke and debris. It was a monstrous thing, like a gelatinous polyp, black in places while seemingly invisible in others; it twisted and turned in the sky, roiling in apparent agony. Whip-like tendrils flailed from its body smashing against the walls and nacreous structures, and wrapping around those poor souls who were too slow to escape its attentions.

"Then, as if some threshold had been reached the thing ceased moving. It hung there in the sky like a twisted mockery of a moon. It shuddered there, shuddered and then seemed to shrink, implode, before finally with a great and horrid sound it exploded, disintegrating into innumerable pieces that tumbled from the air and covered the city in slime and gore. The pieces, strange amalgamations of bladders, muscles and cartilage writhed on the ground for a few moments before finally collapsing into masses of quickly desiccating mucus. Doctor Hu cursed and spat a word I was not familiar with, but which still filled me with fear and loathing. I needed to know what it was that created in me such terror, that filled me with such anxiety and dread. With the strange high pitched alarm still ringing in my ears I screamed that strange word that Hu had cursed just moments before. I screamed it and demanded an explanation.

"And then he tells me, and I could no longer hear the workers below crying out in terror and agony over the sound of my own screams! Screams that force me to flee back to the waking world, where I wake up in a cold sweat, my heart pounding. But though I have dreamed this dream countless times I cannot tell you what he told me. I can only remember the name, that horrid name that Hu spat out in disgust. I remember it, but it still fills me with dread. Perhaps you can tell me Doctor Peaslee. Do you know what horrid monstrosity Doctor Hu was referring to?"

Peaslee shook his head. "Do you know where this dream took place Captain Troy?"

Troy shook his head. "He said this word, a word I didn't understand."

Peaslee fumbled with a map. He pointed at a spot. "Was it here? This is where Intelligence says Doctor Hu has been excavating, a place called Hwadae. Is that where you were?"

"What does it mean Doctor Peaslee?" Troy was ranting. He rose up from his chair and tore at the sensors. There was foam at the corners of his mouth. "What does it mean Peaslee! Tell me. WHAT IS A SHOG-GOTH!?"

December 23, 1953
Jack Base 2 Codename: Candlestick

"I'm going to be honest with you Captain Troy, You are in it deep." Peaslee took a drag off his cigarette. "You left your accommodations, in the middle of the night, jumped the fence into a restricted area, and sabotaged some very delicate and expensive equipment. Would you care to explain yourself?" There was no reply. "Captain you are facing charges of sabotage and treason, the penalty for which is death. Would you care to explain yourself?"

Captain Troy glared at Peaslee with tired eyes. "You know what I was doing there. You've known all along why I am here."

A smile came across Peaslee's face. "Of course I know, I've been waiting for you for a long time. Well, you or someone similar. I have to admit, you had us confused for a while. Your repressed memories were backwards. The memories are supposed to be of your world as seen through a human's eyes, not of our world seen through alien eyes. It was puzzling, until we realized that it wasn't the memories that were being repressed, but rather an entire personality, two minds in one body, one human and one Yithian. You must have been very desperate to attempt such a thing."

Troy strained at his bonds. "You can't hold me forever. I have friends, allies, they'll come for me."

"Do you mean Beria?" Peaslee was suddenly smug. "I'm sorry to tell you, I've just gotten word that the Soviets executed him earlier today. Tell me, what happens to your kind when the body you inhabit is killed inside an ELF field?"

Troy's jaw set. "You tiny little creatures, you have no idea what you've done. You've destroyed one of the Great Minds, an intellect that had existed for millions of years, had traveled through space and time almost at will. Had seen things and done things you couldn't even dream of."

"A Great Mind? I seriously doubt it. You've made too many mistakes." A look of incredulity came across the prisoner's face. "See, like that. I've studied your kind for decades, ever since one of you inhabited my father, you don't do emotions. Oh I think you have them, but I don't think you've figured out how to translate them into a human response. Never have and never will. You on the other hand, seem quite expressive. It makes me think you aren't like those that came before you. It was one of the clues that gave you away to my partner. He thinks you are little more than a common thief."

"How dare you!" shrieked Troy, or the thing that was pretending to be Troy.

Peaslee whipped out a hand and slapped the Captain across the face. "How dare I? How dare you! You come to our world, inhabit hundreds of our people, enslaved thousands more, and forced them to excavate your ruins, and you think you are entitled to be outraged?" Peaslee spat in the thing's face. "We've tolerated the incursions from your kind because in most cases your actions have been rather benign, or at least suitably inscrutable, but this, what you have done here we cannot tolerate."

The faux Troy was suddenly laughing. "You think that you can threaten me, us? I'll tell you what you want to know, but not because of your threats, but because it amuses me." He put his hands on the table, the restraints were gone. "You creatures, you humans, you like to classify things, to lump things together, to split them apart. You find it convenient to identify things and say this is what it is. You say 'communist', but don't imagine that a Russian communist might be different from one from China, or Poland, or even Cuba. You call us Yithians, the Great Race, so named because we learned to leap our minds through time. We learned how when no one else could. We move back and forth through time almost at will, without fear of the things that hound other lesser races. We learned it so that we could survive, so that we could leap from one time to another, and survive while all the other races faded into memory. But we're not a single race. We're millions of minds, but we're thousands of races. Individuals hand-picked from the races that we choose to inhabit. It is our gift to them, that some select number of their ranks should join us in eternity. But our mastery of time is not without limits. There are rules Peaslee, universal laws that even we cannot bend. The leap across time takes energy, precious particles that are rare, and difficult to store. The bigger the leap, the more energy that is needed. We are a patient race, we built collectors, batteries, and then planned to make the leap en masse."

"But something has gone wrong?"

"In the far future, the battery is damaged. There aren't enough tachyons for all of us to migrate. There was talk of a culling, of leaving some behind. Of marooning them in realtime forever. The very thought led to dissent, to conflict, to armed rebellion, and inevitably to war. Some of us, a mere handful, were able to come to this time. We've built an army, a nation, and with our superior knowledge and technology we'll soon come to dominate this age. And you, and all like you will learn your place, and serve your rightful masters."

Peaslee stood up and turned away from his prisoner. The door opened and Hollister came in. Peaslee yielded the floor to his assistant.

"Do you think we are fools? Do you think we would allow you to come here, to do this without permission? You think these people, these humans weak, but it does not occur to you that we spend an inordinate amount of time studying them?" The thing that was pretending to be Hollister sat down.

"But the leadership rejected them for the migration!" Troy replied.

"Because we could not subjugate them you fool. Not because they were too weak, but because they were too strong! They learn, they adapt, they overcome. They are more than worthy enough to contribute to our ranks, but we feared what inhabiting them might do to us, and them. So we chose not to, but always regretted not adding their uniqueness to our own. You have solved that problem. When the time is right, Peaslee and his kind will turn off the ELF generator and we will forcibly separate you and your kind from the human minds."

"You are taking us back? We would rather die."

Hollister shook his head. "We aren't taking you back, we're taking the humans. You will remain here, surrounded by military forces you cannot hope to defeat. Trapped by the technology that we ourselves have supplied to the humans. You will be marooned here, and you will live out your traitorous lives in realtime. Oh, I am sure that you will be able to rebuild some of the technology. You might be able to move from one body to another, but for how long? How long do you think you can last, trapped in this world?"

December 27, 1953
The Bridge of No Return

Wingate Peaslee stood watching as the prisoners trundled slowly across the bridge and into the trucks that waited on the northern side. There was a man there, a small Asian man, old, but seemingly spry. As the last prisoner was whisked away he gave an odd three finger salute which Hollister returned quickly. Then the little man, who Peaslee recognized as Doctor Hu, turned and walked out of view.

"We don't trust you," said Peaslee.

Hollister nodded. "We know, that is why we gave you the designs to the ELF generator, so you wouldn't have to."

"I've read Hu's file. He's been here a long time, longer than the others. He's smart. We think he's a liability. He'll figure a way out. We have plans to eliminate him preemptively."

Hollister shook his head. "I wouldn't try that if I were you. You are right about Hu. He is smarter than the others, and he will probably figure a way out, in fact I'm counting on it."

Peaslee was suddenly annoyed. "The deal was that we were to keep them contained, if Hu gets out . . ."

"Calm yourself my friend. Hu isn't your enemy."

A look of confusion crept across Peaslee's face. "But he's been working with them, planning, rebuilding. He was one of the first."

Once more Hollister shook his head. "He's been working with them yes, planning, and building. But what has he built, but simply a very comfortable prison." He looked at his watch. "Hu is not their ally Peaslee, he is their warden, and will be for what you would consider a very long-time." The alien took a small device out of his pocket, it was a strange conglomeration of spheres and rods. "You will excuse me

Doctor Wingate Peaslee, but the field is about to drop and I have a very important appointment that must be kept."

Peaslee drew his gun. "I don't think so; we would like you to stay."

Hollister flicked a switch and the tiny machine began to move. "You will let me go Wingate, you have no choice. I must keep my appointment; everything we've done here in the last few days depends on it."

He cocked the pistol and pointed it at the whirling machine. "You're lying."

"No, I am not. If I do not make this leap, you will not be here, you will not have done these things or any of the work you have done for the last forty-five years, and all of our efforts will have been for naught. Unless you let me go, the rebels will be free to move as they please."

Peaslee took a step forward and placed the muzzle of the gun as close to the spinning machine as he could. "Impossible, you can't have been manipulating me for the last forty-five years, I would have noticed."

"You are correct Wingate, we haven't been actively manipulating you, but we did set things in motion, set you on the path, pointed you in the direction that brought you here today. We did interfere with your life, but only once. Don't you remember?"

Peaslee lowered the gun. "Where are you going?" There were tears in his eyes. "Please, I have to know!"

The machine was nearly invisible now, it moved faster than Peaslee would have thought possible. He could barely hear Hollister speak, "You already know, I have to go to where it all began for you Wingate. I'm sorry, but it's the only way."

The Terrible Old Man fell to his knees, "Tell me!"

The Hollister-thing's voice seemed to grow weak, and as the Yithian left and the body it inhabited collapsed he spoke one last time. "I have to go to your father Wingate, I have to displace him. It's the only way to make sure you'll grow up to be the man you are, to gather so much information about us, to help us build a trap for our criminals. We need you Wingate Peaslee, we need you to fulfill your mission, to do that we must displace your father, and destroy your family. In order for us to use you, we must teach you to hate us. It's the only way."

And as the man that was Hollister came back to his own time and body, Doctor Wingate Peaslee, the Terrible Old Man, could do nothing but weep.

NAMES ON
THE BLACK LIST
BY ROBERT M. PRICE

"Look, Senator, I'm just a retired bus driver!"

"Let me repeat the question, Mr. Sargent. Are you now, or have you ever been, a member of the Esoteric Order of Dagon?"

"'F' Pete's sake! That must have been thirty years ago!"

"Twenty-six years, to be exact. So I'm to take that as a yes?"

"C'mon, it was just a social club. It was just like the Rotary or somethin.'"

"Perhaps the Odd Fellows would be a better comparison, Mr. Sargent?"

"Bah! Whatever y' say!" Joe Sargent exclaimed, waving a slightly webbed hand in the air dismissively.

Joseph McCarthy shuffled some papers from the file folder on the podium before him. "Oh, I think it was a bit more than a harmless moose lodge, Mr. Sargent. I see here that you appeared eight years ago before the House Committee on Inhuman Activities…"

"Dun't remind me! That was near about as foolish as this!"

"It seems you were reported as using your jalopy of a bus to smuggle some of your Dagon brothers out of town while Federal agents were closing in on the place."

"What smuggle? I told you, Senator! I was a bus driver! I was just making my scheduled run! We didn't even know your G-men were on their way! M' passengers were just headed out to Arkham and Ipswich on errands. What, I dunno. Ain't my business to pry."

"Come now, Mr. Sargent! You mean to tell us you had no knowledge of the goings-on out in the sea off Devil Reef? The massing of the creatures you call the Deep Ones, and the, er, Shoggoths?"

"You called 'em that, I didn't. I said all this before. You probably got it all typed up right in front of you. I never see'd any o' those things. Sounds to me like some folks watched that new motion picter about

258

the Critter from the Black Lagoon and thought they was seein' a news reel!"

"There's something *to* that, Mr. Sargent. In fact, it may interest you to know that we are right now investigating Universal Studios. That 'make-up' looked a little *too* real, though I doubt that surprised *you*. Why, just look at you! And the rest of you there in Innsmouth! You ought to be marked Exhibit A! What exactly *is* your ethnic background, anyway?"

"Yeah, yeah, we got, I got, that 'Innsmouth look' yew outsiders talk about. But that's just cuz m' pappy was an old New England salt and m' ma was from the Polynesian islands. Same as most o' th' Innsmouth folk. Can't help it if you all think anybody but white folks is suspicious. You 'n the Klan!"

"I'll ignore that insult against this committee, Mr. Sargent. But why won't you tell us what goes on in the Dagon Hall?"

"I done told ya! Told ya thirty years ago! There ain't many of us left. Yer G-men saw ta that thirty years ago!"

"Twenty-six, Mr. Sargent."

"We mainly drink and play cards. Always have. And we spec'late on why the gov'ment torpedoed the Reef, and why they took away most o' our young people. We're a dyin' town, Senator, and it's the fault o' the US gov'ment. Why cantcha leave us old folks be?"

"I think you're not exactly being straight with us, Mr. Sargent. You can't be unaware that more and more people with the so-called Innsmouth look have been popping up in harbor cities on both coasts and the Gulf of Mexico, and that wherever they move in, mysterious disappearances increase. And the names! 'Gilman,' 'Marsh,' 'Fisher.' These aren't real names! They're jokes! Do you think we're that stupid?"

"Whatcha mean, they ain't names? Why, you got some senators with them names, if I ain't mistaken."

"We'll get to them, Mr. Sargent. But you seem to know something about them. This committee would very much enjoy hearing more."

At this point, Senator Smollet from Rhode Island was heard to groan with barely-suppressed indignation, then: "Damn you, McCarthy! This has gone too far!"

Turning to look behind him, McCarthy shot back, "Or maybe not far *enough*, eh, Smollet?" Joe Sargent, who was beginning to enjoy the whole show just a bit, started to snicker, then thought better of it. But he did speak up.

"Jest what is it you're so all-fired afeerd of? That we'll marry yer daughters? We keep to our own kind. They's few enough of us."

"But more all the time! Haven't you been listening to me, man? What can you tell us about your kinfolk who've recently arrived in New Orleans, Boston, Providence, and so on?"

"Dunno, Senator McCarthy. I reckon they's the sons 'n daughters o' the good Innsmouth folks what done ran off when the G-men overran the town all those years ago. But I never met a one of 'em."

***

During a recess in the proceedings, once Joe Sargent had been dismissed as a witness, one of Senator McCarthy's colleagues, not one of his Committee members, approached him. "Joe," he whispered, with a quick look around to make sure no reporters were snooping, "I don't see why you're opening this thing up again after all this time! I mean, Sargent's right, isn't he? He's a poor half-breed hick! And why this vendetta against his dying town? Just wait—it won't be long before they're all dead."

McCarthy's beady eyes narrowed even more. "Chuck, did you ever read the reports on the 1928 raid? It reads like science fiction. It's our men who described these giant amoebas, the Shoggoths. And the two-legged fish! These can't be trustworthy reports! If you ask me, it means the men who filed these crazy documents were co-conspirators with the people we sent them after! How they wormed their way into that position, I have no idea. But that just goes to show how far-reaching the conspiracy must be! What on earth could they be after? It's subversion, sure, but why? What do they represent? I'm stumped. But I'm also worried as hell! Are you beginning to see?"

The other's eyes were wide, though not as wide as Joe Sargent's.

"I don't know, Joe. It's the first I've heard of this. You sure it wasn't some practical joke?"

"If it was, it wasn't very funny! And did you know the guys who filed those reports, the ones on the subs, have all disappeared? Well, time to start again."

***

It had been a long day. And it wasn't over yet. When Senator McCarthy got back to his office to make a few preparations for the next day's hearing, he saw that he must have left his desk lamp on after turning out the other lights. Well, he didn't really need the ceiling light, so he sat down, reaching for a folder within the circle of the lamp's illumination. But before he could read it, he was startled by a rasping voice from an unseen figure that had to be sitting in the chair over in the far corner of the room.

"Quite a performance today, Senator!"

McCarthy recoiled, backing away from the desk in his rolling chair. Away from the direct glare, his eyes began to adjust to the outlying shadows. He could see a man slumped in the chair. He looked as if wearing an enveloping overcoat or robe, like a boxer. The outline of the man's head was indistinct, perhaps surrounded with a towel, though the voice was not muffled.

"No, Senator, don't get up. And don't come any closer. Not to worry; I'm not armed. Except with the truth."

"Who…?"

"I knew you wanted to speak with me, but you didn't know where to send the subpoena. The name's Arnie Eldridge. You know, I was assigned to one of the subs that attacked the Reef. Off Innsmouth. You were talking about me earlier today."

"How did you…?"

"Guess. You'll probably be correct, as correct as you were about some of that stuff you said earlier. Let me get to the point. I and some others were assigned to the mission for the very good reason that we grew up in the area. I'm from Innsmouth itself. The other commanders were from Ipswich and Newburyport. We knew the whole layout, the depths off shore, and what was hidden there. And once we got our orders we contacted the higher-ups in the Dagon Hall. They couldn't get *everybody* out, but most of the older folks who never used to leave their boarded houses got out through a network of tunnels. Many of the common folk followed the old train tracks out of town, and a few more got out on the rattletrap bus. And others, well…just…swam away. There were a number of undersea refuges. Yha-N'thlei was just the tip of the iceberg, you see. We had to buy some time for all this, so we summoned the sea-shoggoths—you know about them, I believe—to keep the subs busy, at least *looking* busy, as long as we could. We hadn't wanted them to be seen, but it couldn't be helped."

"Sounds like a bad dream to me. A fairy tale. You expect me to believe this? How do I even know you are who you say you are?" McCarthy was raising his voice to cover the sounds of his fumbling through a desk drawer. "But I have seen your picture. Maybe I'd recognize you..."

Here he clicked on the flashlight he had fished out of the desk. No sooner had he done so than he dropped it, shaken.

His visitor rose to his feet, sloughing off the overcoat.

"I wish you hadn't done that. But perhaps it's for the best. The only way you'd take me seriously. Might as well turn on all the lights now."

"No thanks! I've seen enough!"

"No, I don't think you have. I've brought something for you to see. It's on the floor in front of your desk. Tell you what: I'll be on my way. Look at the evidence by yourself, and you'll know what to do next."

Short of breath, Senator McCarthy sat as immobile as Lincoln in his Memorial. He said nothing, made no motion, as Arnie Eldridge shuffled past him and into the lushly carpeted hall of the Senate office building.

The Senator's head pounded, his breath short. He tried to calm himself, to brace himself against whatever revelations the box might contain. From the shape, size, and color of the deep green cardboard cube, it looked to be a standard evidence file box. The FBI housed thousands of these things.

He got up unsteadily and flicked the light switches on. The added illumination did not comfort him much. He picked up the box and placed it on a cleared area of his mahogany desk.

Off with the lid. Why was he suddenly remembering that old story about Pandora?

There were heavily redacted copies of the original reports of the mission commanders, with whole paragraphs blacked out. There was a pair of broad bracelets and a pectoral, all fashioned from a peculiar gold-silver mixture, or so it appeared to be. There was a separate set of papers about these artifacts. The world 'electrum' with a question mark caught his eye. There was a wrinkled paper bearing the letterhead of the Director of the Smithsonian Institution declining the gift of these articles for display in the museum. Holding the items to the light, Senator McCarthy could see the elaborate workmanship depicting crude, yet somehow lifelike, scenes of sexual congress between humanoid forms and less identifiable creatures. It was plain now why the Smithsonian had said 'Thanks but no thanks.'

A jade statuette looked like a totem pole such as one finds among the Indians of the Pacific Northwest, but the effigy atop the column was a tentacled octopus. Underneath it was something suggesting a toad, though it possessed bat-like ears. Under that was a random collection of bulging eyes and fanged orifices. The detail was startling, though the style was altogether different from that of the pectoral and wristlets.

There were other, smaller items in the box, but McCarthy's eyes were drawn to a six-inch tall jar which seemed to glow softly with an inner radiance. This he picked up gingerly and watched as something swirled slowly within. He felt an odd compulsion to shake the jar, but he managed to resist. At the same moment he heard the muted whisper of his better judgment telling him to put the jar back in the box and leave the office. But curiosity had begun to rise within him as if it had been sexual arousal, and all hesitations evaporated. He began unscrewing the jar.

It was old and long unopened. There was rust in the lid. Residue of the contents looked to have hardened in the grooves, and it took all his might to twist the lid off. The glow increased in intensity as the gelatin within met the air for the first time in who knew how long. And it was definitely moving now, shifting in a slow spiral. Now the Senator felt a black cloud of intense dread settling over him, as well as a sense of wistful regret…but he stood transfixed.

He did not move an inch even when the silvery gel spewed like a geyser from the jar mouth and enveloped him like the molten salt encasing Lot's doomed wife. It seemed impossible that such an amount of living mass could have been confined to such a tiny prison. But there was enough of it to cover him—and to devour him. He sank to his knees as he lost consciousness, becoming one with the shivering, quaking, grinding mass. It sprouted eyes and mouths, human facial features that quickly sank back into the jelly, then reemerged, too many of them. Hair sprouted like grass, then fell out. The mass contracted and shuddered. Finally it settled into a stable form.

And that form stood to its feet and stepped briskly into the office bathroom. It looked in the tall mirror and realized it had better cover its nakedness. The Senator always kept a closet with spare suits, shirts, and shoes. He went downstairs and had the attendant summon a taxi. It took no time to arrive, and the figure, as if used to every detail of its unaccustomed world, climbed into the back seat. He gave no directions, but only looked at the driver's identification plate. He could see the driver was not the man depicted there, but he did look familiar. When the cabbie turned around to speak to him over his shoulder, the passenger recognized the greasy face and bald pate of Joe Sargent.

"FBI Headquarters, right?"

He nodded.

***

The man was shown at once into Director Hoover's office, still occupied at this late hour. The tall, heavy man standing behind the desk did not at first turn to face him.

"It's done," his visitor announced prosaically, as if some minor errand were now to be checked off a list. "I'm McCarthy now."

"Good," the man said and turned, focusing his protuberant eyes on the new McCarthy. "I suppose now we can drop all this damn nonsense and focus on a real conspiracy—the god-damn Commies."

THE END OF THE GOLDEN AGE

BY BRIAN M. SAMMONS
AND GLYNN OWEN BARRASS

The thick manila folder hit the conference table with a heavy *thwap*. From it a few small, thin, magazines with brightly colored covers spilled out.

Special Agent Donald Carson of the FBI looked at his partner, Special Agent Robert Moore, a large bear of a man three years his senior who sat across the table from him. Bob just raised an eyebrow and quirked a bemused grin back at him. The man who had walked into the room and tossed the file onto the table, Special Agent in Charge Mike Bateham, took a moment to light a cigarette before speaking.

"That's your next assignment, boys."

Carson picked up three of the thin magazines and quickly looked at them. The title of the first one read, *The Treader of the Stars* and underneath that was a smaller subtitle; *...and the Slumbering Abomination!* The next shared the same main title but had a different subtitle: *...and the Chaos that Crawls!* The third of these *Treader of the Stars* magazines was subtitled; *...and the Yellow Menace!*

"You want us to look into these funny books, chief?" Moore asked as he plucked the Yellow Menace issue from Carson's hand to look incredulously at it. The cover showed a man in a black cape whose face was concealed within a black hood and goggles with his hands outstretched dramatically. This black clad figure was on all the comic book covers, so Moore took him to be the titular 'Treader'. From the hooded man's spread fingers, wavy lines were drawn representing energy of some kind that flowed towards a second man. This figure was dressed in tattered yellow robes and wore a cracked white mask. The yellow robed man was sending lightning bolts back towards the Treader from his own hands and it was obvious that the two were supposed to be locked in some kind of magical battle. It was the typical kind of kid stuff that you always found in rags like these. Moore wondered what the big deal was.

"Some Kraut egghead wrote a book a few months back called *Seduction of the Innocent* about the evils of those 'funny books', Moore," SAC Bateham said, exhaling a cloud of Lucky Strike smoke. "He claims they're warping the minds of the kids that read them and causing a rise in juvenile delinquency. Well a bunch of Senators agree with him, so they're gonna have a hearing on the matter soon. That means the Bureau has been tasked to look into the matter. Mostly to gather names and evidence should criminal charges start getting handed out, the usual sort of thing."

"For real, chief?" Carson asked. "I read comic books when I was in the Pacific. They used to come in our care packages to help us pass the time between battles. They were always sort of silly, but harmless."

"I don't know," Moore said and held up the issue he was holding. "This 'Yellow Menace' could be about the Chinks."

Carson couldn't tell if his partner was having him on or not.

"Well the senators want us to look into it and so that's what we're gonna do. The boys in New York have their hands full because most of those things come out there. However in our neck of the woods we've got a little publisher called Funny Time Comics. They're the ones who put out that Star Treader crap and that's got someone, somewhere worried enough to have us look into it. So you've got some of those comic books to read and the name and address of the guy that runs the publishing company. The boys in background couldn't find anything on the guy that writes and draws the comic, so I want you two to go talk to that publisher, lean on him a bit, and see if you smell anything funny or red. Get him to spill on the creator of that comic book. After that, go see that guy and determine if he should be someone worth keeping an eye on. Any questions?"

Both agents shook their heads.

"Alright then, get to it."

***

An hour later Moore was behind the wheel of their government issued black sedan while Carson sat shotgun, reading through issues of *The Treader of the Stars*.

"So how are the funny books?" Moore asked.

"Weird, and not funny at all. From what I gather this 'Treader of the Stars' is some kind of bodiless, alien *thing*. It's really old and from 'between time and space' and it went into the body of a professor of advanced mathematics named Langham. Now together, this Treader keeps running into weird things like aliens, ancient gods, monsters, things from dreams. Sometimes the Treader helps the things accomplish whatever they're trying to do. Other times he fights with them. It's all over the place and I really can't make much sense out of it."

"So he's like a superhero or something?"

"Kind of, but not really. He 'knows the absolute truth that lies at the center of all space and time' whatever the hell that means. But that means he reshapes reality as he sees fit because what mankind knows as reality is just a lie. So he sometimes melts people into goo, or summons disgusting things with tentacles on their heads to eat his enemies. Most of the time he just tells people 'the truth', that drives them crazy and they usually end up killing themselves in some way."

"Yeah, that does sound pretty weird. Anything in there about commies, crime, drugs, homosexuals, or anything else that would get people in a twist?"

"No, nothing like that. It is against religion as it says the earth is older than humanity thinks and that all the gods man has ever prayed to either never existed, never cared about us, or are just masks of the 'The Formless One.' Maybe that's why the Washington Boys wants us to give the author the business." Carson said.

"Hmmm," Moore sagely commented before slowing the sedan and turning the wheel. "Well time to get serious, this is the place."

Moore pulled the car into a weed-specked dirt parking lot next to a small brick building in need of a new paint job. A faded sign out front read *Funny Time Comics* and there was a rusted green 1940 Plymouth in the lot. There was also a kid with a long, thin case of some kind under one arm, banging on the building's side door.

The two G-men got out of their car, put on their hats, and sauntered up behind the teenager without the boy even noticing them. The youth was banging on the door fit to break it and shouting, "Come on, I know you're in there. I saw you through the window looking at me. You've got to listen to me, it's important!"

"What's so important?" Carson said through his best no-nonsense expression.

The teen whipped around with a start, his eyes wide and lips trembling in mid-shout. His blond hair was lanky, unwashed, and in need of a good cutting. His twitchy face was pockmarked with zits, had a shiny film of oily sweat coating it, and he had a few straggly hairs over his upper lip. The teen's clothes were unkempt, stained with food, and a nose hair curling stench of body odor wafted off the boy in waves.

Everything about the kid rankled Moore who did nothing to hide his contempt. "My partner asked you a question, answer the man." He said through a sneer.

"You…you guys make comics too?" The kid asked, his face twitching into a thin-lipped smile. "You wanna take a look at my work? It's really good, honest. Here let me show you."

The kid then fumbled with his long, ratty case, tugging on the stuck zipper.

"No son, we don't write comic books. Go on home now, we've got business here," Carson said in a firm but friendly manner.

"No wait, you've gotta see this. It's amazing. Let me just get this open… I swear, you'll love it. Ain't no one ever done stuff like this never."

"Scram, kid." Moore said, grabbling the reeking, disheveled youth by the arm and pulling him out of their path.

The teenager's beady brown eyes darted back and forth between the two men in front of him and his protruding Adam's apple bobbed as he gulped. Then his brow furrowed and a look of rage bloomed in his face. Carson could not remember ever seeing anyone so young look so mad.

"Beat it, already," Moore said and took a menacing step towards the boy.

The kid got the message at last. He turned and slowly walked away in a sulk, muttering to himself as he went, tossing baleful glances over his shoulder at the two FBI men as his shoes shuffled in the dirt. Carson and Moore watching him hop a three-foot wooden fence and shamble away through the neighboring vacant lot.

"Weird little punk," Moore said.

"Come on, let's get this over with," Carson said. He then turned back to the building, pounded on the door, and yelled out, "Mr. Abe Smilansky? Open up, it's the FBI."

After a moment the door cracked opened a few inches and a wrinkled, bespectacled face crowned with wisps of white hair peered out at the two agents. "That *meshuggina* kid gone?" the old man asked with a thick accent.

"Yes sir. Agents Carson and Moore, FBI. Open up, Mr. Smilansky, we've got to talk to you."

The older man shut the door to undo the chain, then opened it wide and told the two government men to come in. "I'm sorry about that. That damn kid has been hounding me for weeks. He thinks—"

"We're not here about some kid," Moore cut him off as he pushed roughly past the smaller man and went into the building. "We're here about the books you've been printing."

"What, my comic books?"

"Yes sir," Carson said, stepping inside and closing the door behind him.

"We want to know everything about the one you're putting out called the 'Treader of Stars.'" Moore said.

"W…why?" Abe Smilansky stammered.

"We'll ask the questions here, pal!" Moore, well into his role as bad cop, emphasized the point by jabbing a thick finger into the man's chest.

Carson calmly added, "There's been some talk in Washington about how comic books are no good for kids these days. They're full of sex, drugs, violence, and pink-o propaganda. Your Treader comic has got some people worried, and when they're worried, they send us to look into things. Make sure things aren't hinky with the guys making the stuff up."

"Look, I didn't write it—"

"No but you publish it," Moore cut the little man off. "And that makes you just as responsible for the filth."

Carson took a moment to light up a cigarette before giving a well-rehearsed sympathetic sigh. "Look, Mr. Smilansky, we know you didn't write this thing, and you know you don't want to stand before the Senate and have to defend yourself like the folks in Hollywood had to do, but that's where this thing is heading. America is at war with the Commies, and whether it's shooting them in Korea, or making sure their dirty ideas don't corrupt the minds of the youth back here, it's a never-ending battle. And all those not on the right side of things will be treated the same. So, are you on the side of America?"

Abe Smilansky looked bewilderedly from one agent to the other. Both G-men could smell the fear seeping through his pores, which meant a quick and easy day for them.

"Of course I'm on the side of America. I love America!" Smilansky said emphatically.

"Good to hear that. Now, tell us everything you know about the guy who writes and draws this rag, a T. Buckwell," Carson said as he pulled out a note pad and a stub of a Berol Black Beauty pencil.

"Well I don't know much about the man," Abe began. When both agents gave him a dubious look he quickly went on. "Honest I don't. I've never met him. About a year back I got a box from him in the mail with the first four issues of his Treader all drawn out, worded, and ready to print. A letter with it said that if I wanted to publish his stuff that he had three more issues done and was working on more of them."

"That seems like a strange way to do business, Mr. Smilansky," Carson said.

"Oh it's very strange, but just a month before that I lost a couple of my regular guys to the big shots in New York, I was desperate for something to put out. So I read what he sent me. Honestly, it didn't make any sense to me, I don't get a lot of that horror and sci-fi stuff, but it sure sells like hotcakes at the theaters. So I took a chance and published it and it soon became the best seller of all the titles I put out. The kids just love it."

"And you still haven't met Mr. Best Seller?"

"No. He always said he was too busy 'transcribing the messages' to come to the offices. That's what he called it, like he was having visions or something. The guy is a real odd duck. He often writes crazy stuff like that in the letters he sends with his new issues. For example, when I sent him the contract for his Treader stories, he said he would only sign it if his stuff was listed as nonfiction. I told him I didn't make such distinctions in my comics and he wrote back that made him happy as there were no distinctions between fiction and reality. Weird stuff like that was common with him. But he always delivered fully written and drawn issues ahead of deadline and, well, he worked cheap."

"So you never met him, you two ever talk on the telephone?" Moore asked.

"No. I mentioned it to him once, but he said he didn't trust telephones. The only way we ever communicated was through letters that accompanied the issues he sent in, and the ones I'd send back with his monthly check."

"You got any of his letters?" Carson asked.

"Oh, maybe his last one, but I don't know. Once I read 'em, I usually tossed 'em in the trash. No reason to keep 'em."

"What about his address?"

"Yeah, that I got. Here, let me get it for you," Abe said and then walked into his tiny, cluttered office. The two agents followed close behind. The publisher cleared his desk of piled newspapers to uncover a rolodex. A quick flip through it and he pulled out a card with a name and address on it and handed it to Agent Carson.

"Thomas Buckwell," The agent said and then read the address. "This is about eighty miles away from here."

"Yep," Abe added.

"Swell, another long drive," Moore muttered.

"You got any of his comic book stuff that he sent you around here?" Carson asked.

"No, as I get them in, I send them to the printer. It's a month-by-month thing. Kind of scary not having anything in advance by the guy, but then just dealing with the man is kind of scary too."

Carson nodded. "Thank you for your cooperation, Mr. Smilansky. We'll look into this, but rest assured, we will get back in touch with you soon. This isn't over," Carson said, delivering the standard FBI farewell threat. With that the two agents let themselves out.

On their way back to the car, Carson asked, "So what do you think?"

"He's sort of a weasel, but probably not a subversive. All he cares about is money." Moore said.

"My take on him too. It's this Thomas Buckwell that's got all the crazy ideas."

As Agent Moore opened up the driver's side door to the car he said, "Let's go sort him out, but first let's stop for lunch. I'm starving."

Carson got into the car, grunted an acknowledgement, and the two G-men drove off.

***

After nearly two hours of driving north, the agents had left Detroit long behind. Even the new suburbs that had been slowly but steadily spreading out from the Motor City since the 40s were now far to the south of them. Out here it was farms, apple orchards, and tiny town-ships. A slice of small town America as anything Norman Rockwell ever painted for the Saturday Evening Post.

"Okay, this little spit of nothing is Clio, keep your eyes peeled for Woodside Road," Carson said, looking up from the open map in his lap.

"There it is," Moore said and turned off the highway that had only finished being paved four years back onto a single lane dirt road. "I would never have expected a writer or artists living this far out in the sticks."

"I think that will be the least of Mr. Buckwell's eccentricities." Carson said, folding up the map.

The black sedan pulled up to a clapboard, cracker box of a house hemmed in on all sides by tall grass and weeds. An old tire swing hung from a tree out front, making lazy circles in the breeze. The front porch had lost one of its banisters that held up its roof, so half of the porch was a crumpled mess. One of the side windows had been broken and now a piece of cardboard covered the hole. The house was the picture of neglect and there was no car parked on the two dirt ruts that served as a driveway, but thin threads of smoke drifting out of the chimney told the agents someone was home.

Moore and Carson carefully approached the front door, both duck-ing under the sagging porch roof, and Moore pounded on the door hard enough to rattle the windows in their frames on either side of the entrance.

"God damn it, I'm coming," someone bellowed from inside.

The door was wrenched open with the squealing protest of warped wood and a blubbery man in stained dungarees and a blue work shirt with its sleeves rolled up stood on the other side.

"Yeah?"

"Mr. Thomas Buckwell?" Carson asked.

The man took a moment to look at the two men, rubbing a hand over his chin stubble, before answering. "Yeah, who the fuck are you two?"

Moore shoved the man inside, following. "We're the FBI, pal. Stow that talk or we'll bring you in for indecency."

Buckwell barked out a single laugh but quickly stopped and looked both confused and wary. "You two for real?"

"Yes sir we are," Carson said, stepping into the house and showing the man his ID. "We want to ask you a few questions about the comic book you write."

"What for?"

"Because we think it's a filthy rag full of filthy, un-American ideas, that's why. Tell us, Thomas, you one of them pink-os?" Moore said as he looked around the gloomy front room.

"Hey I ain't no Commie!" Buckwell said indignantly. "I stormed the beaches of Normandy, damn it."

"You sure you and your neighbors aren't part of the Communist Party of America? Out here in the sticks, who knows what you all could get up to?"

"What? Hell no, we'll all just farmers and such. Good God fearing folk, that's all."

"But you're not a farmer, are you Thomas? You're a writer and an artist. An *intellectual*," Moore jabbed, stressing that last word that to J. Edgar Hoover and most of his Bureau Boys was just another word for a dirty red.

"Huh? What, wait, you—"

"And don't give us that 'we're farmers' bull! Most of the Ruskies who started the Communist party were farmers." Moore continued the intimidation. Keeping the perp reeling and off his game was a sure way of making him slip up and say something he otherwise wouldn't. "As far as being 'God fearing' we know that's a lie. We've read your sick little funny books and we know all about what you really think about God, Thomas."

"But wait, you don't understand."

"We want to understand, Thomas." Carson spoke up now that Moore had softened the man up with his verbal blows. "Why don't you tell us about your comic book? Maybe we got it wrong and it's not as subversive as we think it is."

"That's just it, it's not my comic book. I didn't write it, my brother did. I'm Henry Buckwell. Tommy was my brother."

The two agents exchanged glances for the briefest of moments.

"But you told us you were Thomas at the door," Carson said.

"You trying to pull a fast one?" Moore reached out and grabbed Mr. Buckwell by the front of his shirt and pushed him up against a wall. "Lying to a Government Man will get your ass tossed in the joint before you can say 'I like Ike.'"

"No, wait, stop." The chubby man blubbered, his face red and his eyes watery. "Look, my brother is dead. He was living here with me and writing those crazy books and was making good money for doing it too. So after he died, one of his checks came in the mail. And then another and another. So I…well I sort of cashed them. Look, he was my little brother, he would have willed them to me if the fool had ever done a will. It's not like I was hurting anyone. So when you two showed up here in your suits and driving that big, fancy car, I thought you were bankers or accountants or something, so that's why I said I was Tommy. Honest to Christ that's why."

Moore let go of Henry's shirt. The man was broken, no need to keep menacing him. He nodded at his partner. Carson would take the lead in the questioning now.

"What do you mean your brother is dead?"

"He's dead. He killed himself three months back. Went out into the field one night with my shotgun and blew his damn head off," Henry Buckwell said. "He was crazy, as in *really crazy*. The doctors said he was a schizo. Ever since he was a boy he heard voices. Made our lives hell, me and my folks, having a loony in the family. No matter how we tried to hide it, people knew. They snickered behind our backs and steered far clear of us, like we all had the crazy and it was contagious. My damn brother couldn't keep quiet about it. Always telling anyone that would listen about the 'voice from the stars.' That's what he called it. That's why he named his comic book what he did. That's why he started doing it in the first place. He said that he had to, that the Treader told him secrets and that others had to know them too. So they could 'become like they are' or something."

"Sounds like a Grade-A loony," Moore said without a hint of sympathy in his voice.

Henry nodded. "And then three months back all of the sudden he said he was finished. The Treader told him he was done and Tommy was happy for the first time I could remember in a long time. He came out of his room and even had a beer with me. We watched the Jack Benny show on the TV I had talked him into buying. He didn't talk much, he never did, but it was a good night. Then around two in the morning I was woken up by the shotgun blast. After looking all over the house for him, I found his trail through the tall grass outside and eventually what was left of him. He still had both barrels rammed into his mouth and the top of his head was nothing but a pile of wet pulp."

Henry had tears trailing down his face and he wiped his runny nose on the back of a bare forearm.

"I'm sorry about your brother, Mr. Buckwell," Carson said earnestly. "Did he leave a suicide note?"

Henry shook his head.

"Could we have a look at his room, at any of his possessions or work that he left behind?"

"Ain't nothing of his left. He didn't have much to start with, just a few clothes and some art supplies and I sold both off after he was dead. As for his work, I told you, he said he was done. When I was cleaning out his room after his... afterwards, I found that he had the last six issues of his comic book finished and in a box ready to be mailed to Detroit. There was a note on top asking me to take it to the post office like I always did for him. So I did. I didn't do it so I could keep getting his checks. Honest I didn't. I did it because he was my brother. Yeah he was crazy and all, but damn it, he was still my little brother."

After a quick inspection of Thomas' now empty room, the two agents said that they had all that they needed from Henry for the moment and that if they needed anything else, they'd come back. Henry sheepishly asked about 'the check stuff' but Carson told him to forget it. Check fraud was not high on their list of priorities this day. Once outside Moore lit up a cigarette and turned to his partner.

"Now what?"

"Now I say we go back to Mr. Smilansky and find out why he didn't tell us that he had at least three more issues of The Treader of the Stars all ready and waiting to come out. 'Kind of scary not having anything in advance' my eye."

Moore shook his head and said through a smirk, "You can never trust a Jew."

The two then got back into their car and started their long trip back south to the city.

***

The return to the city was a quiet one, the agents saving their energy for their upcoming encounter with Smilansky. When they turned onto the publisher's street, Carson said, "We should have gotten the guy's home address, you know."

His partner shook his head. "No, he's in, if that rusted piece of shit Plymouth is his car anyway."

Moore pulled up into the lot and a minute later they were heading towards the building. As they walked, Carson pulled his pencil and notepad from his pocket and scribbled down the Plymouth's number plate. Moore grunted in approval.

Rat tat tat. Moore pounded on the door. When no answer was forthcoming, the agents shared an uneasy glance. "Let's check out back," Moore said and turned. Carson went to follow when the door flew open, pausing both men in their tracks.

"What the? Can't a man use the can in peace?" Smilansky, red-faced and angry, paled considerably when he saw who'd been knocking. "Oh, I wasn't expecting you two again," he continued, his words innocent sounding. "Forget something?"

Moore stepped past Smilansky into the building while Carson ushered him in, kicking the door closed with his shoe. All subterfuge of 'good cop, bad cop' gone, Carson snarled, "You can drop the act, Mr. Smilansky."

"What, what?"

"Just say 'what' again you little weasel and see what happens." Moore said and stepped up close to the publisher.

Smilansky looked to Carson for help but the grim-faced agent shook his head.

"You lied," Moore said, looking down at the far shorter man.

"No more issues of The Treader?" Carson added. "We spoke to 'Thomas' about that."

Smilansky backed away from Moore. "You actually met him?" The surprise was evident by his tone.

Moore gave him an ugly grin. "Sort of."

The publisher looked quizzical for a moment then raised his hands in defense. "Okay, okay. I have more issues. I didn't tell you because you know, this business is my bread and butter. I didn't want 'em taken away from me."

Carson scanned the room. "They here then?"

The other man quailed. "You can't have 'em—it's my best-selling title… and… and I made a call to my lawyer while you were gone."

Moore looked to Carson and raised an eyebrow. "A relative, I bet."

Smilansky ignored the stereotype quip and continued. "Those comic book hearings of yours don't start till next year, and I'll be done with the Treader by then." His confidence growing, the old man stood straighter. "So, there's nothing you can do about it."

***

Moore was fuming when they left the building, his face twisted into a scowl. "Damned lawyers!" he said and spat on the asphalt. Carson shrugged his shoulders and said, "We can still bring him in you know." His partner paused and Carson followed suit. Moore thought for a moment and replied, "Aw screw it," before continuing towards their car.

"Hey, hey?" Moore was just opening his door when a rasping voice appeared behind him. Beyond Moore's bulk Carson saw the unkempt kid from earlier rush across the lot.

"Oh brother," Carson said.

Moore was far less eloquent. "Scram you little shit or else!"

Undaunted, the kid continued his approach, panting as he spoke. "I thought you said you didn't work here?" he whined. "I knew you were lying. You're just like everyone else. Always putting me down, laughing at me, lying to me, never listening to me." He stopped before Moore and from Carson's line of sight, disappeared beyond the big man's shoulders.

Moore sounded exasperated, "Look kid just—"

"Well you've got to listen to me now," the kid said, cutting Moore off mid-sentence. "Now I've got something important to say and you're all gonna listen."

"Huh?" Moore said in a surprised voice. There was a sudden scuffling sound and Carson, darting around the car, witnessed his partner trying to push the kid away, his big hands pressed against the teenager's bony shoulders. To Carson's horror, the kid, his spotty face twisted in rage, had a switchblade pressed into Moore's gut. Carson froze. The kid withdrew the knife and a fountain of blood followed.

Carson's world slowed down. The kid looked at him, his wild face blood-spattered, as beside him Moore collapsed slowly to his knees. Fighting through his shock Carson pushed his hand into his jacket. It reappeared holding a heavy black revolver: his Smith & Wesson Model 10. He aimed, pulled the trigger, and with a cannon-like boom the kid's face impacted, the back of his head exploding in a cloud of red mist. Time reasserted itself, the kid collapsed backwards, and Moore issued a loud groan. Carson lowered his gun and took the few steps needed to reach his partner, crouching beside the injured man.

"Agh, the little shit knifed me!" Face glossy with sweat, Moore looked to Carson with panicked eyes. "I'm gonna die!"

Carson re-holstered his gun and removed his jacket. Balling it in his hands he pressed it against the ugly flower of blood forming across Moore's chest. "I'll get on the radio," Carson said urgently, and thought rather than move his partner to reach the door he'd run round to the other side. A movement caught his eye and he saw the kid's portfolio at Moore's feet, the contents partially spilled to the asphalt, blowing in a slight breeze. He saw random frames from comic books there, glued haphazardly together, images of a black hooded superhero battling unearthly foes.

***

"Crazy." Carson said as he examined the kid's portfolio. The incident now eight hours behind him, Carson sat slouched at the pool table in his den. His partner was in hospital, stable and getting better despite the kid's attempts to murder him, and Carson, unable to sleep, his mind still filled with the events of the day, had tossed and turned beside his wife's sleeping form before he had given up, risen and walked downstairs in slippers and pajamas to his den.

He'd signed the portfolio out of the evidence locker after a quick interview with Bateham. There were procedures to follow, when an agent shot a citizen dead, but with the violent assault and hospitalization of Moore it had gone smoothly enough. Still Carson had trouble escaping the fact he had killed the kid, hence the insomnia, hence the reason he sat here, a scotch in one hand and an eight ball in the other, the kid's disjointed scrapbook flat on the pool table between them.

He was struggling to make sense of it all. Perhaps there was none. The pages were out of order and from different issues. Some had words crossed out, others were underlined, but they were all from *The Treader of the Stars*. Carson blinked. His vision blurred and the room seemed to spin for a moment. He'd only taken a sip of scotch so it wasn't that so… The pages throbbed, or at least, that's the impression his skewed vision gave him. The next moment, he was screaming himself hoarse.

"Honey? Honey!" his wife's voice appearing through a black haze, a sudden splash of wetness across his face halted his screams. Carson opened his eyes to find her staring down at him, her long red hair disheveled around a petite, worried face. She had an empty glass in her hand.

His face wet from what she's done to bring him around, his body was soaked in sweat, his hands shaking and... he looked down and found a broken pool cue clutched in his right hand.

"You probably woke half the neighborhood!" she said. "Are you drunk?"

He couldn't reply, for adding to his confusion was the horror of discovering the den utterly demolished.

"What the hell got into you?" his wife continued, her voice filled with exasperation and not a little fear. Carson wanted to reply but found himself transfixed by the carnage around them. The pool table was on its side, cracked in the center with two legs smashed. The floor was littered in broken glass and pool balls, the wall behind the bar damp with spilled alcohol. His framed Pollock prints there were smashed and askew, chaotic reminders of the strange seizure that had consumed him.

"Judy, damn," he sat up and his limbs ached like he had been through a day's field training. Despite his confusion and horror, he was quick to make an excuse now. "Sleepwalking. Must have had a nightmare. I'm sorry hon."

It was a pathetic excuse, but she nodded in sympathy. Putting down the glass she rubbed his knees. "You look half dead, Don. Let's get you back to bed and we'll talk about this in the morning."

"Yes, yes." Carson tried to compose himself further but as she helped him to his feet his mind whirled with horror.

That blasted kid's comics, he thought, they did something to me!

"Watch your step, don't step on the glass."

"Yeah thanks," Carson replied absently. The way the comics had been cut and pasted, the way they were altered, had altered *him* somehow, and brought about a break of extreme psychosis. And what if Judy had appeared in the room while he'd been wrecking it? Carson shuddered.

"It's okay Don, really." As his wife patted his hand and led him through the door, Carson had difficulty holding back his tears.

***

A few nights later Carson took his wife to see a Vincent Price movie, filmed in some new, '3-Dimensional' technology. He did it in way of an apology, as his conscience at what could have happened in his den weighed heavily on him, so much so it completely obliterated his thoughts concerning the shooting of the deranged kid. The portfolio had been returned to the Bureau without a word about his seizure as Carson thought his theory, of how the configuration of words and pictures had initiated his mental derangement, just might send him on a one-way ticket to the nuthouse.

House of Wax, the movie was called, and Judy got a real kick out of the new 3-D technology. Carson didn't see anything special about it at the time, until the next week they returned to the cinema because Judy wanted to show her sister the amazing new thing, and this time, he saw it. When the guy whacked the paddleball right at the camera, Carson, like many other movie patrons around him, found himself ducking. It was a strange sensation, something he knew wasn't real causing this involuntary physical reaction, and he couldn't help but be reminded of the incident with *The Treader of the Stars*.

The remainder of the movie left him deep in thought. On the previous showing, he hadn't gotten the trick, but once his brain got use to it... It made Carson think: is that what the comic book was like, that you had to see the trick in order to get it? He'd been unfortunate enough to receive a concentrated dose through the kid's mangled portfolio, so what if some people got it right away, and turned nuts like he had? That's what really scared him.

Or was he just going crazy? As far as he was concerned, those committee hearings couldn't come fast enough.

***

Some months after his episode with insanity, Carson was involved in a disturbing case of a teen brought in for beating his mother to death with a hammer. A standard, albeit bloody, murder case that fell under local police jurisdiction, the FBI nevertheless got a courtesy call because the woman had worked as a secretary in the Detroit bureau field office. Carson didn't meet the kid in person, but he saw a mug shot. A spotty, snotty nosed juvenile, it was the Funny Times Comics incident all over again. It came as no surprise then, that the kid owned copies of the *Treader of the Stars*. Carson later found out that the little bastard even had an issue of it folded and stuffed into his back pocket when he was busted.

Then the Senate Subcommittee on Juvenile Delinquency arrived, and comic book publishers were brought to account on their comics' effects on juvenile delinquency. Following the proceedings, Carson found some of it to be complete hokum. Batman and Robin faggots? Wonder Woman a bondage freak? But darker issues were covered concerning the depiction of murder, bloodshed, and torture in comic books, and by the end of the proceedings a Comic Code Authority was created and certain publishers were forced to drastically censor their comic books. Some titles, too graphic to be censored without cutting them to pieces, were cancelled altogether.

Funny Time Comics wasn't mentioned during the hearings, for compared to the likes of EC Comics, their covers and interiors were rather tame to the eye and didn't create an instant abhorrence in those running the committee. Carson went to his superiors trying to give evidence against the publisher: after all, they had a near fatal stabbing and a dead mom in their favor, but red tape and jurisdictional issues stopped him and Moore from ever getting near the hearings.

The hearings did good, Carson couldn't doubt that. They perhaps went a little far in some cases, with werewolves, zombies and vampires being banned from portrayal in comics, but gone were the comics that depicted bondage, excessive gore and sexual violence. But, what of those comic books out there already, in the hands of America's youth? Nothing could be done about those, and as far as Carson knew, the damage was already done.

One thing he could do however, was find back issues of *The Treader of the Stars* himself and destroy them. This he did, buying them from used bookstores, garage sales and by placing ads in newspapers, beginning what would become a lifelong obsession.

A few days after the final issue of *The Treader of the Stars* was released, Funny Time Comics suffered a fire that turned the building into a burnt out wreck, with Smilansky the only victim. An apt end, though a little late in coming, but at least fate brought some justice to the world for a man that published such deranged trash.

Over the following years Carson's grim interest in comic books grew, especially where murders were involved, and when the most extreme cases of violence and murder appeared, he made a point of searching the case files for evidence that fueled his own personal obsession. It wasn't hard to find.

In 1957 the country was shocked to silence when a weird but harmless looking fellow from Wisconsin was arrested for murder, grave robbing, desecrating corpses, cannibalism, and necrophilia. This farmer, Ed Gein, had turned his home into a house of horrors with cut off lips dangling from strings, upturned skulls used as bowls, human skin stretched over furniture, ten severed female heads, a box full of tanned and treated lady parts, and more grotesqueries. And while everyone in law enforcement who didn't personally inspect Ed's horrible house poured over the hundreds of crime scene photos with morbid curiosity, Carson was sure he was the only one who fixated not on the ghoulish decorations, but on a copy of *The Treader of the Stars* that could be seen in one of the photos right next to Ed's belt made out of women's nipples.

A year later, Charles Raymond Starkweather, a James Dean fixated killer, murdered eleven people including his girlfriend's two-year-old sister. After his first killing, that of service station attendant Robert Culvert, Starkweather claimed he had transcended his former self and now lived on a higher plane of existence where he was above humanity's morals and laws. It came to no surprise to Carson, as he delved into the case notes, that Starkweather's fourteen-year-old girlfriend Caril Ann Fugate had been an avid reader of boys' comic books, including *The Treader of the Stars*. Carson guessed she had shared her interest with Starkweather too.

Then there was the Texas Tower Sniper, Charles Whitman, who in 1966 massacred and killed fourteen people after murdering his wife and mother. In an interview, one of his buddies from the Marines said, "Old Chuck was sort of quiet, kept to himself. A nice guy, just sort of odd. While all of us would blow off steam playing cards and drinking, he would usually be off in a corner reading one of his funny books. Yeah, that's pretty much all he did, read those stupid funny books."

Carson found and burned more issues of that damn comic in his furnace, but it seemed a never-ending task. As the years passed and the horrors mankind perpetrated against his brothers grew, real life monsters appeared to replace those banned from comic books.

Many killers Carson read about in biographies, for after retiring from the FBI in the 1970s he had no further access to the case files. Still, he found enough.

Charles Manson, a burglar, rapist and a pimp in his younger, troubled years, was a deranged monster that moved on to more heinous crimes that ended up tainting America culture for decades to come. In a biography, Carson read this disconcerting quote from Manson: "I tried desperately to live a normal life as a boy, but the world wouldn't let me. Still I tried following the rules, read comic books and bought baseball cards, things I treaded into the dust of my childhood as being a man of power became my true calling."

Another human monster, Ted Bundy, the serial killer, rapist and necrophiliac, spent a disturbed childhood in Tacoma where he later described to biographers that he would roam the neighborhood searching through people's trash for lurid comic books and detective magazines. Another youth tainted by The Treader of the Stars? To Carson's eyes, it was certainly a possibility.

***

An old man in a world he barely recognized, Carson, a widower of some fifteen years, went through a daily routine that while not exactly stimulating, at least gave his lonely life some meaning. As the 1980s arrived he continued his search for the comics, and spent a good portion of his bureau pension buying comic store catalogues and making phone calls to stores across the United States and Great Britain. It seemed the supplies of *The Treader of the Stars* were finally running dry. He hadn't incinerated a copy for over two months now, and with every comic shop listed in the phone directories he diligently searched at the 96th Street Library, Carson felt he finally had a handle on things.

The library being a daily goal for as long as he could remember, Carson walked to the building by cutting though Midtown Park, walking slowly so as to avoid slipping on the icy footpath. The cold spell this January played havoc with his arthritic knees, and while walking, he looked to the frost encrusted grass and thought of warmer days when he could sit on one of the graffiti-scarred benches and watch the world go by. He left the park, looked both ways before crossing Lexington Avenue (for the drivers these days were utter maniacs), and went to continue another part of his daily ritual: buying a paper from Geoff's Magazines, a small stand that had appeared on the avenue a few years previously. He could just read the papers for free in the library, but Geoff was a friendly face and he liked to chew the fat on occasion.

Geoff, completing the sale of a magazine to a sallow-faced priest, saw Carson's approach, his brown face forming a toothy grin. "Hey Mr. G-man! Braving the weather too huh?"

"As always," Carson replied and returned the smile. He usually bought a copy of *The Times*, *The Post* too if there was something interesting to follow, and he was about to ask for the former when he stopped dead in his tracks. A line of comic books hung near the top of the magazine rack, dangling from clothes pegs on a piece of string. There was the usual fare, *Batman*, pictured battling some gaudily clad villain, *The Amazing Spiderman* fighting his own garish enemies, and between those two comic books he saw *The Treader of the Stars*. He even recognized the issue, despite the fact the cover art had been updated. It was number three, the Yellow Menace issue. The cover depicted the Treader standing over a cowed enemy dressed in yellow rags and a cracked white mask, both men trapped in a battle of wills with black energy bolts pouring from the Treader's hands, white ones from the Yellow Menace's.

Carson's blood ran cold. "No," he said. "It can't be." It was too horrible to be true.

"Hey Mr. Carson what's up? You've gone pale. You wanna sit down?" Through a haze Carson heard Geoff pull his plastic chair out from behind him.

"The Treader of the Stars," Carson said, the words more ominous now than ever before.

"Oh that?" Geoff said. "Comic books are hot again since the Superman movie was a such a big hit. They've even gone back and reissued a load of old titles bought from out-of-business publishers. *The Crimson Ghost*, *The Deadman Detective*, *The Black Cat*, and *The Iron Golem* they're all back. But that Treader one, that's the best seller by far. I hear it because it's got a dark edge to it. You know, that's what the kids want these days. The days of good guys punching bad guys for the American way is on its way out. Now everything's got to be dark, and it's just getting darker."

"Darker," Carson repeated and his legs went weak at the knees.

"Mr— Hey!" Geoff sounded panicked, his voice coming from a distant shore as Carson collapsed, face down into oblivion.

***

Apart from a few scrapes, Carson had suffered no real injuries from his fall. This felt like no consolation as he sat brooding at the dinner table in his small apartment. The only item on the table was a large tin box, scratched and battered, and Carson stared at it as he had done for the past two hours after being discharged from the hospital. He'd taken a taxi home alone, for he had no one now, cancer having taken his wife all those years ago, and even Moore, Moore had been killed during a shootout on an Indian Reservation back in '73.

He gulped, swallowed heavily, and opened the tin, the lid creaking upwards with a whine of rusted hinges. Inside lay his old Smith & Wesson Model 10 service revolver, the brown wooden handle worn but the black gunmetal barely aged from when he had last used it, all those years ago in the parking lot outside Funny Time Comics. Carson lifted the gun reverently from the tin, checked that it was still loaded, and pressed the barrel into his open mouth.

CPSIA information can be obtained
at www.ICGtesting.com
Printed in the USA
BVHW090031110721
611481BV00003B/87

9 781568 823980